A Letter To Die For

Joe Shumock

A Letter Series Novel

Publisher: Silver Sage Media LLC

**Scan this QR code to visit
www.Silver-Sage-Media.com**

A Letter to Die For

ISBN-13 9780983793915
ISBN-13 9780983793908
ISBN-13 9780983793922

Book Web site:
www.Silver-Sage-Media.com
E-mail: info@Silver-Sage-Media.com

Give feedback on the book at:
feedback@Silver-Sage-Media.com

Publisher: Silver Sage Media, LLC

Printed in U.S.A

To Kathryn K. (Kathy) Shumock
(1940 – 2010)

She always thought we could do it.

Joseph E. Shumock
P. O. Box 173
Coker Creek, TN 37314
joeshumock@tds.net

Prologue
October 1982

Janice searched her pockets without success. *Never a tissue when you need one.* She gave up the hunt and wiped her teary eyes and damp nose on the sleeve of her sweater. Almost immediately, new tears made their way down her face in a cascade of despair.

Shivering in the breeze, she crossed her arms and, following a life-long habit, tucked her chin inside the neck of her sweater, hoping to warm herself in the unexpected chill. The drop in temperature had surprised the two women as they strolled the streets of New Orleans on this late October evening.

Her friend Carolette shivered, too, then buttoned the collar of her long red coat against the cold wind. As they often did, the women were walking along the neutral ground, a tree-lined strip of land dividing the traffic lanes of Esplanade Avenue.

"I love twilight. It's such a nice time of day to walk in the Quarter," Carolette said. "Quiet, pleasant . . ." *Bless her heart* – Carolette was making a special effort to lift Janice's spirit.

"Except when it's cold and windy . . . like now," Janice said, looking over at her friend and forcing a grin, then focusing down at the grass again.

Carolette laughed, catching the irony of Janice's words. Then, in a more serious tone, Carolette said, "You know it's for the best – what you've done. A baby would be too much responsibility."

Too much responsibility? When was a child ever too much responsibility?

"I know, but that doesn't make it easier," Janice replied without looking up. "I just can't get past knowing I'll never see her again." Her voice aching with sadness, she added, "But I *am* leaving my hopes and dreams for her . . ."

Chapter One

Twenty-two years later. . .

In the moments before the accident, there had been no fog. Then suddenly Kenneth Warren couldn't see the road ahead. It was like a curtain had been dropped beyond the windshield. Alice had been sleeping but jerked upright as her husband instinctively hit the brakes.

"Oh my God!" she screamed.

Then they plowed into the truck.

Loaded with cargo and headed into Washington, DC, on I-66, the driver had braced as his big eighteen-wheeler jackknifed on the slippery pavement. Without warning, he had run into the fog bank and tried to slow down. His rig, though twisted and broken, had stayed upright but now sat blocking the east-bound lanes of the Interstate. He was climbing down from his cab when he saw an automobile skid out of the fog and under his trailer. He felt the impact as metal struck metal with fearsome tearing sounds.

Then all hell broke loose as four more vehicles suddenly burst from the night, following the first one into the already ruined truck and into each other. As the wreckage settled, the fog rapidly began to dissipate – leaving the highway clear in the night except for the debris surrounding the big cab and trailer.

Apart from some minor cuts and bruises and being scared out of their minds, the people in the last four vehicles walked away from the disaster.

Not so for the passengers of the new Toyota Avalon. The roof and front compartment were crushed. Doors all around were jammed. Rescuers were unable to reach the couple inside until later when the car could be pulled from under the trailer.

But it wouldn't have mattered anyway. Emergency responders on the scene had crawled far enough into the vehicle to know that they were recovering, rather than rescuing, the two people inside.

***

The doorbell rang a little after eleven. Cary Warren rubbed her eyes, rolled out of bed, and grabbed her robe. *Allie had probably forgotten her key again.*

But it wasn't her roommate standing in the hallway. Instead, two Tennessee state troopers were waiting when Cary opened the door. One of them was a woman.

"Miss Warren? Cary Anne Warren?"

Cary's eyes darted back and forth between them for a moment before answering. Her mouth suddenly dry, she was having trouble breathing. *Something's happened!*

"Yes," she managed to say. "I'm Cary. Why are you here?"

"May we come in?" the male officer asked, his face grim and his eyes avoiding hers.

"Yeah . . . sure." Cary stepped out of their way.

"Could I bother you for some water?" the female trooper asked.

Cary went to the kitchen and, with a trembling hand, drew a glass of water at the sink. She returned to the living room and handed it to the woman. They sat down, the officers on the sofa, Cary in a chair facing them.

"Miss Warren, we have some bad news," the male officer told Cary. "Are your parents' names Kenneth and Alice Warren, and do they live in Farragut?"

Cary had held herself in check as long as she could. "Yes, for God's sake. Tell me what's happened!" she demanded, hovering at the edge of her chair.

The woman spoke up. "There's been an automobile accident near Washington, DC, tonight, Miss Warren. Your parents were both killed in that accident. We're sorry." The woman tried to hand Cary the untouched glass of water.

"Oh, God," Cary said, shaking her head, refusing to believe the officer's words. "Oh, God." An uncomfortable silence ensued. Cary was stunned, disbelieving. She couldn't even cry. She just sat there, arms stretched across her chest, a bewildered feeling sweeping over her.

"Is there someone we can call to come stay with you?" It took a few moments for Cary to understand the woman was speaking to her.

"No," she mumbled. "No, there isn't." Looking up, she said, "My roommate should be home soon, though." It was a lie, but she wanted the troopers gone.

The officers glanced at each other, then back at Cary. Clearly they were uncomfortable leaving her alone.

"It's okay," Cary told them as she stood and walked toward the door. "I'll be fine . . . really." Cary closed the door behind them and leaned against it. After a time – she didn't know how long – Cary realized hot tears were coursing down her cheeks. Without intending it, Cary's knees buckled and she slid downward until she was sitting on the floor with her back to the door.

It can't be true. Not Mom and Dad.

Cary had been at her parents' home in Farragut that morning when they were leaving for their outing to the Capital. An action person, forever stepping out and leading others, she had been so proud of herself. Always planning things and making arrangements, the trip had been her idea. She had organized it, made their reservations, suggested places they should visit, everything. Worse yet, she had talked them into going. They deserved a getaway, she'd told them.

At nine o'clock that morning she'd waved goodbye to them and driven back across Knoxville to her dorm at the University of Tennessee. She was a senior and already a week into her last semester. She remembered thinking that morning, she was twenty-two years old and ready to step out into the world. But that was all before . . .

Guilt washed over Cary as she remembered, and she buried her face in her hands. *Could her enthusiasm have caused this tragedy?* Her parents were a big part of her world. Now they were gone. All because of her.

At some point after midnight, exhausted and drained of tears, Cary rolled to her side in a fetal position and dozed off.

That was how Allie found her when she returned to the dorm at one-thirty in the morning. "Cary? Why are you sleeping on the floor? Have you been drinking?" Allie was teasing but then she saw Cary's eyes. "My God, Cary! What's happened?"

The next several days were a blur. There were few relatives for Cary to turn to. Her dad's older brother lived in Seattle near his two children. Uncle Ellis had recently undergone heart surgery, so he wouldn't be coming to the funeral. His children weren't close so Cary didn't expect them either. Kenneth and Alice were the youngest in each of their families. Her mom's last sister had passed away during the previous summer in Phoenix where she lived. And Cary had no siblings. Allie was her only close friend.

She called her father's attorney the morning after the accident. He made arrangements to have her parents returned to Knoxville. He made the interment preparations, too.

A service was held five days later. The wake and double funeral were both well attended. Many of the mourners were patients of Cary's father, a popular family doctor. Several ladies who played bridge with her mother were there, too. And Allie's boyfriend Jed came with her.

As Cary sat in the church fighting back tears, Allie held her hand, an arm around her shoulder. Allie had been by her side since finding Cary on the floor that first night. Before the accident they had been busy with their separate lives, but since then they'd formed a tighter bond. Cary didn't know what she would have done if Allie hadn't been there. She squeezed her friend's hand, thankful for her presence. Glancing over, Cary hoped she and Allie would remain close after college, but doubted it – Allie was returning to her home in California. They might never see each other again. *Another* tear . . .

During the days and nights after the accident, Cary had told Allie all about her parents. But what she didn't tell her was that her mom and dad had adopted her when she was an infant. After a friend in whom she'd confided told several others in high school about her adoption, Cary had never revealed it to anyone else. And her mom and dad had never told anyone other than family, as far as Cary knew. They didn't consider it anyone's business. Cary was their daughter and they were her parents, end of story.

A new round of tears welled in her eyes as she gazed at the two caskets near the front of the church. Another thing Cary hadn't told Allie was that she felt responsible for her parents' deaths. Not in real terms, but in the funny way things happen when you don't mean them to.

Cary hoped she could get past this.

After the service, when everyone had left the cemetery, Cary stayed to say her own goodbyes to her mom and dad. The afternoon had turned warm with just the slightest breeze. The fragrance of lilies filled the air: they were her mother's favorite. Grief welled up inside her and she dabbed at her eyes. She couldn't imagine the house without her parents there. With a knot in her throat, she realized for the first time that she was now alone. At that instant, Cary felt different, somehow changed: empty and, she realized, guilty.

Cary gazed back over the cemetery to the twin mounds of fresh earth covered with flowers. She stood still for that moment, then touched the tips of her fingers to her lips, kissing them gently before tossing the small expression of her love to the winds.

Then she turned and walked to the roadway where Allie and Jed waited. The three of them drove to the house in Farragut. With Jed remaining in the car and

Allie at her side, Cary went in and picked up a few things to take with her to the dorm. They quickly returned to the car. Cary wasn't ready to face the house, knowing her parents were no longer there.

As they drove back to the UT campus, Cary gazed out the window. Out of the corner of her eye, she occasionally saw Allie and Jed exchange glances but was relieved when they didn't say anything to her.

In the following days, working around classes, Cary took care of necessary details. Lon Jackson, her father's attorney, kept her informed of the many details that needed to be handled. He also set her up with a folder for paying the household expenses. Lon did all that he could without interrupting, but her signature was required in many cases.

"You'll need these insurance forms, deeds, titles, and other papers," he said, as he pushed a manila envelope toward her.

She thanked him. It all seemed overwhelming.

"And here," he added, giving her a copy of her parents' wills and explaining them to her. "You were their only heir, other than a few charitable gifts. Your parents made sure you would be well cared for."

With a heavy sigh, Cary looked down at the crisp white paper. If she was reasonably careful, she understood she would be okay financially. But emotionally . . . that was another thing.

In the weeks after the accident, Mr. Jackson also negotiated the sale of her dad's medical practice to his associate. Cary was kept aware of the process but stayed out of the discussions until it was time for her to sign the papers. She had met the young doctor and her family during a reception at her parents' home a few months earlier. Cary thought her dad would have been pleased with the way things were working out.

Exhausted at the end of most days, life was tough, but Cary found she could be tough, too. She tended to stay with a project until it was handled, even if it proved unpleasant. Some would call it "dogging something to death." Cary thought of it simply as getting the job done. She knew her dad would be proud of her. He had worked hard to instill these traits in his daughter.

One night Cary lay in bed thinking of all that had taken place. She realized she had learned to be task-oriented through her parents' example. Because of them, Cary had been that way, too, for as long as she could remember. Hopefully, she had learned enough. Cary realized she would be proving herself to her parents long into the future. *I hope I got it, Mom and Dad.*

Days ran into weeks, weeks into months. Spring came, and graduation. Cary walked across the stage and picked up her diploma, almost expecting to see her parents smiling and waving from the audience. But the tightness in her chest reminded her they were gone. How she wished they could have been here.

She had her first job lined up before graduation. Her undergraduate majors were in advertising and marketing, and Trebeck Corporation wanted her to take a position in their advertising department. The corporation's headquarters was in Knoxville, so she wouldn't have to move away.

When she had finished her course work, Cary looked for an apartment. She found what she wanted in the western section of Knoxville near Turkey Creek. She looked forward to being in a place of her own. Gathering everything she had accumulated in four years, she moved it from her dorm room over to the new apartment.

She still needed furniture. On the Saturday morning before she was due to start at Trebeck, she rented a U-Haul truck. Then she commandeered Allie and Jed to help her. They went out to her parents' house and loaded the furniture she had decided to keep. The three of them moved her bedroom furnishings and several other pieces into her new apartment.

That first night in her own space, Cary looked around at familiar objects from her past and sighed, especially happy to be sleeping in her own bed. Whatever else she might need would have to be purchased when she had the time. The shopping could wait until after she received her first paycheck, too. She planned to live on what she earned.

The curious feeling that had come over Cary in the cemetery returned and became more pronounced after she started her job at Trebeck Corporation. The emotion had expressed itself as a driving force, a compulsion to succeed, she realized as she placed a stack of paperwork in her briefcase to take home that evening. And with heightened ambition, loneliness returned, too.

Having pushed her emotions aside, Cary managed a swift pace as she climbed the corporate ladder. With friendly help and guidance, she was now in an office of her own. There was even a window. Cary often glanced out at the trees and lawns surrounding the buildings that included Trebeck's home office. Having just finished her latest project, she decided on a short mental break, something she did periodically. Sometimes those breaks lasted for as long as three or four minutes. Cary smiled at the fact she considered them breaks at all.

Turning to her credenza, Cary picked up a framed photograph of the family on a cruise. The three of them were standing on a beach in Jamaica at sunset. When her mom and dad were alive, Cary and her parents had shared a sense of family. With them gone, she no longer had that feeling.

But at least she had friends at the office now. At the sound of a light rap on the open door, she put the photograph back on the credenza and looked up.

"Hi, Rita," she said, happy to see her friend. "Get in here. You don't have to knock."

"Look at you sitting here in your *big* office," her friend kidded her. Rita Ammons had become her pal. Four years older than Cary, she was very different in stature. Cary was tall, at five-ten plus without her shoes, whereas Rita was just over five feet. And while Cary was a brunette with dark eyes, high cheek bones, and a slim athletic build, Rita was blond and petite with a cute round face and a big smile.

Rita had been in the advertising department for a couple of years when Cary started at Trebeck. Initially assigned to work with Rita, that gave them time to get acquainted.

Slowly the two women had started doing things together outside of the office. Rita was single, too, and didn't seem to be in any big hurry to change her status, although she did like to date.

Seeing forms in Rita's hand, Cary asked, "What now, girl?"

"Erica needs you to sign off on these travel vouchers." She placed the papers on Cary's desk. "What are you doing after work?"

Although Cary had gone out occasionally while in college, she didn't date as often now. It was a conscious choice. She was more interested in her job. She worried sometimes about her compulsion to succeed, but she hadn't figured out what to do about it.

"Let me get started," Cary said, reaching for the forms. She began signing them as they talked.

Rita was interested in plans for the evening. "Get your work done early. It's Friday, our night out on the town, and I want lobster."

"Lobster?" Cary had to laugh as she thought of her dad. He called lobster "po' man's food" because he'd had it so often while in the navy.

Cary and Rita had dinner out at least once a week, usually on Friday. Their conversations almost always got around to men. Every month, without fail, Rita tried to fix Cary up with some new guy. More often than not, she refused, but occasionally took a chance.

Tyler, one of Rita's possibilities, had become a good friend. He was a successful businessman with all the trappings. Rita had been sure Cary and Tyler would become an item, but Tyler was career oriented, too. A long-term connection wasn't in the cards.

Cary had considered it. In her heart, she had to admit that she longed for a relationship like her parents had experienced: to fit together like two pieces of a puzzle. That's what she hoped would come her way – some day.

So, what do you say?" Rita asked, sitting on the corner of Cary's desk.

"It's a date," Cary said. She could use the reinforcement of a night out. Tomorrow she would finally tackle her parent's house and her dad's papers.

The next morning, a Saturday, Cary had breakfast, then drove out to Farragut. She had dragged her feet as long as she could, putting off the chore for several months after starting her job.

After her parents died, Cary never spent another night in their house. She went there occasionally but couldn't bring herself to stay over. Before, when Cary lived at home, she had always known that her mom and dad were just down the hall. *Maybe it's the guilt that keeps me away.*

Lon Jackson had explained the situation. The property was in her name. She could rent it or sell it. But for her to do anything, she had to go through her parents' personal belongings. That would require looking at pictures, papers, books, clothes, all those private items she'd put off going through since their deaths.

Cary pulled around behind the house and parked in front of the garage. Once inside, she went directly to the kitchen and started a pot of coffee. A few minutes later, carrying a cup of fortification in her hand, Cary walked down the hallway to her dad's study. Armed with a set of keys he had given her for emergencies, she sat at his desk and found the one that opened his file drawers.

She thumbed through the tabs to see what was there. Most of the files were ordinary – paid bills, bank statements, that sort of thing. But back toward the rear of the first drawer was a folder with a tab marked *Cary Anne's Papers*. A tingle of anticipation crept through her as she removed the folder and placed it on the smooth desk surface. With trepidation, she opened it. On top was an insurance policy taken out on her life when she was a child. Cary glanced at the main page, then laid it aside. There were papers about college, a registration on her vehicle, and several pictures of her when she was a baby.

She found her passport. They hadn't needed it since her parents took her to England the summer after Cary finished high school. She smiled, thinking about the outing. That had been fun. For part of the trip they had rented a car and driven out in the country, staying at quaint inns. She dropped the passport back into the file while feeling that now familiar pang of loss.

The last envelope in the folder caught Cary by surprise. It was marked *Cary's Adoption Papers – October 14, 1982.* Her dad's handwriting. She picked it up, pausing before she opened it. The first papers she saw were a set of legal documents setting forth the adoption of one Cary Anne Warren by Kenneth and Alice Warren. She touched her nose to the faded yellow text that smelled musty with age, then placed it back in its envelope.

Then Cary saw another document in the file, a birth certificate. She picked it up, glancing at the information. The spaces for the mother and father showed Kenneth and Alice Warren. Thinking about it, she understood the need, maybe even a requirement, that their names be shown rather than her biological parents. What surprised her was the city of birth: New Orleans, Louisiana. Cary had never thought about where she was born, always assuming Knoxville. It had never come up in conversation. Considering it, Cary realized her parents must have adopted her when her dad was in medical school in New Orleans. Her emotions did a little flip.

New Orleans . . . Huh!

As she dropped the birth certificate back into the file, something caught her eye. On a sheet torn from a small memo pad, there was a short note in her dad's handwriting. It read, "Birth mother to leave a note in folder."

What a strange message. What folder did he mean? Where? And how could she get it? That would take some thought.

Cary started to put the note back into her dad's file but paused as she spied a word written lower on the sheet – something she hadn't noticed before. There, almost hidden in a wrinkled fold, was a single word penned in red and in her dad's handwriting: *Murdered?*

Cary felt a chill run through her body. *Who* was murdered? Her birth mother? Couldn't be. Someone else? But if it *was* her biological mother, why hadn't Dad written more details? And why had it never been mentioned?

Dread crept over her as she dropped the note into the folder. Quickly closing the drawer, she stood up, unwilling for the time being to further ponder the note's implications.

Chapter Two

Several months went by as Cary tried with little success to put aside the discovery she had made in her adoption file. It was difficult. A single word, written in red, seemed stuck in her consciousness. Even sleep didn't help – it was always there. *Murdered?* The word just wouldn't go away.

Cary became a trusted member of the supervisory staff at Trebeck Corporation. Seasons had come and gone as she took on even more responsibilities with her journey upward to management in the corporation. Another autumn, with its cooler temperatures, bright colors and falling leaves, had come to East Tennessee. Everything was spectacular, but . . .

Other developments were requiring her attention.

This year's seasonal transformation coincided with potential changes in Cary's status at work. For several weeks she had been consumed with the likelihood of becoming Vice President in charge of Advertising. This was a new VP slot in the corporate structure. She wanted to be in her new office by her twenty-fifth birthday.

Time had flown by since Cary finished college and started her career. Though it seemed much shorter, she had been at Trebeck Corporation for over two and a half years now. With her remarkable work ethic, natural intelligence, and ability to deal with people, she was roaring up the corporate ladder.

Good fortune had been with her, too. Shortly before Cary was hired at Trebeck Corporation, the company had been bought out. The new owner was a holding company ruled by a group of private investors. Scuttlebutt had initially argued there would be significant changes in the company's direction and management. The rumors had proved false. No one was fired, and operations continued basically as they had prior to the buyout. Cary had seen nothing but benefits.

Now, approaching three years after the change in ownership, no one even discussed it. Trebeck Corporation was growing and prospering. The advertising department was busier than ever. And Cary was an important part of that. Over the last eighteen months she had been promoted three times. Things were good.

In late summer, the HR department had announced plans to interview for the new V.P. position. With Cary's birthday less than a month away, the goal was within her grasp. Before leaving home the morning of the interview, she ran a quick brush through her hair and stepped away from the mirror to take in her image one last time.

She wore a blue outfit she'd recently purchased. The new suit, along with a light blue blouse, fit her flawlessly and highlighted her features without suggesting she was pushing charm rather than ability. With her dark eyes and high cheekbones, Cary's long wavy dark hair framed her face, making it the focal point of attention. Rita often teased her, saying she should become a model.

"You'll do," she told her likeness in the mirror. Then, grabbing her briefcase, Cary headed out the door, her thoughts turning to the interview. She practically ran the Advertising department now and continued to work toward her MBA. She was a couple of classes short of the degree, and she also needed to finish her thesis paper. *All in good time.*

Traffic out to Trebeck Corporation was light that morning, and though the drive was short, it gave her time to think. Pressure on the job was an everyday occurrence. Cary rubbed her stomach, surprised she didn't have an ulcer. And even with Rita as a close friend and Tyler to do things with, Cary still felt alone. She had never been able to shake the self-imposed guilt for her parents' deaths, either.

Though Cary thought of her mom and dad almost every day, since their deaths she had begun to wonder about her biological parents. She often considered the memo in Dad's file and wondered what it was all about. *Birth mother to leave a note in folder.* Such an odd message. And the notation, *Murdered?* – and in her dad's handwriting. Why was it there? Maybe she should spend a few days in New Orleans, searching for answers and hunting for her biological mother and father. She had considered it numerous times before. Perhaps she could use the opportunity to find out about the strange message, too, and see if it involved her.

Those thoughts faded as she pulled into the parking lot. A couple of fellow workers wished her well as she headed for her office. Then, before the interview, Rita stopped by and they talked for a few minutes.

"Break a leg," she said, giving Cary a wink.

"I'd rather not have that as one of the options," Cary called after her, but Rita was already gone. Though anxious about the upcoming interview, she used the time to handle a few tasks that had accumulated on her desk. Then she checked her watch. Eight-thirty.

Thirty-five minutes later, seated at a wide table with a group of executives facing her, Cary handled all the questions well, she thought, despite her internal jitters. On the surface, she remained calm and focused, anticipating a number of question lines before being asked. When the meeting was over, she received congratulations.

Later, going over the meeting in her mind, Cary decided she had done all the right things. As it turned out, everything, that is, but one. She didn't get the job.

Ten days after the interviews, on a Friday morning, Mr. Stocks, the CEO, prepared to make the announcement. Promotions at this level invariably went to someone already in the company structure. Everyone in the meeting room was excited.

Rita grinned at her. Cary's new position was a foregone conclusion as far as Rita was concerned. Cary, on the other hand, remembered how she felt on the day of the interview. She managed to remain calm on the outside, but her nerves were another matter.

"We've had a number of great applicants," the CEO began. "Several of them from Trebeck Corporation." He seemed to glance in Cary's direction as he said that. She couldn't help smiling and even relaxed a little.

"But in the end, one applicant stood out among the rest."

Rita smiled at Cary and squeezed her hand.

Say it, Cary willed. *Say it.*

"I won't leave you in suspense." She held her breath as she waited to hear the words that would assure her advancement.

"The new head of Advertising for Trebeck Corporation is . . . Mike Webster."

For a second, it didn't register. Then almost everyone began clapping. Glancing around, several of Cary's coworkers seemed as astounded as she felt.

Mike Webster? Who the hell is Mike Webster?

Rita stared at Mr. Stocks, and then turned toward Cary with a frown on her face. "What did he say?"

While everyone was standing, Cary slipped out of the meeting to catch her breath. She saw someone, probably the new guy, start toward the podium as she left the room. She knew she shouldn't leave the gathering without saying hello to him. After a couple of minutes, Rita hurried up to her in the hallway. "You okay, kid?" Cary nodded. "I guess."

"I asked around about this Mike Webster," Rita told her. "Turns out he's single, thirty-one, and from Atlanta. He has a Master's Degree in advertising. That's all I could get and that's all they seem to have. I thought that was strange." Rita frowned, obviously puzzled about the lack of information.

"You found out all that in just a few minutes?"

With an air of importance, Rita said, "You just have to talk to the right people."

Cary knew the right people meant the CEO's secretary.

"You know you're going to have to meet this Webster."

"I know."

Taking a few more moments to compose herself, she swept her hair back with her fingers, then walked back into the meeting room with Rita at her side. Heartfelt or not, she needed to offer her congratulations to the new head of her department.

A rather large group stood with Mr. Stocks near the podium. Cary gently elbowed her way forward. She eased around the last person . . . and tripped over an unseen briefcase, all in the same motion. Her last thought as she toppled toward the floor was – I needed *this* today?

An instant before she hit the deck, Cary felt a hand under her shoulder, another at her waist. Then her body was being lifted upright. Moments that seemed like an eternity passed as she balanced herself. Presently, she found herself looking into the eyes of a stranger as he steadied her.

Clearly concerned, he asked, "Are you okay?" He held her arm for another moment, then released her. Cary quickly flipped her hair over her shoulder and into some semblance of order. Then she glanced down, easing the offending briefcase out of the way with her toe.

When she turned back to the stranger, she was silent for several seconds. He was taller than her by at least six inches. And it had been a long time since she'd met anyone this handsome, though-be-it in a rugged way. She realized he must be one of the people she had noticed earlier, but hadn't recognized. No . . . she would have remembered this one!

"Thank you," she managed. "I'm usually not this awkward."

His demeanor was friendly. "And I'm almost never in a position to aid a pretty lady in distress," he answered softly. Then he smiled.

And . . . *she* blushed. The words "tall, dark and handsome" came to mind.

At some point, Cary realized that Mr. Stocks was speaking to her. Finally, she turned, directing her attention to the CEO.

"Cary," he said, "I'd like you to meet Mike Webster. He's the new Vice President of Advertising." Then Stocks leaned in close and said in a voice lowered so only Cary could hear, "I wanted to tell you earlier."

"I understand," she said . . . but she didn't.

Stocks continued, "Mike Webster, I'd like you to meet Cary Warren. She'll be your Number Two in command."

"It's a pleasure," she said, fighting the edge in her voice. It wasn't a pleasure. It wasn't even close – in spite of his helpfulness, *and* good looks.

"I understand we'll be working together," he ventured.

"Yes. Well . . . probably." Cary wasn't interested in making it easy for him. This damn well wasn't easy for her. This . . . this person was holding her future in his hands. *I'm not about to welcome him like a long lost friend.*

Cary paused then, and took a breath. She studied him. So this is Mike Webster. Her frustration level was rising. Mr. Stocks and the rest of management had let her think she was going to get the job. Well . . . that wasn't exactly true, she knew. *But they sure as hell didn't put much effort into keeping me from thinking that way.* She grew more aggravated as everyone stood there making small talk. She wanted to lash out at someone – anyone. Her future was severely altered, and she wasn't inclined to think the fault was hers.

Cary listened to their idle chatter for as long as she could. After a few minutes, she excused herself. She left the meeting room, her long stride taking her swiftly toward her office.

Damn it. Damn it. Damn it, Cary thought as she marched along the hallway. The remainder of the day was a blur. Thank goodness the announcement came on Friday. She needed time to regroup. She hadn't landed the job. That was it – end of chapter. She refused to dwell on it.

"It's Friday night, and I have a spare shoulder. How 'bout dinner with an old friend?" Rita stood in Cary's doorway late that afternoon. "Well . . . strike that part about *old*. Let's just go out for a bite to eat and some small talk." Cary knew Rita would understand if she wasn't very chatty tonight.

They decided on a little Chinese place near the office. After being served wine and appetizers and placing their order, Rita cautiously asked Cary about the future.

Cary took a sip of wine before answering. "I haven't thought about it because I expected to be busy in the new job. Then Mike Webster shows up." They discussed him and the lack of biographical information. Rita had tried several other sources but had come up empty – data on Webster was in short supply.

"Will you stay in the department?" Rita asked as she popped a won-ton into her mouth.

"I don't know," Cary said, shaking her head. The egg roll on her saucer lay untouched. "Everyone knows how much I wanted that job. I've been acting like it was already mine." Cary couldn't help the edge in her voice.

During the conversation, their entrees arrived.

When they were alone again, she continued, "It's going to be awkward at best. At worst, it could be downright embarrassing, for me *and* for Mr. Webster."

"How so?" Rita asked as she poured them each a cup of oolong tea.

"Well, the way I see it," Cary said, taking a sip, "when the situation becomes apparent to Webster, he's going to feel uneasy." She paused. Then, snapping her fingers, she said, "I think I've just figured out what to do."

"What?" Rita frowned. "You'd better stay out of this, girl."

"No, it's okay. This will work," Cary told her as she placed some Szechuan Kung Pao chicken on her plate.

"I hope so." Rita was skeptical. "I don't want you in over your head."

"Just listen," Cary said as she laid out her plan for Rita. "If I go to Webster and offer to help him in the new position, it could be good for both of us. Right?"

"Yeah. Okay," Rita offered tentatively. "I think I see where you're going."

"Stay with me. Everyone will pitch in when they realize I'm on board with the new guy. The upside for me is a chance to learn. That's always good, right?"

Rita was nodding now. She took a swallow of tea as Chinese music played softly in the background.

Cary continued. "You said he has a Master's Degree in advertising, didn't you?"

"Yes."

"Well, it's obvious Webster must have been doing something right for Mr. Stocks to go outside the company. Where did he work before coming to Trebeck?"

"That's where it gets strange." Rita tugged at her ear. "Someplace in Atlanta, I guess," she paused, taking a sip of her hot and sour soup. "Ellen didn't have a record of his work history."

"Hmm. That *is* odd," Cary agreed, frowning. "Anyway, he must be good or they wouldn't have hired him."

Pensively, Rita studied her for a moment. "I know this is going to sound like I've suddenly switched sides," she said, "but what about giving yourself time to cool off – maybe take a couple of weeks to look for your biological parents?"

Cary had confided in Rita, giving her some basic details about being adopted and about her dad's papers.

"This would be a good time to do that," Rita continued. "Did you ever figure out what the note in your dad's file was about?"

"No," Cary told her as she speared a morsel of chicken. "I've thought about going to New Orleans, but I haven't made up my mind. It makes me feel disloyal to my parents' memories. And if I do go, I'll want to follow through with everything. On the other hand, if I leave now, everyone will think I'm doing it because of Webster. And . . . I'm no quitter."

"Of course you're not. Everyone knows that," Rita told her. "But this is something you need to do for yourself, and this could be the perfect time."

Cary listened, thinking about what Rita was saying and how it all made sense. Still . . .

Rita put it into words. "You should ask for a leave of absence. Tell him you'll work with him, but let Webster get on his feet while you're gone. You've been putting this off for a long time. You've said so yourself."

"When have I ever said I wanted to go?" Cary asked.

"You know you've been thinking about this since you found your birth certificate and realized you were born in New Orleans. And that little slip of paper about your mother stirred your curiosity. You *need* to do this."

Cary dropped her hands to her lap and sat quietly for a moment, her food forgotten. Her parents' deaths had been eating at her. She needed to deal with her anxiety.

With some hesitancy, she began. "I'm going to tell you some things I've never told anyone before," Cary said, immediately getting Rita's attention. "You've heard me talk about my parents. And you know that I was adopted." "Yeah, I know all that."

Cary continued. "And you remember I said Mom and Dad adopted me when I was an infant. I never knew anyone but them as parents."

Rita listened, sympathetic, but not saying anything.

Cary hesitated, wondering how much to tell her friend. Just then, the waitress arrived with more tea and refilled their water glasses.

When the waitress left, Cary took a small bite of egg roll and continued. "It's interesting that you brought up going to New Orleans. Since Mom and Dad died, I've wondered more and more about my biological family. I don't think it would have bothered me as much if I hadn't lost both my parents. But since that happened, I've been at loose ends. Even with a close friend like you, it's been tough." Cary reached over and touched her hand.

"I know," Rita said, smiling.

Cary looked at her, sadness in her eyes. "I've also let this job become the most important thing in my life." She shook her head, then took a bite of her chicken, giving herself time to control her emotions. Rita had her chopsticks working now and was picking at her main course.

Cary touched the corner of her mouth with a napkin, then said, "So maybe you're right. If I take some time off, I can look for my biological family and see if I have a history in New Orleans. At the same time, I'd be giving Webster a chance to get his feet on the ground."

Rita remained silent, chewing and thinking about what Cary had shared.

Finally, she managed, "Wow! So, you're going to do it? Consider it . . . I mean?"

"Yeah, I guess I've been thinking about it long enough. Besides, my cat's tired of hearing about it." They both laughed. Cary didn't tell Rita, but if she planned things carefully, she could be in New Orleans for her birthday and on the anniversary of her adoption.

"Okay, let's say you get the time off. What exactly will you do?" Rita asked. "What *can* you do?"

"The first thing is try to get my adoption file opened. If I can do that, I may be able to learn everything I want to know from it. And, hopefully, whatever my mother wrote will be there – mystery solved. If I can't get into the adoption file, I guess I'll do it the hard way, starting with the records department."

Rita laid aside her chopsticks. "Cary, I know I've prodded you into going. Just be sure you're not just doing this because of me – this needs to be something you really want to do for yourself." Rita chewed her lower lip as she gazed at Cary. "You realize you could learn more than you want to know."

"I've thought about *that*," Cary said, eyeing her friend. "But you're right. I have to do it."

"What happens if it's a loss, and you can't find out anything about your birth parents?"

"Then, at least I'll know I've tried."

Rita cracked open her fortune cookie. "You should refrain from meddling in the affairs of others." And Cary's read, "You will be lucky in love." They had a good laugh. Who would believe such nonsense?

Cary went to her new boss's office early on Monday morning. Webster's door was open, but she stopped and knocked. He looked up from something he was reading and, upon seeing her, slipped the documents into a folder and smiled. He was dressed in tan slacks, a blue button-down with a striped tie, and navy blazer – the picture of a young professional.

How nice he looks sitting there at *my* desk, Cary thought, then wondered if her face had taken on a green tint with the momentary envy she felt.

"Come in," Webster said, rising from his chair.

They shook hands, nice and cordial. Cary looked at him. *His nose is a little crooked.* It had been broken at some point. Her immediate unkind notion was that it served him right. She instantly regretted the inappropriate thought, acknowledging that it probably wasn't his fault he had been given the job instead of her. At least she couldn't imagine he would have had anything to do with it.

"Good morning, Mike, ah . . . Mr. Webster," Cary began. "I don't know if you remember me. I'm Cary Warren."

"The lady in distress," he said smiling, clearly not intending to embarrass her.

She was still uncomfortable about tripping and falling in front of all those people on Friday, especially him. On impulse, she decided the best way to handle his comment was to ignore it.

"If you have some time today," Cary said in her best business voice, "I'd like to talk with you."

"Now's as good a time as any. I have some things I'd like to go over with you, too"

Motioning her to a chair, he led off. "I'm aware you expected this position would be yours. I've checked your qualifications. You would've done a great job."

She glanced away, then back again. "Yes, I think so, too. Maybe it wasn't my time."

"I doubt if timing had anything to do with it." It was as though he knew something she didn't. "There could be other reasons," he added. Then, after standing and walking to the window, he continued. "I hope you'll consider working with me. We can help this company."

She stared at him for a few seconds, evaluating his motives. "I'll help you," Cary offered tentatively, and then threw out her conditions: "but I can't do it right away. First I need to do something for myself, something I've been putting off for a long time."

His eyes narrowed as he gave her a questioning look.

She continued. "You'll need time to get organized here."

Webster nodded, willing to listen.

She had his attention now. "Since everyone thought I was going to get this position, I think it would be best if I stay out of the picture initially. Giving you time to settle in will work to everyone's advantage."

His eyebrows rose as he considered her proposal. *Visions of Groucho Marx danced across Cary's mind.* Finally he spoke. "I understand where you're coming from," he said, "but I'm not sure I agree."

Cary attempted to interrupt, but he held up a hand, cutting her off.

"I follow your point about getting settled," he said, "but if you take time off right now, people may see it as a split between you and me." His forehead wrinkled into a frown. "That concerns me. A good start is important."

Hesitating, he glanced out the window. After a moment he turned back to her. "I have plans for Trebeck Corporation. I'm betting you do, too. I was hoping you'd share your plans with me. You'll get the credit. That's the way I work."

Then he changed subjects, asking, "Other than letting me get settled, would I be prying too much if I asked your purpose for taking off right now? You appear determined. I'd like to work with you, but it's going to be awkward at best. Put yourself in my position." He walked back and sat in his chair.

Cary wondered if she could tell him her reasons. Rita was the only person who knew. However, Webster *did* seem sincere and this was important to both of them. But she couldn't share the details. Not right now.

"I need to go to New Orleans," she said in a calm voice, "to try to find someone." That was the most she was willing to give him. "I'll need a couple of weeks. Then I'll return and work with you. By then you'll be established. " She made sure her words and their tone left no room for argument. "I really do need to make this trip."

She was a little surprised at his reaction. He seemed to be trying to read her thoughts, and his eyes had narrowed when she mentioned New Orleans. They stared at each other for several moments before Cary broke the silence.

"So, do I get the time off?"

He frowned. "Do I have a choice? I mean, if I say no, does Trebeck Corporation lose you?"

After a moment, she nodded. "Yes."

"Is two weeks enough?"

"I hope so – I think it will be," Cary told him. "I'll take two weeks vacation and also leave a request with you for a short leave of absence. That will cover both of us if I need more time." She hesitated, and then said, "One more thing. Can we just say I'm going to New Orleans to shop for antiques? I'd like to keep the real purpose to myself."

He leaned back and laced his fingers behind his head. Thoughtfully he asked, "Will you help me get organized before you go?"

"Sure, I can do that."

"Oh, by the way," he said, snapping his fingers, "I'll be at the University of New Orleans in two weeks for a brush-up seminar. If you're still there, maybe I can help with your search." He hesitated, then added, "Also, if the situation requires it, I know some people in New Orleans."

His suggestion surprised her. *What an odd offer.*

Cary didn't like the idea of Webster even being in New Orleans, but she couldn't tell him not to come.

"That sounds fine," she said, careful not to make a commitment. "Let me think about it."

"Okay," Webster said. "Oh, and do you mind if I call you Cary? I like to use first names."

***

When Cary left his office, Webster closed the door and walked to his chair. Sitting down, he turned and propped his feet up on a corner of the desk, frowned, and leaned back.

Cary Warren could be a problem. Webster considered their meeting. She obviously had expected this job to be hers. *Then I slipped in front of her. I'd be upset, too.*

She'd *really* be disturbed if she knew the truth.

It wasn't an accident that he was at Trebeck Corporation. A great deal of planning and forethought had gone on before he walked through the front door. Webster, more than ever, wondered about his assignment – could he pull it off? He knew what was required, but success was doubtful at best. And Cary Warren had already thrown a monkey wrench of her own into the works.

In his mind, Webster reviewed the situation: he would be running an advertising department *and* functioning as a corporate spy, as it were. *And* he would be keeping an eye on Cary Warren. Otherwise, she could screw up the whole damn mess. On top of everything else, the headstrong Miss Warren had now informed him she was going to New Orleans to search for some unspecified person. *Damn! I must have been crazy to take this job.*

He *was* pleased with his quick thinking. The made-up seminar would serve as a cover for his presence in New Orleans with both Cary and the people at Trebeck. It would also allow him to follow some leads in that city. The situation was complicated, but still he was happy to be in a domestic setting, *and* in the U.S. where he could speak English. Played right, the job could lead to a normal life, perhaps even a family someday.

Now Webster had to hope the wrong people didn't figure out where he'd surfaced. To accomplish that, he'd have to maintain a low profile, which shouldn't be too difficult.

Dropping his feet to the floor, he turned and reached for the material he set aside when Miss Warren showed up. Opening the folder, he took out the papers he'd been studying. Webster read the remaining few paragraphs, then reached for a pen and signed them in three places. Interesting – after all this time, it only took a few signatures to cut the ties to his former life. His mind kept jumping back to the task at hand.

Checking out operations and ownership here at Trebeck should be easy enough. Additionally, he had instructions to investigate and confirm or rule out illegal activities in the corporations operation.

Webster knew how to get that job done, too. Overall, he didn't foresee any specific problems even though his work here could change the lives of some high-rollers down in bayou country. All things considered, comparing this assignment to other recent ones, this one should be relatively danger-free. Yet, as he noticed the lingering scent of Cary's perfume, he wasn't quite so sure.

***

To get Webster grounded, Cary arranged for them to combine forces for the remainder of the week. By Friday afternoon, he had met everyone and understood how the department worked. He was well received by the staff – in no small part, she noticed, due to her willingness to work with him.

She packed for New Orleans on Saturday and prepared to fly out on Sunday. Come hell or high water, Cary had decided to satisfy herself about her birth relatives and especially the note concerning her mother. Thinking about the high water part, she wondered if she should pack some waders.

Chapter Three

She flew out of Knoxville's McGhee-Tyson airport on a Sunday morning that couldn't have been more spectacular. Sunlight sparkled on the Little Tennessee River and the cerulean sky held only a smattering of clouds, yet Cary was restless. As satisfying as the flight and scenery were, she caught herself tapping nervously on the armrest. Glancing over at her seat-mate, she wondered if the woman had picked up on her fragile state of mind.

Settling into her seat, Cary thought of Rita. She had phoned her buddy just prior to leaving for the airport. "Watch yourself and be careful," Rita had cautioned her. "You never know what or who you're going to run into in a strange city." Cary promised her friend she would phone often while in New Orleans. Rita had admonished her to make sure she had her cell phone. Cary had checked. It was in her purse.

The flight was due for a stopover in Atlanta. From there she would fly to her destination. Cary hoped she could keep her emotions at bay. To take her mind off the uncertainties, she turned to the lady in the adjoining seat and asked, "Where are you headed this morning?"

"Home," the woman said with a smile and then added, "finally."

Cary sized her up. She was elderly, probably eighty at least. Her long sleeved dress, made of a pretty flowered print, had lace around the collar and cuffs. She reminded Cary of someone's grandmother. A thought crossed Cary's mind, *"Maybe mine."*

"I can't wait to get back," the woman softly told Cary, a sparkle in her eyes. "N'awlins is home to me. Hurricane Katrina chased me out, but I'm going back now an' I'm gonna stay this time." She spoke with her hands as much as with her voice. Cary visualized an earlier time, the turn of the century perhaps. A woman like this would have fit right in: soft spoken, conservatively attired – perhaps in an even longer dress.

"That storm nearly blew the ole place away." The old lady made a swishing sound and waved her arm across her body. Flashing a bright smile, she said, "My boys have been fixing my house up and now it's finally ready."

She eyed Cary and asked, "What's your name?"

"Cary Warren, from Knoxville." Cary quickly changed the subject back, asking, "You've always lived in New Orleans?"

"*I have,*" the woman said emphasizing the two words. "I was born there. I'm Mrs. Roberto Lawrence Kato." Grinning, she said, "How's that for a name." Then she waved her hand dismissively, saying, "But you call me Landie. It's an old family name."

"I like it . . . It's different." Cary again imagined Landie in an earlier time when people took care of each other – an era when neighbors didn't mind being call upon – Southern Hospitality, they called now. Cary twisted, attempting to curl her long legs under her in the seat. Finally giving up, she eased them back to the floor. Her shoes were already tossed aside.

Landie said she was tired and going to rest. Cary leaned back, too, turning to her thoughts as she stared out the window. Relaxing wasn't in the cards.

The stopover in Atlanta was brief, and then they were on their way again. A few minutes before landing in New Orleans, a thought that had been nagging Cary since they first introduced themselves finally came into focus. The lady's surname, Kato, seemed familiar – like she had heard it before. But try as she might, Cary couldn't put her finger on the connection. *Oh, well! Perhaps she was letting her imagination run wild.*

Cary excused herself and went to find the restroom. When she returned, Landie was flipping through a magazine. After another short conversation, the lady returned to her reading, leaving Cary to her thoughts again.

In the silence, she went over her reasons again for the journey to Louisiana. She couldn't bring herself to give a name to the mother who had placed her for adoption as a newborn infant. Even if Cary found her, maybe the woman would want no part of a twenty-five-year-old daughter. But she realized a new family would mean a lot to her. It would also go a long way toward releasing her from the blame she placed on herself.

"Isn't it beautiful?" Landie said, interrupting Cary's thoughts. She pointed out the window. "I never get tired of flying." Then she asked, "Will you be visiting someone in N'awlins?"

"No," Cary said. "I'm looking for someone from my past." The words came out slowly. She wasn't comfortable talking about her search.

Landie glanced at her before commenting. "Sounds a little mysterious," she remarked. "I hope you find whoever you're looking for . . . if that's what you really want." Cary remembered Rita's observation along the same lines a week ago. She wondered if Landie might be guessing at her motives.

As the plane descended, Landie wrote her address and phone number down. "I want you to promise if you have time, you will come and have dinner with me. I'd like to hear more about you and your search. And if there's some way I can help, let me know." The old woman sounded sincere.

Cary promised, thinking how Landie really seemed from another place and time. *Kato . . . Kato?*

Their Captain turned on the "Fasten Seat Belts" sign and a short time later they were on the ground and exiting the aircraft. Reaching the main terminal, Cary saw a large, joyful group of people holding a huge sign proclaiming: **Welcome Home, Landie!**

Cary felt a catch in her throat. Landie's family was waiting for her. The elderly lady had been leaning on Cary's arm as they came off the airplane, and now she pulled her toward the waiting group.

"Grandma," a little blonde girl yelled, as the family rushed toward the old woman. Several children crowded close, looking up at her and waiting for the frail arms to encircle them. Adults, too. Everyone wanted their own private moment with this little woman.

Cary stood among those gathered around Landie, an emptiness inside her that wouldn't go away. She caught herself wishing this was her family, that she could be a part of this homecoming. But this *wasn't* Cary's family. Finally, when Landie had been hugged and kissed by everyone, she took a moment to introduce Cary as her *New Best Friend*. She told them Cary's name, and announced, "We discovered each other during the flight." Then, taking Cary by the arm, she said, "This is Andy, my oldest son, and Greg, the youngest. This one here is Kathryn, Greg's wife." She even took Cary to meet a tiny baby held by her grandson's wife.

Of all the family, Greg, the youngest son, left the most lasting physical impression. She would remember two things about him: a scar along his cheek and his inquiring eyes. He seemed to take in everything around him.

Cary was finally able to say her goodbyes and make her way to the baggage area. She gathered her luggage and headed out to look for a limo or taxi. Even though it was October and not as warm as she expected, the humidity still seemed oppressive as she walked outside.

"Limo's the best, Miss," a porter told her as he followed along with her bags. "Where to? Uptown, downtown, lakeside, riverside, or over to the west bank?"

Cary stood with her mouth open, wondering what he was talking about. "Ahh . . . Downtown? To the Sheraton New Orleans. On Canal Street," she finally said. He grinned, revealing a sparkling gold front tooth. "Downtown, it is." With that, he loaded her bags. When the limo pulled up to her hotel, Cary climbed out and entered the lobby, followed by a bellhop carrying her bags. She checked in and the same young man led the way to her room.

"Where are you from?" he asked cheerfully as he opened her door and stacked her things inside.

"Knoxville," she said. ". . . Tennessee."

She tipped him, then closed and locked the door. Cary's room was on the eighteenth floor with views out toward the foot of Canal Street where it ended at the Mississippi River. She could also see over into the French Quarter.

"It's gorgeous," she uttered aloud. Then she thought about her parents. Cary felt a tug at her heart. This is where her mom and dad had lived a generation earlier, walking these same streets. They had loved each other and, wanting a child, had adopted her. She felt as though they might be looking over her shoulder, understanding and pleased. She believed they would have approved of her search.

Looking down at the foot of Canal Street, ocean-going ships caught Cary's eye as they moved up and down the river. In the Quarter, she could see people leisurely strolling along and peering at treasures in the shops. On a sidewalk in the distance, she could see a street musician playing a trombone; passers-by were dropping money into his instrument case. She imagined her parents strolling hand and hand, listening to the music the man played on his old horn. Cary could almost hear the sounds herself. She would have loved to go exploring, but it was late, and she was tired.

She had automatically picked up her cell phone when she'd first walked to the window. Standing there in thought for another moment, she punched in Rita's number. They said hello and Cary reported on her flight. She even told Rita about Landie. Rita was on her way out, so they only spoke for a couple of minutes. Still there was time for Rita to caution her again about New Orleans. Smiling at her friend's admonitions, Cary closed her phone and tossed it on the bed.

Finally, turning from the window, she began unpacking. It was then she noticed a small fruit basket on a table in the corner. She assumed it was something from the hotel until she saw the attached card. Walking over, she pulled the envelope loose and opened it.

"Good luck with your search," it read. It was from Mike Webster. *How did he know where she was staying?* Cary immediately realized Rita must have told him. *I'm going to have to have a talk with that girl.*

Finished with the unpacking, Cary took a long hot shower. As she was toweling off, her stomach growled. Pulling on one of the hotel's terry cloth robes, she ordered a sandwich from room service and flipped on the TV. The food arrived a short time later, and she ate while watching a couple of sitcoms. Giving up on the reruns, she switched it off in favor of the Grisham novel she'd brought with her.

Later, dead tired and knowing that Monday would be busy, she closed the book, turned off the lights, and crawled into bed.

At last sleep was starting to overtake on her. With heavy eyes, she peered over at the fruit basket one last time. Though he seemed shrouded in mystery, Webster was trying hard to be a decent guy, she decided. Not bad looking, either. She conceded she should try to get along with him, even if he did have her job.

Chapter Four

Monday morning found Cary awake and eager to start her search. After a light breakfast in the Starbucks Coffee Shop off the lobby, she ventured out of the hotel. The sun pounced on her as she walked out, causing her to look up at a magnificent sky. It was a brilliant day, crisp, with just a few soft clouds scattered here and there. The weather had been fantastic for two days in a row – maybe that was a good omen.

She tucked her chin down into the loose-fitting neck of the sweater she wore. It was a habit she almost believed she'd been born with. She had slipped on the sweater as an afterthought, but now, with the morning chill, she was glad.

People rushed along the sidewalks, trying to make it to work before eight. *Why don't they just leave earlier?* She realized her mind was jumping at anything it could to stay off her real purpose for being here. Cary walked along the sidewalk in front of the hotel, studying folks as they hurried to their destinations. Any one of them could be from her own family. She remembered the line: "Rich man, poor man, beggar man, thief." *Thief?* Where had that come from?

Glancing down Canal Street, she saw a streetcar stopped a block or so away, passengers climbing on and off. The trolley reminded her of ones she had seen in old, late night TV movies. New Orleans was an old city, some three hundred years, if memory served her, and teeming with history. Streetcars were part of the lore.

 Her short walk finished, Cary went back inside the hotel to ask directions to the State Adoptions office. A reservations clerk checked the phone book. "You can walk there," she said. "It's only six blocks away, down in the French Quarter."

No need to rush, the adoption office probably didn't open until nine. She walked slowly, using the down time to relieve stress. She'd been tense since she'd learned her job had gone to Webster. That and the decision to come here and search for her family had Cary in knots. Anything to divert her attention was welcome.

For the present, she savored the sights and sounds of storekeepers readying their shops for the day's customers. Cary could see activity through the windows. Some individuals were cleaning and rearranging furniture. Others stocked shelves with new merchandise. Still others cleaned windows and washed down the sidewalks. A couple of them smiled and said hello, turning the water away as she passed by.

An elderly black lady greeted Cary with, "Mornin', Darlin'. Now ya'll have a blessed day, ya heah." Cary smiled and waved in reply, feeling more at home than she had expected.

Several elderly men, obviously down on their luck, wandered by. Cary saw one old fellow digging in a garbage can. These could be her relatives, too, she realized with a fresh jangle of nerves that caused her to quicken the pace.

Cary located the adoption office without difficulty. It occupied an entire two-story building, the front of which was weathered stucco. Working shutters festooned each of the windows. Cary went inside. "May I help you?" the young receptionist asked.

"I hope so," Cary told her. "I need to speak with someone about opening an adoption file."

"Take a seat, please. I'll get you in to speak with Mrs. Hebert. She's in charge. Here's one of her business cards."

Cary took a seat, glancing at the card. Along with the standard information was a drawing of a bear cub. The little animal was pointing to the woman's last name – *Hebert*. Emily Hebert. *Ahhh* – French – *a bear!*

Cary repositioned her chair to face the street. Alone and nervous, she picked up a magazine and waited. Who could tell what this visit might bring? She was tempted to get up and leave, but instead, she thumbed through the magazine, not really paying attention but needing something to do with her hands.

After a few minutes, the telephone buzzed. "Mrs. Hebert can see you now," the receptionist said, pointing to an opening. "She's through there, first door on the right."

Cary made her way to the office and knocked.

"Come in," she heard a gruff voice say. Opening the door, she entered a spacious room furnished with attractive antique furniture – not what she would have expected in a state office. A large aubergine oriental rug covered most of the oak floor. Pictures on the walls, Cary noticed, reflected the history of New Orleans and the countries that had claimed the city over the centuries. A large roll top desk, the main feature of the room, sat against a long wall, clutter covering most of its surface: a computer monitor, keyboard, mouse, numerous files, papers, pens and pencils. Nearby tables were covered with files, too.

An older woman, in her early sixties maybe, was seated at the desk. She looked as though she might have been delivered with all the other antiques. The woman turned her wooden swivel chair and peered at Cary in a way that made her wonder again if she should have come to New Orleans. Mrs. Hebert was stout, her hair pulled back into a tight bun. Looking Cary over, she shoved her spectacles up on her nose before she spoke.

"What cha want, Honey? I'm real busy an' I got a bunch of people coming in to see me this morning."

The abrupt greeting took Cary by surprise and she stammered, "I'm ah, I'm . . . searching for my mother."

The woman stared at Cary for a couple of seconds. Misinterpreting or uncaring, she said, "Well, she's obviously not in here and I have a mountain of work." The woman gestured at the stacks of files.

All the emotions Cary had been holding back bubbled to the surface. She covered her face with both hands as a sob escaped and tears glazed her eyes.

Cary's breakdown got the woman's attention.

"Oh, Sweetie," she said, handing Cary a Kleenex. "Sometimes I just get overwrought and . . . oh for heaven sakes. How 'bout if we try again?" This time she grinned, and the whole room seemed to warm a few degrees. Smile lines at the corners of her mouth and eyes appeared well used. The effect was dramatic and lifted Cary's spirits immensely.

Dabbing at her eyes, she returned a weak smile, answering with more confidence this time. "I was adopted through this agency when I was an infant," she told the social worker. "I want to try to trace my birth family."

Mrs. Hebert studied Cary's expression, then motioned her to one of the large overstuffed chairs in a corner of the office.

"Want some coffee? I'm not worth a hoot in the morning 'til I've had mine."

Cary shook her head, wiping her eyes again as Mrs. Hebert picked up the phone. She punched in a number and told someone on the other end to get her some coffee in here right now, and didn't they know what time it was anyway.

Her coffee arrived quickly. She took it, picked up a writing pad and joined Cary, dropping her ample frame into the other chair.

"Why do you think you need to do this?" Mrs. Hebert asked.

Cary was ready. "My adoptive parents were killed in an accident a few years ago," she said, wiping her nose. "Since I don't have any siblings or, for that matter, any other close relatives . . ." she hesitated, glancing down at her hands. "I feel like I'm adrift. Given the situation, I think I'd like to try to find my biological family." Pausing for a moment, she then added, "I suppose I'm on a mission to find out who I am and where I came from." When she finished, Cary glanced up and was surprised to see tears on Mrs. Hebert's cheeks.

"It hurts, doesn't it, Dawlin'," the woman said softly. "I was adopted, too, but the laws were different in those days. There was no way for me to find out about my family."

"I'm sorry," Cary said. Then, with renewed hope, she asked, "But does that mean maybe I can find mine?" She caught herself twisting her hands in her lap.

"It's possible. Depends on several things."

"Like what?"

"Well, there's a voluntary registry here in Louisiana. Your mother or someone else may have signed up with the registry so you could contact them. If not, then you have to hope for the best with the adoption file and whatever is there."

"Such as?" Cary asked.

"Well, like whether or not your biological parents gave their permission for you to trace them," Mrs. Hebert answered. "Sometimes . . . no, make that most of the time, a mother who allows a child to be adopted doesn't want to be traced later. It's such a difficult decision that usually they want to put it behind them forever. On the other hand, some just fail to leave permission in the file. The question is left open." She made some notes on the pad.

"What happens then?"

Raising her eyes back to Cary's, the woman said, "You'd need to petition the courts to open the file; there are reasons that allow this. If the file is opened, we trace the parents through this department. If we find them, we ask permission for you to contact them. If they okay it, we set up a meeting."

"Sounds simple enough," Cary said, somewhat encouraged. Now she caught herself rubbing her hand back and forth along her leg. She stopped but not before Mrs. Hebert noticed.

"Yeah, it sounds simple," Mrs. Hebert agreed, then with her eyebrows drawn together, she continued. "But often there are snags. People die or move and don't leave a forwarding address or, quite often, they just refuse to see whoever's searching for them."

"What do I need to do to find out about my particular situation?" asked Cary. "Can we get things started, and how long does it take? I only have a couple of weeks to do this. After that, I'll need to take a leave of absence from my job."

"Slow down," Mrs. Hebert said, smiling. "The first thing we'll want to do is check the voluntary registry, then locate your file. Let's get some information.

What's your full name?"

"Cary Anne Warren."

Jotting down more notes, the social worker asked, "Date of birth?"

"October 12, 1982."

"Do you – and this is important – do you know when the Warrens signed papers and picked you up?"

Cary leaned forward, remembering. "I sure do. It was always a special time for us. Mom, Dad, and me, we celebrated it like a birthday or an anniversary. It was the fourteenth of October. Twenty-five years ago this coming Thursday." In response to the woman's raised brow, Cary said, "I planned it . . . to come here on my anniversary."

"Well, Happy Anniversary in advance," Mrs. Hebert said, then pushed her glasses up as she added to her notes. "Okay, let's see if the computer has ever heard of you."

"Think it would help if I cross my fingers?" Cary asked, only half joking.

Mrs. Hebert grinned. "Couldn't hurt." She motioned for Cary to keep her seat and headed for the computer. Cary watched her working and later heard her on the phone.

Left alone, Cary wondered again if she was doing the right thing. She realized she might find information that would trouble her for the rest of her life. Unable to sit still, she stood and began pacing in front of the windows. As she saw her image in the glass, she wondered, as she had many times before, if she looked like her birth mother. Was her mother tall, also? Did she have the same dark hair and eyes? Was her hair wavy, too? Maybe they even shared mannerisms. After a few turns in front of the windows, she sat down again.

Mrs. Hebert spoke, startling Cary. "Well, at least the computer has heard of you. It even thinks it knows where they stored your adoption file up in Baton Rouge. The other news is there are no inquiries on the voluntary registry. I'm sorry."

"Is there anything else we can do?" Cary asked.

"You can put your data on-line and if anyone searches for you, they'll find your information and contact you. But since no one has signed up yet, let's try to get your file to our office."

Cary's heart felt like it was on a roller-coaster ride, up one minute, dashed to the bottom the next. "How long could it take?"

"Well, for starters, the file has to be dug out of storage," Mrs. Hebert said. "The warehouse is in Baton Rouge, as I said, but there are thousands of files like yours. Thank goodness the storm didn't get to them. Sometimes, though, they're out of place, or our information is wrong about their location. All kinds of things can make them difficult to find. But I've already called to get our people searching. Let's see how we do."

"How long should I wait before I get in touch?" Cary asked.

"Call me tomorrow morning. Maybe I'll have some idea by then."

"Thanks, I will," Cary said, rising to leave. Like her heart, her stomach was rolling, too. She didn't know whether to feel happy or troubled about the things Mrs. Hebert had discovered.

The social worker must have sensed her concern because she said, "We'll find it, Honey. I told them to hurry. I know you're in a rush and don't have much time. I truly understand how important this is."

"Thanks," Cary said as she let herself out the door.

Outside on the sidewalk, Cary walked a few feet and stopped, wondering how she should proceed as they waited for the file. She had come all this way to learn something about her biological parents. Waiting for answers – in this case, the adoption file – wasn't her strong suit.

If only she'd brought her laptop . . .

Cary decided to stroll through the French Quarter. Maybe she could locate an internet café. Ambling along, she admired the old buildings, many with tiny gardens or small courtyards between them. Reaching the expansive plaza between Jackson Square and the Saint Louis Cathedral, she stopped to take in the awesome sight of the Cathedral and its triple spires.

She walked to the end of Jackson Square and crossed the street. Down to her left, she could hear a trumpet playing a soulful rendition of "When the Saints Go Marching In." To her right, midway down the block, was a wide set of steps leading to a viewing platform overlooking the area, a perfect spot to get a better view of the street and the river below. Maybe from there she could pick out a likely spot for an internet café. Cary climbed the steps and joined a throng of people gazing out over the Mississippi River.

On her right was a large commercial building with crowds of people going in and out. Behind that building was a dock with a riverboat tied alongside. The craft, complete with a large red paddle wheel, was mostly white but trimmed in bright red and blue. Maybe her mom and dad had brought her there after they adopted her.

As she admired the boat, its whistle suddenly blew and released a large blast of steam. The loud sound reverberated along the waterfront, scattering her thoughts like pigeons fleeing a rooftop. From her vantage point, Cary noticed the Jax Brewery sign on the commercial building, indicating its earlier use. Maybe there would be an internet café inside.

She made her way to the street and headed that way. Inside the building, the first thing to catch Cary's attention was a young mother with a little girl in tow. That could have been Cary and her mom many years ago. As the child and her mother entered a toy store, Cary tucked her feelings away and moved on.

The interior of the building was open and lined with all sorts of shops. Many were small stores of different types: jewelry, hats, clothing – you name it. Some of the establishments were enclosed while others were open to the interior of the building. Then there were the small restaurants. Separated from other shops by side walls but with open fronts except for counters, food vendors hawked their offerings to passers-by. Enticing smells coming from their stalls made Cary's stomach rumble. How long had it been since she'd last eaten? A nearby sign proclaimed the eatery to be "Home of the New Orleans Po' boy." But better than that, on a different wall, there was Wi-Fi and a bank of computers. She decided to get a sandwich and use one of the stations to visit the internet.

After she ordered and paid for her food, Cary took her tray, found an open computer and then went in search of the woman running the place. She paid for an hour of time. Logging on, she quickly found the Louisiana Adoption Service site and keyed into the Voluntary Registry. To her disappointment, the information she pulled up merely gave her a telephone number where she could request an application for registering.

"Bureaucracy," Cary growled, then pulled out her cell phone and called the number, asking that an application be sent to her apartment in Knoxville. She moved on, disappointed at not being able to register on-line. She clicked through several other adoption information sites and other material she thought might be applicable Nothing. . .

She was ready to give up when finally, as if of their own accord, her fingers tapped in her parents' names. There was little on her mother. No surprise there since her mom hadn't worked outside their home. Then Cary punched in her dad's name. She could kick herself for not having thought to do this earlier. His old website popped up along with his image. She scrolled through, reading a sentence here, an item there, stopping when she came to his bio. It noted he had decided to become a doctor when he watched a friend die in a hunting accident and had been helpless to do anything.

Cary stopped reading, turned, and stared toward the river. Suddenly her dad's words had new meaning for her. She refused to go through life in a helpless state: Cary *had* to find her birth mother. She only hoped there was no connection between the mother she'd never met and the note in her dad's file.

Suddenly, Cary was not hungry. Dumping her tray, po' boy and all, she made her way through the rest of the building. Worrisome thoughts kept her from enjoying what should have been a leisurely afternoon. Questions kept popping up. The one that seemed most urgent was the one that might prove most difficult to answer: Her dad's obscure notation – Murdered?

Please don't let that be my mother . . .

***

Elsewhere in the city that afternoon, half a dozen men gathered in a small boardroom at Harrah's Casino. The discussion topic was the profitability of their holdings. They had been partners for more than twenty years and held a myriad of companies and properties of different sorts.

"Overall," their spokesman told them, "it's been the best quarter we've had in two years."

Several of them clapped, while one tapped the table with his knuckles. There were smiles all around. Each of them had a cocktail at hand and silent toasts filled the air.

The holdings they had accumulated were scattered from New Orleans to several southeastern states. The latest, Trebeck Corporation in Knoxville, Tennessee, was doing quite well financially. The spokesman said so. But that acquisition had not been for profitability alone. There were other motives that had nothing at all to do with monetary gain: ones directed toward political objectives and that involved an employee at the company. And the time was at hand for this investment to bear political fruit.

One of the participants asked the question on all their minds: "It's been nearly three years now – how's she doing?"

The spokesman's answer caused a stir.

"Interesting you should ask that," he said. "She's doing great, but that isn't the point. We bought Trebeck, hired and promoted her to make sure she doesn't give us any problems. She's done a great job *and* stayed home – so far. Yet, as we speak, she's in New Orleans." There was an audible intake of breath around the table. A couple of the men sat up straighter in their chairs.

The speaker continued. "She arrived yesterday afternoon," he said, "ostensibly to shop for antiques."

The man who asked the initial question then followed up . . .

"Are we sure that's all?" The speaker stared his way for a moment before answering.

"Can one ever be sure?"

Another man asked, "Do we know where she's staying and do we have someone watching her?" He hesitated. "Under no circumstances can we let her cause a problem – especially now." The man's face was drawn, eyebrows almost touching. He glanced around the table.

Everyone nodded in agreement.

Chapter Five

Tuesday morning Cary was out of bed early – again. Though it was her birthday, there was no time for celebrating. She showered, toweled her hair dry, and combed it, then hurriedly put on her makeup. She dressed casually, opting for slacks, a buttoned pastel top, and her ever-present heels. Downstairs at the coffee shop, she hurried through a light breakfast, then rushed back to her room and called the social worker.

"You better get on down here, Honey," Mrs. Hebert told her – no explanation, nothing.

Sounded like bad news to Cary. "I'll be there as quick as I can."

Minutes later, Cary was in the social worker's office. That uneasy feeling was back. As soon as they were seated, the woman told Cary, "We received your file and I've set aside time for us to talk." She paused. ". . . I've already had a look." Then Mrs. Hebert asked, "Can you take bad news, Dawlin'?"

Cary nodded as she felt the blood drain from her face.

Without preface, the social worker told her, "Your birth mother's dead, Cary and has been since you were an infant. I'm sorry."

Cary was silent, her hopes fading. Questions she had hoped to ask would now go unanswered. With misty eyes, she glanced out the window, then back. "How do you know?"

"Your file – it was all there."

Cary took a few moments. Most her adult life, she'd been in control. With her parents gone, and now her biological mother, she felt abandoned: adrift, like a boat after a storm. The guilt she felt about her mom and dad flooded back, too. Now this – a loss that had been there all along, but this one, she hadn't known about.

Mrs. Hebert continued: "There was a newspaper article in the folder from twenty-five years ago. Someone in our office must have clipped it and dropped it into your file. They probably thought the story closed your case."

"Ho . . . how did she die?" Composure was proving difficult.

"Are you sure you want to know everything?"

Cary didn't hesitate. "Yes."

Mrs. Hebert placed her hand on Cary's arm and said, "She was killed by a hit-and-run driver a few days after you were born. Only a couple of people saw the accident. They couldn't even agree on the color of the automobile, only that it was new."

"Is . . . that all there was?"

"Pretty much," Mrs. Hebert told her. "The rest was details. When and where, that sort of thing."

Cary stared down at her hands.

"Would you like to go for a walk? The Quarter's nice this time of year." Mrs. Hebert motioned her up. "Come on," she insisted. "I don't have any appointments until this afternoon." Cary let the woman lead her through the office and out the front door. The adoption file was tucked into Mrs. Hebert's large handbag. Outside, they strolled without speaking for a time. Others passed by them, but, drained as she was, Cary hardly noticed.

After several minutes, Mrs. Hebert suggested they go and sit in the park. Once military parade grounds, Jackson Square encompassed a city block and was now surrounded by ornate wrought iron fencing. The park was filled with flower beds blooming year round and there were sago palms, southern magnolias, old oak trees, and other assorted plant life.

They ambled over and sat on one of the iron benches facing the large statue of Andrew Jackson astride his horse. The smell of the river came to them faintly on the breeze from the port of New Orleans. And somewhere near the park, "A Closer Walk with Thee" was being played softly on a violin.

"Would you like to talk about it?" Mrs. Hebert asked.

"Why not." Cary said. "And I'll be okay. It's just that I thought I could come to New Orleans, and . . . well, I guess I expected to find my mother and ask her . . ." she breathed a long sigh, ". . . maybe ask her some questions. I imagined that meeting her would help me make sense of what I've been going through for the last three years. But it isn't going to work that way, is it? She's gone, and I'm right back where I started."

Mrs. Hebert didn't reply. Instead, she pulled a wrapped sandwich from her handbag, opened it, and handed half to Cary. "Peanut butter," she said. "My morning snack."

"Thanks." Cary eyed the offering, then took a tiny bite, chewing it slowly, waiting.

"Well . . . you're not quite back where you started. Your file does give us some details I can share." Mrs. Hebert paused, swallowing a bite of her own sandwich, then continued. "For instance, your mother left home after she finished high school. She was second of four children and had three brothers." The social worker referred to the file. "Both parents came from large families. Her father, unfortunately, was an alcoholic. The notes indicate her brothers were headed in that direction, too." She glanced at Cary. "That's probably why she left home as soon as she finished high school." Closing the folder, Mrs. Hebert said, "That's all the family details she provided." Mrs. Hebert held up her snack, eyeing it before taking another bite.

Cary tore the crust off her sandwich and tossed it to nearby pigeons, then asked, "Did it say where she came from?"

"No," Mrs. Hebert told her. "And we wouldn't have tried to trace her. She told us she had gone to a lawyer and legally changed her name three years earlier. She didn't want her family to find her."

"Where did she work? She must have had a job." Cary stuck the last morsel of the sandwich in her mouth, wishing she had some water to wash it down with.

Mrs. Hebert opened her handbag and dug through the papers. "According to this, she worked for a temp agency when she came to us – secretarial and bookkeeping jobs."

"So she worked in offices."

Mrs. Hebert brushed off crumbs before answering. "Yes, and she went to college at night. She had about two and a half years of credits toward a degree."

Cary smiled, strangely proud of the accomplishments of the mother she would never know.

"What about my father and his family?" Cary asked. Funny, she realized, she had spent most of her time thinking about her mother and hadn't given much consideration to him.

"There's nothing about him in the file," Mrs. Hebert said. "But that isn't unusual. Your mother didn't tell us who he was. We get that all the time. They just refuse to say. There's no information about your father on your original birth certificate, either."

"So, my mother's dead, and I don't even know my father's name." Cary glanced at the social worker. "I guess that's the end of my search."

For a few moments, Mrs. Hebert stared at Cary, then, appearing to have made some sort of decision, said, "Maybe not." The woman reached into the adoption file yet again, retrieving an envelope this time. It was discolored and appeared to have been in the file a long time. Without explanation, the social worker handed it to Cary and said, "This is for you."

As Cary stared at the envelope, she remembered the memo in her dad's file. *Mother to write a note to leave in folder.* Her heart skipped a beat. Reaching out with tingling fingers, she took it, asking, "What's this?"

"I don't know," Mrs. Hebert told her, "but it was placed in the file by your mother. As you can see, she wanted you to have it if you ever tried to trace her."

Cary looked at the yellowed envelope. On the front her mother had written: *To My Darling Daughter.*

Cary ran the tips of her fingers across the words, fighting back tears.

Nodding at the envelope, Mrs. Hebert said, "Normally we couldn't give you anything from the file, but this was put there expressly for you. And it's been twenty-five years. I've checked and it isn't inventoried. So if you don't tell, I won't either."

Cary then carefully ran a finger under the flap, loosening the brittle glue. Opening the envelope, she unfolded several pages of a letter. Clutching it to her breast, she just held it, thinking – *This is the only thing I've ever touched that's been held by my mother.*

She turned to Mrs. Hebert and asked, "May I take this with me?"

"Of course, child. It's been here all these years waiting for you to come and collect it. Now it's in your hands, where it belongs."

Cary put the letter back into its envelope. Slipping it into her purse, she rose to her feet. Extending her hand toward Mrs. Hebert, Cary said, "Thanks for all your help. I think I'd like to read this in private, back at the hotel."

"I understand. Call if you need me," then, a little teary-eyed herself, Mrs. Hebert added, "or if you just want someone to talk to."

Back in her hotel room, Cary removed and carefully unfolded the letter. She lay back on her bed and began to read.

> **My Dearest Daughter,**
> As I write this, you are only three days old. Just yesterday morning I signed the papers releasing you to your new mom and dad. The social worker said they were very nice. I'm counting on it.
> I had come up with lots of reasons why I shouldn't let you go. And many of them are good. But I also know I don't have the means to give you the life you deserve.

So I'm letting you go because I love you.

Cary looked away, imagining her mother, all those years ago, alone somewhere, trying to find the words to tell her daughter goodbye.

A solitary tear ran down Cary's cheek. She wiped it with the back of her hand and continued reading:

> *Since this may be the only communication I'll ever have with you, I want to tell you some things about your family and me.*
>
> *I left home eight years ago when I was only seventeen and just out of high school. I'd secretly saved enough money to get started, and I've been working and going to school since I arrived in New Orleans. That's enough about me.*
>
> *Your daddy's name is Johnny Periot. I probably shouldn't tell you, but I thought you deserve to know.*
>
> *I met him one Sunday morning when I was out with a girlfriend. He and I hit it off immediately. Unfortunately, he neglected to tell me he was married and had two small daughters. When I found out, it was too late. I was expecting his baby.*
>
> *Johnny's a young lawyer and our affair would hurt his career. I understand that, but his reaction to my being pregnant scared me. Although I love him, I didn't want to put you at risk, so I've stopped seeing him.*

At risk? What had her mother meant by that? Now Cary understood why there was no information in the adoption file about her father. *Her mother had been afraid to name him in any official way.*

She read on:

> *I thought everything concerning him was over, but then last week I got a threatening phone call from someone. They told me in no uncertain terms to stay away from Johnny.*

And a threatening call. Why would anyone do that? She glanced out the window, thinking. Her father's name sounded familiar. Periot? Johnny Periot?

Cary felt sure she had heard it somewhere. She would remember, sooner or later.

Only a few more sentences:

In the end, I gave you up so that you could have a better life. Someday I hope people will look at you and see a young lady who's very successful. Maybe some of that will have come from me.

I love you with all my heart,

Your mother,

Janice Talmer

So that was her name. Cary tried it aloud, listening to the words roll off her tongue, *"Janice Talmer."*

Still holding the letter, Cary turned to face the window. She lay quietly for several minutes, her head on her arm and tears on her face. She envisioned her mother lingering over each word in the letter written to a daughter she never expected to see again. Cary held the pages in her hand, imagining the emotions involved in writing them. *My mother's hopes and dreams for me – from yesterday.*

After a time, she got up and walked to the window overlooking the city and the gray waters of the Mississippi. For several minutes, she stood looking out at passing ships and thinking about her mother. Janice had only lived a few days after writing the letter.

Finally, Cary shuffled the pages to find Janice's reference to Cary's own safety, or as her mother had phrased it – she didn't want to put Cary at risk. Her mother's concern bothered Cary. Could it have led to Janice's death? Had Janice become a liability to someone? *Cary's biological father, perhaps?*

She spent the next several hours trying to sort out her life. She was feeling lonely and lost, yet also angry and unforgiving, knowing someone might have killed her mother because she had become an inconvenience. But *had* she been killed, or was the hit and run really an accident? She wondered after reading the letter. And then there was that note in her dad's files in Tennessee. *Murdered?* Had her father meant Janice Talmer, after all?

Cary lay awake late into the night, thinking of her mother and trying, without success, to adjust to a world gone wild.

Early Wednesday morning, Cary called Mrs. Hebert. After having read the letter several times, she needed answers to the questions rolling around in her mind – one in particular.

When she got Mrs. Hebert on the phone, Cary asked, "Are you familiar with an attorney named Johnny Periot here in the city?"

There was a short pause. Then Mrs. Hebert chuckled. "You're kidding, aren't you, Darlin'? Lord, yes . . ."

"And? How do you know him?"

"Honey, Johnny Periot is the Mayor of New Orleans."

 **Chapter Six**

Cary almost dropped the phone. Mrs. Hebert must have wondered about her. "I'm sorry. You said he's the Mayor. Th . . . the Mayor of New Orleans?" *My mother's lover, my own biological father . . . is the Mayor?* She could feel perspiration on her forehead. Still seated on the bed, Cary pulled her knees up.

"What's wrong, Honey? You sound . . . out of sorts."

Cary, her emotions all over the place, fought to recover.

"My mother . . . mentioned him in her letter," Cary prevaricated. "She said she met Periot once, along with some other people." It sounded unconvincing, even to her. "I just thought you might have heard of him and decided I would ask." Cary said goodbye as soon as she could and hung up. Her nerves were on edge. She had come to New Orleans to look for her biological parents. *And now all this.* It wasn't at all what she'd expected.

Her hand was still near the phone when it rang. Cary jumped. *Damn!* She wasn't sure how much more her nerves could stand. Would this be more bad news? After a second ring, she picked up the receiver. "Hello?" She sat back against the pillows, an arm around her knees.

"Cary?" A male voice.

"Yes?" The caller sounded familiar.

"Cary. It's Mike. Mike Webster . . . You do remember me?"

"Mike. O-oh, now I recognize your voice," she stammered. "I had just hung up the phone when it rang again. It startled me."

Cary heard him chuckle.

It's not funny, damn it! Cary ran her long fingers through her hair, flipping it back over her shoulders.

"How are you making out? Any luck with your search?"

"Nothing yet," she lied. Cary wanted time to sort things out before she told anyone. *Especially him.*

"That's too bad," he replied, compassion in his voice. "Any leads?"

"Some," she said. "I'm still looking." Now she felt bad about the negative thoughts she'd had. He was trying to be nice.

"Well, good luck." Then he added, "Look, I'm flying into New Orleans late Friday afternoon. How about having dinner with me? We can talk about things here at Trebeck, and you can let me know if there's any way I can help you."

Cary thought for a moment, and then said, "Can I let you know when you get here? Everything is unsettled right now."

"Sure, that's fine. I'll call you when I get to the hotel."

"Where are you staying?"

"Same place as you. At the Sheraton."

Damn! Cary got up and walked to the window.

This wasn't part of the plan. It was bad enough having him take over at work. She didn't need him intruding into her personal life, too.

Listening, Cary stood at the window watching a large ocean-going cargo vessel surrounded by tug boats slowly making its way down the river.

Webster pushed it. "I'm going to be disappointed if you don't have dinner with me."

"I'll *work* on it," Cary told him in a not-so-friendly tone. She flipped her hair again, a nervous habit.

They said goodbye and Cary returned to the bed. She sat, feelings about her mother competing with thoughts of Webster. And there were certainly more thoughts of him than she cared to admit. That she was thinking about him at all confused her. She wanted to be angry. She really did, but she found herself *almost* looking forward to seeing him on Friday night. *What's wrong with me?*

Her interest in him, if she could call it that, bewildered her – particularly now. She knew virtually nothing about him. Sure, he seemed nice, but so what? *Oh, well.*

Cary sighed, then turned her attention to other matters. She called Rita. "Just checking in," she told her. They spoke for a short time, then said goodbye. Within minutes, she decided what she would do next. Cary rang the hotel desk and asked for the location of the nearest library.

"The main branch is only a few blocks away," a clerk told her. He gave her directions and said, "You can't miss it." Cary grabbed a light coat and her purse and headed for the elevator.

***

When they hung up, Webster rose from his desk and closed the office door. Walking to the window, he stood there – trying to clear his mind. Fingers hooked in his rear pockets, his thoughts returned to the restless night he'd had and to his vivid recurring nightmares.

When he awoke at two in the morning, Webster had been drenched in sweat, his sheets and blanket tossed about. He'd found himself sitting upright in the middle of the bed. The dream, once again, had been too real – or maybe *surreal* was a better term. It was actual events, replayed in his mind – in a dream.

He was back in Columbia, outside Bogotá on the edge of the fortification when the shooting started. He'd been trying to get to the kid, just like he had five months ago. And just like then, Webster saw three figures come out of a window on the second floor of an interior building and start to run across the *Spanish tiled* roof. He recognized Juan as the boy scampered along the building's crest with two bodyguards. Carrying automatic weapons, the men were spraying bullets at Federal Police as they clambered over debris and into the compound. Explosives had taken out large sections of the walls.

The police were firing back, and Webster saw one of the men on the roof go down and slide over the edge, leaving a smear of blood behind. The other one, in his bid to escape, pushed the boy ahead and continued firing toward the men coming over the wall.

Then, as Webster watched, a line of bullets walked their way up the roof tiles toward the two remaining figures fleeing along the ridge line. He remembered the action as though it had been in slow motion. The rounds reached the man with the weapon first. The shock of copper striking flesh caused the man's arms to jerk upward, his reflexes holding his weapon's trigger in the firing position. Bullets sprayed into the sky as his body danced like a puppet, with unseen strings attached. An instant later, the same volley of death reached the boy. That's when Webster always woke from his nightmare.

Sometimes he could still hear echoes of "Nooo!" reverberating in his bedroom. Often his eyes were damp with tears. Thankfully, though, the nightmares were coming less often now.

In those moments, five months ago, the boy had died in his father's fortress because Webster had not removed him from danger the previous day. It would have been so easy, but Webster had been concerned the move would tip the boy's father off to the raid. Then, on that fatal day, the Federal Police started their action a few minutes early. *Just a few minutes too damn soon.* In another ten minutes, he would have had Juan and they would have been out of the compound.

Webster walked back to his chair. Sitting down, he laced his long fingers behind his head and threw his feet up on the corner of the desk. He expected the boy's father to come after him some day. The man headed a strong cartel furnishing a large portion of the drugs finding their way into the U.S. from the south. Word had reached Webster that Juan's father blamed him for the boy's death. The man hated Webster for other reasons, too, but that was just a consequence of his old job.

He wondered how long he would feel guilty. He wondered, too, if Juan's death had prompted him to say he would help Cary. He had been told about her parents. A few months ago he wouldn't have allowed that to sway him. Yet, here he was, making the offer even as he recognized the danger.

But for now, he needed to get on with his work here at Trebeck Corporation. Checking his watch, Webster realized he was due upstairs to meet with the boss. The CEO thought this morning's appointment was to familiarize Webster with certain details of the corporation. To some degree he was right, but Webster was also at Trebeck to probe deeper than who reports to whom.

A number of other individuals would be surprised, too – some would be shocked – to know the Advertising Department was the least of Webster's concerns. Trebeck's New Orleans-based investor group would be furious if they knew his true background and present interest in their company. The outcome of his efforts could be felt a long way from Knoxville, Tennessee.

And Cary Warren was smack dab in the middle of all he intended to do.

***

Cary was on her way to the library. The weather had grown brisk; rain was on the way. She wished she had an umbrella. In spite of the conditions, the walk was refreshing, and it allowed some time to clear her head.

The call from Mike Webster had been a pleasant surprise, though she wished it hadn't. The unforeseen part was she almost enjoyed the attention. She wondered what it would be like to have him around for a few days.

As she walked, the two pieces of information from her dad's folder kept surfacing. The one concerning the note from her birth mother *had* to be about the letter. No real doubts there. The other was less clear. The article from her adoption folder told about Janice Talmer's death – the hit-and-run accident. That explained how she died. But murder? If it *was* murder and not an accident, then what was the purpose, the why? *Her mother couldn't have come to New Orleans only to be killed for no reason.*

The letter to Cary appeared to be the only link to justice for her mother. And Cary was clearly the only person who cared enough to look for answers. Her search, she realized, was quickly becoming what *could* be the pursuit of a killer.

It started to mist. Cary turned up her collar as she hurried along the sidewalk. The library building was large and very visible. Cary saw it a block away. *The clerk at the hotel was right. You really couldn't miss it.* In a very short time, she was racing up the steps, two at a time, to the front door. She went directly to the main desk.

Looking up from newspapers spread across the counter, the young librarian asked, "May I help you?" He was rather thin with one of those spiky haircuts.

"Where can I get some information about the Mayor?"

"Johnny Periot or the Office?"

"Yes. Johnny Periot, *that's* the one."

"A number of places." He crossed his arms, then tapped his nose with a finger as he considered the possibilities. "First, we have several books about him," he said, then added, "and there was a good article in *Newsweek* recently. You probably already know this: he's being mentioned as a possible candidate for Governor." He went on. "Also, there's been some talk about him being considered for the Vice Presidential spot on the Democratic ticket."

"Wow. No, I didn't know any of that." She really was surprised. "You're full of information."

"Well, the Mayor's very popular," the young man said with pride. "And you know what?" He reached up, making an attempt to smooth his hair.

"What?"

"I think Mayor Periot will be able to choose which job he wants," he said.

"No doubt he can if a lot people feel the way you seem to." Cary squinted to see his name tag, then looked him in the eye and said, "Bob."

He threw his head back and laughed "Shows, huh?"

"A little," she said, enjoying Bob's take on Johnny Periot.

Bob blushed and walked from behind the counter. "Come on, I'll show you the books and the magazine section. That article is in one of the last two issues of *Newsweek*," he said, pointing toward the racks. "Are you writing a book?"

"No, just personal curiosity."

Cary found what she was looking for in *Newsweek*. The article was a brief bio of the man and his climb to power in the city. She took the magazine and went looking for a secluded chair. Shoes off and one leg underneath her, Cary started to read.

"Johnny Periot," the article began, "was born in the New Orleans area. He grew up in Algiers, a community on the west bank of the Mississippi River across from downtown New Orleans. As a youngster, Periot often rode the Canal Street ferry from Algiers to the city. From there, he explored the streets of downtown New Orleans and the French Quarter."

Her body growing tense as she continued to read, Cary moved her leg from underneath her and placed both feet on the floor. "Sometimes venturing out," she read, "young Johnny Periot took streetcars and buses to such far away locations as Carrolton and the banks of Lake Pontchartrain. He dreamed," the article pointed out, "of one day being an important person in New Orleans, maybe even the mayor." Now she caught herself leaning forward, elbows on her knees. Cary realized she was becoming more interested as she learned about her father. She glanced around, thinking someone might be watching. *Nothing. Come on, girl. Finish the article.*

Periot's family was discussed next. He and his wife, who had been his high school sweetheart, had two daughters. Cary frowned. *High school sweethearts.* Her mother had said he was married when they met, yet he kept it a secret. She read on. The daughters were adults now and out of college. A thought suddenly occurred to Cary. These are her half-sisters. Her family. She forced herself back to the article.

The commentary told of his rapid rise to power in city government a few years after he finished law school in 1981. *So he had just become a lawyer when he met Janice.* Johnny Periot, Cary read, had worked for a large, prestigious local law firm for two years before going into politics. He moved up quickly, both in the law firm and in politics, according to the journalist. That same law firm presently served as legal council for the city. *Interesting!*

The article further indicated Johnny Periot was leader of a small group of politically like-minded individuals who had been together for years and had set the Mayor's office as its goal years earlier. The group did whatever was necessary to achieve their goals. Cary thought of her mother and held the magazine tighter. If Periot's group existed back then, could they have thought of Janice and her daughter as obstacles to be gotten out of their way?

The next few paragraphs really got Cary's pulse racing. Questions had cropped up concerning the group's actions and methods. Suspicions surfaced about the way potential opponents sometimes mysteriously dropped out of races that included Periot and a few other politicians. There were suggestions that Periot, especially, had been a dangerous adversary in the earlier years. *Could this be a connection to what happened to Janice Talmer?* It sounded like the person in the letter who threatened her mother, might have threatened others, too.

Then the commentary changed. According to a new section of the article, as mayor, Periot had become someone the average Joe could go to with a problem. There was an instance several years ago when Periot made an appeal to find a donor for a young boy dying of kidney failure. The article described several other situations in which the Mayor had put himself on the line to help *his* people. "And they love him for it." Cary glanced back at the front desk, wondering if Bob had been a beneficiary of the Mayor's help.

Next, Periot's chances of becoming Governor were discussed. Almost a shoo-in, the writer indicated. Reading on, Cary found Periot had become well known all across the State and even nationally when he was asked to head a special committee by the President. The committee's responsibility was to study ways of more efficiently using the country's inland waterways for exporting the Mississippi valley's farm products. Periot had gone directly to the citizens of Louisiana and neighboring states, asking for their suggestions. Many responded, and the Mayor had given credit to the people with the ideas. Again, "Everyone loved him."

The writer also mentioned Vice Presidential possibilities. Cary glanced back to the paragraphs that called Periot "a potentially dangerous adversary." Reading between the lines, one could almost come up with a Jekyll and Hyde personality for Cary's biological father. *Hmmm!*

Cary thought about his name again. She *must* have heard it on the news. There was no other explanation. She knew it sounded familiar when it surfaced in Janice Talmer's letter.

Reading the last few words, she closed the magazine and sat thinking. This was the man her mother had fallen in love with. There must have been some good in him. Cary then remembered the individual in the article was also the man her mother feared. According to Janice, he was also Cary's father. She shivered, wishing she had brought a heavier coat. Weather or emotions? – she wondered. Cary remembered other words from the letter:

His reaction scared me. And Janice died a few days later – *with injuries resulting from a hit-and-run accident.*

Then Cary wondered if the driver who struck her mother had ever been arrested. It was time to find out.

Chapter Seven

Cary put the magazine away, called for a taxi, then walked outside and waited. When it arrived, she asked the driver to take her to Police Headquarters. There, Cary paid him as he smiled and said, "You're mighty young and pretty to be in trouble with the law." She grinned as she watched him drive away.

Though nervous, she went inside and approached the main desk. The place was bustling, loud, and reeked of sweat, cigarettes, and stale coffee. She had to wait for several minutes before it was her turn. A drunk was sitting on a nearby bench. Apparently having trouble remaining upright, he nonetheless smiled a crooked smile, then winked at her – twice. Cary looked away but couldn't help grinning. *At least he has good taste!*

She watched people come and go, some in cuffs with officers holding their arms and others who looked like they *should* have been in cuffs. When the sergeant manning the desk asked if he could help, Cary told him she was looking for information on a hit-and-run accident that had happened a long time ago.

"How long?" he asked, an eyebrow rising skeptically.

"Twenty-five years?" she said, tilting her head and giving him her most winning smile.

"Geeezz, that *is* a long time," the sergeant agreed. "Let's see." He leaned back in his chair, considering her question. "Well . . . if the case is still open, it'll be on the computer up in records or maybe on microfilm." He paused. "If it's not there, who knows? But anyway, you'll need to start there."

"Okay. So, where's records?"

"That's on the third floor." He pointed to an elevator. "Good luck."

Cary went upstairs and inquired about the information.

The clerk, a middle-aged black woman, named Bradford, asked, "What's your connection, Dawlin'? Why do you want to see this report?"

"The victim was my mother." *Does everyone in this city call everyone else Dawlin'?*

"Oh . . . I'm sorry," Bradford said, now appearing more interested in helping. "When was the accident?"

"Approximately twenty-five years ago."

"*When?*" The clerk's surprise echoed that of the sergeant downstairs.

"I was adopted. I'm just now getting the details," Cary explained.

"Oh! Now I understand." The woman turned to her computer.

"Okay, what was your mother's name?"

"Janice . . . Janice Talmer. That's T-A-L-M-E-R."

"Date of death?"

Cary told her the date, remembering it from the newspaper article.

"Okay, let's see if we have anything," Officer Bradford said. "Sometimes the old ones are here and sometimes they're not. Makes no rhyme or reason."

She typed a few strokes and waited. "Nope, not there." She immediately started again. The second attempt brought no success, either. Cary began to worry.

Finally, the clerk snapped her fingers, a big smile on her face. "I was afraid we'd need to resort to microfiche, but its here. We got it! What do you want to know?" She kept on talking. "We lost a lot of our records in Hurricane Katrina." Then she gave Cary a wink. "Your luck's running hot, Dawlin'. You better go by Harrah's when you leave here and play the slots."

"I might just do that," Cary said. "Does it say if the driver was ever caught?"

"Probably not, since the file's still open. If they had caught the perp, it would have gone to a different file." The clerk struck a few more keys and stood, reading the information off the monitor screen, her hands on her hips. She started shaking her head. "Didn't get him. Not according to this."

"Any particulars about the accident?"

"Yep, it says your mother was walking along the neutral ground of Esplanade Avenue. A car swerved off the street and hit her." Officer Bradford glanced over, checking to see how Cary was taking the news.

"It's okay, I can handle it," Cary told her.

The officer cocked one brow as if to say, "You're sure?" then continued, reading carefully. "Your mother was thrown against a tree. The driver veered back onto the street and kept going. Never slowed down."

Once again the clerk waited, giving Cary a chance to decline more details. Cary motioned for her to continue. Officer Bradford summarized the report. "No one really got a good look at the car although several people were in the area where it happened. According to the report, some of them tried to help, but everyone thought they saw something different." Bradford looked up at Cary. "That happens a lot with accident witnesses." She scanned the monitor again. "Says it was late in the afternoon, almost dark – that's pretty much everything."

"Can I get a copy of the report?"

"Sure. Costs three bucks." Then she was no longer paying attention to Cary. Her eyes were zeroed in on the monitor now, her forehead furrowed and she was frowning. "This is interesting."

"What?" Cary asked, feeling Bradford's excitement.

"The investigating officer, guess who that was?"

"Who?" *Why would it matter?*

"Edward R. Breunoux," Bradford said, glancing at Cary. "Make that Patrolman Edward R. Breunoux."

"So, who's that?" Cary asked, still not understanding.

"Let me put it this way," Bradford stated. "Now everyone calls him 'Big Eddie' Breunoux, Superintendent of Police, New Orleans, Louisiana. That's who he is, Sweetie."

"Ohhh, I see," Cary said, not finding the fact as fascinating as the clerk evidently did. So this Big Eddie is the Superintendent now. So what? She pulled three one dollar bills from her purse and placed them on the counter.

Then Officer Bradford dropped the big one. "Superintendent Breunoux and the Mayor are best buddies, you know. Always have been," Bradford added in explanation. "They grew up together over in Algiers."

With a hand to her chest, Cary took in a deep breath, fighting to control her raging emotions. Cary couldn't let Bradford know how much this disclosure had shaken her. It was a good thing the money was already on the counter. She'd have dropped it otherwise.

But Officer Bradford did notice. "You okay, Sweetie? You're awfully pale."

"I'm okay," Cary assured her.

Keeping an eye on her, Bradford took the money and dropped it into a cash box. The report had finished running on the printer. The officer reached over, picked it up, and handed it to Cary.

As she started to walk away, Bradford spoke to her again, this time in a confiding way, "You didn't hear that from me, okay?" Bradford glanced around as though someone might be listening. Then she continued. "The word on the street is that the two of them, the Mayor and Big Eddie, have always taken care of each other – especially Big Eddie taking care of Johnny. Just gossip, but remember, you didn't hear it here. Clerks in records don't know anything, and they never gossip. It's a rule." Bradford laughed, then waved.

"Y-yes," Cary stammered as she walked away. "Thanks again," As she went out the door, she thought of her mother's caller and his threat. And now she discovers Big Eddie has always taken care of Johnny Periot. *A coincidence?*

Returning to the elevator, Cary punched the down button. She waited, wondering what she should do next. Then she realized the answer was probably right there in the building. The elevator door opened as she made her decision.

I'm going to find Superintendent "Big Eddie" Breunoux. Best friends – always looking after each other. I wonder what else they've been doing for each other. Perhaps Breunoux would let something slip, but she needed to be careful. It was a little early to be making judgments, but it did seem a strange coincidence, Periot's best friend being the investigating officer when Johnny's girlfriend was killed.

Cary rubbed her arms, suddenly nervous, realizing she was doing things she would never have considered before – potentially dangerous things. Being alone was the scariest part, with no one on her side and no one to even know if she went missing. *Where were the police when you needed them?* She smiled at the irony of standing in Police Headquarters, while being concerned for her own well-being.

And the really bizarre part? She was going looking for the man in charge: the man who might also have been involved in her mother's death. Cary walked out of the elevator on the first floor and went to the main desk again. There were only a couple of people ahead of her this time.

"I'm back," she said to the sergeant when she reached the desk.

"Did you get your information on the hit and run?"

"Sure did. Your clerk was very helpful. Now I need *your* help again."

"Name it. That's what I'm here for."

"Where could I find Superintendent Breunoux's office? Is he in this building?"

The sergeant, his eyebrows raised, looked at her for a moment. "I don't get many people looking for the boss." He frowned, as though trying to determine if Cary was a threat. Then he decided, "Top floor."

"Thanks again."

Cary went back to the elevator, stepped inside, and pushed the button for the sixth floor. As the door was closing, two men got on, one of them punching the fifth floor button.

"Have you gone back out to the scene?" one of them asked the other.

Cary listened carefully .

"Not yet," the younger one said. "How 'bout you?"

"Yeah, but I haven't found anyone who saw the guy. Funny how that happens, you know?"

The other one chuckled. "Yeah!"

The elevator stopped at their floor. As the men walked off, Cary heard the older one say, "We'll just have to keep looking. Big Eddie sent the word to stay on it."

Detectives, thought Cary. *And* Big Eddie.

The doors closed and she felt the elevator travel up one more floor. When it opened, she was surprised to see a well-dressed receptionist sitting behind a mahogany desk in a large, opulent reception area. The woman's huge desk was the centerpiece of a workspace that would have put to shame many of the corporate offices Cary had visited during her three years at Trebeck. Anyone arriving here would believe someone very important was behind the large double doors off to her right. When she glanced in that direction, she saw an armed officer sitting at a small desk. She'd bet no one walked through those doors uninvited.

"May I help you?" the receptionist asked, catching Cary's attention.

"Yes, please. I would like to see Superintendent Breunoux."

"Do you have an appointment?"

"No. I was just in the area and hoped I might get a few minutes of his time."

"Could I get your name, please, and the nature of your visit." The receptionist was polite but firm. "I'll see if the Superintendent can accommodate you. He was just on his way out."

"I'm Cary Warren. I'd like to ask him a couple of questions about a hit-and-run accident he investigated some years ago." She added, "My mother was killed in the accident."

"I'll see if I can get you in. Please have a seat." The receptionist spoke to the guard, then opened one of the doors, disappearing inside. A short time later she returned to Cary. "He'll be out in a moment. Can I get you a cup of coffee?"

"No, thanks," Cary picked up a *Times* magazine and waited until she heard the doors open. Glancing up, she watched a middle-aged man dressed in a tailored gray suit approach her. She could see why he was called "Big Eddie." He was tall, several inches over six feet; his body was big, too, with arms that stretched his suit jacket. *Probably a weight lifter.*

He stopped in front of Cary and held out his hand. "Hello," he said, looking down with a smile. "I'm Superintendent Breunoux. How can I help you?"

Cary stood and took his big hand. His grip was firm but gentle.

"I'm Cary Warren." She paused, unsure how to tell him what she knew. In the end, she decided to confront the situation head-on.

Glancing to see if they could be overheard, Cary began, her voice soft: "My mother was killed by a hit-and-run driver when I was an infant. She had placed me for adoption, so I never knew her. I didn't know that she had been . . . killed." She took a calming breath. "I came to New Orleans hoping to find her, but all I've been able to find so far is a police report. It gives the details, and it also indicates you investigated the accident." She stopped, giving him time to catch up. Cary wondered if he could tell she knew more than she was saying. "The accident happened twenty-five years ago."

A frown wiped the smile from his face.

"I know that it's a long shot, but I'm hoping you might remember something about it." She stood gazing up at him.

He crossed his arms, touching his chin with a finger. Finally he motioned her toward the elevator. The smile had returned, though it seemed less sincere this time.

"Why don't you walk along with me," he told her. "I'm on my way downstairs to the gym. We can talk on the way, and I'll see if I can remember anything." He led Cary to the elevator. "Miss Warren's going with me, Ann," he told the secretary as they walked past her desk.

When they were on the elevator, the Superintendent told her to continue.

"As I said, all I've found so far has been this." She took the copy of the police report from her purse and handed it to him. "Since you were the investigating officer, I hoped you might remember something that wasn't in the report."

"I'm afraid your compliment to my memory isn't deserved," he told Cary as he glanced at the report. "Besides, I didn't actually go to the accident site. I was the investigating officer and coordinated the search for the car that hit your mother. The report indicates we never found the driver *or* the car." As he examined the report further, Cary thought she saw a fleeting look of surprise on his face when he saw Janice Talmer's name.

The elevator stopped, and they walked off on the second floor. Still holding the report, Breunoux started toward a set of double doors that served as an entrance to the gym. Cary followed him, a half step behind.

"Can you tell how long you looked for the driver?"

"The report wouldn't say," he told her. "There's no normal time period. We investigate as long as we have leads. In this case, and from the information here on the report, that wouldn't have been very long.

The witnesses didn't even agree on the type of vehicle." He studied Cary for a moment. "Is there something you haven't told me?" he asked. She wondered if he sensed more than normal curiosity in her questions.

Cary hesitated, not wanting to tell him about the letter, but then said, "My mother wrote a short note to me just after I was born. She must have had it forwarded to my adoptive parents. They died three years ago, leaving me to go through their papers. I recently found the note in my dad's desk." Cary was lying through her teeth but she didn't care. No one else was going to try to find out what happened to her mother.

"Go on," Breunoux said.

"When I went to the adoption agency and had my file opened, they said my mother had been killed in a hit and run just after I was born. In the note, she indicated she was afraid. A couple of days later, she was killed."

"Did the note say why she was frightened?"

"She was having an affair with a married man and became pregnant. He hadn't told her he was married, but when she told him she was expecting, he became very upset. Then a few days before I was born, she said someone called and threatened her."

"What about the man?" the Superintendent asked. "Did she name him?" Cary thought his voice broke a little.

"No." She lied again. "She just said he was a businessman, and he was concerned that her being pregnant with his child could cause problems."

Subtle changes in his expressions were like Christmas tree lights blinking on and off.

"Do you have the note with you?"

"No," she told him. "It's back home." Cary didn't like the way Big Eddie was staring at her. She now had real concerns about Periot's friend.

"What can you tell me about the threat?"

"Just what I said," Cary told him. "Someone called and said she would be sorry if she caused trouble."

"And you say your mother didn't name her lover, this . . . this businessman?"

Cary hoped the twitch in her eye wasn't noticeable. She wasn't used to lying, yet she forged ahead.

"No." *Sorry, God!* "Just that he was married and ambitious."

She noticed his shoulders. They seemed to relax a little. "That's not much to go on," he told her. "An unnamed lover and an unsolved hit and run won't even get you a cup of coffee."

"I know. But it's not coffee I'm after." Cary gave her most determined look to 'Big Eddie' Breunoux, the Police Superintendent of New Orleans. ". . . I'm after a murderer *and* whoever that person may have worked for. That's why I had hoped you might remember something about the accident." The ball was in his court now.

They had been standing in the small lobby of the gym for several minutes. Several people had walked by, giving space and deference to the Superintendent.

"Sorry, I wish I could give you more," he told her finally, holding his hands out, palms up, the report still in his fingers.

"Well . . . I knew it was a long shot." Actually, Cary was coming away with more than she expected. *And,* she'd be willing to bet it was more than he realized.

"I'll walk you out," Big Eddie told her. He was still holding the police report.

As they reached the elevator, Cary hit him with one last jab. "I understand you and the Mayor were childhood friends."

He paled, she thought, stopping and turning toward her. ". . . Yes, we were." Then after a moment, "Still are. Friends . . . that is." His look was hard, perceptive. "How did you know?"

"Someone . . . mentioned it. I don't remember who."

"You don't think the Mayor is your mystery man, do you? It would be a huge stretch to believe that."

Interesting leap in suppositions.

"I didn't say I thought that," she told him. ". . . You did."

The big man watched Cary for several moments. Then he said, "You're right, of course. I have known the mayor for most of my life. That's common knowledge. Given that, I can guarantee he would never be involved in anything like you're insinuating."

"I didn't say he was. I only said I think it's odd that Janice Talmer was killed shortly after she was threatened, and the hit-and-run driver was never found."

He studied Cary, his eyes narrowing almost imperceptibly. "I really do understand your concerns, but it's not all that unusual for us not to solve a hit and run – especially one twenty-five years ago. Often we're totally dependent on witnesses; if there aren't any or they're not sure of what they saw, as in your mother's case, our job can be impossible. As you saw in the report, we didn't have much to go on with your mother's case." He finally noticed the report and passed it to her.

Cary returned it to her purse. She smiled at the Superintendent and said, "I'm sure you did all you could, and I've taken enough of your time." She reached out and shook his hand.

"Is there somewhere I can reach you if I think of anything?" he asked.

"I'm at the Sheraton." Cary immediately wished she hadn't told him. "But I don't want to trouble you."

"No trouble," he said, holding the door open. "I hope I've been able to help you rest a little easier. If you knew Johnny, you'd understand."

"Yes, I'm sure you're right," Cary said and turned toward the door.

The Superintendent smiled, touching her shoulder in a fatherly gesture as she entered the elevator. "I hope you have a good stay in our city. Are you going to be here long?"

"A couple of weeks, depending on what I find. I'd like to know more about my mother."

The Superintendent watched as Cary punched the button for the lobby. He waved as the door closed.

***

When she was gone, Big Eddie continued standing there, his hands stuffed in his pockets. Finally, reaching up with his right hand, he stroked the gray at his temple.

She's not here looking for antiques, that's certain. The girl's here to find out about Janice Talmer. This was what they had worried about all these years and why they'd kept tabs on her. Her timing couldn't have been less convenient with Johnny at the peak of the mountain. *She can't be allowed to become a problem.*

He glanced back at the gym, then walked over and stuck his head through the door.

"Allison," he called to the young lady behind the counter.

"Yes, sir?"

"Tell Hot-Dog I'm going to skip out on our session today. Something's come up. I'll see him Friday for sure."

"I'll tell him."

Big Eddie headed for the elevator.

Back in his office a few minutes later, he gave instructions to a small man sitting across the desk from him. "I need you to make sure a young woman who left here a few minutes ago doesn't cause trouble for Johnny. It's Cary Warren and she's staying at the Sheraton."

"Ahhh. Any details I should know?"

"She's asking about things that happened a long time ago."

"I see . . ."

"Can you handle it for me, Marion?"

"How far can I go?"

"Nothing too harsh . . . At least for now."

Marion Douglas Cobreaux assured Big Eddie the matter would be handled.

***

Cary felt uneasy. Big Eddie hadn't put any of her previous questions to rest. He'd only added to them. On the way down in the elevator, she considered her next step, deciding to go back to the hotel and try to sort out her thoughts and organize her plans.

When she reached the first floor, Cary asked the sergeant if there was somewhere she could call for a taxi. As she had hoped, he picked up the phone and dialed for one.

"I hope your visit with the Superintendent went well," the sergeant said as he dropped the receiver in place.

"Oh, it did," Cary told him. *It really did!*

She rode most of the way to the Sheraton before she asked the driver to pull over and let her out. Cary had decided to walk a little and relieve some stress. The session with the Superintendent had been very disturbing. The look he had given her at the elevator was frightening. But he had flinched when she mentioned his relationship with the Mayor. If it really was only friendship, there should be no reason to be defensive. And he had been! Very defensive!

As she walked toward the hotel, Cary passed a Staples. On the spur of the moment, she decided to have copies made of her mother's letter and the police report. She didn't want to chance losing them, *or* having them taken from her.

Cary decided to mail the originals to Rita. She asked the clerk to make six copies of each. Cary then bought stamps and an envelope and prepared the originals for mailing. She stuck the copies in her purse and dropped the envelope into a mailbox outside. Then she opened her cell and called Rita, leaving a message when her friend didn't answer. Now Rita would be expecting the envelope.

At her hotel, Cary went directly to the reservations desk.

"I want to leave some papers in your safe."

The woman reached under the counter for an envelope. "Get this ready," she said, "and I'll have the manager lock it up." Cary folded three copies of the letter and report. With her name and room number on the envelope, she returned it to the clerk.

Back in her room, she read her mother's letter several times, searching for hidden meanings. Then she unfolded the police report and looked it over, too. It was probably a coincidence that the deadly hit and run had happened only a few days after Janice had written about her fears in the letter. But Cary couldn't get the possibility that her mother had been murdered out of her mind. Her visit with Big Eddie hadn't helped. She now believed there was more between him and Johnny Periot than met the eye.

Now I've got to see Periot— but how? She *could* tell him she knew he was her father and that he had scared Janice Talmer with his reaction to her pregnancy. That ought to start a fire under somebody's chair.

Cary wondered if she could pull this off. She was a self-starter and known for achieving goals, but this was different. This involved other people, some long gone like her mother and others who may have thought they had gotten away with murder. However, if she could get in to see Johnny Periot, maybe she'd get some answers.

Then another thought occurred to her: she probably couldn't have done this two weeks ago. But two weeks ago, she hadn't known someone killed her mother. And . . . she hadn't known about Johnny Periot! This situation *could* get tense.

Knowing that, Cary make a list of possible questions, then practiced tossing them at the Mayor. Gradually, she relaxed. Now she had a plan.

Cary knew she wouldn't be satisfied if she left New Orleans without facing up to him. But in doing so, she could be putting herself in jeopardy.

Chapter Eight

Things heated up on Thursday. Cary arrived at the Mayor's office early, gave the secretary her name, and told the woman she wanted to see Mr. Periot.

"I'm sorry," she was informed, "but if you don't have an appointment, I can't get you in today. His schedule is full." Clearly, she wasn't going to help. Cary's vehement plea didn't seem to make any difference, either.

She had been afraid this would happen. What now? Cary turned slowly and headed back toward the elevator. Her planned list of questions would go unanswered if she couldn't get in to see Periot. Arguing with herself all the way down in the elevator, a solution didn't come until she was in the lobby. *Bingo!* Cary turned around and headed back up.

Facing the secretary once more, Cary said, "Tell him I'm here to ask about an old friend of his. Tell him the friend's name was Janice Talmer." She gave the woman her sternest look. "I *think* he'll see me." After a moment, the secretary rose and went into the Mayor's office.

"He'll give you five minutes," she said upon returning. Cary knew she had his attention now. She wondered if Superintendent Breunoux had alerted him.

The secretary motioned for Cary to follow her. As they approached the Mayor's office, she urged Cary, "Please don't keep him too long. He really does have a tight schedule today." She waved Cary into the office and closed the door. Cary stopped for a moment, steeling herself to meet the man Janice Talmer said was her father. Scarcely noticing the surroundings, Cary zeroed in on Johnny Periot.

The man standing behind the large desk didn't appear pleased to see her. Although her nerves were on edge, Cary looked him over like she was shopping for a used car. Johnny Periot was a little over six feet, with dark hair going salt and pepper. She noticed the up-turned nose and the dark penetrating eyes. *Not unlike her own.* He was handsome in his own way, and he dressed stylishly. He appeared to be someone who was always in control.

Periot was staring at her, too. Eyes locked with his, Cary unexpectedly realized she had no personal feelings for him. Nothing. That surprised her.

"What can I do for you?" His tone was hard, almost threatening. He held her eyes for just a moment, then took a puff on the large cigar he held. Casually he tapped ashes off into an ashtray.

Cary studied him, hoping to gain some clue about the man. "I want to ask you some questions about Janice Talmer." She had entered the office determined to push him.

"Why would you care about Janice Talmer?" His tone was restrained, but he still sounded intimidating.

"She was killed in a hit-and-run accident. At least that's how it was classified." She was telling him things he already knew. After all, he and Janice were lovers according to the letter.

"The driver of the vehicle that ran her down was never caught," she continued. "I want to find out what you know about it." Cary was glad she had rehearsed.

He hesitated – not a question he expected. *Gotcha'!*

"I don't know anything about it. What made you think I did?" Then, almost as an afterthought, he added, "And *who* are you?" His face posed the question almost as much as his words

Cary continued pressing. "I have a letter Janice Talmer wrote to her infant daughter before she was killed," Cary told him, not answering his question, yet pursuing hers. She watched his expression. "In the letter she said she had been threatened." Then Cary threw out her trump card: "She was afraid of someone. I believe that person was you."

He didn't react, not even a flinch. Instead, "You didn't answer my question. Who are you?"

Their conversation reminded Cary of a fencing match – thrust, then evade.

"I'm Cary Warren."

"Okay . . . so you're Cary Warren?"

She paused before delivering the knockout punch: ". . . I'm Janice Talmer's daughter."

His eyes changed – a glimmer of recognition? – then it was gone. He attempted to hide it and, for the most part he did. But Cary had been watching. She'd seen the momentary flash of alarm. *Gotcha' . . . Again!*

She knew she had touched on something way back when . . . Back before he'd become the Mayor – or even a politician. Back twenty-five years – back when it was just Johnny and Janice.

She continued to dog him. Staring into Periot's eyes, she decided to push him further with a half truth. "Janice also hinted that you're my father." Tension filled the room as they measured each other.

After a lengthy pause, he averted his eyes. "Sit down, Miss Warren." They had been standing since she arrived. He motioned Cary to a chair. When they were sitting, he stared at her for what seemed an eternity. Although anxious, Cary waited, ready for anything now.

Finally, he said in a low voice, "I . . . knew your mother." His tone indicated he was troubled, but now he also sounded . . . defensive? Surprising Cary, he then tried to explain: "She worked for me for a while as a contract secretary. She was with a temp agency."

Cary played along. "Which one, and why did she quit?"

Periot appeared a bit rattled when he answered. "I don't remember which agency. As I recall, she couldn't handle her assignments, so I let her go."

He's lying. If Janice had worked for him, she would have known he was married.

Periot continued, interrupting her thoughts. "If you think I'm your father, you're wrong. And if your mother told you that, it's an outright lie." Cary's anger surged toward overload . . . yet she waited, listening.

"I was married when she worked for me," he continued. "I took her to lunch a few times when we needed to talk about particular projects, but that's all."

She couldn't believe her ears. He was going to deny everything. "My mother clearly saw it differently," Cary said, her face flushed, her mind almost overcome by her fury. She struggled to control her emotions. "Janice said she loved you, but it's easy to see she was the only one who felt that way."

"Wait," he said, his hands up as if to keep Cary at bay. "I don't want to demean Janice. Maybe she had secret feelings for me. I'm just saying I was never involved with her."

He thought he could lie his way out of this. Cary's emotions were virtually consuming her. Angry almost beyond words, her next utterance was little above a whisper. "Do . . . I . . . look like a one-sided love affair to you?"

"No . . . but . . ."

"You're going to tell me," louder now, "that my mother lied in what she expected to be her only communication with her daughter? I don't believe that, and I can't imagine you do either." She shook her head and stood.

He stood, too, lifting his hands in a defensive gesture. "I didn't mean . . ."

Cary was deadly calm now. Her voice conveyed that composure. "You are a sad human being! I don't know what I expected when I came here today, but it wasn't you." Cary's voice was low and steady now. She looked at this stranger, the man she believed to be her father. *How could my mother ever have loved you?*

"This isn't over." Cary said it like a promise. "I'm going to find out what really happened to Janice Talmer, and I suspect you're going to be right in the middle of it."

"What could possibly make you think I did something to your mother?" he asked, anger causing a quiver in his voice.

"I'll tell you what makes me think that. In my letter she said someone called and threatened her. She was *scared*."

Periot remained behind his desk, his eyes fiery as he ground his teeth. Cary thought that must have been the way he had looked at Janice Talmer when she told him about his child – *their* child.

Cary's legs grew weak as she glared at him. It was impossible to read his thoughts. A chilly sensation swept over her when she realized he must perceive her as a threat to his dreams, to everything he had worked for. That must have been how he felt about Janice when she became pregnant.

Cary's imagination was running wild. What kind of person could kill someone like her mother, a woman who loved him? Cary's own dreams of love had never allowed room for hatred or death. But for her mother, that possibility may have been all too real. Janice had died a sad death twenty-five years ago. And she had been afraid of Johnny Periot.

"You need to go," he said, breaking the silence. "I had nothing to do with your mother's death, and you'd better leave it at that."

"Or what? Will I end up the victim of a hit-and-run accident, too?" Cary stared back at him defiantly.

She suddenly felt the need to address her situation. "In case you or your people think you can deal with me that way, you should know something. I've mailed copies of Janice's letter to three different people back home, including my attorney," she lied. Panic ran through her as he stubbed out his cigar. She continued the charade. "If I don't check in with them each day, all hell's going to break loose." Cary hoped her words didn't sound as absurd to Periot as they did to her.

He reached over and touched a button on the telephone console. A moment later the secretary opened his door.

"Show Miss Warren out," he told her. "We're *finished* here."

"You haven't heard the last of me," she said, her voice barely above a whisper.

Cary stared at him with loathing and more bravado than she felt, then she turned away. She looked back at him once as she reached the doorway. Instead of the anger she expected, she thought she detected a flash of fear as he stared after her.

***

Periot lit another cigar, took a puff and glanced over at the framed photograph on a table near the window. His family. *Well, most of his family.* He involuntarily glanced toward the closed door. After a few quiet moments of thought, the mayor picked up his phone and punched in a number.

"We have a problem," he said. "Can you come over here right away?" He listened for a moment longer before he disconnected. Then he made a second call, giving some instructions before hanging up.

That finished, he turned and walked over to the window. The girl was crossing Perdido Street, walking away from City Hall. He watched her, visualizing Janice Talmer the last time she walked away from him. The daughter would be surprised to know how much she resembled her tall slender mother, those penetrating eyes, the set of her chin . . . the way her dark hair blew in the breeze.

He took another puff on his cigar and blew out the smoke. When it had cleared, he saw that Miss Warren had stopped and was looking up at him. Defiant! *Just* like Janice! It was like seeing a ghost. But Miss Warren's timing was as bad as her mother's had been. *And anyone in politics knew that timing was everything.*

Chapter Nine

Outside City Hall, Cary's legs were weak from the confrontation with Periot. She wanted to sit down, but first she needed to put some distance between them.

As she crossed the street, Cary had the sensation of someone's eyes following her. When she reached the far sidewalk, she glanced back, looking for his office window. She saw him there, cigar in hand, watching her. Cary stared back as he studied her. She wondered briefly what he might be thinking. Then she walked away, knowing whatever he was considering, it wouldn't prevent her search.

Once she turned the corner, she went over and sat down on a bench. Cary thought about their confrontation; Johnny Periot had slipped up at least twice. There was no doubt in her mind that he knew what had happened to her mother. If she was to believe the Police Superintendent, finding the car's driver was pretty much a lost cause. Too many years had passed. That was especially true if her father or Big Eddie was involved.

As she rested, Cary noticed two young women walking together along the sidewalk. Watching them, she remembered something. Opening her purse, she removed a copy of her mother's letter. Unfolding it, she scanned for a certain phrase: "I was out with a girlfriend . . ."

Glancing up at the women again, Cary thought, *the girlfriend*. She whispered aloud, "If I could find Janice's friend . . ." As she struggled for a way to trace the woman, Cary thought of the adoption file. Maybe there was something in it.

A taxi happened to be passing. She flagged it down and gave the driver Mrs. Hebert's address. At her destination, Cary paid the driver before the taxi stopped; she jumped out, hurrying into the adoption agency. Moments later, she was in Mrs. Hebert's office.

***

On the street, another automobile pulled to the curb moments after Cary entered the adoption agency. The two men in the vehicle waited until she was inside before one of them got out and slowly walked along the sidewalk. He glanced at the sign on the office building before returning to join the driver. The vehicle moved further down the street and slipped into a parking space.

***

Inside the agency, Mrs. Hebert was accompanying an obviously pregnant woman out of her office as Cary entered the reception area. The social worker said a brief farewell to the woman, then turned to Cary. "Mornin', Honey. What can I do for you today?"

"I need your help again," Cary said, speaking rapidly in her excitement. Mrs. Hebert motioned her into the office and to a chair. "I need to see my file. Specifically, I'd like to see if there's any information about a girlfriend of my mother's. This particular person was with her when she met my father."

"Whoa. Slow down, Darlin'," Mrs. Hebert told her. "I can't keep up with you."

Cary grinned. Taking a deep breath, she said, "If I can find the friend, I think she could help me."

Mrs. Hebert studied her for a moment. "We'll look in the file, but first, I want to ask you a question? You don't have to answer. Okay?" She paused for a moment, then asked, "Did your mother tell you Johnny Periot is your father?"

Cary hesitated, then said, ". . . Yes."

The social worker was slow to continue. When she did, she spoke softly. "Be careful, Dawlin', there are people in this town who think Johnny and the men around him are dangerous."

Cary only nodded, thinking of her own altercation with Johnny Periot only a few minutes ago.

"Now," Mrs. Hebert said, pulling Cary's file from a desk drawer. "Let's take a look." She opened it, sorting through the papers.

"I can't let you have your file, but we can go through it together." Mrs. Hebert pulled several sheets out, spread them on her desk, and started reading. "This form is information we asked for when the file was opened. It says here if our office had trouble reaching your mother, we should contact Carolette and Alex Shapiro. I'd be surprised if the information we had twenty-five years ago is still good. But . . ." She came up with a telephone book. "There can't be that many Shapiro's in New Orleans."

Cary thought they couldn't be lucky enough for the couple's number to be in the phone book. She was right.

Mrs. Hebert ran her finger down a page, then said, "Not there."

Cary felt tears start to well. "I knew it was a long shot," she told the woman, eyes downcast.

"Well, wait a minute, Honey," Mrs. Hebert said. "When you're in this business as long as I have been, you learn a few tricks. Let me try a couple of places online."

She turned to her computer. For a moment, Cary felt hopeful, but then Mrs. Hebert clucked and shook her head. "Nope, huh-uh. Nothing."

What had Cary thought she could accomplish? Her mother's friend had been in New Orleans twenty-five years ago. She could be anywhere in the United States now, or the world, for that matter.

"Sor . . ." Cary heard Mrs. Hebert start to say, then she let out a "Glory be. I don't believe it."

"What?"

"This could be them: A. and C. Shapiro. Right here in one of my people finders. And guess where they live?"

"Where?" asked Cary, wondering. It could be anywhere, another city or another country.

"St. Charles Avenue," Mrs. Hebert told her, a tone of approval in her voice.

"Is that good?" asked Cary.

"Honey . . . based on this street number, I'd say it's as good as you're going to get in New Orleans."

"Well, what do I do now?" asked Cary. "Do I call her, or should I just go out to her house and knock on the door?"

"Neither. You better let me call. I just hope the initial is for Carolette. I'll try her now," she said as she picked up the phone. She punched in the number, glanced up at Cary, and held her gaze as it started to ring.

Cary listened. "Ahh, yes. My name is Emily Hebert. I'm with the state adoption service, and I'm trying to locate a Carolette Shapiro?" Obviously she had reached an answering service. "Again, that's *Carolette* Shapiro. Mrs. Shapiro was listed as a contact several years ago for someone we are presently trying to get in touch with." The social worker gave her phone number and hung up. "Maybe we'll get a callback, maybe not," she said.

Cary had tears in her eyes now – she couldn't help it. Mrs. Hebert handed her a tissue. "Don't give up, dear. I'll try some other sources, too." She reached across and touched Cary's arm. "Why don't you call me in the morning?"

Cary dried her eyes and headed for the door. She had no idea where she would go. Mrs. Hebert reminded her that it often takes time and you frequently hit dead ends in a search like this. Her words didn't help. Cary didn't know how she would proceed if they were unable to reach Janice's girlfriend.

But everything changed when she reached the front door and started out. She heard the intercom ring. The receptionist answered, then called out for Cary to hang on. She waved Cary back to Mrs. Hebert office.

The social worker was on the telephone and appeared excited. "This is Mrs. Hebert," she said into the phone. Holding her hand over the mouthpiece, she whispered, "It's Carolette Shapiro. She's calling back." Removing her hand, she paused, then added, "Yes, I'll hold." She smiled at Cary and held up her fist, thumb pointed skyward.

Once again, Mrs. Hebert introduced herself, then after a brief pause, explained the situation. Finally, she got around to the difficulty. "There's a problem," she said. "A woman gave us your name twenty-five years ago. You may not remember her. The name was Talmer, Janice Talmer."

Mrs. Hebert frowned and tapped her pen on the desk, clicking the point in and out. "Yes. Yes, we're aware of all that."

As the seconds ticked by, color seemed to drain from the social worker's face. Finally she said, "You what?" Another pause. Then, "Mrs. Shapiro, may we come out and talk with you – immediately, if it's convenient?"

After a brief farewell, Mrs. Hebert hung up the telephone, gestured to Cary and said, "Let's go." Then she added, "Carolette Shapiro was *with* your mother when she was killed."

***

The two men who followed Cary earlier pulled into traffic, keeping the women's car in sight.

"Wha'cha t'ink they up to?" the driver asked his passenger.

"Let's see where they go," his partner replied. "They were talking and waving their arms like they were excited when they came out of that office."

"Yeah, Cher. I seen 'em," the driver agreed. "Mus' be reeeel important, whatever it is."

"Yeah." The passenger kept his eye on the other car as he slid his fingers across the pistol nestled under his left arm.

***

The women left their vehicle parked at the curb on St. Charles Avenue, then walked the short distance to the Shapiro's address. The house was a large, ornate mansion set back from the street in an area Mrs. Hebert called "The Garden District." Entering through an iron gate, Cary and Mrs. Hebert walked toward the large porch. When Cary rang the doorbell, a young maid dressed in an immaculate black and white uniform opened the door. Mrs. Hebert gave the woman her business card and said Mrs. Shapiro was expecting them. Taking the card, the woman nodded and led them into the house. She gestured them forward along a hallway to a beautifully furnished sitting room.

The maid asked them to take a chair, saying, "Mrs. Shapiro will be wit' 'cha shortly." Then she vanished down the hallway.

Moments later, a slim, middle-aged woman entered the room. She was dressed in casual, but obviously expensive dark slacks and a long-sleeved sweater. She wore an intricately woven gold chain around her neck. In heels, the woman was almost as tall as Cary.

"Good day, ladies. I'm Carolette Shapiro. How may I help you?" The woman motioned for them to sit and took a chair near Cary.

Cary was thrilled. She reached across and thrust out her hand. "Mrs. Shapiro, my name is Cary Warren." When her name passed unheralded, she added, "Janice Talmer was my mother."

Carolette Shapiro's eyes and expression registered surprise, but she recovered quickly. Without taking her eyes off Cary, she said, "Yes, now I can see Janice in your features. She was pretty, too – *almost* as pretty as you. Janice had the same dark hair, but she wore it a little shorter."

"Had you known her for a long time?" Cary asked.

The woman paused before answering. "Yes, and no." Then she chuckled at the puzzled look on Cary's face. "Would either of you care for coffee?" she asked, still without answering Cary's question. After a positive nod from both Cary and Mrs. Hebert, Carolette rang a small crystal bell. The maid appeared as though she had been waiting outside the door. "Coffee all around, please, Meredith. And bring us some of those brownies you baked earlier."

After the maid had gone, Mrs. Shapiro returned to the question. With a faraway look in her eyes, she answered, "No, Cary, I hadn't known your mother for very long, maybe two years. But it seemed as if I had known her all my life." Carolette folded her hands in her lap. "We met on a park bench in the French Quarter. We were both out for a walk, and we became immediate best friends. Janice was working and going to school, and I was working. This was some time before I married Alex and before his business started to prosper. Your mother and I were just two young women with big dreams."

Carolette smiled and her voice became gentle as she spoke of Janice. Obviously she had been fond of Cary's mother.

Continuing, Carolette said, "Janice and I never talked much about where we had come from, but we spent hours talking about where we were going. Most conversations involved our hopes and dreams."

She shifted in her chair, glancing back and forth between Cary and Mrs. Hebert as she reminisced about the past.

"Alex and I married about six months before your mother's accident," she said. "Janice was my maid of honor." Touching Cary's arm, she told her, "Your mother envisioned a better life. She had rather a rough upbringing – alcoholic father and such. She wanted a different life for herself and for her daughter." She looked kindly at Cary.

"Were you the girlfriend she was with when she met my father?" Cary asked.

"Do you know your father?"

"I know who he is. That's about all I know. I met him this morning and talked with him for a few minutes."

Mrs. Shapiro pursed her lips as though wondering how she should answer Cary's question. "Yes," she said finally. "I was with her when she met Johnny. Janice and I had gone out to City Park for a picnic one Sunday. We had set our sandwiches out when Johnny ran out of bounds and into our lunch. He was playing touch football with a group of young men. I didn't know him, but it turned out Alex did."

"And my mother liked him?"

"Oh, yes," Carolette said. "It was 'love at first sight.' Of course, your mother didn't know he was married at that point. She didn't find that out until she told him about you."

"Did Janice ever work for my father? Like in the law firm?"

"No . . . Why do you ask?"

"He said she did. Are you sure?"

"Sweetheart, take my word. I would have known."

There. Now Cary had the word of someone she believed.

"Do you think my mother's death was an accident?" Cary asked, carrying the conversation in a different direction.

Before Carolette could answer, the maid returned with coffee and brownies. As she placed the tray on the table in front of them, the maid bent close to Mrs. Shapiro and said, "Telephone for you, ma'am. It's Mr. Shapiro."

"Excuse me, ladies," Carolette said, smiling. "The boss beckons." She walked to a table in the corner and lifted a receiver. After a short conversation, she returned.

"I'm sorry, but I'm going to have to leave you," she said apologetically. "I have to meet my husband to sign some papers. It seems our appointment has been changed. I do hope you'll forgive me. Please stay and enjoy your coffee and brownies. Meredith has a knack for making them. I *think* it's the bourbon," she added with a wink.

Laughing, Cary and Mrs. Hebert rose from their chairs. "Thank you for your time," Mrs. Hebert said.

"No trouble at all," she said. "Why don't you call me tomorrow morning? The two of you can come out for lunch and we'll talk some more about Janice." She looked at Cary then, and added, "Oh yes, Cary. Let me answer your earlier question. No, I don't think your mother's death was an accident, and I told that to the police on the night it happened." She glanced at her watch. "I'll tell you more about that tomorrow." Without further conversation, she left them.

Cary and Mrs. Hebert sat and enjoyed their refreshments before being shown out by the maid.

Outside, Cary turned to Mrs. Hebert. "She didn't think it was an accident. She said so."

"But saying it and proving it are two different things."

***

Later that evening, just after dark, Carolette Shapiro returned home. She pulled her car into the garage as she had done countless times before. Then, as she opened the car door and stood up, she saw a movement in the corner of the garage.

"Who's there?" she called.

No sooner had she spoken when she heard a sound and was seized from behind. A chill ran the length of her body. From the shadows, a second person moved toward her.

"Take my purse," she managed to say. Her heart felt as if it would burst from her chest. "There's money in my billfold. Please, just take it and don't hurt me."

"We're not here for your money, Carolette." A hood hid the face of the man in front of her. "We're here to make sure you don't do any more talking to the wrong people." She tried to scream, but was too late. The man reached out, slipping his fingers around her neck and tightening them.

Carolette died there in her garage, unable to escape or call out – not understanding why this person whose voice she recognized wanted her dead.

Chapter Ten

Cary invited Mrs. Hebert out to dinner that evening. The social worker suggested Russell's Marina Grill out near Lake Ponchartrain. Over seafood and salad, they discussed what Carolette Shapiro had said about Janice Talmer's death not being an accident.

"I wonder if there's something specific that makes her think that," Cary said. "Do you suppose she knows something, or was it just the circumstances and an opinion on her part?"

"It could be either," Mrs. Hebert said. "Hopefully, we'll find out tomorrow."

"Maybe she'll remember some detail from that evening, something that became lost along the way."

"Perhaps, but I wouldn't count on it," the social worker said.

Cary wasn't able to finish her dinner. Finally, she shoved her plate back and called it quits. Her nerves had been on edge since she arrived in New Orleans, and the events of the last several days hadn't helped.

After dinner, Mrs. Hebert drove Cary around the lakefront showing her the view. Lights reflected from boats on the water cast a dreamy ambiance on the shore. The contrast to Cary's real world tribulations was almost startling.

After the tour, Cary's new friend returned her downtown to the Sheraton. As she walked through the lobby and onto the elevator, Cary's thoughts were already on the next day and the answers it could bring. She hoped she was close to learning important details concerning her mother's death. Carolette Shapiro could be the key.

Deep in thought, Cary exited the elevator when it stopped on her floor. As she prepared to unlock her door, she noticed it was ajar – just the slightest crack. She froze, staring at the opening. She specifically recalled locking the door; she had hesitated before pulling it closed, thinking she might need a heavier jacket. At that moment, as Cary considered her options, a couple staying in the room opposite hers stepped out into the hall.

"Excuse me," Cary said, turning to them. "I just returned to my room and the door was open. I'm sure I left it locked. Would you mind waiting while I check it out?" She was relieved someone else was there.

"Certainly," the man said. "I'll look with you." He sounded braver than he appeared. The woman waited by their doorway, her arms tight across her chest.

Cary pushed her door open, reached inside and flipped on the light. The room was a disaster. Her clothing and other belongings were strewn all over. Her briefcase and luggage had literally been torn apart. Someone must have been searching for the letter.

Periot's people. She had a strong suspicion but knew there was no way of proving it. Better keep it to herself, Cary decided.

In her bewilderment, Cary had forgotten about the couple from across the hall until she heard the man whistle softly. She turned, realizing they were both standing in her doorway staring at the shambles of her belongings. "Wow," the man said. "We're lucky they didn't hit us. We've been gone most of the afternoon. Hope you didn't have anything valuable in there."

"No . . . No I didn't," Cary stammered, grasping her purse and thinking of the copies she had inside it. "May I use your telephone to call the desk?"

"Sure," the man said. He turned and walked over to unlock the door for Cary. The woman was attached to him now, clinging tightly to his arm.

The hotel's security people came quickly. They searched the room, and then the man in charge questioned her. The other two were dispatched to knock on doors along the hall, searching for potential witnesses.

"Are you sure you locked your door when you left the room?" the man asked.

"Yes," Cary assured him.

"Can you tell if anything is missing?"

She did a quick assessment. "It's all here. Nothing to steal but my clothes. There was only a note pad and a small calculator in the briefcase. I had emptied the suitcases."

The man filled out a report but indicated nothing would probably come of it. "Hotel robberies sometimes occur," he told Cary, "but the people who do this sort of thing are seldom caught in the act."

"Will you inform the police?" she asked.

"Oh, yes. We've called them and they'll get a copy of our report."

After the police arrived and took a statement, Cary was told she could pick up her things. She folded some and hung others until everything had been put away. She managed to keep her emotions in check, but Cary felt exposed and even violated. One of the security men especially had bothered her. He had perused her things, going through them, handling this one, holding that one up, a slight smirk on his face most of the time. She had considered slugging him.

The hotel's assistant manager arrived as the others were finishing up. "We can move you to a different room, even a different floor, if you would like, Miss Warren."

"No," she said, "but I want the lock changed." Cary suspected the people who had ransacked her belongings wouldn't be deterred by a change in rooms. Staying where she was might even throw them off if they were so brazen as to come back tonight.

"I'll take care of the lock, and there will be a generous credit on your account for the damage to your luggage and briefcase," he said as he took his leave.

The lock was changed five minutes later.

When everyone had gone, Cary made sure the door was secure, even placing a chair under the handle. She jerked the door a couple of times just to be sure.

Finally able to concentrate on herself, she undressed and prepared to take a shower. As she removed her earrings, she realized one of the gold loops was missing, the one from her left ear. Dad had given them to her. Cary thought back to the last time she had them both, recalling touching them in the elevator as she returned from dinner. *It's here somewhere.* She had to find it.

Turning on all the lights, she searched the floor. Then Cary remembered the wastebasket. She had gathered scraps from her luggage and tossed them in along with other trash. She upended the can, dumping everything on the carpet. Sorting through the debris, Cary spotted something shiny and squealed. There it was. She smiled, kissed the small gold loop and set it on the side table. She then started tossing the trash back into the can; halfway through, a glint from another shiny object, a piece of metal, caught her eye. It was lodged in a small chunk of the briefcase. Unable to work it loose with her fingers, Cary went into the bathroom and got a pair of tweezers. She quickly had the object in her hand, turning it over and examining it from all angles. It was a broken knife blade.

Just as she had thought, someone had entered her room with a specific purpose. They had been searching for something. It also made clear the danger she faced if she stayed in New Orleans and searched for her mother's killer. Cary rubbed her shoulders. These people are serious . . . *Deadly serious.*

With everything put away this time, she showered and climbed into bed.

Once settled, Cary thought about the day and all that had happened. She tried to convince herself the people who had broken into her room were just hotel thieves seeking money and other valuables. Yet the only reasonable answer, given the evidence, was that someone was looking for her mother's letter.

But who, and for what reason? She kept coming back to Johnny Periot. The irony that he was her father wasn't lost on Cary. He was the only one who knew about the letter other than Mrs. Hebert. Well . . . and the Police Superintendent.

Cary closed her eyes and tried to force herself to relax. If she had any hope of sleeping tonight, it needed to happen soon. She thought of calling Rita but decided there was no reason to give her insomnia, too.

Then her thoughts turned to Mike Webster. Tomorrow evening they would be in the same hotel. She didn't really want him here. Why couldn't that seminar have been held somewhere other than New Orleans? She hesitated. *But he had offered to help with her search.*

Then she stretched and, with a loud yawn, thought of Carolette Shapiro. What a nice woman. For her mother to have had friends like that, she must have been special, too. Cary hoped Mrs. Shapiro had remembered some details, *anything* that would help in the search. She was looking forward to lunch with Mrs. Hebert and Carolette tomorrow. Maybe then she'd have her answers.

Chapter Eleven

Cary slept well and awoke refreshed. She dressed, then checked herself in the mirror. She looked nice decked out in dark denim pants, a creamy long sleeve top and a light jacket. Her only jewelry was a colorful stone necklace her mom had given her. She felt good about the luncheon with Mrs. Shapiro. Cary was finally making progress.

Careful to lock the door when she left her room, Cary went downstairs for breakfast. As an afterthought she picked up the *Times-Picayune* from a stand in the gift shop.

After being seated by a hostess, she ordered, then settled back to sip her coffee and scan the newspaper. She opened it and glanced through the headlines. As she reached the lower half of the front page, a photograph jumped out at her: *Carolette Shapiro!*

What followed was like an explosion in Cary's world. The headline for the accompanying article made her feel lightheaded. The caption with Mrs. Shapiro's photograph proclaimed, **"PROMINENT BUSINESSMAN'S WIFE FOUND MURDERED."**

Cary could literally feel her heart start to race. Fighting to regain composure, she forced her eyes down and began to read the article.

> **Carolette Shapiro, wife of prominent New Orleans businessman Alex Shapiro, was found dead Thursday evening in the garage at the family's home on St. Charles Avenue. Mrs. Shapiro's body was discovered by her husband when he returned home at approximately 9:00. Mrs. Shapiro appeared to have been strangled, though the exact cause of death has not yet been confirmed. An autopsy is pending.**
>
> **Police gave no motive for the murder but did say Mrs. Shapiro's purse was open and the contents scattered about, leading to speculation of robbery as a possible motive. Mr. Shapiro stated his wife often carried significant cash in her billfold, but police said it was empty when found.**

A leader in New Orleans society, Carolette Shapiro had served on the board of directors for many social organizations and charities.

Funeral arrangements will be announced when they are complete.

Cary had just finished reading about the murder when the waiter brought her breakfast. He had placed the food in front of her before he noticed her expression. Her apparent dismay caused him to ask, "Are you all right, Miss?"

"Yes." She glanced at him. "Yes . . . I think so." She shook her head in an attempt to clear it.

As the waiter slipped away, Cary noticed two men sitting a few tables away. They appeared to be watching her. When she glanced their way, the men turned back and started to talk. Maybe she had imagined it, but the thought that they could be watching her was unsettling.

Cary picked at her food; any appetite she had was now gone. Placing her fork down, she gathered her things and paid the ticket. As she left the dining area, she noticed the table where the two men had been sitting was vacant.

Anxious to call Mrs. Hebert, Cary returned to her room. She could hear the phone ringing inside as she reached her door. She opened it and ran to catch the phone. Cary expected it to be the social worker.

It wasn't . . .

Another shock! A man whose voice she didn't recognize began talking immediately – not even giving her a chance to say hello. "Miss Warren, you had better get out of New Orleans and leave things alone that aren't your business."

She gulped a breath before answering. "What? Who *is* this?" Cary's voice was shaky.

The man continued as if she hadn't spoken. "You're digging up old coffins that are of no concern to you. Listen to me carefully. If you stay in this city and continue asking questions, others will be hurt and you could be one of them. *Drop it now!* This will be your only warning." The telephone clicked and Cary found herself listening to the dial tone. She held the receiver out and stared at it for a moment before dropping it back on the set.

She couldn't believe what she'd heard. She had actually been threatened – and not just her, but others, too. Her thoughts swept back to the dining room downstairs: the two men. Cary wished now that she had paid more attention to them.

First her hotel room had been broken into and searched last night, then Mrs. Shapiro, her mother's friend, had been killed – now this new threat. *What had she stumbled into?* The possibilities sent a chill running through her. She sat down on the side of the bed. *I just wanted to find my mother . . . to find myself.*

She had never felt so alone. Everyone she had been close to in life was gone. First her mom and dad. Now the mother she had never known was gone, too, and someone didn't want her to know why.

Well, to hell with them, whoever they are. It isn't going to work that way.

Cary didn't consider herself especially brave, but now she was mad. Fighting damn mad!

She had been sitting there, thinking, for several minutes when the telephone rang again. She hesitated, staring at it as it rang three . . . four . . . and then a fifth time. Finally, she reached over and lifted it off the hook. Brushing back her hair, she placed the phone to her ear.

"*Hello,*" she said with an attitude.

"Cary? Is that you?" She recognized Rita's voice.

"Yes, Rita . . . it's me. What are you doing calling on this phone?" Cary breathed a sigh of relief hearing her friend's voice after all the craziness.

"No particular reason," her friend said. "What's wrong?" Rita asked, concern evident in her words.

"Rita, I should have called you." She began to explain the whole, horrible mess.

"Oh, Cary!"

"That isn't all." She described her room break-in and the threatening telephone call.

"What do you mean? What kind of threats?" Rita asked nervously.

"They said if I keep 'digging up old coffins' as they put it, I could get hurt. Others, too"

"Cary, tell me you're making this up."

"But I'm not," Cary said. "I was reading the newspaper at breakfast this morning and I saw a picture of a lady I had talked with just yesterday. And Rita, she was *killed* last night. She was my mother's friend twenty-five years ago, and we had talked about my mother. I was supposed to go and see her again today. But she's dead, Rita. *Murdered.* The article said robbery was the likely motive, but I don't think so after the phone call I just received."

Cary lay back on the bed, the receiver to her ear, and closed her eyes. She threw an arm across them, wishing she could block out the world.

"Oh my God, Cary!" Rita exclaimed. "At least tell me you're being careful."

Changing the subject, Cary told her about the envelope she had mailed. "Just put it somewhere safe and keep it when it gets there."

"Will do," Rita said. "And Cary, *please* be careful."

"I will," Cary said and was about to hang up when she remembered something and snapped her fingers. "Mike Webster is coming into New Orleans today. *How* did he know where I'm staying?"

"Uhhhh! I can't imagine," Rita lied. They both laughed though Cary's was a little shaky.

"Well, he's staying here at the same hotel," Cary told her. "He even offered to help with my search . . . if I decide I want him to."

"*Right!*" Rita said sarcastically. Then she added, "You better look out for that one. Those blue eyes will get you if you're not careful. Murder and threatening telephone calls might be the least of your worries."

Cary smiled as they said goodbye. Rita was good for her spirits.

She decided to go to Mrs. Hebert's office. Maybe she could take time to talk with Cary about all the alarming things that had taken place since their dinner last night. Lord knows she needed to bend someone's ear. Cary gathered her purse and jacket to leave, but, as she started toward the door, the phone rang yet again. She picked it up.

"Have you seen the morning newspaper?" It was Mrs. Hebert. She sounded upset, too.

"Yes. I was on my way to your office."

"Come on. And hurry."

"I'll be there in a few minutes." Anxiety had her pulse racing.

Outside, people were everywhere. It was mid-morning, and the shoppers had flocked downtown in force. Cary walked fast, weaving her way through the crowds to the corner. As traffic permitted, she hurried across Canal Street and into the Quarter. Her thoughts returned to this morning's discovery. None of it made sense.

As she rushed along, Cary started to imagine she was being followed. Two men, she decided, were after her, one on each side of the street. She didn't think they were the same ones she'd seen at the restaurant. Nonetheless, she quickened her pace. Then, just as she suspected, they were trailing behind on a couple of occasions as she glanced back.

When she reached the adoption agency, concerned about the two men and heeding Rita's words of caution, Cary peered out through the blinds. She chuckled. One of the men who had *trailed* her, got into a taxi as she watched. The other one went into a tobacco shop. Still on edge, she decided not to mention the incident to Mrs. Hebert.

The social worker suggested they walk in the Quarter again. Before they could leave, her friend realized something was wrong. "You're pale and shaking," she said. "Is there more going on than Mrs. Shapiro's death? Judging from your looks, you might've seen a ghost."

"I received a threat this morning." Cary told her about the menacing call and the stranger's message.

When she finished, Mrs. Hebert stared at her, apparently stunned. Finally she asked, "Do you think it's safe to go on with your search?"

Gesturing, her hands spread wide, Cary said, "Truthfully? I don't know. But I can't stop now."

"Oh, child," Mrs. Hebert said wearily. "It's hard not knowing who you are. But it's even worse having someone tell you you're not allowed to find out."

She could see tears in the old woman's eyes. Cary reached over and hugged her. "I'm sorry if I've brought back old memories."

"It's all right," Mrs. Hebert told her, blinking back the tears. "I just remember a time in my life when I . . . well, I wanted to know things, too."

Standing, she said, "Now let's go for that walk."

With her friend's experience on her mind, Cary trailed her through the office to the front door.

"I love walking in the Vieux Carre," Mrs. Hebert said as Cary followed her outdoors. Curious, Cary asked about the name. "It's French for 'Old Square'. The Vieux Carre is the site of the original city. Dawlin', you're walking on history."

The day, like several of those before it, was gorgeous – cool and clear.

"I saw the article about Mrs. Shapiro at breakfast," Cary said, once they had walked a short distance. "I couldn't believe it."

"I couldn't either," Mrs. Hebert said, "but it's not unusual for someone to get killed in a robbery here in New Orleans these days. It *is* unusual for the Garden District, however. It's been bad everywhere since the storm. There are more gangs and more violence than ever."

"I don't think it was a robbery," Cary said without looking at Mrs. Hebert. "I think she was killed because of what someone was afraid she might know or say about my mother's death." She kicked at a stone on the sidewalk. Cary was having trouble getting her mind around it all: Carolette Shapiro's murder, the menacing phone call, the burglary last night – everything.

Mrs. Hebert stopped, turning to look at her. "You're serious." Evidently Mrs. Hebert was having trouble getting a handle on everything, too.

"Serious as I can be," Cary said, taking her arm and crossing a busy street amidst the honks and noise of mid-day traffic. When they were on the other side, she turned to Mrs. Hebert and asked, "Should I go to the police and tell them we talked to Mrs. Shapiro yesterday? I don't think I should."

"They may already know," Mrs. Hebert said. "They surely asked her husband and the maid who Mrs. Shapiro met with yesterday."

"Then you think they'll be looking for me?"

"They'll probably call both of us if the maid remembers our names," Mrs. Hebert said. "Mrs. Shapiro must have talked with her husband about us," she added. "And remember, I left my card."

"Then maybe I *should* call them," Cary said. "I suspect the part about my mother is going to really blow things open. That is, if they believe me."

"I'll back you up," the woman said, reassuring Cary, "but I think you should wait for them to contact you."

"Why?" she asked.

"Call it what you want to," she told Cary, "but what you've said about your conversations with the Police Superintendent and the Mayor makes me wonder about the whole police force."

Cary nodded, thinking deep down she agreed.

For over an hour, the two women continued talking as they walked slowly through the Quarter. They passed several small cafés where Cary suspected shrimp and crawfish were boiling for the day. Her eyes watered on more than one occasion when the heavy scents of Tony Chachere's Cajun and Creole seasonings drifted onto the sidewalks and streets. Almost unconsciously she had started to notice the appearance, sounds, and scents of the Quarter and its unique neighborhoods.

Finally, they made their way back to Mrs. Hebert's office and stopped outside. She said goodbye and left Mrs. Hebert in front of the building.

As she walked back toward her hotel, Cary wondered how to make the police believe her if they called. She had the letter from her mother, but they might think she had written it herself, making up the story. She doubted if the Superintendent had believed the tale about her mother's note, but she also had doubts about him.

As she neared Canal Street, the crowd on the sidewalks started to press in on her. She eased her way through to the curb where she waited for the light to change. The streets were busy in all directions, and vehicles were passing very close to her. Stepping back wasn't an option. A car brushed Cary's pant leg as it went by. She wondered why someone wasn't struck.

Uncomfortable this close to the traffic, she glanced to her left and saw a transit bus coming toward the curb. It was moving fast, Then, as it approached, Cary felt a push – someone shoved her. The next thing she knew she was falling into the street in front of the bus. She felt a strong tug at her left shoulder, the stout leather strap of her handbag was holding and spinning her around as she fell. Then she was on the pavement.

As she went down in the street, Cary could hear the screech of brakes and saw the big front wheel of the bus speeding toward her. She tried to roll away but couldn't. Then everything went black.

Cary woke up gazing into a sea of faces. She blinked her eyes, focusing. Several individuals, concern etched in the creases of their brows, were leaning over her.

"Are you okay, Miss?" The bus driver seemed ready to cry. "Try not to move," he said. "An ambulance is on the way."

Cary realized she wasn't hurting – at least she didn't feel any pain. She tried moving her fingers and toes, then her arms and legs. They all seemed okay. Everything below her neck appeared to work. She tried turning her head – just a little at first. That seemed okay, too. So far, so good. She felt a burning sensation on the side of her forehead. Cary touched it gently then looked at her fingers. *No blood.*

"The tire must have grazed you there," the driver said, watching her. "Didn't even break the skin, just a red mark."

"I think I'm all right," Cary said in a halting voice. She could still feel the pressure, a hand in the middle of her back. *Someone tried to kill me!*

"Lady, you're lucky you rolled as you fell." Cary looked up. The little man didn't realize she had been pushed by a person who had also tried to steal her purse. Thank goodness the strap held. *That's* why she rolled. Cary checked. Yep! Still had her purse.

"Could you help me up?" she asked the driver as she reached for his arm.

"Oh, no!" She thought he was going to panic. "You shouldn't move," he told her. "You should let the paramedics get here and check you out."

"But I'm okay."

"You gotta stay put," he pleaded. "My supervisor will fire me if I let you leave now. I'll need to file a report, too. You know how it works."

"No, I can get up, really," she told him again as she rolled over onto her knees and then climbed to her feet. She made sure she was steady before she brushed herself off. Her slacks had a small tear at the left knee and there was dirt and grease in several places. Cary checked her purse again and then faced the crowd of onlookers. They watched her with worried expressions. She smiled and said, "Thanks, everybody, I'm fine."

Cary knew she would need to let the police fill out an accident report. She could already hear sirens.

The driver helped her onto the bus. A man moved, giving Cary his seat in the front row. The driver seemed to relax a little, apparently no longer afraid she was going to slip away before the EMTs could examine her.

The medics and police came at about the same time. Cary was checked out, and they asked their questions for the report. She actually had to refuse a trip to the hospital.

She told them she thought the push of the crowd had caused her to stumble and fall in front of the bus. She didn't mention the hand on her back or the attempt to take her purse, feeling sure she would only sound paranoid if she said someone may have shoved her.

When they were finished with their examinations and reports, Cary thanked everyone and headed for the hotel.

Her legs trembled as she made her way across Canal Street to the Sheraton. Common sense required her to tell the police about being pushed, but she recalled this morning's threat and her concerns about Big Eddie and his close ties to Johnny Periot. She decided to pass on making *that* call.

When Cary reached the hotel's entrance, something caused her to glance back across the street. She was stunned. The two men from the restaurant that morning now stood near the bus that had almost killed her. They were watching her, and this time there was no doubt that they had been following her.

Chapter Twelve

Back in her hotel room, the stress of the last several hours swept over Cary like a sudden tsunami – overcoming all anger, all emotion, all guilt – everything. Void of feelings, she kicked off her shoes and slipped out of her clothes, aberrantly tossing them here and there. Though she normally showered, this time Cary immersed her body in the Jacuzzi, turning it as high as it would go – it was luxurious.

After a few minutes in bubbling hot water up to her chin, she rinsed, dried herself and pulled on a soft white robe. Then she crawled under the satin sheets of the bed. Glancing at the clock, she was surprised. It was almost three-thirty in the afternoon.

Reality returned. She tried to relax but her thoughts wouldn't let her. Cary was still having trouble with the notion someone might kill her for trying to uncover the circumstances surrounding her mother's death. Something told her Big Eddie and the police were involved. She couldn't explain it, but in her heart, she knew it was true.

Now she also believed Carolette Shapiro had been killed because of her search. Such a beautiful person. So gracious and outgoing. *And now she's dead.* Cary laid her head back on the pillows, took a deep breath and finally, in spite of all that puzzled her, she was soon fast asleep.

Later – she had no idea how long – the phone rang. Startled from a deep slumber, Cary rose into a sitting position and reached for the receiver.

"Hel . . . Hello?"

"Good evening," Mike Webster said. She recognized his voice. "Are you ready for a fantastic dinner and night on the town?"

Evening? "Webster? Is that you?"

"In the flesh," he laughed. "And in New Orleans, too."

"I'm glad you made it in," she told him. She *didn't* tell him how wonderful it was to hear a strong voice that might be on her side.

"I can tell," he kidded. "Sounds like you're bounding around the room with enthusiasm,"

"It's just that, well . . . you woke me. But I *am* glad to hear from you." She'd have been happy to hear from almost anyone not connected to the things that had happened in the last few days, especially the last several hours. "When did you get in?"

"Just got to the hotel and unpacked," Webster said. "I'm starving so I thought I'd see if you're hungry too."

"What time is it?"

"Six-fifteen in the evening . . . Friday evening," he added.

"It can't be," Cary said. "I couldn't have slept that long."

"How long?"

"Almost three hours."

"You should go to bed earlier."

"It's not that, I promise," Cary said. "And yes, I'd enjoy having dinner with you." She had made up her mind earlier, after the bus incident, that not only would she go out with him if he called, but that she'd let him help her find her mother's killer – if he was still willing.

"Great. I'll pick you up in five minutes."

"Whoa," Cary said quickly. "Give me time to look presentable. How 'bout hmmm . . . seven o'clock?"

"Seven it is. What do you feel like eating? I'll see if reservations are in order."

"Surprise me. I don't want to make decisions tonight."

"Good enough. See ya' soon."

To wake up, Cary took a quick shower, then dressed. She pulled on a silky chartreuse blouse and a black skirt, tossing a sweater on the bed to take with her. A couple of run-throughs with a brush and her hair fall into place as always. She touched the red mark on her forehead, relieved that it seemed okay – just a little sensitive. *I clean up pretty good,* she thought, glancing in the bathroom mirror. She realized she might appear okay, but she felt like hell.

At exactly seven o'clock, there was a soft knock at her door. After checking through the peephole, Cary opened it. There stood Mike Webster, looking even better than she remembered. He had dressed casually, too, slacks and a dark, loose sweater. His sleeves were pushed up to the middle of his muscular forearms. *He looks good!* Damn it, she shouldn't be having these kinds of thoughts

She wasn't even sure she liked the man, though she'd never really given him a chance. And, she realized, not liking him might be a bit of a stretch.

"Ready?"

"Sure," she said, glancing up at him. She wasn't accustomed to looking up to a man, either. In heels, she was taller than most of them. But not him.

She grabbed her sweater and purse off the bed and walked into the hallway. He closed her door, making sure it was secure. Then he took Cary's arm and they walked to the elevator. Moments later, it deposited them in the lobby downstairs. They walked out onto the sidewalk where Webster motioned for a taxi.

Climbing in, he asked the driver, "Do you know a place called Ruby's Grill?"

"Down at the edge of the Quarter, on Esplanade?"

"That's the one."

After a short ride, the taxi stopped and Webster paid the driver. They got out and he led her through an opening between two buildings and down a dimly lit alley away from the street.

"You sure you know where we're going?" She had noticed people who appeared to be homeless on the street outside.

"Absolutely."

At the end of the passage, there was an open area. Here, the lighting was a little better. Webster led her through a back door into a small café that looked as old as the Quarter itself. Dusty lamp shades on strange antique lamps and bar stools dating back to the fifties filled the dining area which, though small, was quite busy.

As they headed toward a couple of empty spaces, Cary noticed a large grill and smelled beef cooking. They took seats at a table with straight-backed chairs and a red-and-white-checkered tablecloth. The small table was one of several placed along a wall. There was just enough space for the one row of tables and a walkway along a wooden bar that ran almost the length of the room. The waiter seemed to be doing double duty acting as both server and bartender.

He came over, lit the candle on their table and asked what they wanted to drink.

Webster looked at Cary, "Draft beer or a glass of wine?"

"Wine," she said.

"Make that two," he said.

"Red or white?" the waiter asked.

"Red," Webster said. With a raised brow, he told Cary, "It's house wine. You only have one choice, red or white."

"Red." There was something sensual about his smile that made her flush as she choked out the word.

With the waiter gone for their drinks, Cary asked him, "Sooo . . . Did you call ahead for reservations?"

Webster smiled, playing along with her. "Yep, but I still had to tip the maître d' to get this particular table. Did you notice how well you can see and be seen from here?" They both laughed. Cary watched him, noting he had mesmerizing eyes. *Ooops, there I go again.*

As they talked, it became apparent to Cary that her dinner companion seemed to be aware of everything going on around them. She thought that a little odd. She began to notice that he had a casual way of keeping an eye on the door *and* on other customers, while giving her the impression that she had his complete attention. The concept troubled her. She shook her head; was she being paranoid again?

But then again, after today, Cary believed she had reason to be. In her mind's eye, she could still see the two men standing near the bus that nearly ran her down on Canal Street.

The waiter appeared again, this time with a container of peanuts, still warm in their shells. Webster cracked one and tossed the nuts into his mouth. She watched him drop the shells on the floor and followed his lead. The floor was littered with the shells from guests long gone, maybe by as much as a week or so; the floor didn't appear to receive a lot of attention.

Their wine came, as if on cue. This waiter was good.

"You ready to order?"

"Do you have a menu?" Cary inquired.

The waiter smiled. "We only serve Steak Burgers and fries, ma'am. Your choice is how you want it cooked."

"Oh," Cary said as she noticed Webster hiding a grin.

"In that case," Webster cut in, taking the lead, "just dehorn the steer, hose him down and run him in." He paused for emphasis. "I like mine rare. How 'bout the lady?" He winked.

As soon as Cary could stop laughing she told the waiter, "Make mine medium well. I'm hoping the steer has been hosed down for some time now." The waiter left their table with a big grin on his face.

When they were alone, Cary wiped fun tears from her eyes and said, "Well that was certainly interesting. I may get to like you yet." Then she flushed, realizing she had let true feelings show. But, like a gentleman, Webster merely smiled, causing her to flush even more.

Later, after they had finished eating one of the best hamburgers Cary could remember, he ordered more wine.

Webster brought her up to date on things that had happened back at Trebeck Corporation during the week. Deep in her own thoughts, she listened but her heart wasn't in it. She soon realized Webster was peering at her in a peculiar way.

"Okay, what's up?" she demanded, finding herself the object of his stare.

"You're here, but you're not here," he said, "if you know what I mean." He paused. "Why don't you tell me about *your* week?"

Cary tilted her head. The man was full of surprises. In just a short time, and, as far as she knew, through no fault of his own, Webster had touched her life and caused significant changes in her future. Now she found herself changing the way she thought of him. Much of her earlier anger was gone. Cary realized that whatever problems existed between them now were hers and not Webster's.

Besides, she was alone in New Orleans and almost certainly in over her head. Like him or not, she could use a confidant. So much had happened, things she couldn't control. Cary needed someone; Webster seemed a logical choice. He appeared responsible, but could she trust him enough to reveal everything? She had always been a good judge of character, but . . .

Finally she looked him in the eye. "You wouldn't believe me if I told you about my week."

"Try me."

Her eyes held his. "Well, for starters, I was almost killed today, and I don't think it was an accident." She watched for his reaction.

Webster's eyes went immediately to the red mark on her forehead.

"Surely you're kidding," he said, but he reached out and lightly touched her injury with his fingertips. With their eyes locked, he turned his hand and slowly swept the back of his fingers across her forehead. The fluttering of butterfly wings couldn't have been softer.

She drew in a breath, surprised at the tender display. Recovering from his touch *and* her feelings, she lowered her gaze to the wine glass.

"That's only the latest," Cary said as he withdrew his hand. From his expression,

Cary guessed the moment had affected him, too. The wine suddenly seemed important: They each took a sip.

Then Cary told him about her week *and* her life, starting with the fact that she had been adopted. He listened, asking questions occasionally and nodding from time to time in understanding. Cary told him about her meetings with Mrs. Hebert and what she had discovered. She described in detail what she found out about her mother's death, the letter, and how her mother had met her father.

At last she looked at Webster and said softly, "You won't believe who my father turned out to be."

"Who?"

"Have you heard of Johnny Periot? Janice Talmer revealed his name in her letter." She didn't expect Webster to be familiar with the name.

"The Mayor of New Orleans?"

Cary was surprised. He sounded genuinely taken aback.

"Johnny Periot is your biological father?"

"Ahhh . . . Yeah!"

Webster's forehead creased and those blue eyes hardened on hers. He seemed to consider his next question carefully. "What do you know about him?"

She wasn't sure what he was after. "Not much except what I read in a *Newsweek* article. How did you know the name?"

He seemed reluctant to answer at first, and then said, "I've read about him, too." His answer seemed to have deeper meaning.

Cary waited for more, but it didn't come. When Webster remained silent, she continued. "I went to see Periot and confronted him. We ended up in a fight and he threw me out of his office."

"What was the fight about?"

"I told him some of the things I had discovered, then I mentioned what my mother had written to me. I didn't exactly say he was my father, but I left that possibility open."

"I'll bet that left him mumbling to himself."

"Yeah . . . kinda'. We argued some, and then he suggested I leave and not come back."

"You're lucky that's all he did." Webster said it under his breath.

Cary picked up on the undercurrent. "What do you mean by that?"

"Oh, nothing in particular." He tried to pass it off. "I can just imagine how he might react if someone came into his office and jumped him about the things you had on your mind even if you didn't accuse him of being your father."

Now Cary felt sure Webster knew something he wasn't saying. That annoyed the hell out of her, and she wasn't about to let it pass unanswered. She leaned forward, set both elbows on the table, and locked her fingers.

"First of all, Mister Webster, I didn't *jump* all over him. I'm not some hysterical female." She could feel the goose bumps on her skin rise in proportion to her anger.

"Wait a minute," Webster said, holding up his hands. "That didn't come out exactly the way I intended."

"I should hope not."

"What I meant is that you must have caught him off guard even if you only implied you might be his daughter."

She leaned back, just a bit. "That could be. I . . . guess I did," Cary said, taking a deep breath. "He wasn't pleased to see me. He finally told me in no uncertain terms to get out and not come back. I got the feeling he wasn't just talking about his office."

"What will you do now?"

"I'm still going to try to find out who killed my mother."

"That's not something you should attempt alone, and with so little to go on, particularly in a city like New Orleans." He hesitated. "You'll need help," he told her. "You have no idea the type of people you're up against."

She had that hunch again. "And you do?" He definitely knew more than he was saying.

Webster was silent for several seconds before he answered. "Maybe." Even then it was only one word.

Something . . . hmmm . . . about him. An illusion – the flickering candlelight in the room or simply her own fear? Somehow a transformation had taken place; for a moment, Webster appeared dark, maybe dangerous. The impression passed quickly when he smiled again.

They finished the wine, paid the check, and then went out for a stroll in the Quarter. As they left Ruby's Grill, Webster led her across Esplanade Avenue to the far sidewalk. There, in front of them in the night, the old New Orleans Mint loomed, dark and foreboding. Webster commented that it was a national landmark.

They turned on Decatur and walked to Jackson Square. There, they opted for a quaint mode of transportation that had been used in the old city. Webster helped Cary aboard a carriage, whereupon a spirited horse and driver took them for a short tour of the Quarter. They saw Pirate's Alley behind the Cathedral and Madame John's Legacy. "The Legacy," their guide told them, "has been mostly used as a residence over the years and is reputed to be the oldest structure in the Mississippi Valley, the original house having been built in 1726. The present structure," he added, "dates back to construction in 1788 when fire destroyed the original building."

Their driver was obviously knowledgeable, but Cary soon tuned him out as she enjoyed the ordinary sights and sounds of the evening. This carriage ride was a welcome change from so much that had happened over the preceding days. Maybe the two men would believe they had scared her into leaving New Orleans. No doubt they were waiting and watching for her next move. Unable to stop herself, Cary glanced around the darkened sidewalks. She would have to be very careful. She hoped Webster could at least take care of himself.

She leaned back into the arm that Webster had placed around her and drank in the sights. As she snuggled down in the seat, the closeness of the carriage and the heat from Webster's body started to awaken feelings that had lain dormant for a long time. Recognizing danger and fleeing from an intimacy she craved, Cary bolted upright, reluctant to let the feeling take hold. She couldn't deal with it – not here, not now.

Webster, feeling her apprehension, asked, "What's wrong? What did I do?"

"Nothing," she told him. "I just couldn't see. I'm okay now."

She could feel him watching her. Then he dropped his arm to his side.

Many of the buildings they passed had wrought iron balconies above the sidewalks, and by their appearance, most of the structures here were very old with both French and Spanish architecture evident.

Music, Jazz *and* the Blues, could be heard from any number of small clubs along the way. After her earlier moment of self-induced panic, Cary was closer to being relaxed than she had been since she arrived in the city. She wondered if it was the wine or the man who sat beside her.

"Crawfisshhh! Hey, cum' git yo crawfish heah." Yes, they were surely in N'awlins.

Later when they returned to the hotel, Webster walked her to her room. Cary was surprised when he stopped at the door and reached out to shake her hand.

"I've had a really nice evening," he said. "I'm glad you went to dinner with me." He took a step back. "I'll make some phone calls and see if I can come up with anything for your search." Then he added, "Let's meet downstairs about nine in the morning. We'll get some breakfast and talk about tomorrow." *He could at least have asked to come in so she could have said no.*

"Sounds good," she said, feeling a little disappointed, but uncertain as to why.

Webster turned and walked away.

Once her door was closed, Cary leaned back against it with old feelings returning. *Tomorrow?* With her luck, she'd be fortunate to make it through the rest of the evening.

# Chapter Thirteen

Webster returned to his room and sat down at the desk. He moved his laptop computer over in front of him, booted up and entered his password, then pulled up a short telephone list from a buried subdirectory. Quickly scanning the file, he jotted down three names and numbers on a pad from the desk.

Once he had his numbers, Webster leaned back with his eyes closed. *What have I gotten myself into?*

He had only recently met this woman; she wasn't his to save. Her problems were her own. He had enough to last without digging for new ones. His task was to find out if the owners of Trebeck Corporation were linked to New Orleans and its crime structure and to find out how Cary fit into all this.

There were already indications that crime in the city had inroads into the political organization, maybe even going all the way to the top. And now Cary drops the fact that the Mayor is her father. Not only that, she hints that she could use a friend in her search for her mother's killer. His first thought was that this was more than he'd bargained for. He could end up at cross-purposes in handling his assignment and also helping Cary.

But he'd already indicated he would help. Besides, it couldn't be as bad as it sounded. He could handle double duty; he'd certainly done it before. Using the nonexistent seminar as a reason for being here, he could keep an eye on her and still keep a low profile . . . couldn't he?

Ahhh, hell! He sat up and studied the list. He needed to tell his people about Cary and her connection to the Mayor and New Orleans. He probably needed to tell them he had agreed to help her, too. Having come to a conclusion, he reached for his cell phone and punched in the first number. He listened for a few seconds and then said, "I need you to have Jim Carson call me at this number." Webster read off the number. "Got that? Just tell him it's his friend Darcy from Chicago. He'll know me." He listened for another moment or two. "No. It's not a joke. Just tell him. He'll understand, I promise."

Webster made two more calls, one to Jack Robbins and another to Ray Ward, essentially saying the same thing each time. After the contacts were made, he took the pad and jotted down some notes as he waited for the phone to ring.

He continued sitting at the desk, but kicked off his shoes and rested his legs on the edge of the bed. Fifteen minutes later, Webster's cell phone rang. After the initial greeting, he got up and started pacing between his bed and the window.

"Yeah, I know, it's been a while. I can't explain right now, but listen. I need a favor." He sat at the desk again, pulling the note pad in front of him. "I need you to check out some things on Johnny Periot, the Mayor of New Orleans. Here comes the weird part, Ray: I need to know what was going on around him twenty-five years ago." He laughed. "Yeah, you heard me right. My specific job is to tie down my company's ownership. We think there's a connection to New Orleans. Call when you have something. Thanks, Ray. Oh, and one more thing, this needs to be kept as quiet as possible for now. I don't want to rattle anyone's cage here in the city."

Webster received two other calls, back to back. The conversations were short and very similar to the first one. The reaction he got from two of his contacts was that they could use anything new he could find from his connection with Cary.

Jack Robbins worried about Webster jeopardizing his cover as the new head of the Advertising Department at Trebeck. Webster assured him he would be careful. He jotted down some additional notes about each conversation, then after the third call, he tossed the pad on the desk and went to brush his teeth.

Later, as he walked out of the bathroom, the cell phone rang unexpectedly. He stared at it. It was a new phone.

Other than the three people he had called tonight, only a select few had this number – oh, yes . . . and Cary Warren.

He stared at the display. "Blocked call."

Webster punched the connect button, putting the phone to his ear. He listened for a couple of seconds, then said, "Hello?"

Thinking he heard breathing, Webster tried again, "Hello? Is someone there?" Then he heard a click and the phone went dead. *Maybe* someone had a wrong number. Then again, *maybe* not.

Kind of like the old days when you were never quite sure who was on the other end.

As a final act of the evening, Webster called a number he didn't need to look up. Having phoned his mentor many, many times over the years to seek advice and direction, the number was ingrained in Webster's memory. Sitting down at his laptop, he punched up Skype, passed his call through three anonymous IP addresses to hide its origin, then heard it connect.

The call was answered after only one ring.

"Ha'low?" The accent never failed to amuse Webster – deeply southern and never changing. Good English, but *deeply* southern. Raegene Dorryen Doyle was probably close to seventy but didn't look it. He was still dangerous if you crossed him, but that didn't show either. He had been Webster's friend since . . .

"Hello, Rage. I hope I didn't wake you." Webster was aware only a couple of people called him that. Most only knew him as "The Author" for his ability to script covert operations however he wanted them.

Rage knew his caller was Webster. "No, son . . . You didn't wake me. I was reading. Did you know that Katmandu, Nepal, has a population of nearly one million people even though it's high in the Himalayas – as the crow flies, only a hundred miles from Mt. Everest?" He always had something interesting to convey to Webster.

"No, I didn't know that," he told Rage. Then, "Why are you reading about Nepal?"

"I'm learning," he said. "So much out there and so little time." Webster heard Rage breathe a long sigh. Then his friend said, "How are things going with you?"

"That's why I called," Webster said, "I need your counsel."

"Speak."

"Something has come up." He brought his friend up to date. There were no secrets between them – confidentiality not an issue. He told Rage about Cary, that he was considering helping her.

"And you want me to tell you if you're doing the right thing."

"I guess that's it."

"Can you put your hands on a bible?"

"Yes," Webster said as he opened a drawer containing a Gideon bible.

"Luke, Chapter ten, verses 29 through 37," Rage told him. "Let me know how it turns out."

Webster heard a click, then the dial tone. His friend had gone back to reading.

Luke 10:29. Webster opened the bible, turning to the four gospels, then to

Luke. He started to read – *The Good Samaritan*. Webster remembered the parable and its lesson. *Okay . . . he would help Cary.*

***

Cary stepped off the elevator in the lobby promptly at nine the next morning. Not surprisingly, Webster stood waiting. She wouldn't let him know it, but Cary was happy to have someone with her after yesterday's attempt on her life.

She had slept poorly, dreaming of being chased through darkened streets and alleys by people who wanted to kill her. She felt exhausted, and the day was just beginning. After her restless night, she now had real questions about continuing her search.

She smiled and said hello, thinking Webster would direct her to the restaurant there in the hotel. He didn't.

Instead, he took her arm, leading her outside where they scrambled into a taxi. After a short ride into the French Quarter, they climbed out near Jackson Square. Webster led her into an open-air café where crowds of people were sitting at tables casually drinking coffee and eating some sort of pastry.

A chill of apprehension ran through her. They were out in the public where everybody could see them. But, she realized, it would be difficult for anyone to bother them with so many others around them. Cary felt better until she remembered how many people were present yesterday when she was shoved under a bus. Recalling that, she realized there was no such thing as a safe place.

They had to wait in line for a table and as they did, Cary surveyed the crowd. Obviously this was a gathering place for natives and tourists alike.

She liked the place; one couldn't help it. Yet she felt unhappy. A sense of depression seemed always to be with her now, even with the festive atmosphere of this place. Maybe she was just tired but she thought it was more than that. What could possibly come from staying in New Orleans?

Her dreams had kept Cary awake. She'd gone over everything and was close to deciding that it was time to raise the white flag and go home. With no idea where to turn, Cary had to admit she'd failed.

As she looked around, Cary started to imagine problems. Behind them in line was a man reading a copy of Friday's *USA Today*. The camera over his shoulder and his backpack, not to mention his casual manner of dress, branded him as a typical tourist.

Cary wouldn't have noticed him if he hadn't turned his head when she looked his way. *There, he did it again.* He folded the paper and stuck it under his arm, glancing around as though waiting for someone. He seemed nervous and Cary decided to keep an eye on him. Two could play this game.

Webster worked them to the front of the line and hurried to a table being vacated by an older couple. Holding a chair for her, he brushed crumbs and powdered sugar over to the side of the table. A waiter finally arrived, cleared their table, and took their order. Webster said they would have two cafe au laits, and two orders of beignets.

"French donuts," Webster explained, seeing her raised brow. "I thought you could use a little cheering up. They're square pieces of dough, deep fried and sprinkled with powdered sugar."

"Ymm!" she said. "Deep fried." Cary winked so he would know she was kidding.

He grinned back and continued his explanation. "Oh, and the coffee – its strong chicory mixed with boiling milk, so it's easier to handle the chicory."

As she listened, Cary kept an eye on the man she had noticed earlier. He had taken a table three rows over and seated himself so he could watch them. Just as she was about to warn Webster, the man obviously realized she had spotted him. In an effort to distract her, he started waving as though trying to get someone's attention. *Right!*

On impulse, Cary glanced in the direction he was motioning. Weaving their way through the crowd was a pretty blonde mommy followed by twin girls about five or six years old. "Daddy, Daddy," one of them called as they both climbed up on his lap. The blonde stooped and gave her man a kiss.

Cary grinned, almost laughing out loud, as she thought how her search and the events of the week were causing her to see things that weren't real.

Webster noticed the smile. "What's so funny?" he asked.

"Me," she said without explanation. He shook his head and let it go.

When their order came, Cary decided she liked everything but the powdered sugar on her dark slacks. She sneezed once and white stuff went everywhere. So much for the smart outfit she had picked for today.

Donuts or no donuts, and try as she might, Cary was unable to get into a positive mood. Everyone in the Quarter seemed happy. A dark-skinned guy was playing jazz on his trumpet and collecting money in the open instrument case. Kids couldn't help dancing as they walked by.

The waiter returned with their second coffee. Cary sipped at it listlessly as the music played in the background. She tried, but couldn't resist searching the crowd for the men who had followed her yesterday. She could still feel the pressure of a hand on her back.

Webster jarred her back to reality. "I made a couple of calls last night," he told her. "Some old friends are making inquiries about Johnny Periot. I asked them to look at his activities around the time your mother died." He nodded his head reassuringly. "I'm expecting to hear from them this morning."

"Really?" She wondered what kind of connections enabled him to make that kind of call. But this *would* be a direction for them to take if he came up with something. *If only.* She really didn't want to give up on the search for Janice's killer. With his help, maybe she'd give it another day or two.

Cary realized as she glanced over at Webster that he hadn't smiled once this morning. Maybe something was bothering him too. His mood appeared subdued and thoughtful – much like her own. His light spirit from the night before was gone.

"You must have influential friends," she said, "or at least some that are well placed. Who could someone in advertising know that would have access to the kind of information you asked for?"

"I have a few connections in law enforcement," he said without clarification. She studied him but decided not to push it, for now.

"If you can stand it, I'm going to stay close to you for the next couple of days," he told her. "If someone really is trying to hurt you, maybe they'll think twice if you have someone tagging along."

"But what about your seminar?"

"I'll cancel it if I need to. Let's see how things go. It doesn't start until Monday." He finally smiled, and then reached for his cafe au lait. Cary watched as he peered into the cup. One would think it might hold the answers to his future. *Or* maybe hers.

Catching her eye, he said, "You know . . . maybe I could pose as your boyfriend." He chuckled, then paused, staring at her with a raised eyebrow before saying, "That works for me, how 'bout you?" Then he flashed her a wide grin. *That's more like it!*

But was he simply joking around, she wondered, or could there be some hidden implication behind the notion? It might take her a while to figure him out.

"I don't know about the boyfriend thing," she shot back, hoping to ease him off a little, "but I could probably live with the 'staying close' part."

"Done," he agreed and held out his hand.

She eyed him for a moment, then shook sealing the deal.

At his suggestion, they decided to go to the library where Cary had gone on

Wednesday. Webster wanted to read through some of the material about Johnny Periot and his friends. She suggested he start with the biographical article in *Newsweek*.

Webster found them a taxi and they headed out. Minutes later, they were climbing the steps to the library. Bob, the young man Cary had met earlier, was on duty as they walked past the main counter.

"You're back again," Bob called out to her. "Still interested in the Mayor?"

"Still interested," she confirmed. "Even brought a friend."

"You might want to check the current *Newsweek*," Bob told them. "It came in yesterday. There's an article talking about him as a possible Vice Presidential candidate again and pairing him up with Stuart Daniels, even before the primaries. That's unusual. Be sure and catch what it says." Bob sounded very proud.

"I'll do that. Thanks," she told him.

To Webster, she said, "That's the fellow I told you about."

"I figured that. I can see what you mean about his being a fan of Periot." They walked back to the newspaper files and, after some discussion, decided to check articles written in the last year. There was a lot of material in the local paper. They narrowed it down to Sunday articles and editorials. After finishing the newspapers, they would check out the article Bob had suggested and Webster could read Periot's biographical article.

Cary showed Webster an editorial in the second week of July that talked about the Mayor and his lifelong friend, "Big Eddie" Breunoux. They had worked on a debris removal truck for a day. A series of photographs showed the two of them picking up tree limbs and other pieces of trash and tossing them into collection bins. The writer commended them for their example to other executives and to the community and for helping the City return to normal after the hurricane.

After reading one article, Webster said, "Your friend the Mayor is a publicity hound and a good one at that. He makes the reporters come to him."

After an hour of reading, Cary asked Webster if he'd like some coffee. She asked Bob where they could get some. He brought a cup for each of them from his office, and they walked over near the main entrance doors and stood talking as they enjoyed the coffee. Cary introduced Webster to Bob.

Then Cary asked Bob, "Have you been at the library long?"

"Nearly four years and counting. Most of it part-time while I was going to college full time."

"Are you from the New Orleans area?" Webster inquired.

"Nope. From the country, up in Mississippi," he told them. "I came to the city to go to school. Went to the University of New Orleans, got my degree and decided to stay. Didn't plan on hurricanes, though." He shook his head, remembering.

"I bet you didn't," Webster said.

They talked on, Webster and Cary asking questions, and Bob chatting about the hurricane, the City, and the Mayor. Periot was obviously popular and not just with Bob. Also, Periot's friend "Big Eddie" seemed to be in every story Bob told. Obviously, Periot and Big Eddie were close. *Too close?*

After about thirty minutes, Cary and Webster excused themselves and went back to their research. They worked until noon.

As they were finishing, Cary went to find a restroom. When she started back, she spied a water fountain at the end of a short hallway and stopped for a drink.

She was leaning over the fountain when someone approached. Startled, Cary moved to step out of the way, thinking the individual wanted to get to the fountain. It was a man, glaring *and* dangerous looking, and he blocked her path.

"I guess you didn't get the message," he said in a rough voice. Reaching out, he gripped Cary's arm and forced her toward a supply closet. Before she could even think of screaming, he reached out, clamping a cloth soaked with chemicals over her face. A strong arm encircled her waist to keep her from escaping.

The man elbowed the closet door open, attempting to push Cary inside.

She knew she had only seconds to fight him off before losing consciousness. Desperately holding her breath, she swung at him with her right fist, landing a good hard blow under his left eye. He shook off the punch and kept shoving, slowly but surely forcing her into the closet.

Cary refused to go easily, but she was running out of oxygen. Still, she was all arms and legs, scratching and finally pulling the cloth away from her face in time to grab a breath.

***

Webster finished an article and glanced at his watch. *Where's Cary?* She should have been back. As he stood up, he heard a muffled cry and rushed to where he'd last seen her. As he started past the hallway, he saw her struggling with a man trying to push her into a closet.

A couple of quick, long strides and Webster reached them. He landed a jarring chop at the junction of the man's neck and shoulder. Clearly shaken, the individual turned, still holding Cary. Now Webster slugged him squarely on his lower jaw, this time breaking his grip on Cary. The jolt staggered her assailant, throwing him against the back wall of the closet where he crumpled and slid to the floor. He lay there for a moment, then shook his head.

In an effort to finish the job, Webster leaned in for one last blow. What he saw caused him to draw back, making sure Cary was behind him. Webster didn't think she had seen the big 45 Colt semi-automatic pistol. The man's words were almost as chilling as the weapon he held. "I'll kill you both right here," he said softly, "and some others, if I have ta – up ta you, big fella."

Webster stepped back, pushing Cary ahead of him. By this time a small crowd had gathered, and Bob had called the police on his cell phone.

"Are you all right?" Webster was only concerned about Cary now.

"I'm fine," she said, but her voice was shaky.

After a few moments, the man rose from the floor and staggered forward as he brushed himself off. The gun was nowhere in sight. The thug was a little under six feet but solidly built. Glancing at Webster with glassy eyes, he said, "You're going to regret that one." He glared at both of them for a moment, then shoved Webster hard into the small crowd of onlookers and made a run for it. Knocking people aside, the man headed for the front entrance. Leaving Cary on her own, Webster followed after him with a couple of other men a few steps behind him. Webster made sure no one got too close. He didn't want anyone killed. He watched as the man ran and jumped into a car with someone else. They drove off, too far away to get a tag number.

Cary was waiting where he'd left her. "He had someone waiting in a car outside," Webster told her.

"I think he was one of the men who tried to push me under the bus yesterday," Cary said.

Webster tightened his lips and put an arm around her. He could smell the chemical. "Sure you're all right?" he asked again as he checked out a minor bump on her chin. "What did he say to you?"

"I'm okay." Webster heard her words, but he could see she was trembling. Cary told him what the man had said, then added, "I'm glad you were here."

"Sounds like a continued threat from the phone call yesterday and maybe the bus incident, too," he told her, choosing not to mention the weapon he had just been threatened with or anything about the hang up call he'd received last night. He didn't want to frighten her more. Besides, the call may not have had anything to do with her.

"We'll have to be more careful." He remembered how he had felt when the caller hung up. What the hell was going on? Webster's cell phone rang as they were talking. He glanced at the display. It was Jim Carson, from last night. Jim had been Webster's go-to person for details in an earlier life. Carson ran a large computer data bank in Virginia and could acquire difficult-to-obtain information no one else could get. He had never questioned Carson's sources. Webster excused himself and walked to the portico outside the library entrance doors to take the call.

After greeting Webster, Carson asked where he was located.

"New Orleans," Webster said, "specifically, the main library. We're pulling together some current information on the Mayor. What did you come up with?"

He listened as Carson spoke.

"Tell me that again," Webster said after a few moments. He peered back through the windows at Cary. She was standing alone, off from the others, watching him.

He listened to Carson, a frown on his face. "Let me get this straight – Alex Shapiro was the third man in their little threesome? Johnny Periot, Big Eddie Breunoux, and now Shapiro." Webster shook his head in surprise.

"You sound like you've heard Shapiro's name before," Carson commented.

"I have," Webster told him. "You want to hear something interesting? Shapiro's wife was murdered here in New Orleans on Thursday night."

"Interesting timing."

"Yeah. It had the appearance of a robbery, but I don't think so."

He went on to tell Carson about Cary, then her connection to the Mayor and the attempt on her life.

When he finished, Carson said, "Listen, Mike, you need to get out of there. You're all alone in New Orleans. The last thing you need is for someone to identify you. A number of people would like to collect the reward that's on your head."

"I realize I'm on my own here, Jim," Webster said, "but how do you walk away from something like this? I'll be careful." Then he signed off.

Webster glanced up and saw Cary as he closed the phone. He waved her out and filled her in on some of the details of his conversation .

"Another of Periot's friends from grade school has popped up. Want to guess who?"

"Besides the Police Superintendent?" she asked.

"Besides him," he challenged. She shrugged, clearly without a clue.

"Alex Shapiro." He gave her a moment to process the new info. "Shapiro went to grade school with the other two and lived on Periot's street. Those two went their separate ways after grade school but hooked up again a year before your mother was killed."

Cary started to speak, but a puzzled look spread across her face. Obviously she wasn't sure how everything fit together.

"Yeah, me too." Like her, he was still putting the pieces together.

After a moment, Cary tried again. "Do you think . . . I mean could there be . . . a connection to Carolette Shapiro . . . and to Janice, twenty-five years ago?" Cary looked into Webster's eyes, then shook her head.

"Maybe." But he had doubts.

Webster could tell it was a mental stretch for Cary, even after all that had happened to her. What she'd said left Webster trying to sort it out. She asked good questions. The best he could do was warn her.

"In less than a week this has gotten complicated and dangerous," he said. "And we're not sure what we're looking for yet. You've walked into something," he gave her a warning look. ". . . Something really big."

Chapter Fourteen

The onlookers lost interest after the officers arrived and started questioning Cary and Webster. Now, forty-five minutes later, only the two of them, along with Bob and the two officers, remained outside the library.

Bob signed his statement and went back to work. Cary and Webster each finished giving a description of the man and detailing how Cary had been attacked. Cary left out the part about believing the same man was involved in Friday's bus episode. As she completed her statement, she saw that Webster was finished, too.

The officers released them and headed for their cruiser.

As Webster turned back to her, a stranger approached and tapped him on the shoulder. Turning toward the man, Webster's eyes widened in recognition. He glanced at Cary, then quickly and without introducing the man, excused himself and walked down the steps with the stranger.

Rugged features, graying hair and in his late forties, the man had a decided scar running across his left cheek. His pleasure at seeing Webster was apparent. They laughed, slapped each other on the back, and acted like long lost brothers. Cary strained to hear as they conversed in low tones on the sidewalk. Who is this guy, she wondered – *and how does he know Webster?*

***

"Hey, Ray. I didn't know you were in New Orleans when we talked last night." One of Webster's calls the previous night had been to Ray Ward.

"Why are you here?"

"Same as you," Ward said. "Searching for answers. Jim told me where to find you." Webster and Ward had worked together before, but it had been over a year since they had seen each other. There would be time to chat later. Webster, concerned with Cary's search, asked if Ward had come up with anything on the Mayor. "I'll let you decide. Listen to this."

Webster listened, trying to understand what he was hearing and keeping an eye on Cary at the same time. Ward had a lot to tell him. Finally, well into the conversation, Webster put a hand on Ward's arm. "Let me be sure I'm following you. The three boyhood friends, back together as adults, were buddies again. One goes to law school, another becomes a policeman, and there's Shapiro. He starts a business that's barely paying its bills, but then something changes – we're not sure what. But what we are sure of is Shapiro's business took off immediately after Janice Talmer was killed." Webster took his hand off Ward's arm. After a moment he said, "There must have been something else that caused the change. Did he have partners or investors?"

"Nope. Just him and his wife. The two of them ran the company."

Ward gave Webster a smattering of other information, but it was mostly details, almost nothing of consequence.

Then he asked Webster to do something for him . . .

***

Cary was impatient, ready to start tapping her foot at any moment. It didn't take a genius to know Webster wasn't acting like an advertising executive

Something didn't add up. *There's a lot more to him than he's saying.*

Webster was watching her, too. Cary had seen him glance her way several times. Then something the man said peeked Webster's interest because he turned away and they lowered their voices even more. Even standing up on the portico, she had picked up a few words during their conversation but nothing that made sense. Now she couldn't hear them at all.

Finally, as suddenly as the stranger had appeared, he and Webster seemed to finish their business. The man briskly walked away and Webster called to her, "Come on. Let's go somewhere and grab a sandwich." He took a step or two, then glanced back. "While you were getting mugged, I found out something that might help us. We'll discuss it over lunch."

"Who was that man?" She couldn't wait to ask.

"One of the people I called last night," he told her. "He happened to be in New Orleans."

"How did he know we were at the library?"

"Carson – the call I received earlier." he said, and to her raised brows he simply shrugged.

"Let me tell you what I found out," he said, plunging ahead.

Answers at last – maybe. As they hurried along, Cary listened as Webster explained the reason for the man's visit. She realized Webster hadn't actually told her anything specific about the man, including his name. The only thing he explained was what his friend told him about Alex Shapiro.

She was confused. "So the Shapiros, who were starting a business and were not well off, suddenly came into a lot of money? But how?"

"I didn't say they came into a lot of money. I said their business took off – boomed, whatever. We're not sure why. The money came later."

"So, Mr. Mike Webster, who *is* this we? What's your link with that man?" Cary motioned for him to keep talking, "and how does he know about all these things that affect the search for my mother's killer?"

Webster shrugged. "I can't tell you more than I already have."

She turned on him, grabbing his arm. "*Can't tell me?*"

"Believe me," he said. "It's for your own safety."

"*My safety*," she sputtered, not believing her ears. "In case you hadn't noticed, your presence and information haven't kept me safe so far. When is this safety of yours going to kick in?"

"I'll try to do better in the future." Cary thought he was just saying that to get her moving. He glanced back at her. "I need to tell you some other things."

She hurried to keep up as he moved off down the sidewalk at an even faster pace. "The situation here is even more complicated than we guessed." Now he had her attention.

"Meaning?" Cary had never faced circumstances as complicated as these, or as dangerous. Life had been easier in Tennessee.

"Let's find a place and sit down. I'll tell you while we catch a bite to eat."

They walked – *he* walked, *she* ran – a couple of blocks and went into a small café off Canal Street. After they ordered, Webster leaned close, careful that only Cary could hear.

"As I'm sure you could tell, I received some information on the Mayor's early years. It seems the three friends, Alex Shapiro, Big Eddie Breunoux, and Johnny Periot, had different goals in life. I tend to think that worked to everyone's benefit. We already knew that Periot wanted to be Mayor. That's been his dream. Eddie Breunoux wanted to climb the ladder with Johnny, so he joined the police force. Along the way he may have come up with a plan to help himself and Johnny."

"How could he help Periot?" Cary sipped her sweet iced tea.

"I don't have an answer for that one," Webster told her. "Maybe something came up along the way. Or maybe he just found occasions when helping meant looking the other way. I'm just guessing."

Cary eyed him suspiciously. "What kinds of things?"

"I really don't know. Just . . . things," he said, tracing circles on his water glass with a finger. "Being in the right place at the right time, twisting arms to get things done, that sort of help. Breunoux may have had like-minded friends by that time, too. That's probably how it started. What I do know is that our third friend, Alex Shapiro, started a little import-export warehouse business at about the same time Periot and Breunoux were beginning their careers."

Cary had been thinking, too. "None of what you've said seems all that strange or even related, for that matter. Just three young friends getting their lives going."

"You haven't heard the damaging part yet," he said, glancing around and lowering his voice even more. He leaned in with Cary following suit.

But just then the waitress arrived with the sandwiches, interrupting their conversation. She placed the food in front of them and asked if they needed anything else. Cary shook her head.

Again, she leaned in, ignoring the food. "Tell me," Cary commanded through clenched teeth. Frustrated, she wanted to reach over and grab him by the collar.

He put a hand on her arm, saying, "You're not going to like this."

"Just tell me. I'll decide," she said, shaking off his touch.

"Okay." His eyes held hers. "Like I told you before, right after your mother was killed, Shapiro's business took off. I'm told it exploded, growing by leaps and bounds."

Continuing to look at her, he said, "Now, here's the bizarre twist. My friend said the timing made it appear that Shapiro had something to do with your mother's death. Don't misunderstand – there wasn't any clear connection between Shapiro and the hit and run, at least none that anyone could see at the time. But in looking at the circumstances now, it seems too big a coincidence to overlook without asking some questions."

Cary clutched her arms across her chest, stripped of emotions. Between the attack earlier at the library and now this revelation, she felt numb. She glanced out the window and then back at Webster, saying, "I don't usually drink in the middle of the day, but do you think we could have a glass of wine?"

He leaned back and grinned. "I guess these are special circumstances."

Minutes later they each had a glass of the house white wine in front of them. Cary downed about half of hers when it arrived. As Webster gave her more details, she held the glass, sipping occasionally at the remainder.

"There's also the fact that Carolette Shapiro was with your mother when she was killed. Mrs. Shapiro could have been hit, too." They were both silent for a few moments before Webster finished his thought. "It's interesting that the car didn't touch her." Then he said what they both were thinking: "But I'm looking at the accident from a distance of twenty-five years, and with more information."

Cary leaned back, glancing down, then out at the street. The sky had grown dark outside, not unusual for New Orleans at this time of year. She could see angry clouds billowing over nearby buildings. The wind had picked up, and a storm was brewing on the horizon. Already, she could feel the dampness as people opened and closed the restaurant door. Unconsciously, she reached for a chip and sat there thinking.

"How could there have been a connection?" she asked while continuing to watch the dark rolling clouds.

"I don't know. I just have a feeling," Webster said as he took a sip of his wine. "And now, all these years later, you catch up with Shapiro's wife, and that same evening she's murdered. That's one coincidence too many, don't you think?" His mood seemed as gloomy and disturbed as the sky outside.

"You're scaring me."

"Scares me too," he admitted. Then he added, "Cary, I'm concerned about you. Too much is happening around you. Threats, assaults. And it all seems to center on that letter tying Johnny Periot to your mother."

Their conversation dwindled without further resolution.

"I still plan to stay close and try to make sure nothing happens to you," he promised. "That is, if you want me to."

"But what about you? It's dangerous for you, too. And you don't owe me anything." She felt obligated to give him a way out.

He didn't take it.

"You sound like my friends," he said. "They told me to keep a low profile. I couldn't forget even if I wanted to. Everyone keeps reminding me that I could be in danger, too."

They both laughed softly as Cary wondered why his friends would be telling him to keep a low profile. And who are these friends?

When they finished eating and Webster paid the ticket, they hurried back to the library to avoid the downpour that seemed imminent.

After exploring Periot-related material for a while longer without finding new information, the couple put away the books and magazines. Walking out to the portico, they found the storm had passed, leaving the sidewalks and streets wet.

Evening was coming as Webster suggested they walk down to St. Charles Avenue and take a ride on a streetcar before sunset. An outing after the storm would help to relieve stress. And perhaps one of them would come up with new answers to their current dilemma.

Cary wasn't so sure a ride on the trolley was a good idea. But hopefully they were safe from new attacks now that Webster was part of the equation. Yet, it seemed a stretch.

"What if they're still after us?" she asked. "What if someone's following us right now?"

"Have you seen anyone?"

She glanced around.

"Well . . . have you?"

"No . . . but . . ."

"Come on," he said as he started down the sidewalk. "Trust me. I've been working on a plan." She noticed Webster pass his hand across the back of his jacket at the waist but thought little about it at the time.

They boarded the next trolley that came along and grabbed a seat. Webster seemed preoccupied as he checked out the other passengers. That left Cary to listen to the streetcar clickitie-clacking along.

***

Mazou – young, late twenties, and short – pulled the automobile with its dark windows away from the curb, careful to stay several hundred yards back. "Me, I don' like dis," he said, nervously watching the traffic and the streetcar.

Glancing over at Frank, his partner, Mazou said, "You ought to call Mr. C and fin' out what he wants us to do." Frank agreed, tapping a number into his cell phone.

Frank was older, around fifty, and of medium build. His muscular physique and dark complexion gave him a hard look. And now he sported a swollen and red area along his jaw from the altercation at the library.

His call was answered, and Frank recognized the voice of the short middle-aged man he suspected was sitting at a desk in a downtown office building. Marion Douglas Cobreaux. "Mr. C?"

Frank told him about the young couple leaving the library and boarding the trolley.

"He's staying with her everywhere she goes now."

"Who is this guy?" Cobreaux said. "Whoever he is, he's making it difficult for us to close this thing down." Then he told Frank, "Just follow them for now and see where they're going. For God's sake, don't let them catch you watching them." Cobreaux hung up without waiting for an answer.

Frank turned to Mazou and passed on Mr. C's instructions. Then, without thinking, he reached up and rubbed his jaw where he had taken the punch.

A few moments later, Frank's cell phone rang. It was Mr. C. "I have another idea," Cobreaux said. "I'm sending a couple of our guys with a driver. If we have time, I want our people to take this couple off the streetcar. I'll have them brought out to the warehouse. In the meantime, let me know if they get off the trolley before our guys get there."

"We'll watch 'em, boss!"

"You stay clear of them, Frank. They know you from the library. Once our boys get on the trolley, you can break off and come on back to the warehouse. I'll meet you there."

"We'll handle it," Frank said and hung up.

***

Cary gaped at the views along St. Charles – many of the houses were huge. She also watched with interest as a mixture of riders got on and off the streetcar: Cajun, descendants of the French Canadians, both black and white Creoles, Germans, the Irish, Italians and others among a melting pot of heritages. All these along with just plain old N'awlins folks.

Realizing they were passing through Shapiro's neighborhood, Cary pointed out the large, stately home to Webster. It troubled Cary that she had visited with Mrs. Shapiro on the day she had been murdered. It particularly concerned her that she might have been the cause.

Relieved to be past the house, she attempted to turn the conversation toward more personal questions. Cary wanted to know about Webster.

"Mike?" she said, touching his arm. "Where did you call home when you were growing up?"

As she inquired about his past, the wind from the open window tossed her hair across her face. When raking it back with her fingers proved futile, she let it blow. Without commenting and using only the tips of his fingers, Webster reached over and brushed her long tresses behind an ear. This time it stayed.

He gazed deep into her eyes for a moment. Breathing was suddenly difficult.

Taken aback, Cary sat waiting for an answer to her question. By this time, she realized that for reasons she didn't understand, Webster seemed unwilling to tell her about himself. She wondered if those reasons had to do with choice or circumstance.

She had decided he wasn't going to answer, but then he did.

"I lived all over," he finally said. "My dad worked several different sales jobs when I was a kid." He certainly sounded truthful. Cary hoped he would tell her more. He didn't.

Instead, he asked, "How about you? Did you always live in Knoxville?"

She chose to let his quick change of direction go. *But she would get back to his life.*

"Yes, Knoxville's always been home for me. Mom and Dad moved us there when my dad finished medical school. I even went to college at The University of Tennessee, but you probably already knew that," she said.

"Didn't you ever want to travel – to see the world?"

"Oh, I love to travel," Cary said. "But I've never had the time. I went on a few trips with my parents." She hesitated and then added, "I guess there are some places I would like to see when I can." She understood he was only making small talk.

Glancing at him, Cary wondered why he chose to reveal so little of himself. Most men she knew were more than willing to talk about themselves if she appeared the least bit interested. *Webster*, he was different, and she thought that was an interesting characteristic – or maybe he was simply hiding something.

***

Frank and Mazou continued to follow the streetcar, but now they had been joined by a blue van. "Laissez les bons temp rouler." Mazou was getting excited.

Let the good times roll.

 **Chapter Fifteen**

As the streetcar swayed along St. Charles Avenue, it became obvious Webster wasn't going to talk about himself. Cary though, was too uptight to sit there in silence. As they had left the library earlier, she remembered, he had said he had a plan.

"So what's this plan of yours?" His blank stare indicated he had something else on his mind now, having forgotten what he said earlier.

"When we left the library, you said you had a plan. That's why we're on this trolley. Remember?" She was becoming frustrated.

"Oh, yeah." he said with a grin. "Sure you want to know?"

"**Yes!**"

"You and I are going to act as bait." Incredulous, Cary exclaimed, "We're what?" She turned to face him on the slippery wooden seat. At that same moment, the streetcar jerked to a halt for a couple of new riders to get on. Losing her balance, she slid to the edge of the bench. There, to her embarrassment, Webster caught her in an outstretched arm. For a moment, they stared at each other in silence. Then she pulled herself away, reluctant to admit how good it felt to be in his arms and safe, despite the many questions she had about him.

"Sorry," she said.

"I'm not." He said. When he looked at her, there was something new in his expression, something that hadn't been there before. Turning then, he looked out the window, scanning the street in both directions.

Taking her cue from him, Cary became watchful too, gazing at the people getting on and off the streetcar. She noticed Webster checking the vehicles following the trolley. She didn't really think Periot, or for that matter, anyone else, would send someone after them so soon. Apparently Webster saw it differently.

After riding in silence for several blocks, Cary glanced ahead and saw that the streetcar would be making a turn. As it neared the Mississippi River, she could see the levees here were high, and some of the houses had been built close to them. As the streetcar neared it, she realized how massive the mound of earth was that contained the river. With a nervous sensation, she wondered how chaotic the day had been in 2005, when levees broke all around the city.

Cary's mind jumped to a different time – the day her mother died. Not unlike the muddy river waters, something unknown had been beneath the surface there, too, something unseen and certainly not understood by her. Something she couldn't quite grasp – at least not yet.

Cary then made a small, unspoken vow to herself: No one was going to stop her from discovering the truth about her mother, not even Johnny Periot. Especially not him!

Without giving specific thought to the matter, Cary realized she was changing. Perhaps it had to do with this man who sat beside her when he didn't have to. She wasn't sure what had caused the change, but she was now just as determined as Webster to see this through. If someone wanted to attack her for that, then bring it on. She glanced at Webster, pleased that he was with her. This was turning out to be a satisfying jaunt.

After another ten minutes, they came to the end of the line. The streetcar shifted over onto the last of the tracks that had run parallel to them in their ride out St. Charles and Carrollton. Everyone exited the car except the two of them. The conductor began to flip the seats so they faced in the opposite direction for the trip back to Canal Street.

"You folks just touring?" he asked. "If you are, you're gonna have to pay again to go back to downtown N'awlins."

Cary watched Webster count out the fare as other passengers crowded onto the streetcar.

***

The blue van had caught up with Frank and Mazou a few minutes before the trolley reached the end of its route at Carrollton and S. Claiborne Ave. Then it pulled around on the opposite side of the streetcar. Frank watched for the two men who would be boarding.

"Can you see them?" Frank asked.

"I t'ink so," Mazou told him. "They walkin' up to da' trolley over on da' other side, Cher."

Hugh and Tee-do were preparing to board the car and remove the young couple when they reached Millaudon near Broadway. Their driver would be waiting for them there. Mr. C had given Frank all the details.

"What gonna happen to 'dem?" Mazou asked.

"Mr. C didn't say and I didn't ask," Frank said in a tone that told Mazou that wasn't their affair.

The boss had said he and Mazou should break off when Hugh and Tee-do boarded the trolley. Frank watched and waited until the two men were sitting with their targets: Hugh directly behind them and Tee-do across the aisle on the boyfriend's left.

"That ought to do it," Frank said aloud.

With the two men in place, he breathed a sigh of relief and told Mazou to drive them back to the warehouse. Frank was satisfied that things were under control.

***

Twilight approached and rain clouds appeared as they often did late in the day in the city. The streetcar filled rapidly. Two casually dressed men boarded and took seats near Cary and Webster. Like the other passengers, they appeared harmless enough at the moment. But it was a long way to Canal Street.

The streetcar had only traveled a couple of blocks when the man behind them leaned forward, his head between Cary and Webster. Cary stiffened. He was in his mid-thirties, not a large man.

"Listen to me," he told them in a low but firm voice. "There's a gun pointed at you."

Cary cut an eye at Webster, who held up a hand, palm down, motioning her to stay calm.

The man spoke again. "Look to your left. See that dude? We're together, him and me."

Cary leaned forward and looked at the man. *Maybe I'm not obsessed.* At least she wasn't alone this time. She was somewhat reassured, having Webster with her. She hoped by now he had developed a plan to support his idea.

The man across the aisle had his right hand in his jacket pocket and was staring at them. He was burly, using most of the two-person seat. The jacket was plaid like a lumberjack would wear. Paul Bunyan came to mind.

The individual behind them wore a tweed sport coat; a pipe was sticking out of the upper pocket. If he hadn't spoken, she might have mistaken him for an instructor at one of the colleges. The Professor said, "We'll be getting off in another block or so. Don't do nothin' stupid and everything's gonna be cool. Understand?" Cary and Webster both nodded. "Good. Now, when I tell you, just get off like it's your stop. My buddy and me will be right behind you. There'll be a blue van down the side street. You'll see it."

The Professor glanced ahead, then reached up and tugged the cable to signal a stop. The trolley driver eased to a halt and the doors opened.

"Let's go."

Cary and Webster got out of their seats and walked to the rear door. She felt a slight push as Webster made sure she went first. The Professor stood, too. He was a little shorter than Cary. He kept his hand inside his coat as he followed Webster to the door. Paul Bunyan brought up the rear.

Cary had just stepped to the ground when Webster shoved her to the side. Stepping down and without a backward glance, he jerked both feet from under the Professor. Falling hard on the steps of the trolley, the man let out a deep groan. Before he could recover or Paul could pull his weapon, Webster drew a pistol, crouched and pointed it at them. Cary opened her mouth to yell a warning, but then realized Webster was already in control. His weapon had materialized from somewhere in his belt.

The Professor groaned again as Webster grabbed a handful of collar and dragged him upright and out of the way. To the would-be abductor who had been sitting across the aisle, Webster said, "Show me your hands. Then walk off the streetcar – nice and slow." Webster's voice had changed, becoming hard and threatening, a tone Cary hadn't heard before.

The man who had borne the brunt of Webster's unexpected attack moved slowly and with obvious pain. He was holding his right shoulder, his own weapon now forgotten. Webster took handguns from both of them, sliding the weapons into his belt while keeping his own pistol trained on the men. The early evening darkness covered most of the action.

"What the hell is going on here?" the streetcar driver said, rushing from the front of the trolley to see what the commotion was about.

"Everything's under control," Webster assured him. "Keep everyone on the streetcar and call the police. Tell them three men in a blue van will be waiting for them. Then go on with your route." The trolley driver looked at Webster and then at the other men. Webster kept his pistol out of sight. After a few moments, the driver nodded and walked to the front of the streetcar.

Cary heard him say, "Everything's alright, folks. We're on our way." The streetcar then pulled away, continuing its run toward Canal Street.

Cary stayed out of the way, keeping her eyes on Webster as well as the two men. Motioning toward the blue van parked midway down the block,

Webster told the men, "We're going to walk to your vehicle now. If your driver sees us coming, I want him to think everything's fine. So keep your right hands inside your pockets." Webster then tucked his hand and the pistol into his own pocket.

When they reached the van, Webster motioned for one of the men to open the sliding door. Hearing it open, the driver glanced around, asking, "Everything go okay?" Then he saw Webster's pistol and started to reach down into the van's console.

"Don't," Webster warned him and pointed his pistol at the driver. "Pick it up by the barrel with two fingers and hand it to me." The driver did as he was told, carefully passing his weapon back. Webster passed the gun to Cary, telling her to hang on to it. With a startled glance at him, she took it and gently eased it into her handbag.

With all the weapons secure, Cary watched as Webster glanced around the truck. There was a roll of duct tape on the floor. He motioned toward the driver.

"Get it."

After the driver had the tape, Webster instructed him to secure the other men's arms with their backs together. That done, Webster handed his pistol to Cary and told the driver to sit with his back to the others. "Shoot them if they try anything," he told Cary. Then he taped the driver to the others. Using both hands, Cary pointed the big pistol into the van, secretly hoping it didn't go off accidentally.

The men remained still throughout the process, all the while glaring at Webster and mumbling among themselves. When Webster finished with the driver, he wound several strips of tape around all of them, tying them into one big bundle and then securing their feet. Before taping their mouths he said, "This is your one chance to tell me who sent you. You say the word, and I'll let you go." The men merely stared at him. "No?" He taped their mouths.

Webster stepped out of the truck and looked at the men. "I don't know why you and your people have been following this lady around and harassing her – even pushing her in front of a bus," he added, "but what you've just attempted is called kidnapping. I'm going to be staying close to the lady and I'm giving you this one warning: screw with her again and someone's going to get hurt. Understood?" They just glared at him.

"I'll take that as a yes," Webster said, smiling at them. "Oh, and by the way, the police know you're here. You can try explaining what happened to them."

Webster gathered their pistols, including the one in Cary's purse. He emptied the weapons and stripped the magazines. Using a rag he'd picked up from the floor of the van, Webster wiped the weapons down. He then dropped the cartridges into his pocket and put the three empty weapons in the console of the truck. Then Webster stepped into the van and locked all the doors. Cary hoped the dark windows would keep the men hidden until the police arrived.

"Let's go," Webster said and started down the street.

"No problem." She hurried after him as he turned the corner on St. Charles Avenue.

"What do you think that was all about?" she asked when she caught up, a thousand other questions swirling in her head.

"The kidnapping? More of the same, I suppose."

"What are we going to do?" she asked. "And why are you carrying a gun?" Cary was having trouble keeping up with the action.

Webster ignored her last questions. *No surprise there.*

When he stopped at a storm drain, she almost ran into him. Reaching in his pocket, he collected the cartridges. A quick look around, then he tossed them down the opening.

Cary was almost trotting as they started off down the sidewalk again. They were a block away from the van now, and they could hear the police sirens coming their way. Webster cut across St. Charles and the trolley tracks onto a side street.

"We'll have to make some changes in our living arrangements," Cary heard him say. He was already way out in front of her.

Chapter Sixteen

"Where are we going now?" Cary reached for Webster's arm. By then they were several blocks from the action, and she thought they could slow down a bit. Breathing hard, she stopped and leaned over, resting with her hands on her knees.

"We're going back to the Sheraton and get our things," he told her as he stopped and turned. "Those people will be back. I guarantee that. Whatever you've stirred up isn't going away with just a warning. We need to get off their radar."

Cary nodded her head, her thoughts racing. Where would they go? What would they do?

"Any ideas?" he inquired.

She stared up at him, wondering if she had missed something.

"Any ideas about what?"

"A place to stay. We need to disappear." He seemed to be talking to himself yet expecting answers from her.

She had hoped he already had a plan, but Cary gave it her best shot: "Can't we just move to another hotel?"

"We could, but we won't be able to use our real names. Given all that's happened, people are going to be out there looking for us. Probably already are."

"Oh, great," she said. "Now we won't even feel safe in a hotel."

"Let's go get our things, then we'll find a place to stay. One thing at a time."

"How are we going to get back to the hotel?" Cary asked. "Can we flag us a taxi?"

"I don't want a taxi driver who can identify us and say he picked us up near the blue van."

"Why not?" She felt a chill of fear sweep over her and wondered if they had done something illegal. The guns were still on her mind, too. *And Webster also had a gun! What about that?*

"I just think it would be better," he told her without answering the question. "I saw a large intersection a couple of blocks ahead before we cut off onto this side street. We'll be several blocks from where we were pulled off the trolley. Maybe we can catch a bus.

A thought occurred to her. "If we appear to travel separately, we'll be less noticeable," Cary ventured. She was almost running to keep up.

A step ahead of her, she heard him grumble, "Good idea."

Wow, I had a good idea . . . Fancy that!

Minutes later they had worked their way out to Broadway. It was a main street, and they were several blocks from St. Charles. There were bus stops here and a transit bus was approaching. They hurried to the next stop and boarded, sitting in different seats. The bus took them further away from the three men and the police sirens. A couple of transfers later they were back to Canal Street.

When they reached the hotel, Webster stopped her and said, "Go to your room and pack your things as fast as you can. We need to be gone from the hotel before the police can figure out who we are. They may come looking for us. Remember, we gave them our names and other information this morning at the library."

"Why, Webster? Why would they come after us? We're the victims here. We didn't do anything wrong." She hesitated, *"Did we?"* Agitated, she gripped his jacket, determined not to let go until she had her answer.

"Because," Webster said, "those three men will be missed by whoever they work for and ten bucks says they'll have someone tailing the police. Our hotel would be the first place anyone would look."

Cary slowly released him. What he said made sense.

She went to her room and started gathering her things, throwing them into her bags as quickly as she could. She was glad she had already picked up some new luggage at a shop downstairs. As she packed, Cary tried again to make sense of it all.

The difficulties were continuing to increase – almost by the minute. Thank goodness Webster was with her now. Having survived by sheer luck before he arrived, Cary recognized that without him, she wouldn't have made it through today. Too much was happening, and the situation had become too dangerous for her to be alone.

As she packed, Cary began thinking about Webster again. She really had to know more about him. She had literally put her life in the hands of a stranger. She realized, too, that she was starting to put more than her life in his hands. In situations like this, attachments formed; she was already starting to think of him as a friend. But he was still an unknown. They would have to change that. Whether he liked it or not, she had to ask hard questions and some how force him to give difficult answers.

Finished with the packing, she called Webster's room. He answered on the first ring. "I'm ready," she told him.

"Sit tight," he said. "I'll come and get you. Don't let anyone in but me." The line went dead.

A couple of minutes later there was a soft knock. She looked through the peephole – Webster. Cary opened the door, and he gathered up everything but her briefcase. "Let's go," he said. In the hallway, he grabbed his own bag, leaving his briefcase and laptop for Cary.

He had left the elevator on hold with the doors open when he came for her. Cary punched the button for the lobby and glanced nervously at him. Adrenalin had them both operating on full alert.

They had checked out and were ready to leave when Cary remembered her papers. "You're holding something for me – an envelope. Could you get it?" Cary described the envelope. "It's in your safe."

After several minutes, the clerk returned, a concerned expression on her face. "When did you leave your package, Miss Warren?" Cary's stomach tightened.

She thought about the previous several days and said, "Wednesday, I think. Yes, it was last Wednesday evening. Why?"

The clerk smiled unenthusiastically, "I didn't find it in the normal slots. Let me look again." She disappeared back into the office.

Cary's thoughts immediately went downhill. Had someone taken her envelope? *Why? Who?* As Cary's mind sifted through the limitless questions, the clerk returned, smiling big this time, Cary's envelope in her hand.

"The night manager found it for me," she said. "It was with some of the hotel's papers that had been copied today. We don't know how it got there."

Now Cary was really disturbed. "Could someone have made copies of my papers?"

"Oh, I don't think so," the clerk said reassuringly. "Has it been opened?"

Cary examined the seal. "No, I guess its okay," she told the clerk. "Thanks."

Finally ready to leave, they carried their luggage outside and placed it in the trunk of a taxi.

"Take us to the Hotel St. Marie," Webster told the man. The hotel was a small one Cary had walked past in the French Quarter. Ten minutes later they were standing in front of the old building.

When Webster paid the driver, he asked if they needed help taking their bags inside. "We can handle it," Webster said.

As the taxi pulled away, Cary turned to him. "Won't we be just as easy to find here?" she asked.

"We might if we stayed here, but we're not. Let's take a walk," he told her, and started gathering up the bags again. Not wanting to be left behind this time, she grabbed the briefcases and laptop and followed him as he explained what they were going to do next.

They had only walked a short distance before they found a small convenience store. Webster led them inside and straight to a pay phone on the back wall by the coolers. He looked in the phone book for a number, then dropped in some coins and made a call. Cary could hear him talking to the police, explaining what had happened on the trolley. Cary was certain they would read about the blue van in the *Times-Picayune* the next morning.

"Why didn't we just wait and talk to the police out on St. Charles Avenue? Surely they're not all crooked."

Webster stared at her. "Probably not, but this is New Orleans, Cary. Why chance it?"

They left the store and walked toward Canal Street. The moon was out and the sky had finally cleared. After a while, they saw a taxi and Webster started to wave: Cary gave out a loud piercing whistle. With a startled glance at her, Webster waved it down and they loaded their bags. He directed the driver to a La Quinta Inn out in Kenner near the airport. The taxi headed out.

When they reached the hotel, Webster checked them in as Mr. and Mrs. Frank Johnson, saying they would pay with cash.

"I need a credit card for an imprint and also need to see some identification," the clerk said.

Webster surprised her when he took a drivers license from his wallet and showed it to the clerk. Then he handed him a credit card. Sure enough, the license had Webster's picture, but the name on it was Frank W. Johnson. She didn't have time to see the address, only the city – Alpharetta, Georgia.

The clerk finished and gave them keys. Once again, they gathered everything and headed off.

When they got to the room, Webster opened the door and held it for Cary. They piled bags inside and each picked a bed and flopped down.

On the way to the room, they picked up some snacks. Cary tossed a few over to Webster and then tore into a pack of crackers. He opened one, also. As he munched on a cracker, Webster eyed Cary, waiting for the questions to begin.

For a long moment, she took stock of him and the situation, then demanded, "Who are you, Mike Webster? I need answers."

An uncomfortable silence followed. Cary fumed, not exactly sure why she was so angry with him. Maybe it was the Frank Johnson identity and how easily he played it.

Finally, "Are you sure you want to know about me?"

She nodded. "I didn't know much about you before to the last several hours and now even what I thought I knew seems confusing . . . You're not Mike Webster, Advertising Exec . . . are you?" It was a rhetorical question. She stared into those blue eyes, trying to determine if there was any chance he would tell her the truth.

He glanced away. "I really can't tell you much. Nothing of real value. Too much is at stake, for you . . . and for me."

Irritated and tired, she said, "You're not going to tell me anything, right?"

Webster sighed, also frustrated. "You're going to have to trust that I'm a good person who's trying to help you. I've been very honorable, haven't I?" She couldn't disagree with that.

He stared across at her. "You already know too much about me for my own good – probably for yours, too." She suspected he was telling the truth there also. "I'll tell you a few things. I'll have to trust you to keep them to yourself."

"Well, fire away."

He paused, "If you don't keep this to yourself, I'll have to kill you." He grinned. She didn't . . .

Cary worried he just might be telling the truth about *that*, too. She crossed her arms, then one leg over the other. *Waiting here.* She didn't say it, but she wanted to.

"I've had some jobs over the years where I worked undercover." Webster got up and drew himself a glass of water from the bathroom sink before strolling over near the door. He peeked out between the curtains, then came back. Cary waited patiently as he sat there for a few moments looking at the glass he held with both hands.

"That kind of work has made it necessary for me to be careful where I go and what I do. There are some unsavory people who would like to find me." He glanced toward the door. "I can't say much more without putting you at risk." Then he told her one last thing. "I had significant problems just staying alive before I met you. What we've been doing doesn't make it easier." He glanced over, his expression suggesting she probably shouldn't ask any more questions.

Cary believed him. However, she had told him almost everything about herself; yet, at this point, she didn't even know his real name.

"Okay, but just answer this for me. How did you end up working for Trebeck?" She didn't really expect an answer to this one.

To her surprise, he explained - sort of.

First, though, he studied her, seeming to settle something within himself. "Let's just say I needed a job quick, and I needed to be in a different location. The opening at Trebeck came up and . . ."

"And someone helped you get it."

"Yes."

"And you can't say who."

"No."

Some answer. She didn't like it, but she guessed she would have to accept it .

Her eyelids drooped unexpectedly. Now that they were settled in their room, Cary realized she was dead tired.

He seemed to be dragging, too. Then he asked, "Do you think we could get some rest and have another go at this tomorrow?"

She placed her suitcases on the bed. "Great idea," she said as she opened one of the bags. She found a T-shirt and a pair of sweatpants she could sleep in, given that she would be sharing the room with this stranger.

Cary went into the bathroom and changed clothes. When she returned, Webster was in a light robe, his toothbrush in his hand. The closeness of the situation and seeing him like this stirred her emotions. Sleep would be difficult, if not impossible. She was relieved when he disappeared into the bathroom.

As he returned, he said, "We need some help if we're going to find out what happened to your mother. We also need to find a better location – some place where we're hard to find." He yawned and sat down on his bed. "You okay to call it a night?"

"Sounds good to me," Cary agreed, moving to her own bed. She switched the light off. It felt good to stretch out and get her head on a pillow.

She could hear Webster as he settled in, too.

"You really can trust me," she heard him say in the darkness.

"Hummh." *I hope so.*

***

Frank crossed his legs again as he kept an eye on the clock. Mr. C and

Mazou were anxious, too. Where were Hugh and Tee-do? They were supposed to bring the young couple directly to the warehouse and they were way overdue.

"They should have been here by now," Cobreaux said as he paced the floor of his office. "What the hell happened to them?"

"I don't know, Mr. C," Frank said, dropping his feet to the floor and standing. "We watched them get on the trolley."

Mr. C glared at him. "Well, don't just stand there, go find them." With that, the boss grabbed his coat and left the office, slamming the door behind him. The last thing he told Frank was he would return early on Sunday, "and this little problem better be resolved by then."

A few hours later, Frank imagined the situation across town as the phone rang beside Mr. C's bed. Frank was sitting in a liquor store parking lot. The store's neon sign winked on and off, and he could almost feel the devil sitting on his shoulder. Frank had a bad thirst and had considered going in and making a purchase. No doubt it was a bad idea, but damn, he could use a drink. *Ahh, well.*

The call to Mr. C was one Frank would rather have not made. The boss was *not* going to be happy.

"Hello."

"Mr. C, this is Frank."

Sounding groggy, the boss said, "It's three in the morning, Frank. I'm assuming you already know that."

"Yes, sir."

"Hmmm! Then this must be an emergency . . . and at this time of the morning that would include a body. So, Frank, who's dead?"

"Nobody, Mr. C, but . . ."

"But what, Frank?"

"Well . . . Hugh and Tee-do screwed up the job we gave them," Frank said. "The boyfriend took on all of them: Hugh, Tee-do, *and* the driver."

"You're kidding me."

"No, sir." Frank said, gazing wistfully at the liquor store again. "He whipped all three of them."

"How the hell did he manage that? No, never mind. I probably wouldn't believe that either. Where are they now?"

"Well, that's where we got lucky. One of the cops who works with our people was dispatched to the scene.

It happened on the streetcar out on St. Charles." He told Mr. C what he'd heard.

"Shit!"

"Mr. C, I did some checking and found out the guy with her is named Mike Webster. He's her boss back in Tennessee. At least, we have a name now.

We lucked out because he left our people tied up in the truck. That's where the officer found them. Only problem is, the girl and Webster was gone. When we got to their hotel, they had checked out and disappeared. That's where it stands now. We're looking for them."

"Okay," Mr. C grumbled. "Get everyone on the streets: start with hotels in the area where they were staying. I want to talk to that young lady and her boyfriend. Meet me at the warehouse at nine o'clock. We'll see what we've got then."

Frank could hear Mr. C swearing as he hung up.

Chapter Seventeen

The weather had turned dark on Sunday morning; rain was falling again. The sound of a storm outside matched Cary's mood as she struggled to wake up. She hoped her frame of mind wasn't an indication of what was to come.

When she first awoke, Webster's bed was empty, but the shower was running. She stretched, waiting for him to vacate the bathroom. He came out looking fresh and wearing casual slacks with a blue sweater, his hair still wet.

"Don't you look handsome," she complimented him. She had decided, for the moment, to give him the benefit of the doubt for last night's question and answer session.

"Thanks," he said. "Your turn," nodding toward the bathroom.

She glanced over to where her bags were. After their close call, Cary had literally dumped her clothes into the luggage. Dreading the results, she rolled out, threw the bags on the bed, and opened them to pick something for the day. Finding them rumpled as she expected, Cary fussed at herself, knowing she should have hung them up last night.

Deciding on an outfit became a matter of choosing among the less wrinkled pieces. Kristofferson's song "Sunday Mornin' Comin' Down" came to mind, something about picking out his 'cleanest dirty shirt.' She chose a sweater and slacks and placed them on hangers.

Cary noticed Webster watching her with raised eyebrows.

"What? You've never seen a girl do two things at once?"

"Two things?"

"Yeah," she said. "I'm going to take a shower and steam the wrinkles out of these clothes at the same time."

"And I get to watch?"

"What?"

"You asked if I'd ever seen a girl do two things at once. I thought you meant. . ."

"*Yeah!* You think too much."

Cary stood there staring at the mess still in her bag. Out of the blue, an idea hit her that had nothing to do with the clothes.

"I'm going to try to see Johnny Periot again," Cary said. "You can go with me.

Given the right circumstances, he can help us."

Webster stared at her, his head tilted as though he hadn't heard her correctly.

"I'll tell him after thinking everything over, I decided I don't believe Janice Talmer's story." She dumped the remaining clothes out of her bags and began sorting them. "Since he knew her back then, I'll say I was hoping he could tell me what she was like and help me understand her – things a daughter would want to know." She started refolding her clothes.

"Going back will be like walking into the lions' den," Webster said. "They might even have us arrested." He had dropped down on the edge of his bed.

Cary paused in her repacking, her eyes coming up to meet his. "I know I'd be taking a chance but the best defense is a good offense – right? Still, I'll be surprised if he agrees to see me. Things were pretty tense when I left there." Her stomach tightened just talking about going there again.

Then Webster dropped a new one on her.

"I think we should pay a visit to Alex Shapiro, too," he said. "After his wife's funeral, of course."

"Yes," Cary agreed, making the mental leap with him. "As close as Mrs. Shapiro and my mother were, her husband must have known Janice, too. We'll find out when the funeral takes place and then call him."

"I should go with you for both visits." He wasn't asking.

Before heading in for her shower, she said, "I had another idea before I dropped off to sleep last night. Oh, and by the way, you snore."

"Then that makes two of us," he countered. His crooked half grin shot a warm sensation through Cary.

"And what's your idea?" he asked.

She told him just enough to peak his interest. "I think I may know where we can get some help and a place to stay," she said. "I'll tell you about it over breakfast." With that, she carried her belongings into the bathroom and turned the water on.When Cary opened the bathroom door a few minutes later, a cloud of steam preceded her into the room. When it cleared and she could see, Webster was gone. Momentarily disappointed, she saw a note on her suitcase: "See you in the coffee shop."

She was relying on him already, getting used to having him around. It wasn't half bad, either.

Minutes later Cary entered the coffee shop. Webster was seated at a small table in a back corner. He was kicked back, his legs stretched out crossed at the ankles, and reading a newspaper with a cup of coffee and a half-eaten donut at his elbow. To anyone who hadn't spent the last day and a half with him, Webster would have seemed totally at ease. But Cary could tell he was surveying the room, keeping a wary eye on his surroundings as though he had done this countless times before. She was willing to bet he had checked the restroom, too, before he sat down.

Again, she wondered who this man was that she had taken up residence with. Had he done something awful, maybe even killed someone involving organized crime. Or perhaps he had been in a position to know something that put his life in danger.

"Is this seat taken?" she asked, indicating the other chair.

"I'm waiting for my girlfriend, but you can sit here until she shows up," he said with a wink. His hair tended to be a little unruly this morning with a lock of it loose over his right eye.

Seeing him that way, Cary's throat went dry. She had to admit, he was sexy, and he *probably* didn't even know it.

She left her purse hanging on the chair and went to get some coffee and juice. A chocolate éclair would be good, too. Her hands were full when she came back to the table.

Once she was seated, Webster held up the newspaper. "Nothing in there about the blue van," he said. "That bothers me more than an article giving our descriptions." He shook his head, clearly surprised at the omission. "I thought the police would be all over it, and the newspaper would have the story."

Cary scanned the sections of the paper Webster handed her. Maybe he missed it. But there was nothing about the attack anywhere in the paper. Not a line. Zilch.

"Maybe it was just too late to make the deadline," Cary said.

"Yeah . . . maybe," he said, letting the matter drop.

"Want to hear my idea about getting some help?" she asked. Cary opened her silverware and sweetened her coffee as she laid out the plan. "I met a lady on the flight here from Knoxville. She introduced me to some of her family at the airport." Webster was looking bored.

Cary continued. "Her name sounded familiar; I've been trying to place it since we met. I think I worked it out last night." She thought he was starting to show some interest. "I'm certain her husband was one of my dad's advisors in medical school. He even visited us once when he was in

Knoxville." Cary sipped her coffee. "Mrs. Kato – Landie – offered to lend a hand if I needed anything while I'm in New Orleans. If I'm right about the connection, she might help us. It's worth a shot." *He had to be interested now.* "What do you think?"

Frowning, Webster put the newspaper down. He had questions. "What makes you think you could trust this person? You don't even trust me!"

She had him! "You'd have to meet Landie," Cary told him. "She seems to be a true southern lady. I think *anyone* would trust her." She jabbed a finger at him. "Even you."

Webster reached over with his napkin. "Chocolate, here." She started to back away but he dipped his napkin in her water and delicately touched her upper lip.

"There," he said, "all better." His eyes lingered a bit too long. She had to look down or be lost in them.

Cary wiped her lips and continued but not before she felt a flush of warmth. "I'm going to call her." She started digging for her phone. Webster looked at her for a moment, his eyes still questioning, but he didn't disagree.

Finally he took a sip of his coffee and leaned forward, saying, "Before you call anyone, let's get cell phones that can't be traced to us."

"How?" She dropped the old phone back in her purse.

"Wal-Mart," he said. "We'll buy some throwaways and purchase our minutes as we need them. Also, we'll use fictitious names and addresses when we activate them. No one will be able to trace us."

Cary had read about those phones but had no experience with them.

"Okay," she said, anxious to call Landie. "Let's do it!"

***

Across town, Marion Douglas Cobreaux was meeting with Frank and Mazou at the warehouse.

"Something about the guy that's helping her strikes me as being peculiar," Cobreaux said to Frank. "He's too good. It's like he's done this before."

"Yes, sir."

"Have you found anything at all? Where they went? How they traveled?"

"We traced them to the Quarter," Frank told him. "Nothing after that. They've disappeared."

"Keep searching and call me at home when you have something."

"You got it, Boss."

Finished with breakfast, Cary called a taxi and told the driver to take them to the nearest Wal-Mart. Webster asked him to wait while they picked up a couple of things. He agreed, even lending them an umbrella.

The electronics department had what they needed. Webster picked two phones and a minutes card for each of them.

Back in their hotel, he began the activation process. It took a half hour to handle the details. Then Cary waited for the phones to come online while Webster scanned through the newspaper again. Finally, when they were sure the new phones worked, Webster turned his regular cell phone off. Cary did the same.

At last Cary could call her new friend.

"Don't mention that you have someone with you," Webster cautioned. "If it appears Landie and her family are open to helping us, then you can tell them about me."

"Okay."

"If it's a go, call me and I'll join you."

Cary dug the paper with Landie's information out of her purse. She punched the number into her new phone.

The old woman answered and after a brief greeting, said, "Cary! Of course I remember you. Have you found the person you were searching for?"

"Well, sort of," she said. "I'd like to come see you and talk about it if that's possible."

"Certainly. I'm leaving for church now. How about one o'clock. Or I could skip today if you need to come sooner."

"No. One o'clock is fine. I have your address. I'll be there." They hung up, the meeting set.

Cary refolded the rest of her clothes while Webster reworked his own suitcase. Finished, they walked outside their room and settled into chairs that overlooked the pool area.

The table between them was small. As they were getting settled, their legs touched and static electricity popped, causing both of them to jump. Their eyes met and a short awkward silence fell between them.

Webster broke the unsettled quiet. With a mischievous grin on his face, he ventured a cause for the electricity – *"It's a sign!"*

Cary didn't buy it. *"I don't think so!"*

"Can't blame a guy for trying."

They were both quiet for several minutes, each deep in their own thoughts.

Webster broke the ice. "You really think you can work things out with Landie?"

Cary struggled to find her voice. "Yes. Uh . . . I'm thinking that I'll tell her what's been happening, then ask about staying with her for a few days."

Webster flipped the maverick lock of hair from his forehead and said, "What will you say when it's time to tell her about me?"

"The truth. That we work together and that you're helping with my search."

"Okay."

Studying him, she said, "We've been lucky so far, haven't we?"

He peered at Cary for a moment before nodding. "Yes . . . I'd say we've been very lucky."

She looked at him, a serious expression giving emphasis to her words.

"In case I forget to tell you later, thanks. I'm grateful for what you're doing." Skipping a beat, she threw in, "Whoever you are."

Then, with her emotions already confused, he reached out, gently touching her cheek with his fingers and stilling her heart with the same movement.

After a moment, he dropped his hand, saying, "Just a part of the job, ma'am." It was a poor imitation of Clint Eastwood – or was it John Wayne?

The sensation of his touch lingered, making concentration difficult as they discussed her narrow escape with the bus. A lot of things were going on. Webster brushed at imaginary lint on his trousers. She could tell he was feeling the strain, too.

Soon it was time for Cary to leave for her meeting with Landie. She phoned for a taxi, and shortly afterwards they heard a horn beep in the parking lot.

"I'll call when I know something," Cary said. As she rose from her chair, Webster stood too, gathering both of her hands in his. She looked up as he brushed her forehead with an unexpected kiss. Pleased, she lifted her face. She would not have been displeased if there'd been more. But that was all. He simply stared at her, a poignant expression on his face.

"Whether you mean to or not, you're making this difficult," he said with sadness in his eyes. "For both our sakes, we can't let it happen." He softly pressed a finger tip to her lower lip, then released her. "Be careful . . . for me."

Responding took a moment. "I . . . I will," she promised, and then reluctantly moved to the door. She hurried downstairs and climbed into the taxi, giving Landie's address to the driver.

Webster stood at the top of the stairs, watching as her taxi drove off.

It took most of the ride for her to calm herself. Cary didn't know if she was hurrying to Landie's or away from her emotions. She suspected it was the latter.

The heated emotions and intimate contact of the last few minutes with Webster had almost done her in. Cary had never known these kinds of feelings. She wasn't sure if it was the situations they'd faced since Friday night or Webster himself. She didn't know and was afraid to find out.

After about twenty minutes, the driver pulled over in front of a cute little cottage. Shrubs and a few fall asters filled the yard. The light rain had ended and the sun was peeking through broken clouds. There were a number of older homes in the immediate neighborhood. Landie's house and most of the others looked great, considering Katrina. Only two FEMA trailers were still sitting in neighboring front yards.

As the taxi left, Cary walked up the sidewalk and climbed the four steps to the porch. The house was a small white shotgun structure with working shutters, and there were flower pots with geraniums on the porch. Landie had obviously been watching for her and opened the door before Cary had time to ring the doorbell. "Come in, Dawlin', come in," she said. "I'm so excited that you remembered me and called." Landie reached out and give Cary a big hug.

Cary instantly felt as if she had known the elderly woman for years.

"Thank you for inviting me over," Cary said. "I hope it's not an imposition."

"Nonsense, child. I wouldn't have given you my number and address if I hadn't wanted you to call." The old woman still wore what appeared to be a Sunday dress; a kitchen apron, white with embroidered flowers, covered the front of it. Smudges near the top evidenced its usefulness. "I've made us some coffee and I have some lemon squares I baked last night. I hope you'll have some with me," she said. "Sounds wonderful," Cary told her. Her stomach growled, reminding her that she and Webster had skipped lunch.

Cary checked out the living room as Landie went to get their refreshments. The furniture – a sofa, four chairs, and an assortment of tables and lamps – made for a cozy atmosphere. The upholstered pieces were worn but clean. Cary wondered if the storm had damaged many of Landie's things.

They settled on the sofa and Landie poured their coffee. While Cary was spooning sugar into hers, Landie scooped a lemon square onto a plate for her. Landie gave herself a dessert and sweetened her coffee.

Relaxing, she studied Cary, a serious expression on her face. "Now, tell ole Landie what you've found. You didn't sound happy when you called."

First Cary wanted to establish a connection with Landie. "I'd like to ask you something before we talk about that. Is that okay?"

"Certainly," Landie said. "What is it?"

"I've been thinking about your name since we met on the plane," Cary told her. "After we parted, I remembered something. Was your husband a doctor?"

Startled, Landie looked at her, "Why, yes. Yes, he was. How did you know?"

Touching her arm, Cary said, "I think I knew your husband, at least my parents did. When I was little, he used to visit my father when he was in Knoxville. My parents talked about him." Cary frowned, recalling the circumstances. "Did he teach at the Louisiana State University School of Medicine here in New Orleans – about twenty-five years ago?"

"He did." Landie hesitated, recalling things, too. "And you said your last name is Warren?"

"Yes, ma'am."

Landie smiled then. "I bet you're Kenneth Warren's daughter, aren't you?"

Now Cary was surprised. "That's right. Did you know my dad, too?"

"Not well, but Reberto did. And I met your father a few times at receptions out at the medical school."

"But how did you know about me?"

"Well, your father told us they were adopting a baby. I still remember how excited he was. It was near the end of medical school for Kenneth. When they got you," she touched Cary's hand, "he brought Reberto a cigar wrapped in pink cellophane. Reberto brought it home. I think I still have it in a box of his things."

Cary's eyes grew teary, and she wiped at them with the back of her hand. "I'm sorry. These darned tears . . ."

Landie patted her forearm. "How is your father? Is he still practicing?"

At the mention of her dad, Cary reached for a tissue.

Landie squeezed her hand. "What is it, dear? Has something happened to your father,"

Cary dried her eyes, taking a moment to compose herself before answering. The old feelings of guilt gnawed at her.

"Dad and Mom were both killed in an automobile accident," she told Landie. ". . . Three years ago."

"Oh, I'm so sorry." Landie held Cary's hand as she supplied details of the tragedy.

When she finished, the old woman patted her arm. "You poor child."

Soon, they were back to Landie's original question about what Cary had found in her search.

"I know," was Landie's spirited reply.

Tears clouded Cary"s eyes."I'm sorry," she said, setting her dessert down."It's been a hard week since we parted last Sunday. "She took a moment to collect herself. "I didn"t tell you on the airplane but I came to New Orleans to look for my birth parents."

"I thought it might be something like that," the old lady said softly as she reached out to touch Cary's hand. Then she motioned for Cary to continue.

"The adoption agency located my file, and I learned some things on Tuesday." She explained about the hit and run.

"You poor thing!" Landie patted her arm.

"One of the most intriguing things I've found so far is a letter my birth mother wrote to me. She had it placed in my file in case I ever came looking for her."

Landie's eyes grew wide, but she continued listening without interrupting.

Cary told Landie some of the details in the letter but not the part about her birth father. Then Cary said, "In the letter my mother sounded frightened. Then, she was killed a few days after I was born."

Landie held up a hand to stop her. "Did she tell you about your father?"

"Yes . . . she did."

"Have you tried to locate or make contact with him?"

"I've talked to him," she told Landie, "and he warned me not to bother him again." Cary had decided she wasn't going to tell Landie his name unless she specifically asked.

"So . . . where does that leave you?" Landie sipped tentatively at her coffee.

"Well, that's part of why I wanted to see you. I need your help." Cary took a sip of her coffee, then picked up her lemon square again.

"Just name it," Landie said as she sat forward on the sofa.

"After reading her letter, I decided my mother's death wasn't an accident. The problem is that my search has made someone uneasy. I've had some close calls."

"What do you mean close calls?"

Cary told her about being shoved in front of the bus and about her room being burglarized. Then, without details, she told Landie about the kidnapping attempt. "I was lucky to escape," she said, carefully leaving Webster out of the explanation. She didn't mention Carolette Shapiro, either.

Landie listened, nodding. She was clearly taken aback but didn't make any comment.

When Cary finished, Landie told her simply, "So you need a place to stay where these people are unlikely to find you."

Cary could sense Landie's hesitation as she weighed the danger.

"I wouldn't ask if I . . ." Cary wished she hadn't called. She stood to leave. "I shouldn't have come. I'm sure we can find something."

"I'm sorry," Landie said, "it's just that, well, I . . ."

"I understand."

As Cary moved to the door, Landie stood and reached out, "Wait!"

Cary hesitated, turning.

"Oh, for heaven's sake," Landie declared, her fists on her hips. "I've survived hurricanes and worse, and it's not like I'm getting any younger." Cary started to protest, but Landie halted her with a raised hand. "I'm not requesting this, Dawlin', I'm telling you. No arguments. Just go get your things. I'll have Greg take you. He's my youngest boo." She grinned at Cary's questioning expression. "My youngest son. He lives two houses down. You met him at the airport."

"Wait," Cary was finally able to say. "There's one important thing I haven't told you yet. Someone has been helping me. A friend. I don't think I would have made it this far, otherwise."

"So what's the problem? Bring your friend with you."

"The problem," Cary said to her, "is that my friend is a man." She waited.

With a glint of humor, Landie looked her in the eye. "If that's a problem, my dear, it's yours, not mine. Bring him with you. I have plenty of room. It'll be nice to have a man in the house again."

Cary leaned over and hugged her. "Landie Kato, you're a special woman."

Chapter Eighteen

Cary listened as Landie phoned her son. "Greg, I know you're watching the Saint's football game, but I need you to do something for me. And bring your . . . your car or whatever you call that thing – oh, right, your SUV."

Cary phoned Webster. "Get our bags ready and check us out of the hotel," she told him. "Landie's son is taking me to get you and our luggage. We'll be there in about thirty minutes."

"Everything okay?" She could hear the concern in his voice.

"Yes. I'll tell you about it later."

"I'll be ready," Webster told her. "That'll give me time to make some calls and leave the new cell number."

Cary peered at her phone as she hung up. What did he say? Something about making calls and leaving his new cell phone number. Who would he need to leave it with – and why?

There's so much he hasn't told me. And, she realized, there was much she hadn't asked. Yet it was nice knowing he was with her. Having him on her mind brought that warm feeling again, remembering the way he'd touched her cheek and the way their eyes had met.

No doubt, being with him felt special – the two of them might even be good together. But then she caught herself.

There could be no future with him. He said so himself.

A few minutes later, Greg knocked on Landie's kitchen door and came walking into the house. Cary nodded to him as Landie said, "You remember Greg. He and Kathryn were at the airport."

Cary recalled how when they met, she had wondered about the long thin scar on his left cheek. He was late thirties, early forties, about Cary's height, with a dark complexion and the beginnings of a beer belly. His probing eyes seemed interested in everything. She remembered that from the airport, too. But she didn't recall his wife.

They shook hands. Then she paced nervously as Landie filled him in on what had transpired in the last forty-eight hours. Finally, Landie dropped the bomb. "I told Cary the family would be happy to help them."

"You told her wh . . .?" he started to argue, then the words died on his lips.

"Yes, *happy,*" she assured him, with a glare that dared him to say more.

Cary could read his wariness as he eyed her. For a moment, she thought he might turn her down, but with a glance at his mother, Cary saw him relent. Landie had spoken. Cary hoped the rest of the family would be as charitable as her elderly friend.

"Mom's made up her mind," Greg said without any measure of warmth or friendliness. He ushered Cary through the living room and out the door. She waved to Landie as they headed to pick up Webster.

"Where to?" he asked once they were moving.

"The La Quinta on Williams Boulevard near the airport."

"I know the place," he said. Greg remained quiet most of the way to the hotel. The only time he spoke was when Cary asked about his job.

"My son and I sell used cars," he said. "We have a sales lot on Veterans Highway."

"Just the two of you?"

"Nah. We got a couple of guys who work for us."

He obviously didn't want to talk and Cary let it drop.

When they arrived at the hotel, Webster was waiting with their luggage stacked on the sidewalk. Cary climbed out and introduced the two men. They shook hands and exchanged small talk as Greg helped Webster load the bags.

The ride back to Landie's house was relatively easy. Sunday's traffic was light.

On the way, Cary tried to get Greg talking by asking about Hurricane Katrina. "Was the storm as bad in your area as I've heard it was in other parts of New Orleans?"

He glanced at her and seemed to know what she was doing. He answered anyway.

"It was bad everywhere," he said, "but it was devastating in the areas where the levees broke. The levee on the 17th Street Canal busted a few blocks from us, but the break was on the opposite side of the canal. The water flowed that way, to the east."

Cary watched his demeanor change as he remembered the storm. "We were lucky. In the areas that flooded, almost everything was destroyed. To even attempt to salvage the homes, people have had to tear everything down to the basic wall structures and start again. Even then, the wood has to be treated to keep out that terrible black mildew."

"That's heartbreaking," Cary observed.

"In many of the flooded areas, if you want to rebuild, you have to raise the entire home up several feet." Greg hesitated, his expression growing dark like the hurricane must have been. Then he said, "I wouldn't want to battle another storm like Katrina. We're *still* dealing with the aftermath."

Cary and Webster listened without comment.

"What the water didn't get, the wind did." He paused. "It was terrible." Greg spoke as though the feeling of devastation was always near. "Several of our neighbors' homes were completely destroyed," he told them. "All of our homes had lots of damage. Kathryn and I lived in a FEMA trailer for months."

"Were contractors available to do the repairs?" Webster asked.

Greg glanced at him in the mirror. "Most of the time there wasn't anyone to help," he said. "No one you could trust, anyway. And the local government hasn't been much help. Johnny Periot, that's the Mayor, supposedly got us all those federal dollars. If he got them, where are they? Where did the money go? Most of us haven't seen much help. My brothers and I, along with our families, did most of the work to get us back in our houses." Wrinkles across his forehead were bunched with anger.

Cary's guard went up. "What do you mean, you didn't get any money?"

"I mean Periot and his people seem to be doing better than ever, and yet we've received almost nothing. Some of our streets aren't even cleaned up yet. How do you account for that?" he asked. Then he added, "Some of our families are still working on the interiors of their houses. A few still live in the FEMA trailers."

Cary glanced at Webster across the seat. She wondered how Greg would take the news that Mayor Periot was her father.

Nearing his neighborhood, Greg pointed out a pile of debris close to the street. "The old man who lived there refused to evacuate," he said. "A big magnolia tree fell across the house and killed him. They didn't find him until a week later. His neighbors thought he had gone to his son's house in Shreveport. People decided he must have hidden so he wouldn't have to leave."

"What about your mother's house?" Webster asked.

Greg's mood changed. He sounded proud when he said, "We all pitched in to get Mom's place ready so she could come back home. Her house was the first one we started working on. Things weren't the same without having her here. We completed it on Friday and got the furniture in on Saturday before Mom returned."

"It must be nice to have her back," Cary said.

"More than you know." He seemed to have softened a little. He glanced at her, then back at the traffic, making a turn down the street to their neighborhood.

They unloaded the bags at Landie's house and carried them in. Landie directed where to put them. Cary's went in one bedroom at the end of the hallway and Webster's in another. Landie hadn't asked if they intended to sleep together, but it was clear by the directions given that in her house that was not an option. Cary smiled at the thoughts that must have gone through the elderly woman's mind.

Cary stood next to Landie as Greg said goodbye. Her thoughts were still swirling over what Greg had said about Johnny Periot. Where *had* the government money gone?

"Nice meeting you, Webster. I'll see you both later." The look in Greg's eyes didn't do much to bolster Cary's hopes that they could count on his assistance. But his attitude and mood *had* softened a little. He gave her a weak smile. Then he was gone.

Landie took over. "Help me set out some things for a snack, Cary, and then we'll talk about your search and what to do next. I'll heat up some Court Bouillabaisse and we'll make some sandwiches."

"Court Bouillabaisse?" Cary asked, unfamiliar with the dish.

"It's a rich, spicy fish soup we make here in N'awlin's. I'm sure you'll like it. And I bet everyone's hungry by now." Cary wondered if the elderly lady had always been such an in-charge person.

Webster followed them to the kitchen and began peeling and slicing a couple of apples for dessert.

Landie and Cary set everything on the counter and then pulled out barstools. Landie said a blessing, praying for safety for her new friends. Cary threw in a silent prayer for herself and Webster, sensing they would need it.

They were all hungry; the food was delicious, especially the soup.

"I can't tell you how much I appreciate what you're doing," Cary told her elderly friend as she wiped her lips with one of Landie's linen napkins. "But there's one other thing. Do you think Greg or someone else would let us borrow a vehicle?"

"Greg can handle that. I may be getting ahead of you," Landie ventured, "but I think you should consider letting the family really help you. What else do you need?"

Cary wasn't as sure about Greg as Landie seemed to be. She glanced at Webster. He narrowed his eyes. Obviously he had concerns, too.

Turning back to Landie, she said, "Well, there'll be some research. We could use help with that." Cary reached for a slice of apple.

"Greg's wife works at the *Times-Picayune*," Landie told them. "She could probably lend a hand with that."

Webster spoke up. "Do you think someone could come with us if we go into the city?"

"I believe they would do that," Landie said. "But I should tell you about my oldest son, Andy." She poured more of the ginger lemonade she'd made for the meal. "He won't be as eager to help as some of the others. Andy called me earlier, while you were gone," she said.

Cary thought of Greg and realized Landie might not be aware of his opposition. She decided not to mention it.

"Then we probably shouldn't be here," Cary said, thinking now of Andy. "We'd never want to cause a problem in your family."

"Nonsense," Landie said, shaking her index finger in the air. "When the day comes that I can't make decisions, Andy and the others can tell me what to do." She smiled reassuringly at Cary. "I assure you that day hasn't arrived yet." She handed the last apple slice to Webster.

Then to Cary's surprise, Landie said, "Tell you what. I'm going to call Greg and some others and tell them to come over here this evening. You can have a planning meeting. And don't worry about Andy. He'll be okay when he realizes the others are in this."

Cary traded glances with Webster. She had never considered this kind of help. Judging from his raised eyebrows and funny grin, he hadn't either. They had only been hunting for a safe place to stay.

But then she remembered the less than open-armed welcome she'd received from Greg. She hoped Landie was right about the rest of the family.

That evening, Cary was overwhelmed as Landie's living room filled with family members. All chairs and the sofa were occupied. Additionally, three very large grandsons stood against the walls. Another appeared to be guarding the front door. Everyone was excited and conversed quietly until Landie indicated it was time to listen to Cary and Webster.

Cary had discussed the get-together with Webster, and they had agreed she should be the spokesperson. When everyone was settled, Cary moved over near Landie.

She began by bringing them up to date. "I was fortunate to fly into New Orleans last Sunday with a very special lady." She motioned toward Landie. "You all must know what a treasure she is." Everyone smiled and nodded in agreement. Even Andy smiled as he glanced across at his elderly mother.

But when he looked back at Cary, the smile was gone. Andy was shorter than Greg, but had the same dark complexion and penetrating dark eyes. Appearing to be in his late forties, he had a slim build without Greg's paunch. For the moment, though, there was no friendliness in his face.

Cary glanced around the room. "Several of you were at the airport and embraced me as though I were a family member." Everyone appeared interested. She told them about her search to date and explained what she needed. Then Cary paused and scanned the room again, her eyes coming to rest on Andy. "I never dreamed then that I would need to ask for help." Andy's dark eyes were locked on Cary – he wouldn't come easily. Several of the others openly nodded and appeared ready to do whatever was needed. Even Greg had softened more during the day. Andy, on the other hand, appeared determined to hold out. Cary pressed forward in spite of his obvious opposition.

Next, she introduced Webster. As she did, their eyes locked for a brief moment. Flushing, she looked away. But not before she'd seen a hint of something more, something she might have wanted to explore. *If only it were another place, another time.* What *was* it about this man?

Forcing her attention back to the moment, she directed her comments to Landie's kin. Time to grab their attention and keep it. "In fact, if it hadn't been for Webster, I would probably have been kidnapped or killed during the last couple of days."

Shock – even disbelief – appeared on several faces. Uneasiness at what she was telling them was palpable throughout the room, especially with Andy and Greg. Cary could almost feel their eyes boring into her. She understood that the possibility of danger made them fearful for Landie, but she wouldn't sugarcoat it. The family needed to know the truth; she'd let the chips fall where they may.

There was a buzz as the family talked among themselves. She stepped toward Landie and raised her voice. "I would never ask Landie or, for that matter, any of you to do anything dangerous. Anyway, that's not what we want. We need research and the use of a vehicle, things of that sort. Oh, and a place to stay temporarily." She smiled at Landie, saying, "We seem to have that worked out."

One of the women sitting on the sofa interrupted. "What kind of information do you need? I do research at the *Times-Picayune*."

Relief surged through Cary as she considered the dark-skinned woman with tawny brown hair and almost gypsy-like features. "Thanks . . . Remind me of your name. We met at the airport, didn't we?"

"I'm Kathryn," she said, "Greg's wife."

Cary couldn't help noticing that Greg's wary expression was back and that he was watching his wife closely. Cary wondered if he was unhappy that she had agreed to help without first speaking with him.

"Kathryn," Cary said, "I appreciate your offer." She looked around again and then said, "Now, there are a few other things I need to tell you."

Everyone seemed to sit a little straighter, expectant, giving Cary their attention. Andy hadn't taken his eyes off her for several minutes now, nor had he uncrossed his arms. Avoiding his stare, she gave a brief rundown of what had happened since her arrival in New Orleans. Cary mentioned her mother's letter without giving details. She included the threat and that her mother's lover had been married. Finally, she told them about the hit and run.

The time had come to tell them her father's name, but she had concerns. No one but Webster knew his identity. She hadn't even told Landie in their earlier conversation. Cary couldn't imagine what Greg's reaction would be, given what he had said on their way back from the hotel.

Might as well toss gas on the fire! "According to my mother's letter, my father was . . . is . . . Johnny Periot, the Mayor of New Orleans." Shock registered throughout the room. Greg leaned forward; Andy, too. Cary thought she detected a slight grin on both their faces. That could be positive.

Then, just as suddenly, she heard a shuffling sound as people changed positions, surprised and caught off guard. There was an intake of air, and no one said anything for several seconds.

Finally, Landie spoke. "Well, my goodness, child. You sure know how to create drama." Several others laughed nervously. The spell was broken. Everyone started to talk at once, questions flying.

Obviously Greg hadn't been the only one touched by Periot's misdeeds when it came to hurricane relief. Now everyone wanted to help. What could they do? Where did Cary and Webster need to go?

Greg spoke up, asking Webster about protection. Andy joined them, still not saying anything, but he seemed ready to listen.

"Cary and I don't want to put any of you in danger," Webster told the brothers. "Thanks for the offer, though."

"Oh, I think we can take care of ourselves." Greg swept his arm around the room, taking in a couple of Landie's grandsons who looked to be in their twenties. Every one of them was well over six feet tall. "What do you think?" He grinned at Webster and punched Andy with his elbow. "Tell him, Big Brother." Andy grunted and grinned, just a little.

The grandsons appeared formidable. Cary suspected they could hold their own in most situations.

Kathryn again asked Cary what kind of research she had in mind.

"We need anything we can get relating to the Mayor around the time of my birth and my mother's death: 1982 and '83.

"I can handle that," Kathryn said. "I'll also look at the subsequent years."

As she talked with Kathryn, Cary noticed Andy had confronted Webster. She joined them as soon as she could break away.

She was in time to hear Andy's question: "Don't you think you could be putting Mom in danger?" he asked, leaning in close.

To stave off a confrontation, Cary answered, "No one should know you're helping us. Besides they're not after you; they want us. I really don't see any of you being in danger."

Andy clearly wasn't satisfied, but Landie's scowl indicated her son had gone too far. He backed off, but Cary doubted they had heard the last from him. He turned to Cary.

"I'm not worried about myself," he said, straightening his jacket, "but Mom's another matter."

"We understand," Webster told him.

"We only plan to stay here a short time," Cary assured Andy. "We don't want anyone to know where we are. That's why I called Landie."

"Okay," Andy said, eyeing his mother one last time.

"But be careful. Please."

" Agreed." said Webster."

When Andy walked away, Webster cornered Greg. "We're going to try to see the Mayor tomorrow morning. Could someone go with us?"

"I'll work it out," Greg assured him. "Just let me know what time." Greg seemed to be on board now that he knew they were after Johnny Periot.

Earlier, Cary and Webster had talked about what they needed to do in the upcoming week. Visiting the Mayor would get the ball rolling.

When all the questions had been answered and arrangements made, Landie's family started back to their own homes.

Greg sought out Cary. "That's my son, Barry." Greg pointed out a tall, strapping young man. "We'll go with you tomorrow. We will take two vehicles and some Nextel radios for communication."

When she told Webster what Greg had planned, he nodded. "Good thinking. Two vehicles will come in handy if someone tries to follow us."

"Don't forget your seminar," she reminded.

"Uh . . . yeah, right. Thanks. I'll take care of it in the morning," he said.

Cary picked up on his hesitation. Something wasn't kosher about that seminar.

Kathryn tapped Cary on the shoulder. She had her instructions for the research. "I can handle it at work without anyone knowing unless they check my computer."

The plan was for everyone to deal with their part of the puzzle without the word getting out that Cary and Webster now had support.

When everyone had gone, Landie set out food and the three of them enjoyed a light supper. Cary was so excited she could hardly eat. Not so with Webster. He had two bowls of fish soup.

By the time they finished and cleared the dishes, it was nine-thirty. They were all tired and ready for some rest, especially Cary.

Landie went to her bedroom, and Webster took a quick shower. When it was Cary's turn, she heard Webster talking on his cell phone. Without meaning to eavesdrop, she heard him tell someone named Jack where he'd be sleeping for the next night or two. He also said he'd keep in close touch. Then he asked that his new cell number be passed on, on a need-to-know basis.

Hearing more than she wanted to, Cary headed into the bathroom. After her shower, she heard Webster tell someone goodbye and saw his light go off. She would have enjoyed a few moments alone with him after their tender encounter earlier, but that would have to wait.

Finally climbing into bed, Cary was asleep almost by the time her head hit the pillow. She slept soundly, not rousing even once, which surprised her. Sleeping through the night was unusual, especially under these circumstances.

***

Webster wasn't as lucky. He lay there, questioning his involvement with Cary. What *was* he doing helping this woman? And he questioned their close encounter earlier in the day. That wasn't like him, but Webster realized the feelings he had were genuine. He liked Cary, but he needed to rein in his reactions. Emotions like these tended to get in the way when living his kind of life. This was not the time for extra baggage.

He was supposed to be keeping a low profile, too. *That was certainly going well!* Webster was pretty sure a visit with the Mayor of New Orleans wouldn't fall in the low-profile category.

Chapter Nineteen

Cary awakened to the aroma of strong coffee and morning sounds coming from the kitchen. She heard Webster come out of the bathroom and close his door. Then she remembered they were going to try to see the Mayor today. Her heart began beating faster. *Time to get this thing started.*

Cary gathered her things and went into the bathroom. She showered, then returned to her room, dressed and headed to the kitchen. She could tell by their conversation that Landie and Webster were waiting breakfast for her. The coffee smelled even better as she joined them.

"Good Morning," Cary said as she entered the room. She claimed a barstool.

"Well hello, sleepyhead." Webster greeted her with a wink.

"Mornin'," Landie said. "I hope you slept well." Landie promptly offered her a cup of coffee and a homemade cinnamon roll.

Webster's expression indicated he liked her outfit. The buttoned light gray blouse had a slight vertical pattern making her appear even taller. The skirt, a darker gray, came to just above her knees and fit nicely where it should. Heels and silver jewelry completed the ensemble.

Webster mouthed "Wow" and gave her a thumbs up. She smiled, a slight blush creeping up from her neck.

Cary stretched again and yawned. "I slept great," she said, "and I needed it."

After breakfast, Cary and Webster started into the living room to plan their day. Landie suggested a stroll in her backyard garden would be better. They agreed and walked outside into the breaking sunrise.

The yard was a charming mixture of shrubs and flower beds, some with chrysanthemums blooming and others with roses climbing along the fence. Boxwood separated the beds here and there. Cary wondered briefly who had kept the yard up after the hurricane. Then she got down to the business at hand.

"I'll call Periot and try to get us in to see him," she said. "It's dangerous, but who could be a better source than my . . . ?" Her voice trailed off.

"What will you say about having someone with you?"

"I won't tell him. We'll just show up together."

Webster voiced her hopes: "City Hall would be a poor location for a kidnapping, anyway." Then he suggested the next step: "After that we should try to reach Alex Shapiro."

Cary had stopped and leaned down to smell one of the many tea roses Landie had in her garden. Before rising, she broke off one of the blossoms, then stood and deftly slipped it behind Webster's right ear.

The act surprised him, but he stood still while Cary leaned back to admire her handiwork. "Looks cute," she told him.

"Always wanted to look cute," he grumbled.

He plucked the rose from his ear and smelled it. As he did, she glimpsed Landie at the kitchen window. She had a big smile on her face. Cary suspected her elderly friend had been watching them for some time.

Webster pulled their thoughts back to business. "I'm still waiting for a phone call from one of my contacts," he said. "I think we'll know more about Shapiro then. And don't forget, Kathryn will be looking through the *Times-Picayune* files today. We may get some new information there."

Cary glanced at him, wishing she could be as hopeful. Instead, she suspected, they were in over their heads.

Promptly at nine o'clock, Cary called the Mayor's office. She phoned from the bedroom in case things got heated. When she told the secretary her name, Cary was put on hold. Then the Mayor answered.

"This is Johnny Periot."

The hard edge to his voice brought a flood of doubt to Cary's mind. This was probably another dead end. But, remembering what her parents had taught her about courage, she pressed on anyway.

"This is Cary Warren, sir. I've been giving a lot of thought to our meeting last week, and I wanted to call and apologize." She paused, listening for a response but hearing only silence. Though difficult, Cary kept her voice even. "I behaved badly," she said. "I was upset after finding out about Janice Talmer's death." She took a deep breath and then said, "I'm afraid I took it out on you. I hope you'll forgive me."

Cary closed her eyes, heat rising up her neck as she waited. Apologizing was more of a challenge than she'd expected.

Clearing his throat first, he finally spoke. "I'm afraid I wasn't on my best behavior either." Periot's admission surprised Cary. His voice had also lost some of its menacing tone.

Not wanting to lose the advantage, Cary added, "I don't know why Janice wrote what she did, but I shouldn't have jumped to conclusions."

"I agree." *Bastard!* So arrogant, when he knew the truth – *the truth about her mother.*

Cary's grip tightened on the telephone as her other hand balled into a fist. "Again, I would like to say how sorry I am for the things I said and for the way I behaved."

Cary unconsciously twirled a tendril of her hair.

"Apology accepted." Periot's tone was more conciliatory this time. "I've been thinking about our meeting, too," he said. "Under similar circumstances, I might've behaved the same – or worse."

Then he really surprised her by saying, "This may not interest you, but I've thought about our conversation, and I can certainly understand how you would want to know everything possible about your mother."

Cary's mind was in a whirl of confusion. She listened as he continued.

"Would you like to come see me again to talk about your mother? Perhaps you'll have some specific questions, or maybe I can remember something that will benefit you."

Cary's fingers were growing numb as she continued her death grip on the phone. "That would be wonderful," she said, throwing herself down on the bed. She couldn't believe what she was hearing.

"How about eleven o'clock this morning?" he asked.

"We . . . I mean . . . yes, I'll be there." She'd almost blown it. Cary hoped he hadn't noticed.

"I'll look forward to seeing you then." She started to hang up, but stopped when he said, "One last thing you should know . . ."

"Yes?"

"Miss Talmer didn't tell you the truth. Regardless of what she may have said, I'm not your father." With that, he said goodbye. *He's really concerned about my believing Janice's letter.*

Frowning, Cary closed the phone and pulled herself up on the edge of the bed. He had professed not to be her father. Okay, if that's true, why was he willing to meet with her?

Doubts abounded. Had it been too easy? Was he leading them into a trap? He could have someone waiting for them. She considered the last twenty-four hours and the danger she had faced even before that. But then she remembered what Webster had said: *They would be at City Hall. What could happen there?*

There was a knock at the door. "Mind if I come in?" It was Webster.

"Sure." She shoved her phone in her purse as he opened the door. "We have an appointment at eleven," she told him. "I almost let the cat out of the bag about your being with me."

"I heard." In response to her questioning expression he added, "I was coming down the hall. Have you decided what you want to ask him?"

She shook her head. "Have you?"

"I'm going to be the quiet one."

"Right . . ."

***

When Periot hung up with Cary, he buzzed his secretary. "Get the Superintendent for me. Tell him I need to see him for a few minutes – right away if he's free."

Big Eddie Breunoux strolled into Periot's office five minutes later. The Superintendent sat down in one of the large leather chairs in front of the Mayor's big desk as though he owned the place. He wore a dark brown suit with a crisp, tan buttoned-down shirt and a gold tie. Leaning back, Big Eddie crossed his legs, his feet parked on the edge of the mayor's desk, the cordovan shoes so polished he could've combed his hair in them. "You wanted to talk?" he asked.

The Mayor got right to the point. "The young lady I told you about last week is coming to see me at eleven. Has she tried to contact you again?" The Mayor looked out the window, his back to Breunoux. He gazed down at the area where Cary had stood on Thursday. In those few moments, Periot almost expected to see her there again, staring back at him, demanding to know about her mother.

The Superintendent watched Johnny, saying, "I haven't heard any more from her. I think she hoped I might remember something about her mother's accident. When I said I didn't, she moved on. That's probably when she decided to come see you."

"Yeah . . . You're probably right," Periot said, still staring out the window, now thinking about the girl's mother.

"Do you think she'll try to pressure you?" Big Eddie asked.

"I don't know. I really don't," Periot said thoughtfully. "I don't think so. I know it sounds strange, but I think maybe I convinced her I'm not her father in spite of what her mother said in her letter."

"That's good. We can't have her nosing around."

Periot turned finally and looked at the Superintendent. "She apologized for the way she behaved last week."

"Did you believe her?"

"She seemed genuine enough on the phone, but who can tell?" Periot strolled back and stood at the corner of his desk.

Big Eddie peered up at him. "You want me to do anything? She could really pose a problem with your announcement coming up. The last thing you need right now is an illegitimate daughter showing up."

"I know," Periot said, picking up a pen and tapping it against his palm. "I'll meet with her and then call you if something needs to be done."

"I can handle that." The superintendent swung his legs off the desk and got to his feet.

"How's Justin doing down at Florida State?" Periot asked as Big Eddie started toward the door. "Think he'll be the quarterback next year?"

"He better. It's costing me a fortune in tutors." Big Eddie walked out of Periot's office and closed the door behind him.

Periot stared at the closed door for several seconds. He had a very bad feeling, and he wasn't sure if it was because of the girl or because of Eddie. He thought about the girl's mother again and wondered what his life would have been like if he had made different choices twenty-five years ago.

Too late for that now.

***

Webster called Greg after the appointment was set. Greg and Barry arrived about ten-fifteen to escort them to City Hall. Cary and Webster were waiting and got into Greg's SUV. Barry followed them in a white business van.

Webster suggested Greg drop them off a block from City Hall. They would walk the rest of the way so no one could see how they were traveling. Webster would phone Greg for a pickup when they came out of the meeting.

They drove downtown, and Greg let them out near City Hall. Cary and Webster entered the government building just before eleven. Since Cary had been to the Mayor's office before, she led the way. Cary also knew they had to pass through a security gate, so Webster left his pistol in Greg's SUV. After the security check, they headed upstairs.

"I'm Cary Warren. We have an appointment with the Mayor," she told the secretary.

"Yes. I remember you." She glanced at Webster and eyed Cary with a frown. "The Mayor didn't mention a second person."

"Yes, well, this is Mike Webster. He's a friend of mine and I need for him to be included," Cary told her. The secretary looked at Webster again, obviously not satisfied.

"Let me check if the Mayor's ready to see you." She headed for Periot's private office.

Returning quickly, she said, "He'll see the two of you now, Miss Warren."

As they entered, Webster surveyed the man and his space at a glance: handsome, well dressed – spacious office, ponderous furniture, formal décor; leather-bound books on law, the environment, the economy, and one other that Webster noticed, *Wealth and Politics.* How very interesting. Webster returned his attention to the man and found himself the focus of a Johnny Periot stare.

"Hello, again," the Mayor said, focusing on Cary. Then he returned to Webster.

"This is my friend, Mike Webster," she told Periot. "I didn't think you'd mind." The two men stared at each other for a moment.

"I see," Periot said as he shook Webster's hand. "Nice to meet you." The Mayor was smoking one of his big cigars. Air in the office smelled stale and the ashtray on the edge of his desk was almost full.

"Likewise," Webster replied.

Periot motioned toward the chairs in front of his desk. "Have a seat. Would either of you care for somethin' to drink?" He kept glancing at Webster, his eyes narrowed. Webster was concerned that the Mayor would recall a brief encounter they'd had some time ago, but he doubted it.

"How about a Coke or some coffee?" Periot asked finally.

Cary refused his offer, as did Webster. As she glanced around the room, Cary noticed a framed family portrait. The grouping included two beautiful young women, an attractive mother, and Johnny Periot. These were her half-sisters – *her family.*

She was so caught up in the portrait that she hadn't realized Periot was staring at Webster again. The silence caught her attention, causing her to turn.

"Have we met before, Mr. Webster?" Periot was digging to find a connection.

"No, I don't think so," Webster said.

"Where are you from?" Periot's gaze never left Webster. "You seem familiar."

He took a puff on his cigar and offered one to Webster. "I seldom forget a face."

Webster refused the cigar. "I don't think we've run into each other. I would remember meeting someone as important as you," Webster said, without answering Periot's question.

"Now you're trying to snow me," the Mayor said with a grin. "I would bet I've seen you somewhere. It'll come to me. Like I said, I seldom forget a face. Part of bein' a politician, I guess," he said, finally turning back at Cary.

Periot sat down, tapped the ashes off the cigar, and glanced across the desk.

"Now, Miss Warren. How can I help you?"

Cary was ready. Carolette Shapiro had said Janice never worked for him. Maybe he would stumble. "You said you employed my mother for a while. I wondered if you remember any of her friends." Cary watched his face for anything that might betray some emotion or thought. Periot kept his composure and seemed in control of his emotions. *He's good.*

"Let's see." He pursed his lips and narrowed his eyes. "She worked for a temp agency at the time, I believe. I don't remember which one. As for her friends, the only one that comes to mind is Carolette Shapiro." He glanced at Webster again, then at Cary. "The two of them seemed close. Unfortunately, as you may have read in the paper last week, Carolette was murdered. Happened during a robbery, apparently." He took a final draw on the cigar, then crushed it out in the ashtray.

"I saw the article," Cary said. "She was killed Thursday night." She paused, then said, "I had visited with her that morning."

Cary detected a reaction this time, his eyes focusing on her with a momentary flicker of revelation. The effect surprised Cary. Was it that she had talked with Carolette Shapiro *or* that he hadn't been aware of it?

She took a new tack. "Do you remember where my mother lived in New Orleans?" And then another. "Did she have any family or relatives here?"

Her rapid fire questions flustered him. "No . . . No, I wasn't aware of anyone. I don't think I ever heard Janice say where she was from either." *Hmm . . . That wasn't what I asked.*

Periot appeared rattled as he stood up and began pacing. "I guess I just assumed she was from N'awlins. And no, I never knew where she lived here in the city." After a couple of turns in front of the windows, he returned to his chair.

Who was he kidding? Janice Talmer's lover would certainly have been in her apartment – many times. He would have known exactly where she lived. Cary was willing to bet on that one. *Your lies are stacking up, Mr. Mayor!*

"How could we find out where she's buried? Cary would like to visit her grave." Both of them turned toward Webster.

Cary thought the Mayor's reply came a little too fast and seemed . . . ill-conceived.

"She was cremated: that's what I was told." Webster had knocked Johnny Periot off balance.

"Where would you have heard that?" Webster again.

"I'm not sure," Periot said, slower with his answer this time. "That was a long time ago. I think someone mentioned it in conversation at some point."

Cary thought that was an unusual piece of information to have heard "at some point."

"Is there anything else, Cary? Any other questions? It's time for my next appointment," Periot told them, effectively declaring the meeting over. Webster's questions seemed to have pierced his armor.

"Could I call you if I think of something?" Cary asked.

"Of course," Periot said, rising from his chair. Back in control now, he handed her a business card. "Just tell my secretary who you are. I'll tell her to expect your call."

Cary and Webster stepped away from their chairs and turned to leave. Zeroing in on Webster, Periot tried one last time. "I still think I've seen you before."

"I have that kind of face," Webster told him.

"I . . . don't think so," Periot said.

As the Mayor walked over to open the door, Cary was surprised when Webster reached across to the Mayor's ashtray and stealthily dropped a cigar butt in his pocket. Though taken aback, her expression didn't change.

"I hope you're able to find out what you need to know about your mother," the Mayor said as they reached the door. He then turned to Webster and said, "I'll see you around." Then to both, "I trust you'll enjoy your stay in N'awlins."

***

Periot stood in the doorway and watched the couple as they walked out of his office suite. The young woman glanced back at him once, enduring his focused stare with no hint of faltering. The young man with her, someone he had almost certainly met, had a presence that concerned him. They appeared to be a formidable team.

This was the second time he had met Cary. Seeing her today was as unsettling as it had been last week. Her resemblance to her mother was striking and uncanny.

For him, she was like a ghost from his past, even sounding like Janice, the same lilt in her voice. Periot rolled his shoulders, trying to shake the feeling of dread that had been building since Miss Warren and her friend arrived in his office this morning.

Today should be one of the best days ever in his dynamic, and, in many ways, remarkable career. Yet the appearance of Janice's daughter and her search for her mother could threaten everything.

The measure of that risk was as certain as a hurricane roaring in over the wetlands to endanger his city.

Johnny sighed deeply. Cary's search couldn't be allowed to continue.

Even though she was surely his daughter, she had to be stopped.

Forgive me, Janice.

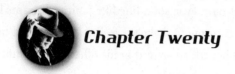

Chapter Twenty

As they left City Hall, Webster took Cary's elbow and hurried her toward the pickup point. He had alerted Greg, and Barry would be waiting for them.

While crossing the street, Webster spotted a well-dressed black man watching them. The individual had an athletic build and was well over six feet. The man turned, appearing uninterested when Webster glanced his way, but he reacted too late. Webster had seen people with much more experience running surveillance.

As they headed for the intersection, Webster kept an eye on him as he tagged along on the opposite sidewalk. Webster didn't tell Cary they were being followed; instead, he kept her close in case they needed to run.

Half a block from the pickup point, they came to a busy intersection. Nearing noon, traffic was heavy. As the light was about to change for pedestrian traffic, Webster nudged Cary and whispered in her ear: "Stay close. Someone's following us. Run when I tell you!"

Cary's eyes grew wide, but she merely nodded.

"Now!" he hissed.

They tore across the street as the light changed, leaving their pursuer momentarily blocked by traffic. Webster and Cary sprinted to the opposite sidewalk and turned the corner where they could see Barry's van at the curb thirty yards ahead.

"C'mon!" She matched him step for step.

Relief flooded through him as Webster noticed the sliding door already partially open. He jerked it back, and Cary dove in. Webster slid in behind her and pulled the door closed.

"Go! Go!" Webster urged, but Barry was already pulling into traffic.

Webster peered through the tinted back windows and watched as their pursuer raced into sight. He slowed to a trot at the street corner, staring in all directions, hoping to spot them.

"Don't worry about him getting our tag number," Barry said as he watched Webster through the rearview mirror. "I took the plates off and put a 'License Applied For' sign in the back window."

Still breathing hard from the chase, Webster smiled. "Good thinking."

Barry made a call, and a few minutes later they pulled up beside Greg on a quiet residential street. Webster and Cary climbed into the SUV with Greg. They left Barry putting his license plates back on the van.

"Let's get some lunch," Greg suggested. He had finally warmed up to Webster.

"Sounds good," Webster and Cary said in unison and laughed, releasing some of their tension.

Greg called Barry and told him to meet them at Deanie's on Haynes Boulevard out near the lake. A few minutes later, Greg was leading Cary and Webster to a table near the back of a bustling neighborhood restaurant. Smells of spices and fried seafood left Webster hungrier than he was already. Barry joined them a few minutes later.

"So," Greg started the conversation, "who do you think was chasing you?"

"Hard to say," Webster told him, "but since we were coming from Periot's office, my bet is on his people."

"You should've seen the guy's face, Pops," Barry told his father. "I could see him in the mirror. He didn't know where they went."

"They'll know we had help, though, and they'll be watching for us." Webster felt certain it was only a matter of time before someone spotted them if they continued searching for Janice Talmer's killer. And he knew enough about Cary now to understand that she was unlikely to give up the chase. Her tenacity was one of the things he liked about Cary. Unfortunately, here in New Orleans, it could get her killed.

Several waitresses were rushing back and forth among the tables. Linda took their drink orders, then a short time later, Jenny – short, blond, and cute as she could be – came to the table and suggested the Seafood Boats if they were really hungry.

"What's a Boat?" Cary asked.

"Darlin', it's just about the best old-fashioned sweet bread you ever had, and it's all buttered up and filled with seafood: oysters, shrimp, catfish. And you get french fries and a salad with it. It's big enough for two," she said, winking at Webster and Cary, who readily agreed to share one.

Fifteen minutes later, Jackie, a third waitress, brought their bounty. As Webster watched the women work their table, his mind kept returning to the chase. He was anxious to get out of here and back on the streets.

Someone was making a significant effort to keep Cary from tracing her mother's killer. If Webster wasn't careful, this unknown person or persons would find out more about him than he could afford, all because he was helping Cary.

Thirty minutes later Webster was stuffed, as were the others. As they walked out to the vehicles, the conversation turned serious again.

Webster put a hand on Cary's shoulder and said, "We need to make a couple of stops before going back to Landie's."

"Why don't you take the SUV if you think you'll be safe," Greg said.

"Can you do without it for awhile?" Webster asked.

Barry laughed. "We have a couple more where that one came from."

Greg shrugged, and said, "Take it. I'll ride with Barry. You're not expecting any trouble, right?" Webster glanced around, then shook his head. "I hope not."

"You won't need an escort then." Greg got into the van with Barry and they pulled out.

When they were alone, Cary turned to him. "Why did you take that cigar butt when we left Johnny Periot's office?"

"I'm going to send it to a lab." He raised his eyebrows. "Don't you want to find out if he's really your father?"

"A cigar butt is going to tell us that?"

"That's what DNA is all about," he said with a twinkle in his eyes.

Driving away, Webster glanced in his rearview mirror to see if anyone was following them, then made a left-hand turn onto Downman Road. "We'll have it analyzed for DNA, then compare it to yours. Watch for a post office. We're going to mail the cigar to a lab I trust. We should have some preliminary results in a few days. We'll get your DNA done locally and have a comparison made. Then you'll really have something to discuss with Periot. That's if they match."

"You don't think they will?"

"On the contrary," Webster told her, "I think he's your father. And, for whatever reason, you seem to have shown up at a very inopportune time. I don't know what he has going on at the moment, but I'm betting you're not in those plans."

For several seconds, Cary studied him, a frown on her face. "Back in his office, he thought he recognized you."

"Yeah, he did, didn't he?"

"You think it's just a coincidence?" she asked. "You do seem to be shrouded in secrecy. Even with my snooping, I haven't found out much about you."

"I know," he said. "But we need to leave it that way for now. Okay?"

"Do I have a choice?"

"No."

"Then okay."

At that moment Webster saw a UPS Store coming up on their left. He swung the SUV into the parking lot.

"Let's use UPS instead of the post office." After making a brief call to his contact to let him know what had happened, he turned to Cary and said, "That's covered." Then he went inside to send his package.

When he returned, Cary, as expected, was ready with more questions, but he didn't give her much. "You sure seem to know a lot about things that have nothing to do with advertising," she said with a touch of sarcasm.

"I've had some experience."

"I'll bet."

***

Twenty minutes after Webster and Cary left Periot's office, Big Eddie was sitting in front of the Mayor's desk again. Periot told him about his discussion with the young woman. Then the conversation turned to her friend.

"She had someone with her this time," Periot told him while tapping a pencil on the desk. "The guy's name is Mike Webster, and I'm pretty sure I've seen him before. You know I don't forget faces. He said we haven't met, but I don't agree."

"What do you want to do?" Big Eddie asked, his eyes on Periot.

"I don't know. Let me think about it and I'll call you." He reached into his desk drawer and pulled out two of the big cigars. He tossed one to Big Eddie and lit the other. Big Eddie pocketed his and walked out of the office.

***

When the Superintendent returned to his own office, he had a visitor. Budrow, the man who had followed Webster and Cary a few minutes earlier, waited in the reception area. The dark skin of his face and hands glistened while his size tested the strength of the reception chair where he sat. Big Eddie motioned him into the office. The Superintendent walked purposefully around the desk and flopped down in his chair. Leaning over, he set his elbows on the edge of the desk and rested his chin in one of his big palms.

"Okay, tell me about it."

The man spoke with a slight Caribbean accent. "I picked them up when they left City Hall," Budrow said, "but I guess the boyfriend saw me and they ran. I lost them in the noon-hour rush. Someone must have picked them up."

"Did you see the vehicle?"

"No, mon."

The Superintendent slammed a fist on his desk. "How the hell could you let them get away? We've got to know what they're doing. If it gets out that the girl or her mother is connected to the Mayor, it will be a disaster." Then he thought about what Budrow had said. "Someone's gotta be helping them."

"Yeah, that's what I think," Budrow growled.

"Okay, tell Mr. C to have his people find them, whatever it takes. We need to know who's helping them. When you spot them, give me a call."

"I will," the man said, "but it's going to be hard to find them, mon. I think we should watch Shapiro's place. They might try to contact him since his wife was her mother's friend and they can't talk to her anymore. We can put someone over at the adoption agency, too. She might go there again. Otherwise, we'll just have to wait until they show up somewhere. We'll keep an eye out for them on the street, and we're still working the hotels. Mr. C is all over this."

"Good," Big Eddie said. "Keep me informed."

"Done."

***

After Webster's phone call to Jack Robbins about the cigar and DNA, he told Cary, "We need to run out to Lakeview. That's where the laboratory is located. We can get your lab work done and when they get Jack's analysis from the cigar, they can make a comparison."

She listened with raised eyebrows, continually amazed by his ability to get things done with a phone call. *Big things.*

They drove to the Lakeview area of the city. Cary had long ago lost count of the neighborhoods and actual cities that make up New Orleans: Downtown, Uptown, Ninth Ward, Lakeview, Lakefront, Kenner, Metairie, and she didn't know how many others. And it all seemed to be N'awlins.

Webster had an address for the lab and, after consulting a map they found in the glove compartment, he drove to the site. It was only a short distance from Landie's house.

Orleans Laboratories, LLC, had only one location and was housed in an impressive compound of stucco and marble buildings. They parked near the tastefully landscaped entrance and went inside. At the reception desk Webster gave his name.

"Ed Lawrence knows we're coming."

An assistant led them into a small room that smelled of chemicals and was furnished with a couple of chairs and a treatment table. A few minutes later, a young woman dressed in a white coat joined them. After greeting them, she instructed Cary to open her mouth. A swab was rolled across her inner cheek for a saliva sample, and the procedure was complete.

The visit over, they were soon walking back to their vehicle.

Cary wondered what the results would be. What if Johnny Periot wasn't her father? That would certainly muddy the search. A couple of days and she would know.

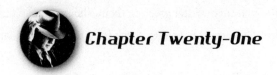

Chapter Twenty-One

A few blocks from the restaurant, they stopped for a traffic light. Cary touched Webster's arm, suggesting: "Let's get a newspaper and check on the funeral."

He swung in at the first convenience store they came to and went inside. Back in their vehicle, he searched the paper for the obituaries. Cary leaned across the console to read with him.

There was a long article with a picture of Carolette Shapiro. According to the commentary, a wake had taken place Sunday afternoon with a graveside service and burial scheduled for eleven o'clock on Monday. This morning . . . a couple of hours ago!

Surprised that Carolette Shapiro had been interred so soon, Cary glanced at Webster, noticing *his* raised eyebrows, too. The quick burial wasn't what surprised her most. "The Mayor didn't attend her funeral," she said. "We were with him at eleven o'clock. I'm stunned. They were close friends."

Webster continued to scan the article and then turned to her, his lips drawn and the muscles tight around his eyes. "It doesn't make sense," he said. "There must be problems between them."

Cary was seeing possibilities in the situation. "Let's call Shapiro this evening while everything is still fresh," she urged. "He might be more inclined to talk."

"The sooner, the better."

Her new cell phone rang, causing Cary to jump. She had only given the number to Kathryn and Landie last night. With some hesitation, she answered.

"Cary, is that you?"

"Who's this?"

"It's Kathryn Kato. I've been working on the research."

Cary breathed a sigh of relief. "Wonderful! How's it going?"

"Fine," Kathryn replied, "but that's not why I called."

Kathryn continued in a breathless rush of words.

"I was having lunch with a friend, Emile LeBlanc. He's a reporter here at the paper. Emile noticed I had some old articles on Johnny Periot." Cary shot a glance at Webster as she listened.

"He asked what was up, and I told him about your search – don't worry, no names." Kathryn stopped, as though gearing up for the punch line. "Cary, when I mentioned that you are interested in events of twenty-five years ago, his face turned white and I thought he was going to pass out." There was a pause on Kathryn's end.

"Go on," Cary said, demanding to hear more. She leaned over and held the phone away from her ear, motioning for Webster to listen.

"And guess what?" Kathryn said, excitement making her words run together.

"What? Say it!"

"Emile said he's been investigating the Mayor for several months. He thinks Periot was involved in some shady dealings in the past. He also says Johnny rose to power and has stayed there because he isn't afraid to twist arms, and, in some cases, break them. Those are Emile's words." She paused again. "My reporter friend considers Periot a dangerous man in spite of his reputation as a do-gooder. He believes the Mayor has dangerous people in his retinue."

"Wow," Cary said. Webster was quiet, looking out the window. He wore a somber expression.

"Cary, my friend wants to meet with you and Webster. I haven't told him who you are and I won't unless you say it's okay."

Webster, still listening, held up a hand. Cary squinted at the phone and said, "Give us a minute to talk and I'll call you back. Where can I reach you?" Kathryn gave her a number and hung up.

Cary felt perspiration above her lip. The temperature in the SUV was warm, but she doubted that was the cause. Anticipation gnawed at her as she glanced at Webster. He suggested they sit at one of the picnic tables the store had out front for customers. They climbed out and walked over. Webster took a spot on the edge of a table with Cary on the bench beside him.

They remained that way for several moments before Webster broke the silence. "You realize this could be the break we've been waiting for."

"How so?"

"Well, what if your mother knew something about Periot and that's why she was killed? This reporter could have your answer."

"Yeah," she agreed. "Now, what's the downside?"

"If he's connected to the people who are trying to stop you, we could be letting them know what we're doing and where we're staying. Right now, they don't know our location and I'd like to keep it that way."

"But Kathryn says he's already been investigating City Hall." Cary made it clear that she wanted to talk with the reporter.

"I know," Webster told her. "I'm only suggesting that we proceed carefully."

"So what should we do?"

Webster leaned forward for a few moments, considering the possibilities. Then he turned back to Cary, a glint in his eye.

"Call her back. Tell her we'll talk to her friend. Explain that we have a couple of things to do first, but we'll call him in an hour or so. Get his name and a number." He was thinking as he talked. "I'll have him checked out. Oh, and tell her not to give him our names or numbers yet." He paused, then said, "And one more thing . . ."

"Yeah?"

"Have Kathryn describe him and ask her how he's dressed."

"Why?"

"Just do it." The words were sharp, commanding.

Startled, Cary nevertheless picked up her phone and dialed. He obviously expected her to do what he said without questioning. His secretiveness and commanding ways were starting to get on her nerves.

When Kathryn answered, Cary told her what Webster had said – omitting the part about having the reporter checked out. Cary then asked for LeBlanc's description. After getting it, she thanked Kathryn and hung up."

"Got it," she said, turning to Webster.

She held the notebook for him to see. Webster glanced at the name, picked up his phone, and keyed in a number.

He winked at Cary in what she presumed to be an apology for his earlier abruptness. She wasn't buying it. *Too late, Bud.*

"Ray, I need you to check out a reporter on the *Times-Picayune* staff here in New Orleans. His name is Emile LeBlanc. I want to know if I can trust him."

"We'll find out in a few minutes," Webster told her as he closed his phone.

They waited for the return call. It didn't take long. A couple of minutes on the phone and Webster had his answer.

"He's okay," Webster told her. "Good reputation. Actually spent forty-five days in jail once protecting a source. That speaks for itself."

Webster called the reporter and set up a meeting for that afternoon.

***

When they reached Harrah's Casino, Cary pulled into the area for valet parking. LeBlanc was waiting for them. Kathryn had described him as short, middle-aged, and balding. She said he was wearing a brown sport coat over tan slacks with a blue button down. Kathryn had added that LeBlanc talked funny. Cary and Webster had exchanged glances over that one.

They said hello, then LeBlanc followed them into the Casino and over to a cozy lounge located near the entrance. Webster asked for a secluded table and they ordered drinks.

After the waitress had gone, Webster began. "Our talk needs to be off the record for now. You have any problem with that?"

"Okay by me."

"We understand you're investigating some dealings by Mayor Periot. Is that right?"

LeBlanc held up his hand. "Jus' a minute. Before I tell you anythin', I got some questions for da two o' you."

"Ask away." Webster picked up a paper napkin, twisting it in his fingers.

LeBlanc took a small notebook and pencil from his pocket, but their drinks arrived before he could get started. Alone again, LeBlanc posed his first question.

"First of all, why y'all interested in Periot?"

Cary fiddled with her drink, eyeing Webster. He nodded.

In a soft voice, she began, "My mother was his girlfriend twenty-five years ago. He was already married but I don't think my mother knew that, at least not in the beginning." She waited for a reaction.

LeBlanc reached for his Scotch, draining half of it before commenting. Then he dropped a big one. "Heart, I'd say your mother was Janice Talmer." It was a statement, not a question.

For several seconds Cary couldn't get her breath; words she wanted to say wouldn't come. Finally getting a grip on her emotions, she said, "I . . . I didn't tell you my mother's name. How did you know that?"

"I'm an investigative reporter, and I'm good at what I do," he told her, smiling. "I knew 'bout Janice Talmer and I knew she had a daughter. Also knew she gave up da daughter for adoption." He looked at Webster, then back at Cary. "You jus' tole me dat da daughter is you." He tossed back the remainder of his drink and motioned to the waitress for another.

"Then you know my mother died in a hit-and-run accident." Cary sipped her wine while she waited. She was calm now. Webster's beer sat untouched.

LeBlanc stared at Cary for a moment, and then glanced back at Webster before answering. "Maybe it's jus' da reporter in me . . . but I don't think dat was an accident. No sir, Dawlin'! I don't think your mother got in da way of dat car anymore than I did." He paused and sat forward in his chair. Then he voiced what he really believed. "I think she got in da way of Johnny Periot and his friends."

"Got any proof?" Webster asked as he took a sip of the beer, his eyes on LeBlanc over the cold mug.

Before the reporter could answer, a scantily clad dancer walked by. His eyes followed her. As the performer disappeared from his view, LeBlanc turned his attention back to Webster and said, "Proof? Not yet, I don't. Nothin' dat'll stick anyway. Nobody really saw da accident but Janice Talmer's girlfriend. And she got herself killed last week."

"Carolette Shapiro," Webster said.

"Cary visited with her the day she was murdered."

Now LeBlanc appeared surprised, his eyebrows pulled tight. He glanced back and forth between Cary and Webster, then focused on her. "She tell you anythin' we don't already know?"

"Not much," Cary answered. "Except . . . she said she didn't believe my mother's death was an accident. She invited us back to talk more, but she was killed that night."

LeBlanc seemed to pick up on the "us" because he said, "Someone went wit' you to see her?"

Cary told him about the social worker. He listened, then made a note in his little book.

While he was doing that, Webster asked him, "What do you know about Alex Shapiro? We understand that he and the Police Superintendent have been friends with Periot since grade school. Were you aware of that?"

LeBlanc finished writing before he looked up. Hesitating as if coming to a decision, he put his pen behind his ear and said, "Da three of them were practically joined at the hip until Shapiro's parents sent him off to boardin' school. The boys didn't see much of each other until Shapiro and Periot finished their educations. Breunoux didn't go to college right away. He started night classes when he joined da police force. Anyway, after Shapiro and Periot got their degrees and came back to N'awlins, they all hooked up again. Da Three Musketeers."

"Sounds like good friends sticking together," Webster suggested. He took a sip of his beer as Cary played with the stem of her wineglass. LeBlanc's second Scotch sat untouched.

"They all seem to have prospered in their chosen fields," Cary said.

"I think it's related," LeBlanc told them. "Their success, I mean,"

"How so?" Webster asked.

"Jus' my opinion, you understand. I haven't tied anythin' down, but, think about it dis way. Periot's da Mayor. He has ways of 'takin' care' o' certain people. Big Eddie is da Superintendent. He can turn da screws in lots of interestin' ways, if you know what I mean. Shapiro is worth millions, and da other two helped him get those millions. He shares da good fortune with his buddies. One big happy family, da way I see it. They're all pretty well off, you know."

"So why did Periot want to get rid of my mother twenty-five years ago?"

LeBlanc answered slowly, speculating, "Maybe he didn't think he could take da chance of a scandal at dat point in his career. Maybe he was just keepin' things clean. Or, to take it a step further – what if someone else felt dat way? Maybe not Johnny Periot, but someone else. What if dat someone thought they were protectin' him?"

"Maybe," Cary said while considering LeBlanc's theory – not exactly agreeing, but not disagreeing either.

Rising, LeBlanc said he'd be right back and headed toward the restrooms. Cary excused herself and followed. Webster took another swallow of his beer, then pushed it away and waited.

When LeBlanc and Cary returned to the table, Webster asked, "So, where does your investigation go from here?"

"I'm goin' to follow up on da idea dat–" he nodded at Cary, "dat your mother got in their way. How about da two o' y'all?"

"We're going to try to see Shapiro," Cary answered. "I want to see if Carolette might have told him anything interesting about that night."

"Good luck," LeBlanc said to them. "I don't think he's gonna talk to you."

"We'll see." Webster tried to sound confident.

"Cary, let's let Mr. LeBlanc get back to work."

They paid their tab and went outside.

"So," LeBlanc asked as they waited for their vehicles, "do you two want to work together on this? We can share anythin' interestin'. Dat okay wit' y'all?"

Webster and Cary both nodded.

"And, nothing will be published until we give the word?" Webster said.

"I'm okay wit' dat," LeBlanc agreed. "If we don't wait too long."

Cary tossed LeBlanc a final thought as they parted: "By the way, the Mayor didn't attend Mrs. Shapiro's funeral today . . ."

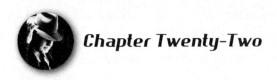

Chapter Twenty-Two

As she and Webster left the casino, Cary decided to try Shapiro's number. It was time for a little truth-telling.

"Shapiro residence." Someone, probably a maid, answered.

Cary gave her name and asked to speak to Mr. Shapiro.

A few moments later, a man picked up. "This is Alex Shapiro." He sounded tired, but when she told him why she was in New Orleans, his voice quickened, "Could you come this evening? Or perhaps this afternoon?" She thought she heard a catch in his voice. Then he said, "I could use a friendly visit to take my mind off of the things that have happened recently."

She couldn't help feeling sorry for him.

"Actually, a friend and I are not far from you now. Would thirty minutes be all right?" she asked.

Surprisingly, he agreed, telling her to come on out.

"That was almost too easy," she said to Webster as she put her phone away.

"Yeah, it was."

***

When they arrived at the Shapiro residence, Webster parked. They crossed St. Charles Avenue and started up the sidewalk to the stately home where Carolette had lived. As a precaution, Webster checked out the vehicles parked up and down St. Charles and on adjacent streets. There were several.

A panel truck sitting on a side street at an angle from Shapiro's place attracted Webster's attention. Its sign indicated it belonged to an electrical contractor. With a side door open, its occupants were probably working at one of the nearby houses. He watched the truck for a few seconds and, seeing nothing suspicious, temporarily dismissed it.

***

"There they are," Frank said, jabbing Mazou's arm and pointing at Cary and Webster from inside the van. "They're heading for Shapiro's. Did you see what they were driving?"

Mazou was pointing down St. Charles Avenue. "Yeah, Bra. It's dat SUV parked over on this side of da street. See da one I mean?"

"Yeah, I got it." Frank reached into the back of their truck and grabbed a GPS transmitter. "Go down there and attach this to their car. Stick it up under the back, but make sure it fastens securely. Get their tag number, too."

"F'sure." When the couple was out of sight, Mazou opened his door and casually strolled along the sidewalk toward the SUV.

As he did, Frank punched a number into his phone and said, "We got 'em. They just showed up at Shapiro's. We're putting a GPS on the vehicle. Even if we lose them, we'll still know where they are."

"Let me know when they leave Shapiro's," Frank heard Cobreaux say from his downtown office. There was a click and the phone went dead.

***

Webster and Cary walked up on Shapiro's porch and rang the doorbell.

Alex Shapiro opened the door. "I'm glad you could come," he told them. "The house is so quiet without Carolette here." He was still dressed as he might have been for Carolette's funeral, except for his tie. It was missing and his shirt was open at the collar. He did a slight double take at Cary as he held the door for them to enter the hallway.

A gorgeous golden retriever sat just inside with a leash in its mouth. Shapiro touched the dog's head and said, "This is Zabeth. She was Carolette's special pet. I was about to take her for a walk. Would you like to join us?" Zabeth dropped her leash and stood and walked over to Cary, nuzzling her head against Cary's leg.

"She likes you," he said as she stroked the dog's head.

"We'd love to walk with you," Cary told him as Webster kneeled to pet the animal.

"Good. It's settled then." Shapiro picked up the leash and hooked it to Zabeth's collar. They walked out the front door and down the sidewalk – the retriever leading the way.

"That's an interesting name," Webster said, pointing at the retriever as they walked toward the street.

Shapiro smiled, "It's a Cajun word for Elizabeth. Carolette named Zabeth after her grandmother."

As they reached the sidewalk and walked along St. Charles Avenue, Cary spoke. "Mr. Shapiro, I was so sorry to hear about your wife. She appeared to be a special lady." Zabeth had her leash stretched as far as she could and was sniffing every nook and cranny along the way.

"She was a special lady," he agreed, "in more ways than you could imagine."

Shapiro waved at a neighbor and then said, "Now who did you say you are again? Tell me your name."

"Cary Warren. We haven't met. My mother was friends with your wife many years ago." She explained about her background. "I'm hoping you can help me."

"I'm not sure what I could possibly tell you, Miss Warren," he said, sounding uncertain. Cary noticed him surreptitiously watching her. She wondered if he was remembering Janice Talmer as he looked at her.

In an effort to get him talking, Cary said, "Your wife invited me and a friend out to your home last Thursday. We had a short talk about my mother."

He glanced at Cary. "Last Thursday, you say. That's the day . . ." He started again. "That was the day Carolette died."

"Yes, I know. But information about my mother is so scarce, and I really do want to learn more about her. Mrs. Shapiro said my mother was in your wedding. If you remember anything about her, anything at all . . ."

He became quiet and introspective as they walked along following Zabeth. Cary allowed him his silence as she glanced at the large houses that graced the street. The mixture of styles spoke of the variety of wealthy families that lived in these expansive mansions so long ago. Obviously, the Shapiro's were relative newcomers to the neighborhood.

When he was ready, Shapiro resumed the conversation. "What did you say your mother's name was? Or did you?"

"Janice Talmer." Cary told him.

She watched for a reaction and saw a glimmer of recognition.

After another few moments of quiet, Shapiro said, "I remember Janice now. And, yes, you're right. She was a good friend of Carolette's. They were close even before Carolette and I married."

Cary watched as a streetcar rumbled past on the neutral ground of St. Charles. Though the afternoon was cool, several windows on the trolley were open and riders sat with their arms resting on the ledges.

"Do you remember much about her?"

Shapiro reached into his pocket, searching for something. Coming up with his glasses, he unfolded and put them on, saying, "I have some vague recollections. What would you like to know?" But Cary believed by his hesitance that he remembered more than he was admitting. His expression seemed guarded.

Zabeth spied a cat crossing a side street and tugged at Shapiro, trying to chase after the animal. The dog barked as the cat ran under a house in the distance and disappeared.

"You and your wife had been married for several months when my mother was killed. Isn't that right?"

He rubbed his chin. "Yes, six months or so, I believe."

Turning, Shapiro nodded toward his house and said, "Let's start back if you don't mind." They turned, Zabeth following along behind.

"Did your wife spend much time with Janice?" Cary asked.

"Oh, they were always together," Shapiro said. "They frequently went shopping, and when they could, they went to antique stores even though we couldn't afford expensive furnishings at the time. They dreamed of how things would be in the future. Often, in the evenings, they went for walks, laughing and talking. We all lived in the Vieux Carre, you know. Your mother, too."

Webster said, "That's what they called the old quarter, isn't it? The French Quarter – where New Orleans started."

"That's true," Shapiro said, before turning back to Cary.

"Do you know where my mother lived in the Quarter?" Cary asked.

"No," he said. "I never went there with Carolette, but I think it was on Barracks. I was busy working in those days, but Carolette would have known." As he said this, his eyes became misty and he sighed deeply.

"Did you know they were going out on the night my mother was killed?" Cary asked.

"Oh, yes. In fact, I watched them stroll off down the sidewalk that evening. Carolette and I lived in a small apartment on Burgundy near St. Ann. I went back inside and was reading when I heard the sirens. It's strange, but I still remember that."

"Did it hap . . . Where . . . Was it near your apartment?" Cary asked.

"Six blocks or so."

"Did you go there? To the scene of the accident, I mean."

"Yes. A neighbor came and told me that my wife's friend had been hit by a car. When I got there, I found out a woman had been killed." He looked at Cary with a sad expression. "It was Janice. Carolette tried to tell me what happened, but she was confused and upset. I stayed until I could bring her home."

They were almost back to Shapiro's house now. Zabeth had tired, no longer tugging at her leash but walking alongside Shapiro.

"Did your wife ever say she didn't think it was an accident? Did she tell you that?" Cary asked. "Because that's what she told me."

"No. She never said that," he replied immediately . . . maybe just a little too fast. He was hiding something. Cary and Webster glanced at each other. He had to be lying.

Probing, Webster asked, "If Carolette had believed Janice's death wasn't an accident . . . if she told that to the wrong person, do you think your wife would have been in danger?"

Webster's question must have mentally blindsided Shapiro because he stopped, appearing stunned. Cary wondered if he had considered that particular possibility. His answer was slow in coming.

Finally he said, "No . . . no, I can't imagine that being the case." He seemed deep in thought, the questioned having rattled him.

"I hope you didn't mind my asking," Webster told him, watching his eyes. "I just wondered . . ."

They had reached Shapiro's gate now and stopped there on the sidewalk. Zabeth sat at Shapiro's feet.

"I'm rather tired," he said. "It's been a grueling several days. I hope I've helped you some." The last statement was directed to Cary.

"Could we leave a number with you in case you remember anything else?" Webster asked him.

"Certainly."

Cary, with a questioning glance, tore a page from her notebook, and Webster gave him the cell number.

They said goodbye as Shapiro opened the gate and headed toward the house with Zabeth trailing along behind. As they walked away, Cary said, "I'm surprised you gave him your number. He may still be with them. What do you think? Will he call?"

"I doubt it. He's been with his old friends too long. You're right; he's probably not going to abandon them now. After Carolette's death, he'll be afraid for his own life, too." Webster took her elbow and guided her across the street. "I think we've heard the last of Mr. Shapiro. Giving him the cell number can't hurt, though. If it becomes a problem, I'll toss this phone and get another one."

Cary also doubted if they would hear from him. Shapiro was lying about what his wife had told him concerning Janice Talmer's death. She was almost certain of that. She wondered what else he might be lying about.

As they got into the SUV and drove away, a light mist began to fall – appropriate for another dead end in their search.

***

"They're leaving Shapiro's," Frank told Mr. C.

"Follow them and see where they go. We need to find out who's helping them."

"You want us to stop them?" Frank asked.

"No, damn it. Just find out where they spend the night, then call me in the morning."

"Yes sir, Mr. C."

Chapter Twenty-Three

Shapiro gazed out through the mist as the young couple drove away. He wondered if Cary had noticed his shock when he first saw her at his door. It was like seeing Janice, back from the grave.

Over the years he had often thought of the girl's mother. Carolette loved Janice – they were more like sisters than friends. Cary was very much like her in looks and in the way she carried herself. She even talked like Janice. He hoped he would be able to get the girl *and* her mother off his mind.

As soon as he let Zabeth into the house, Carolette's retriever headed for her food and water dishes in the kitchen. She would come looking for him when she was ready. Zabeth tended to stay close to him since Carolette was no longer there to care for her. Over the last few days, the dog's presence had been a genuine comfort to him.

Shapiro closed the front door and walked down the hallway to his study where he sat down behind his desk. As he stared across the room and out the window, he was uncertain what to do about this new complication. Again, he caught himself as he ground his teeth together. He'd started doing it again after Carolette . . . died. Now his jaws were starting to ache. Having conquered the habit years ago, he had found himself doing it several times since Webster asked his question. Shapiro pondered the thought again. Could his lifelong friends have killed his wife? Would they have betrayed him like that?

Finally, he picked up a novel he had been reading and opened it. He needed something to take his mind off the reality that Carolette was no longer sitting on the sofa across from him with a book of her own. Taylor Caldwell's *Captains and the Kings*, the one she had been reading last Wednesday evening, lay unopened and untouched on the table where she'd left it. Shapiro knew the story dealt with an Irishman, Joseph Montrose, who had obtained enormous wealth in America but never found satisfaction in life. Shapiro recognized parallels in his own existence.

For several hours he forced himself to read, but his mind kept drifting away from the story, and he'd catch himself thinking of Carolette. The maid had brought him a sandwich and milk some time ago, but it sat, ignored, on the desk.

Finally, around ten that evening, Shapiro marked his spot and closed the book.

Zabeth was asleep in a corner near the door in one of her several beds. She eyed him, her tail wagging before she dropped her head to her front paws.

Shapiro leaned back, deep in thought, with his hands clasped behind his head. At last, having made some decisions, he sat forward and picked up the phone. It was late now, but the time didn't matter to him. He held the receiver, punched in a number, and listened.

"Hello?" A sleepy male voice answered after several rings.

Shapiro muffled his own voice and said, "Sorry. Wrong number," then hung up. He had only wanted to see if Victor was home.

Reaching for his coat, he pulled a key ring from one of the front pockets. Choosing a silver key, he opened a bottom drawer and lifted a lockbox, placing it on the desk. Another key opened the box, allowing him to sort through the papers inside until he found what he wanted. He shoved the metal box aside and unfolded two pages, placing them on the table in front of him. It was a letter he had written many years ago. *Actually, it wasn't a letter – it was a confession.*

After checking the lockbox to make sure he had another copy, Shapiro refolded the one on the desk and slipped it into his coat pocket. He closed the box, locked it, then placed it back in the desk drawer. Then he relocked that, too. Opening the bottom drawer on the other side of his desk, he removed a small .32 caliber pistol and slipped it into his belt. Standing then, coat in hand, he walked through the house toward the rear door.

As he passed through the kitchen, Shapiro paused, turning to the young live-in maid who was having a snack at the table. "I'm going out for a while. Don't wait up." She simply smiled. Zabeth had followed him and was now circling her kitchen bed.

Shapiro continued out to the garage. As he started to get in his car, he glanced over to where Carolette's body had fallen when she was killed. He murmured, "Sorry, Darlin'. I hooked up with the wrong people, and after all these years, you paid the price."

He climbed into the car and leaned back in the seat. Once again looking at the place where Carolette had been murdered, he said, "Now it's their turn to pay." He started the automobile, backed out of the garage, and drove away.

***

Mayor Periot had spent the evening giving a party for a hundred or so of his oldest and dearest friends. These people were also some of his most generous contributors, many of whom had been with Johnny since his first political race. Almost every important individual in the city was there: heads of all the city's departments were in attendance, as were several judges and the District Attorney. Businessmen and labor leaders, builders, contractors and developers, physicians and hospital administrators – all were present.

Constance, his wife, moved from one cluster of guests to another, as always the gracious hostess. Tonight she looked exquisite in a long black fitted gown. Adorning her neck was a thin gold chain embellished with a dazzling array of small diamonds. She strolled about, effortlessly doing and saying little things to make everyone feel they were special.

Johnny knew Constance would do what he expected of her. They were a team.

Servers worked quietly to keep everyone's drink glasses filled. The Mayor wanted his friends to feel generous when it was time to let them in on his news. He flushed with satisfaction each time he thought about the announcement. Johnny realized tonight would be memorable for him and for Constance.

The Governor had even put in a short appearance earlier in the evening before flying on to Washington. Johnny and the Governor were still trying to get a large portion of the funds that had been promised to rebuild the city after the hurricane.

Conspicuously missing from the happy gathering, though, were Alex Shapiro and his wife Carolette. Everyone there knew what had happened to Carolette. They whispered to each other what a shame it was to have lost such a wonderful person from their midst – poor Alex: he must be devastated.

But tonight, Periot had no time to dwell on that.

Even Johnny's old buddy, Superintendent Edward R. Breunoux, was there, resplendent in his dress blue uniform with its four stars attached to epaulettes on each of his shoulders. Johnny smiled, knowing Eddie had designed the uniform himself.

Big Eddie was telling everyone who asked that his detectives and, for that matter, the entire police force wouldn't rest until they found the cowards who had robbed and killed Carolette. He said he wanted the city to be safe for everyone, but especially for wonderful people like the Shapiros. He returned the mayor's wave from across the room.

Johnny made the rounds once more, shaking hands, careful not to miss anyone. He was proud of his ability to attract people like these assembled in his charming home tonight. They were rich and influential, strong leaders of the community. They were the city's movers and shakers. He looked around, smiling at those who caught his eye. These people looked up to him. They made him strong. *These are my people.*

That hadn't always been so. He had grown up across the river where, at night, he could only look at the lights in the city. His father had worked on the docks in those days. Periot could remember many Friday nights when the old man came home, whisky on his breath, and fell into bed without even saying hello to his family.

Young Johnny, Mayor-to-be, had sworn he would go to college and that some day, people in New Orleans would look up to him. He had diligently worked toward that goal. He had struggled for an education and made his mark here.

Johnny had negotiated with some, partnered with others, pulled strings for many, then called in favors as needed, and, when necessary, hadn't hesitated to bring others down – with a little help from his friends. There had been a few shattered kneecaps and worse along the way.

But now he was on top. He could write his own check, so to speak, anywhere in the city.

For just a moment, Periot thought about his visit with the girl and her friend earlier in the day. As he sipped at his chardonnay, worry mixed with other thoughts of them. This Cary Warren, the daughter of someone he had once cared for, was *probably* his daughter. But in his wildest dreams, Johnny would never really let himself imagine that the lady from Tennessee could topple his kingdom. He *refused* to let himself think the impossible.

***

Webster and Cary stopped for a light supper before returning to Landie's for the night. Although hungry and tired, he knew they needed to regroup.

While waiting for their food, they discussed what they needed to do when they got to Landie's. Kathryn would probably have information for them the next morning. With that they could lay out a plan for Tuesday. For this evening, they agreed to call it a day.

When they were back in the SUV, Cary leaned her head back onto the headrest. She was dozing when he glanced over. Webster couldn't help it: he was starting to like her. But he knew that couldn't be. *Wrong time, wrong place!*

Cary had dropped into a deep sleep, not even stirring when he turned a corner. His stomach did a small flip when she slowly slid over to rest her head on his shoulder. She remained that way until he gently shook her as they sat parked in front of Landie's house.

"Wake up," he whispered. "We're home." She woke suddenly, blushing as she realized she'd had her head on his shoulder.

"Don't give it a thought," Webster told her. "I started to nod off myself, but then realized I was driving." He winked at her. She flushed, but he could tell she enjoyed the attention.

Cary caught his eye as she reached for the door handle. "By the way, your shoulder makes a good pillow," she told him. "Very soft."

Landie had waited up for them and fussed because they'd already eaten. After a few minutes of catching up, she said goodnight and went to her bedroom.

"Why don't you have the first run at the shower," Webster said as soon as they were alone. Cary nodded, too tired to argue.

Once she was in the shower, Webster went to his room, closed the door, and opened his laptop. He pulled up a number and called Ray Ward. Because it was only 10:30, Webster doubted he would be waking his friend.

When Ward realized who was calling, he asked, "Isn't it bedtime for little boys like you?"

"One would think so," Webster replied.

"So what do you want now? You always need a favor."

Webster chuckled. "You're right, as always. Could you see what you can find on an Alex Shapiro?"

"Shapiro?"

"Humor me," Webster said. "He's a business owner here in New Orleans. See what's out there on his company, too. It's some sort of import-export thing. Very successful from what I hear."

"I can do that," Ward said, "but if I keep doing these little favors, I'm going to have to start billing you." They both laughed this time, but Webster thought his friend sounded concerned.

"Let me know what you find in the morning."

"Will do. Now go to bed."

***

"Bingo!" Frank said as Mazou pulled to the curb nearly a half block from the small white shotgun cottage. The GPS signal was working fine.

They sat for a while and watched as, one by one, the lights in the house went off. Mazou opened a laptop and pulled up a cross-reference directory. He plugged the house address into the program and up popped Landie Kato's name and enough of her personal information to give them a bead on her. Another Kato family was listed a few doors away. That name was Greg Kato.

"Now we know where they're staying and probably who's helping them," Frank said with a chuckle. That information would make Mr. C happy.

Mazou started the car and made a u-turn in the street.

"Love dat GPS."

Chapter Twenty-Four

When Shapiro left his house that evening, he drove out to Canal Boulevard and then to an area of large homes a few blocks off the shoreline of Lake Pontchartrain. The houses were older, built mostly in the fifties and sixties, and large for their time. The styles varied from Spanish, French Chateau, Fifties Modern, and Cottage to Classical.

Some of the major streets of New Orleans such as Canal Boulevard were wide, with ample space for two lanes of traffic and a lane for parking in each direction. Huge neutral grounds large enough for football games separated the traffic lanes.

Familiar with the area, Shapiro went directly to Victor's house. He and Carolette had been there many times over the years. The house, like most of those around it, sat fifty feet or so off Jewel Street in an area called Lake Shore. Victor often bragged about being able to walk to the southern shore of Lake Pontchartrain in less than ten minutes.

Victor's residence was large and attractive with a Mediterranean flair, the grounds spacious and manicured. Carolette had often asked Victor's late wife Anne about the trees and flowers around the yard. The house was built of brick, a sandy shade of brown, not the usual red so prevalent there. The shutters were black and the front door, a bright red.

Shapiro pulled into the driveway and got out of his car. He glanced at the nearby houses, then walked up to the front door of the sprawling old house. He rang the bell once, then twice more in rapid succession to make sure Victor would hear it. Through thin curtains on side-lights at the door, Shapiro saw a light go on toward the rear of the house and a few moments later watched the man shuffling along toward the front door.

Victor pulled the curtains aside; with dark eyes widening in recognition, he nodded at Shapiro.

Sounds of the safety chain being removed and the door unlocked held Shapiro's attention as he waited. Then the door opened and the sleepy man inside blinked his eyes as he looked out at his visitor.

"Alex! What the hell are you doing here at this time of night?"

"I've come to bring you something, Victor," Shapiro told him. "Can I come in?" Without waiting for an answer, he brushed past.

"I guess so," Victor said, stepping back. "I was in bed, you know."

"I can tell." Shapiro turned to face him. "You'll have plenty of time to sleep when I leave."

"You want something to drink?" Victor asked. "Some coffee? I could make a pot. Or I could make us a drink," he offered.

"You might want to make one for yourself. You're going to need it."

Frowning, Victor closed the door and flipped the lock. "You've got to admit this is pretty late for a visit, Alex."

"Yeah. I'm aware of that, but I had some guests this evening myself. One of them asked me a question that caused me to do some thinking." Shapiro looked at Victor. "You have any idea what that question might have been?"

"Of course not. How could I?" Victor snapped, a touch of anger in his voice. They were still standing in the foyer.

"Let's go sit down and I'll tell you all about it," Shapiro suggested.

"I'm not sure I want to sit down with you." Victor was clearly upset now. "In fact I think I want you to lea . . ."

He abruptly stopped talking and was now staring at the pistol in Shapiro's hand. It was pointed at Victor's chest.

"I'm not asking, damn it," Shapiro said in a forceful tone. "I'm telling you."

Shapiro motioned toward the back of the house. "Move! And keep your hands where I can see them."

Victor obediently led Shapiro to the kitchen where he walked over to the breakfast nook and sat down at the table. Shapiro watched as Victor kept his eyes on the pistol and folded his shaky hands on the table top. Shapiro remained standing.

"What do you want from me, Alex? What's this about?" Fear was evident in Victor's wide eyes and the quaver in his voice.

Shapiro paused before addressing his questions. "You remember I said someone asked me a strange question earlier tonight. Well . . . the question was whether I thought Carolette's murder could have had anything to do with the death of Johnny's girlfriend back when we were all getting started."

"You mean that hit and run when Janice Talmer was killed?" Victor must have realized that he had been too fast with his response because he clinched his fists and momentarily turned his face away from Shapiro.

Shapiro nodded, his gaze never wavering. "Yeah, Victor . . . *that's* the one."

"Now wait a minute, Alex. You don't think I had anything to do with Carolette's death, do you?" Beads of sweat started to pop out on his forehead and above his lip. "Alex," Victor pleaded, hands held out in supplication, "you know Carolette and I were friends."

"Yeah, I know all that," Shapiro said. "Look . . . I know you didn't do this all on your own. I'm also sure it wasn't your decision. Someone gave you the orders." He paused, the gun still pointed at Victor's chest. Then, "Who? Just tell me."

Victor was shaking now, clearly terrified. "You've got it wrong. I didn't do anything to Carolette. I don't know what you are talking about, Alex."

Shapiro suddenly lowered the pistol a few inches and fired. Victor screamed and dropped from his chair, clutching his right knee. Shapiro didn't worry about the sound. The houses here were far enough apart and the small caliber pistol didn't make that much noise.

"No, Alex. Wait! What are you doing?" Victor started to sob. Blood trickled between his fingers as he held his knee, pleading.

"Alex, please don't kill me."

Shapiro was calm as he studied the wounded man. He was past anger, even past caring. His decisions had all been made earlier that evening after the young couple had left him. There was nothing more to consider. Nothing else to plan. Dealing with Victor was just the first item on Shapiro's list of things to take care of. It was like making groceries – a New Orleans' expression. Take the list and put the items in the cart. *Get the job done.*

"Now, do you want to try again?" Shapiro asked. "I think I know the answer, but I want to hear it from you. Who gave the orders to kill Carolette? I'm aware Janice Talmer's daughter has been trying to find out about her mother. I also know Carolette talked with her last Thursday and invited her back on Friday. Someone must have found out about that and decided I might start talking, too."

"No, Alex. You've got it all wrong." Victor's eyes reflected his defeat when Shapiro raised the pistol, pointing it at his face.

Victor lowered his head. Then slowly raised it again, his eyes on Shapiro. "Okay . . . okay," he said, resignation now apparent in his voice, sweat running off his balding scalp and into his eyes. "You're right." He hesitated as though trying to gather his thoughts. "He called me last Thursday afternoon." Shapiro knew who Victor was referring to. "It must have been right after the girl left your place. He told me we had to keep you from talking but that you're too important to lose. He said he hated to do it, but I should take someone with me – go out there and make sure Carolette couldn't talk to the girl again. I understood what he meant."

"Who did you take with you, Victor?"

"Budrow . . . I took Budrow!"

"That was one assignment you shouldn't have taken," Shapiro said to him. He lowered the pistol toward Victor's chest.

"No, Alex. Don't . . ."

Shapiro fired a single shot. Victor toppled backward, silent, relaxing as he continued to stare at the pistol. Then his eyes moved to Shapiro's face and he spoke again, almost a murmur, "I'm sorry, Alex." And for the briefest time, Shapiro hesitated, unsure of himself.

After a moment, he stepped forward and fired two additional shots, one into Victor's forehead, another into his temple as his head dropped to the side. Then Shapiro did a strange thing. He stooped and gently closed Victor's eyelids.

He watched his long-time friend for several seconds before standing. Slowly, he stuck the pistol into his belt, turned, and walked toward the front door.

He had been careful not to touch anything in the house, and now he slid his arm up into his coat sleeve and used the cuff to open and close the front door. Once outside, he used the tail of his coat to wipe off the doorbell.

Satisfied, Shapiro climbed into his vehicle and cautiously backed out of the driveway. He drove with care on the way to his home. He certainly didn't want to get picked up for speeding on this particular night.

On the drive into town, Shapiro wondered, just for a moment, if they had missed him at the Mayor's party. His invitation lay on his desk at home.

***

At the Mayor's home, the time for his announcement had come. He took a position at the entrance to the dining room, up one step from the sunken living room so everyone could see him. He held up a champagne glass, gently tapping it with a piece of silverware. "May I have your attention, Ladies and Gentlemen? I have an announcement." Everyone ceased talking and crowded in, giving Johnny their full attention.

"I'm not going to drag this out," he said. "I received a phone call today from Stuart Daniels. Most of you have probably heard of Mr. Daniels. He's running for President." A ripple of chuckles passed through his audience.

"Anyway," he continued, "Stuart called to ask if I would be interested in the Vice Presidential slot in the race for the White House. He wants us to campaign in the primaries as a team." Before he could continue, his guests broke into spontaneous applause. As he waited for quiet, a myriad of thoughts ran through his mind. He'd dreamed of this night since he was a boy living across the river in Algiers. Now, everything he'd ever wanted was within his grasp – if he could keep Janice's daughter from exposing his one act of utter stupidity.

Periot took a deep breath, then held up his hands, silencing his audience again. When the chatter died down, Johnny said, "Of course, I told Stuart I would need a couple of days to think about his offer." More applause, with laughter this time.

"Seriously," he said, "I told him I would be honored. I hope all of you agree with me. I think we all should be flattered that the party, as well as Stuart Daniels, considers the Mayor of New Orleans qualified to be the Vice President of this great country."

As he stood there, Periot could feel his stomach muscles clench and his breath quicken. Now, more than ever before in his political life, he had to play his cards right. If he did, he could be on top of the world; if not, his world would be destroyed. He fought his rising panic while forcing an outward smile.

"I hope you'll keep your checkbooks handy and support me in this race the same way you have when I've ran for Mayor." From the cheers and applause, there didn't seem to be a problem. He smiled, then winked at his wife, all the while hoping Cary Warren would give up her search soon and return to Tennessee.

***

Arriving back at his home, Alex Shapiro drove his car into the garage and shut off the engine. He didn't open the car door immediately, but instead, sat quietly thinking with his head back against the headrest. Without Carolette, he didn't think life was worth living. They had been partners each step along the way. His dreams had been hers and her hopes had been his.

When they were young, they had not been blessed with children though they had wished for a family. They had tried all the latest medical options available, but nothing had worked. Carolette had finally said enough is enough.

He leaned his face against the driver's side window, feeling the coolness on his skin as he thought about the trip they had taken to Europe. That was when they had put their hopes for a family behind them. When they returned to New Orleans, they no longer talked of having children.

Shapiro had worked at managing their thriving business, while Carolette volunteered for various charities and other projects. Carolette, along with a small staff, kept their home like a king's palace, and she made him the king.

Now she was gone and he was alone. But as of tonight, Shapiro knew the people responsible, and he had a plan to bring retribution down on them. Unleashing his anger, he pounded the steering wheel with a fist, vowing revenge for what they had done to Carolette.

Shapiro no longer cared what happened to him. Those concerns had died with Carolette. He sat forward, his face in his hands, his elbows resting on the steering wheel, salty tears making their way down his cheeks.

He realized he felt sorry for the girl, too. Janice's daughter. What was her name? Cary? Her mother had been a good woman. She had been like Carolette in many ways. Janice had her hopes and dreams, too.

And he had helped destroy Janice and her dreams twenty-five years ago. Again he thought of Cary. She looked so much like her mother. Shapiro wondered if she knew that. He wondered, too, if Carolette had kept those old photographs.

Wiping the remaining tears on his coat sleeve, Shapiro opened the car door, walked out of the garage and into the house. In his study, he went to one of the bookcases that lined two of the walls near the windows. Searching through picture albums on one of the shelves, he found the one he wanted. It contained some snapshots Carolette had taken in the months before and after they were married.

Shapiro carried the album to his desk. He looked through the photographs, remembering each one and where it was taken. There were several with Janice and Carolette posing at places the three of them had visited. Alex was in several of the snapshots, and he recognized others where he had been the one taking the picture.

There were several shots in which either Carolette or Janice had been the only person in the picture. He picked one, a nice image of Janice posing beside a large oak tree out at Audubon Park, and slipped it out of the book. He started to close the album, then changed his mind, picking several more of Janice and placing them with the first one. He even chose a few where Janice was obviously pregnant. Finally, he closed the album and returned it to the bookcase.

Shapiro walked back to his desk and sat down. Unlocking and opening a file drawer, he leafed through folders until he found the one he wanted. Laying it on the desk, he rifled through it. He placed several papers with the snapshots, then closed the folder and returned it to the drawer.

Next, he retrieved the lockbox that contained his documents and placed the pistol beneath them. Then he got the sheets he had placed in his coat pocket earlier.

Combining these with the remaining papers from the lockbox, he placed all of them with the snapshots on top of the desk.

One last folder held a number of old newspaper articles which he placed with the other documents.

All that done, he turned on his computer and booted up. When the desktop appeared, he tapped into his Microsoft Word program, opened a new folder, and began typing. He would be working long into the night.

Tuesday morning found him still at the desk. Shapiro was on a self-imposed mission and he had a deadline. The time had come to make amends for the past. If he had done what he should have then, Carolette might still be alive.

# Chapter Twenty-Five

Webster and Cary were in the kitchen with Landie on Tuesday morning when her doorbell rang. Landie left them sipping coffee and went to see who was there. A few moments later she returned, saying, "It's someone for you, Webster."Cary glanced at him, and asked, "Who?" He answered with a gesture, arms spread, palms out.

"No idea," he said as he headed for the front room. He drew his pistol and held it out of sight as he opened the door.

A man in a dark jacket with an upturned collar stood near the edge of the porch, his back turned, staring down the street.

"Can I help you?" Webster asked as he stepped into the opening. The visitor looked familiar, even from behind.

He turned, and seeing Webster, broke into a big grin.

It took a moment for the face to register. The man was definitely out of place, and he sported a beard Webster hadn't seen before.

"Jack? What the hell are you doing here?" Webster was trying to gain his bearings. He had just spoken to Robbins on the phone Monday afternoon. Jack was in D.C. then. At least that's what Webster had thought.

He slipped his weapon back under his jacket before stepping outside.

"What are you doing out this early?" Webster was still trying to make sense of Robbins being there. He knew Ray Ward must have told Jack where to find him. Only the night before, Webster had told Ray that he and Cary were staying with Landie Kato. *Ray had told Jack.*

"Why shouldn't I be here at this hour?" Robbins said. "You know, early bird and all that."

Over his shock, Webster reached out to shake hands, then bear hugged his friend.

After the embrace, Robbins, his arm still around Webster's shoulders, said, "Come on, let's take a walk." He pulled Webster down the steps.

"What do you want?" Webster asked. "I *know* you want something. What?"

"*Moi?* I'm crushed you would think that." Robbins laughed and glanced over at his friend. Lowering his eyes, he scraped the toe of his shoe across a crack in the gray concrete sidewalk.

"Seriously, though," Jack continued, "we received your package overnight and should have the DNA analysis ready for you by early afternoon. I talked to one of our people in Washington a few minutes ago. I'll have it e-mailed back to Orleans Laboratories. Get with Ed Lawrence for your comparison."

"Your guys are fast. I'll give Lawrence a call later. Hopefully they'll have their analysis ready by then, too."

"Now, how's your investigation going?" Robbins asked. "And by the way," he inquired, "didn't you agree to keep a low profile?"

"Fine, and yes," Webster said, answering the questions. They had walked a hundred yards. Webster glanced back toward Landie's house.

"Same old you," Robbins shot back. Then in a totally serious tone, he asked, "Is anyone watching your back?"

Webster, with a sheepish grin, glanced over, telling him, "Just Cary Warren, and she's kinda new at it."

"Not funny," Robbins exclaimed. "Man, you know that people are out there looking for you. *Bad people.* And you're walking around like it's no big deal."

"I'll work on it," Webster said. "I promise I'll be careful." His tone indicated the subject was closed. Webster turned back toward the house.

Robbins reached out, gripping his arm and stopping him. "Hold up," Robbins said. "I need to talk to you about something else." He looked around as though someone might be listening.

"We've been batting around an idea. Let me get your take on it." He released Webster's arm and they walked slowly back toward Landie's cottage as he filled Webster in.

Fifteen minutes later they finished their business. Before leaving, Robbins had said he would ask Ray Ward to check on Webster and Cary from time to time. Webster had reluctantly agreed. As a last point, Webster asked about the beard. "Needed it for a short assignment – it comes off in the morning. Itches like crazy." Robbins had smiled then, walked over and got into his vehicle and drove away.

Webster stood there for several minutes, mulling over their conversation *and* Robbins request. Webster shook his head. He couldn't believe what Jack had proposed, and he couldn't believe he had agreed. Cary would blow her stack if she knew. He would tell her about Robbins' proposal – at least part of it – when they were finally alone.

Webster had started out tired that morning. His nightmare had returned to haunt him last night. He could still hear the bullets as they tracked toward Juan on the ridge line of his father's house. Webster could still see him as he fell, always in slow motion. The result was the same as it had been in Columbia: Juan was dead, and Webster felt responsible. He yearned for the dreams to end.

The smell of bacon frying greeted him as he opened Landie's front door. She and Cary were moving about in the kitchen and breakfast was almost ready. Webster hadn't realized he was so hungry. Being awake since three in the morning must make you that way.

"Go wash your hands," Landie told him, "and sit down.

Cary motioned toward their friend, saying, "She likes giving orders." Cary popped a dish towel in Landie's direction.

The elderly woman deftly sidestepped and told Cary, "You're going to find yourself over my knee, young lady. Now sit down and eat."

Neither of them asked about his visitor.

Webster tried to keep a positive attitude as they ate breakfast. He was already concerned by the opposition he and Cary had faced regarding her search. Then, yesterday's meeting with the Mayor, coupled with the fact that Periot thought he recognized Webster, heightened his growing concern. It didn't matter that the Mayor couldn't recall where they had met. Periot was almost certain to figure it out, and that could be catastrophic for Webster.

Landie seemed spirited this morning. "I like having people make noise in this old house," she told them, "and you two certainly qualify in that regard." The chatter lightened the morning.

When breakfast was finished, Webster noticed Landie's copy of the *Times-Picayune*, still in its wrapper on the kitchen counter. He opened it as he sipped his coffee. An article telling about the Mayor's big announcement covered nearly the entire front page. Mayor Johnny Periot of New Orleans had hit the national scene. The headline read "Mayor In Line For VP Spot." Extensive commentary said Periot would be joining Stuart Daniels as a Vice Presidential candidate for the White House. Webster told the others that, according to the article, there would be a formal announcement at Periot's office that afternoon.

"I'm not surprised," Landie said.

Before he had a chance to say anything more about the announcement, Kathryn knocked on the back door. Like most of Landie's family, she bypassed the front of the house. She carried a folder and produced several copied articles from around the time of Janice Talmer's accident and later.

The four of them sat down at Landie's table and started to go through the information. A more recent commentary got Webster's attention right away. Kathryn, already dressed for work, tapped a polished fingernail on the article Webster was reading. "Look at this," she told him. "It states that the owner of this automobile paid cash up front for repairs but never returned for the vehicle." Kathryn glanced at Webster and Cary, telling them, "I noticed it because the circumstances were so peculiar: the man brought his car in just a few days after the hit and run that killed Cary's mother. There could have been a connection."

"Look," Cary said, reading aloud over Webster's shoulder. "It says the repair shop owner noticed some stains in the creases of a crushed left front fender. He had shown them to a young friend of his who was a police officer." They were all reading now; according to the article, the young officer thought the stains might be blood. He took a sample scraping for evaluation. When the officer's suspicions about human blood were overlooked by his superiors, he carried the scrapings to a friend who worked in a doctor's office.

Kathryn moved the article closer to Cary and Webster. "It says 'an analysis was made and the substance proved to be human blood,' but that was before DNA analysis could be done. Only blood type could be ascertained." She continued reading. "A sample of the scrapings was placed in test slides and one was given to the officer."

"Hot damn!" Webster exclaimed. Then, turning to Landie, he said, "Oouu, sorry, Landie."

"According to this information," Kathryn continued, "the officer was accepted into the Louisiana Highway Patrol program at about that same time and the evidence he collected was left with others for follow-up."

Cary was troubled by this last detail. "So what happened to the samples then?"

Kathryn walked over and picked up the coffee pot, pouring herself a cup before turning around. Leaning on the white-tiled counter, she said, "Nothing was done." She shook her head, obviously exasperated. "The whole thing seems to have fallen through the cracks. The doctor who analyzed the samples was mentioned by name, but again, no one followed through."

"No one did anything? Nothing?" Webster couldn't believe his ears. He wondered if Cary was right; maybe there had been a cover-up.

"This particular article cited reports available at the time." Kathryn gestured with her coffee cup. "It was one of a series detailing the lack of continuity with Police Department investigations. This article was written about five years ago. I stumbled across it and decided it might tie into Cary's search."

Webster read the commentary again as Cary skimmed several other pieces. He finished, laid the article down and turned, staring out the window at Landie's flower garden and backyard. *The owner of the vehicle had never returned for it even though the repairs had been paid for.* Surely someone had tried to trace him? Hmmm.

After a while Cary noticed him. "What's up?" she asked. "What are you thinking?"

"Just an idea," he said, focusing once again on her and the others. "Pretty far-fetched, but it's a possibility." He walked out on the back porch and keyed in the Orleans Laboratories number on his cell phone. He asked if Ed Lawrence was available and a few moments later, Lawrence answered. "How long could a sample be kept and still be used for DNA analysis purposes?" Webster asked.

"If the sample was kept in reasonable condition, DNA could be extracted after many years. Remember Jurassic Park?" Lawrence joked.

"Oh . . . Yeah."

"If you come up with something, bring it to us. We'll see what we can do. I love challenges," he told Webster. Webster thanked him, then flipped the phone closed. After a few seconds, he went back inside and told Cary, "I've gotta go see a doctor."

"What?"

"Just kidding." He grinned. He then explained, "I'm going to try to find the doctor mentioned in this article, the one who tested the blood sample. If, by chance, they stored the sample and it's your mother's blood, we might still be able to match the blood samples on the car with your DNA. It's a long shot, but if we tie the car to your mother, we might also be able to track down an owner."

"Could it still be traced after all these years?" Cary asked, her forehead crinkled in a frown.

"I said it's a long shot."

***

Alex Shapiro had worked through the night. He now had two large envelopes on his desk. Stacked on each of them were copies of old newspaper articles and several sheets of printed material. On one pile were the photographs Shapiro had assembled the night before. Each stack also included a copy of the confession from the lockbox. He was almost done, his mission complete.

Finally, he picked up the telephone and punched in the number Webster had left with him the prior evening. He set a meeting time and hung up. That finished, he stuffed the material into the envelopes and sealed them. With finality, he placed them on the corner of his desk and went upstairs.

After showering, Shapiro dressed and went down to the kitchen. Meredith, the young maid, moved about preparing food for meals later in the day. She smiled, asking what he wanted for breakfast.

"Toast and jelly will be fine, and coffee, of course," he told her. "Are any others of the staff here today?" he inquired.

"Danny, the yard man, is workin' on some of the flower beds," she told him.

"Well, when you get my breakfast, why don't you tell him to take the rest of the day off. Same for you. I've been working all night and I want to get some rest after an appointment I have at eleven-thirty. I don't want to be disturbed."

"Would you like me to stay for your appointment in case you need something?"

"No, that shouldn't be necessary. If anything comes up, I'll take care of it."

She thanked him and said she would tell Danny. A few minutes later, he watched them as they walked, laughing and talking, out to the street. He finished his breakfast and stacked the dishes in the sink.

When he left the kitchen, Shapiro took a leisurely stroll through the house. He stopped in several rooms and each time he gathered his thoughts. Carolette's touch was everywhere. She had loved this place and it showed. The home was beautiful but not ostentatious. It was a mixture of modern with enough antiques to give it a timeless ambiance. He loved the antiques, too. In one room Shapiro reached out and ran his finger tips along the edge of a table Carolette had purchased in Europe. That was the trip they had taken when they realized they would never have children. He let his thoughts drift for several minutes before moving on.

In time he made his way back to the study and sat down at his desk. He thought of the papers he had assembled and placed in the two envelopes; he was content with his decisions. The girl deserved to know about her mother, and he couldn't tell her without acknowledging his part in what happened. Since Carolette was no longer with him, he found it easier to do what must be done.

Actually, he was pleased because this way, he would be cleaning the slate. Shapiro had always known his actions were both legally and morally wrong. Yet, like the others, he had justified his behavior, believing a certain degree of ruthlessness was required to be successful. It was for the greater good, they said, but he had known the truth all along.

Leaning back in his chair, Shapiro put his feet on the top of the desk, crossing his legs. It felt strange. He seldom put his feet up on a desk, not considering it to be a proper thing to do. But he felt like making an exception this time. He knew he would never do it again.

Shapiro smiled at the irony.

***

Webster went into the living room after Shapiro's call. He had Landie's phone book and was searching for the doctor named in the article Kathryn brought them. The doctor's name was Gerald Davison and he was located in Chalmette at the time the blood sample had been brought in. Webster found a Dr. Davison listed but it was Gerald Davison IV. He was in a practice with a Dr. Samuels, and they were located near the LSU School of Medicine.

When he called, the receptionist told him Dr. Davison's son had taken over his father's practice about ten years ago. Patients, records, furniture, everything. *Maybe we have a chance.*

Cary walked in as he finished the conversation. He told her what he had turned up. They decided if they left soon, they could go by Dr. Davison's office before going to Shapiro's home. After gathering their things, they told Landie goodbye and drove directly to the doctor's location.

Webster decided they would probably make better progress if they just showed up and explained the situation. He doubted if they could get the test slide, even if it had been stored in the doctor's files, but he felt inclined to try. One never knew. He believed Cary was overdue for some good luck.

When they arrived, Webster asked to see the office manager. They were asked the purpose of the visit. Webster smiled and whispered, "It's confidential."

"It will be a minute. Take a chair." The receptionist pointed to a seating area.

Webster leaned over and told Cary. "If we get in at all, it'll be the curiosity factor."

A short time later, an assistant led them past a row of treatment rooms to an office. A well-dressed woman who looked to be in her early forties stood behind a neatly organized desk. She motioned for them to sit.

"I'm Pat Newell," she said by way of introduction. "How can I help you? Our receptionist tells me your visit is confidential. I couldn't pass on that one." She smiled and nodded for them to explain.

Webster told her about the hit and run twenty-five years ago, about the young policeman and how he had brought the blood samples to Dr. Davison's father's office.

"Someone conducted tests back then and determined the sample was human blood, type O. Since DNA analysis wasn't available at the time," Webster told her, "it sort of ended there." He let her read the reports and article as he twisted in his chair, crossing one leg over the other, then back. Cary shot him a look that said *Sit still!*

After Ms. Newell finished reading, Webster asked, "Is there any chance the sample would have been kept? And if it was, are there any conditions under which we could take it and have it analyzed for DNA?"

Ms. Newell listened and then leaned back, giving thought to the questions.

"First of all, I can't imagine a sample of the type you describe being kept that long," she said. "Second, I would be surprised if it was still viable. And third, assuming the first two things happened, how would it have been filed? Where would it have been kept? We have some old files going back to Dr. Davison's father, but I can't imagine how it would have been filed."

Webster, thinking, ventured, "Maybe . . . under the policeman's name?"

"And that would be?" she asked.

Webster looked at the article again and told her, "Troy Weaver."

Ms. Newell turned to her keyboard and activated some type of software. She typed in Troy Weaver's name for a search. After checking a couple of sources without success, she tried a third.

"I found his name," she said after a few moments. "He's in our inactive files. I have another list showing where old patient records are kept. Let me pull it up."

Webster glanced at Cary who held up her right hand, fingers crossed.

Newell typed and clicked several times and then looked up at the two of them. "We have a file. It's off-site in one of three possible locations, but there is a set of records. Maybe, just maybe, there's a mystery test slide in that file. I can't guarantee anything, but at least it's a start if we can find it."

"What about testing?" Webster asked.

"First, let's see if we have anything to test," Newell said. "I'll try to get the patient's record and then talk to Dr. Davison. Call me after three," she told them, then added, "I love mysteries."

They thanked her and left for their appointment with Alex Shapiro. Webster was apprehensive about the reasons Shapiro wanted to see them again.

It could be everything, or it could be nothing.

Chapter Twenty-Six

Arriving at Shapiro's house a few minutes early, Cary was surprised when he, rather than the maid, met them at the door.

"Come in," he said warmly. His golden retriever stood beside him.

"Hello, Zabeth," Cary said and bent to pet the dog as their host reached out and shook Webster's hand.

Shapiro led them down the hallway to his study. Zabeth followed along behind Cary, her toenails clicking on the hardwood floor. As they entered the handsome room, Shapiro told them, "Since I planned to be home all day, I've let the staff have the day off."

Hummm! Cary wondered why he bothered to tell them that.

Two walls of his study were lined with striking dark walnut bookshelves crammed with books of all genres. Flaubert and Hugo mixed with Hemmingway, Faulkner, and Dostoyevsky's *Crime and Punishment*. The irony of *that* title was not lost on Cary. She wondered if he had read all of the novels – especially the last one.

"Come in, take a chair."

Unlike yesterday on their walk, Cary studied their host more closely as they settled into their seats. He was upper middle-aged, she knew, but today he appeared older, tired, as though he hadn't slept. The last few days must have been hard on him. He was of medium height, but erect in stature, almost military-like. His hair was fairly long for his age, silver gray and combed back. Dressed casually, he gave the impression of having spent the morning working in his study with his dog as companion. Zabeth had followed them into the room and gone over to her bed, curling up with her big dark eyes on Shapiro.

Cary looked around the room at the luxurious leather sofa and chairs, the traditional tables and many antiques, lamps, and vases, all in the craftsman style. She noticed Webster checking out their surroundings, too.

Cary had been in Carolette's sitting room the week before, so she examined everything with renewed appreciation. It was a wonderful room and she complimented Shapiro.

"Carolette did it all," he said simply. "She loved making things attractive."

Cary exchanged glances with Webster as they sat in opposing wingback chairs.

Shapiro took his place behind the desk, crossing his arms with his elbows planted firmly on the surface. He came straight to the point. "Cary, I asked you back out here because there are some things I need to tell you."

Her emotions took off immediately. Cary had been waiting for this moment when she might finally learn about her mother. She had dreamed of the possibilities before she'd come to New Orleans. Then, Mrs. Hebert said Janice Talmer had been killed years ago. After that, Cary had hoped someone else would be able tell her what sort of a person her mother had been. But now she had almost given up; every possibility had led to a dead end.

Her hopes renewed, Cary felt as though her world was about to tumble out of control again, but somehow she managed to say, "Thank you."

"I guess I've waited twenty-five years for the right audience," Shapiro said with a wry smile.

He stood up behind his desk and stared down at her. "Cary, the truth is, I knew your mother quite well." He paused, but held her gaze. Then, clearly nervous, he sat down again and leaned forward. "Yesterday I told you I didn't remember much about Janice. That was a lie."

Cary released the breath she had been holding, then anxiously waited.

"How long did you know my mother?" She had so many questions.

Webster touched her arm, flashing a warning. "Let Mr. Shapiro tell his story." It was as though Webster understood that Shapiro was about to reveal something and feared Cary might jeopardize that.

Recognizing Webster's counsel for what it was, she nodded and turned back to Shapiro.

"Carolette introduced me to Janice – ahh, your mother – shortly after they met," he told her softly. "That was a couple of years before Janice was killed. They were both out walking and stopped for a rest on the same bench in the Quarter. Are you familiar with Jackson Square?"

She nodded.

"They started talking," he told her, "and that began their relationship. After that, they were always together." Shapiro smiled as he stared out the window past Cary. "They discussed their hopes and dreams, disappointments, everything. They even shared a tiny apartment on Burgundy Street near Esplanade for a while. As I remember, they moved in together about three months after they met. It was all they could afford at the time. Two twin beds and a hotplate. There wasn't room for much more." He talked slowly, his eyes becoming misty. In telling Cary about her mother, he was apparently remembering a younger Carolette, too.

"The three of us went lots of places together. Janice was very gregarious." He glanced at Cary, recalling another time, a happier one. "Your mother was more adventurous than either Carolette or me. She always had someplace new for us to visit."

Shapiro lifted his elbows from the desk, then leaned back in his chair. The atmosphere in the room changed abruptly; he appeared to be backing away from something he was about to say.

Turning his eyes to Cary, he said, "Then she met Johnny Periot." Shapiro paused, his mouth drawn and his facial expression turning dark along with his mood.

"I had known Johnny since he and I were boys in grade school. We were from the same neighborhood, along with Eddie Breunoux, the Police Superintendent." As Cary listened, she began to tense. Determined to let him tell the story in his own way, she chose not to mention that she and Webster already knew about the three men's history together.

Shapiro steepled his fingers. "I hadn't seen Johnny or Eddie much since my parents sent me off to boarding school when I was twelve.

"When your mother met Johnny, the four of us began hanging out together. That's when Johnny and I hooked up again. Johnny and Big Eddie had kept in touch all those years."

He smiled sadly at Cary, a new memory asserting itself. "You know . . . you could be mistaken for Janice's sister," he said, his voice almost a whisper. Then he stood up and walked to the window.

Cary's throat constricted, her breath coming in silent gasps. She blinked away hot tears that seemed to burn her cheeks as they coursed down her face. Cary could picture her mother – bright, outgoing, nearly Cary's own age at the time of her death. She'd had so much to look forward to, and then in a moment, in a blink of an eye, her life was gone and with it, any hopes and dreams she might have had for the future disappeared, too.

Shapiro, struggling with his own emotions, wiped the palm of his hand across his face, then walked back to his chair. Reaching into a drawer, he found a pack of tissues and handed them to Cary.

Shapiro moved forward in his story. "Janice told Carolette that Johnny got crazy when she gave him the news about being pregnant, said it was like he'd never had any feelings for her. He shouted that he wanted nothing more to do with her *or* her baby. As strange as it sounds, I don't think your mother ever saw him again."

"Do you think he could have had her killed? I mean the hit and run . . ." Cary knew she might have only this one chance to dig for answers and she wasn't going to give it up willingly. Webster glanced at her, evidently protesting, a slight shaking of his head,

Shapiro reached across the desk and picked up a framed portrait of Carolette. He stared at it for a long time. Then he lowered his head, tears again glistening in his eyes. Cary didn't attempt to hurry him.

He set Carolette's portrait back in its place after what seemed an eternity to Cary. Then, lifting his head, Shapiro said in a subdued voice, "It wasn't an accident."

Cary had been holding her breath again. Clasping both hands to her face, she gave out a strangled guttural sound, then sat still for several moments. Although in her heart she'd known it all along, hearing the words from Shapiro somehow made it more real. Janice Talmer had been murdered.

Zabeth barked once at Cary's outcry. Then, recognizing her master's signal, the retriever became quiet and settled back into her bed.

Webster's voice broke the silence. "How do you know it wasn't an accident?"

Shapiro's eyes slowly rose and locked on Webster's. Apparently considering the question, he became still, slow to speak once again. He lowered his eyes for a time and cleared his throat. Finally composed, Shapiro glanced at each of them, then said, "I know because I . . . I killed Cary's mother." Almost a whisper.

All the oxygen seemed to leave the room, followed by a new profound silence.

Cary squeezed her hands together beneath her chin, fighting new tears.

Recognizing Cary's momentary inability to speak, Webster challenged Shapiro, saying, "Surely you're not serious."

Shapiro held up his hands. "Oh, I didn't drive the car. That's not what I mean. I don't even know who did. The people who run things here don't work that way. Didn't then and they don't now."

"Then what did you mean when you said you killed her?" Cary asked, finding her voice.

"You get your instructions on the phone," Shapiro said. "You never recognize the voice, but you learn, early on, to do what you're told and keep your mouth shut."

"So, how could you kill my mother if you weren't in the car?" Cary could feel her chest muscles tighten, anger starting to burn through her body.

"I guess you could say I killed your mother by not refusing to do what they told me."

"Why are you telling us all this now?" Cary wanted to know what was behind his admission.

"It's obvious, isn't it? They took my wife from me. She didn't do anything." Shapiro was becoming agitated. He got up, walking to the window again. This time Zabeth followed him and sat down at his side, looking back at them. Shapiro stood there, his hands out, his expression pleading for their understanding. "Carolette just wanted to talk to the daughter of an old friend. And they came here to her home and killed her." He paused. "First to keep her quiet, and second, to warn me not to talk."

"How do you know someone intended to kill Mrs. Shapiro? You seem sure it wasn't a robbery," Webster said.

He focused on Webster. "I went to see an old associate last night and persuaded him to tell me what happened. He was one of the men in my garage when Carolette came home last Thursday. They killed her because of what they thought she might tell Cary. But Carolette didn't know anything. She just had questions." Looking at Cary, he added, "Like you."

Cary watched him closely. He had calmed down some by now and returned to the desk. Zabeth seemed to sense her master's mental turmoil. She followed him and sat beside his chair, allowing him to gently caress her ears as he talked to them.

"The people who call the shots wanted you to stop asking questions. They were concerned that Carolette could tell you just enough to make you want to keep searching for your mother's killer. And," he motioned toward Webster, "they were having trouble stopping you because he was with you. They moved on to an easier target to stop the flow of information."

An anxious hush fell over the room as Cary thought about Shapiro's admission. Finally, she stood and walked over to the hallway door. Shapiro watched her, as did Zabeth.

After several moments, Webster turned toward Cary, but spoke to Shapiro,

"You keep saying *They*. Who *are* they?"

Cary wondered why she hadn't thought to ask that question.

Shapiro glanced back and forth between them before answering. "I believe it's Eddie and Johnny, but I really don't know for sure. I know that's hard to believe, but I never really wanted to know – until now." He leaned back again.

Cary figured that was all she was going to get from him about the organization. She turned the discussion back to Janice Talmer. "You still didn't say how you killed my mother," she asked, pressing on.

As if his head was aching, he raked his hands across it and through his hair, massaging his scalp. "I might as well have painted a big "X" on Janice's back that night," Shapiro told her. "The person who called asked me if Carolette had a bright coat of some sort. Without thinking, I told him she had a red, full-length one. He told me to make sure she wore it that evening when she went for her walk with Janice.

"They knew the girls went for a stroll almost every evening. I thought they wanted to scare Janice. If I had said 'No', maybe things would have turned out differently." Once again he had tears in his eyes. He swiped at them with the tips of his fingers.

"Why did you go along with them?" Webster asked.

Shapiro took a deep breath and sighed. He folded his hands on the desk, leaving Zabeth to return to her bed. "It started out simple enough," he said. "I did favors for them and sometimes they did things for me. The favors they did for me helped my business. They furnished temporary labor or trucks when I needed them – even sent some new customers my way. Things were already going pretty good, but then after your mother was killed, my business really took off. I had trouble keeping up with it. Carolette had to help me." Cary and Webster exchanged glances, remembering what Webster's friend had told him.

"How did you contact them when *you* needed something?" Webster asked.

"A guy who worked for me acted as a go-between." Shapiro didn't appear inclined to say more.

Cary guessed there was a lot he wasn't saying, but she let him continue at his own pace, fearful now of doing anything that might silence him.

"Sometimes things happened and I didn't know if they were behind it or not. For example, my biggest competitor's warehouse burned down, and it turned out he was underinsured. He wasn't able to get financing to rebuild and restock, so he went under. Most of his customers came over to me. The fire marshals said an electrical problem caused the fire, but I've always suspected it was more than that, like maybe another one of their favors."

He turned back to her. "I've always felt guilty about your mother, Cary."

She watched him, judging his sincerity.

"What kind of favors did you do for them?" Webster asked.

Shapiro shrugged. "There were packages to pick up or deliveries to hold. Sometimes we included a shipment of some sort with one of ours. On several occasions, someone rode to some other city with one of our drivers. It varied, and it never seemed to be a big thing. We seldom had to go out of our way to do anything for them. Someone would just call and say they needed an errand. I always knew it was them."

"That's it?" Cary said. "Pickups and deliveries?"

"Mostly," he said. Then he added, "The other way I've helped over the years is with money. My business has been quite successful. I've made lots of political contributions to Johnny's campaigns for myself and Carolette and for my employees. My money has also been used to build and to buy all sorts of things for Johnny and Eddie. Someone would let me know what they wanted and I would pay to have someone get it. I've paid dearly for their help."

"Did they ever request another *big* favor?" Cary asked.

"Never," Shapiro said. She could tell by his frown and raised eyebrows that he knew what she was asking.

"Do you think there's someone over Periot and the Superintendent?" Webster asked.

Cary leaned forward, eager to hear this answer.

"I don't think so," Shapiro said, "but I really *don't* know. I never wanted to know."

"Why don't you go to the police with what you know?" Webster asked.

Shapiro's shoulders sagged at the question. Cary thought it was because it made him face what he needed to do. "I've decided on a different approach, one that doesn't involve the city government or the police."

"What will you do?" Webster asked him.

"I have plans," he said. "I'm going to make things right."

"Won't that be dangerous?" Cary inquired.

"Not the way I'm going to do it."

Shapiro then reached over and picked up one of the envelopes on the desk. He handed it across to Cary. "This is for you. It's something I wrote after your mother died. There are also some other papers I thought you should have, as well as some photographs. Some are individual pictures of your mother and others include her in the scene. I think you'll enjoy them. I hope so. I've written some things for you, too. It's the least I can do, considering the way things have turned out."

She took the envelope and placed it on her lap. It had her name written on it. According to Shapiro, it would tell her more about her mother. Her eyes were misty again.

She opened her purse, folded the envelope carefully into it, taking care not to bend the photographs.

Webster gently put his hand on her arm. She turned her head toward him and smiled through her tears.

Shapiro, for his part, seemed pleased about his decision.

Zabeth, her ears perked up, got up from her bed and went out into the hallway where she trotted toward the back of the house. She barked once and Shapiro called out her name, explaining to Cary and Webster, "The neighbor's cat comes up on our back porch, and she wants to go out and chase it. Happens all the time."

***

When Shapiro handed Cary the envelope, Webster glimpsed a second one addressed to someone at the *Times-Picayune*. Knowing the situation now, he bet the envelope contained some of the same information Shapiro was giving to Cary. Shapiro had obviously decided to tear a hole in the past and probably in the future, too, for some pretty important people. He must know the possible consequences. He could, and probably would, lose his business. Worse yet, he could even lose his life.

The man appeared to be ill. There were bags under his eyes and his entire body carried a look of defeat. Cary's expression seemed troubled, too. Webster reminded himself to ask her about it later.

"Are you sure you've given a sufficient amount of thought to what you're planning? Is this really the way to handle it?" Webster asked. He nodded toward the remaining envelope.

Shapiro caught Webster's eyes and held them, "I know what I'm doing."

"Can I help? Can I change your mind?"

"This is something I have to do myself. I should have done it a long time ago. I've known it all along. I wasn't strong enough to make the decision until now."

Shapiro rose from his chair, walked around the desk, and shook Webster's hand. "Thanks for the offer. Maybe if I'd known someone like you when all this started . . ."

Shapiro turned to Cary. "As I've said, you resemble your mother a great deal. She was attractive, too. You'll see it in the photographs." He paused, and then said, "I would love to give you a hug, but under the circumstances . . ." He smiled at her.

Webster watched as Cary gazed at Shapiro for a long moment, then stepped forward and put her arms around him, her anger spent. Neither of them said anything, but they both had tears in their eyes. After a few moments, they released each other and stepped back.

Webster could see compassion etched on Cary's face.

"It was another time," she said to Shapiro. "You're a different person now."

"Thank you." He smiled. "I think the information in the envelope will make a difference. I'm doing it for Carolette."

He walked them to the door, said goodbye and waved as they walked away. Webster doubted they would see him again.

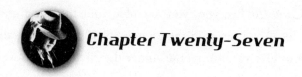

Chapter Twenty-Seven

Shapiro watched Cary and Webster start down the sidewalk toward the iron gate. Closing the front door, he turned toward the back of the house. He needed to hurry; the other envelope had to be mailed, and there was one more visit to make like the one last night. He wanted to go see Budrow, the second person in his garage last Thursday. For Shapiro's plan to work, it all had to be finished before eight o'clock.

As he walked down the hallway, Zabeth didn't come to greet him. *That's odd.* He wondered what kind of mischief she was in.

As he passed his study he heard a sound, and his heart skipped a beat when he realized someone was there.

"Come in, Alex. You have visitors." Recognizing the voice, Shapiro felt a touch of anger that they would invade his home. The feeling intensified as he realized why they were there. He hesitated, then stepped through the door. He was through running.

Two men were waiting for him – one sitting in his chair, the other in one of the wingbacks in front of the desk. Shapiro knew them both; he quickly resigned himself to their purpose for being there. He was relieved the young couple was gone.

The man sitting behind his desk was Frank Pinton, one of the top enforcers in the Mayor's inner circle. The other man was short, younger, probably in his late twenties, and less well known to Shapiro. His name was Mazou.

"What have you done with Zabeth?" Shapiro asked accusingly.

"Dat's your dog's name?" Mazou asked. "Funny name. Da dog's okay. I tied it in da kitchen next to its bed."

Shapiro switched his attention to the other man. Pinton had opened the envelope Shapiro had prepared for the *Times-Picayune* reporter. He had removed the contents, spread them out across the desk and started examining them.

"This isn't a very nice thing to do to the people who helped you succeed all these years, Alex." Shapiro didn't comment.

"Sit down," Frank said, motioning to the other chair in front of the desk as he glanced back down at the papers.

"I don't want to sit. I'm comfortable standing."

"Sit, damn it!" the man roared without looking up.

Shapiro stared at him for a moment and then walked over and sat down in the empty chair. He wasn't afraid of what they would do to him. He was just disappointed that his package wouldn't make it to the newspaper. He felt a twinge of satisfaction, though, reassured that he had put the note in Cary's envelope in case this one didn't make it to its destination.

When they were all seated, Frank spoke in the same calm voice he had used earlier. "What did you hope to accomplish? Did you really think we wouldn't be watching you? Do you think we're stupid?" His voice was rising. "Do you, Alex?"

Shapiro merely blinked. The question didn't require an answer.

"No, I guess you don't," the man said. "You just didn't think we would come calling this soon, did you? Well, obviously we can't allow you to send this to the newspaper, can we?" He shook his head and glanced up at Shapiro. "And what should we do with you?" Frank sat watching Shapiro, apparently expecting an answer.

"You're going to do what you will. I can't stop you."

"No, you can't, can you?" the man agreed in a mocking tone.

He slapped the desk with an open palm, no doubt to unnerve Shapiro. "We should make sure you do what you had intended all along. Yes, I think you should put an end to your sorry life, don't you?"

"How do you suggest I do that?" Shapiro asked.

"I recommend using the pistol you shot Victor with last night," Frank said. Then he chuckled at the momentary look of revelation on Shapiro's face.

"Oh, yes. We knew you were there. I had a couple of our people keeping an eye on you." He laughed again at Shapiro's surprise. "Let me give you this, Alex. I never thought you had it in you. You're a lot tougher than I ever imagined." With a grin he added, "I salute you."

Frank pulled a pair of latex gloves out of his coat pocket and put them on. "Where do you keep the pistol, Alex?" he asked.

Shapiro hesitated, then said, "In the bottom drawer, in a lockbox." He motioned toward the right side of the desk.

"Give me the key."

Shapiro reached into his pocket for the keys and tossed them across the desk. Frank unlocked the drawer, placing the lockbox on the desk. Opening it and rummaging through its contents, he satisfied himself that everything he expected to find was there. Finished, he bundled the papers with a rubber band and slipped them into his coat pocket, saying to Shapiro, "I probably should keep these, don't you think? We wouldn't want them to get into the wrong hands."

When he was done, Pinton lifted the pistol from the box. Shapiro's eyes followed the man's hand and the weapon. Pinton rose from his chair and motioned for Shapiro to come around the desk and sit there. Mazou rose and reached for Shapiro's arm as he stood up. With an angry look, Shapiro shook off Mazou's hand and considered trying to run or to fight them. They were watching him closely, and he realized they would only overpower him. The results would be the same. He might as well retain his dignity. This was what he had planned for himself anyway.

When Shapiro sat down in his desk chair, Frank told him to close his eyes. When he did, he could feel the man gripping his right hand and arm, putting the pistol into his palm and raising the weapon to his temple.

A few moments after he closed his eyes, Shapiro's mind experienced a brilliant flash – then nothing . . .

***

Shapiro's lifeless body slumped to the left and back in the chair. Frank released his arm and the pistol slipped from Shapiro's hand, coming to rest on the floor beneath the desk.

Frank then searched all the drawers in the desk again. He took special care to check folders in the file drawer. Then Frank, with Mazou's help, carefully searched the entire room one last time.

Satisfied they hadn't missed anything, the two men left the house, locking the back door behind them. Mazou untied Zabeth; she watched them from her bed as they walked out the kitchen door.

Frank took one last look around outside. *All clear.*

Chapter Twenty-Eight

Marion Douglas Cobreaux had been sitting in his downtown office for over an hour, waiting for Frank Pinton's call. Frank had suggested they keep a watch on Shapiro after his surprising escapade at Victor's the night before. The watch had paid off.

Frank had kept Cobreaux posted throughout the morning. With the Warren woman and her boyfriend's second visit in as many days, he concluded Shapiro had become too great a liability. Cobreaux's boss agreed.

Now Cobreaux waited. He drummed his fingers on the desk until they were sore. Thinking about other things didn't help either. He realized if this didn't get resolved soon, nothing else would matter. He knew Big Eddie and the Mayor considered the problem his; they expected him to find a satisfactory resolution. Now he could lose everything.

The phone finally rang; Cobreaux scooped it up. "We took care of it, Boss. The 'Shapiro Problem' has been handled."

"Where the hell are you?"

"We stopped for a drink," Frank told him. "We're at The Irish Pub a few blocks from the office,"

"You can celebrate later. Did you find anything in Shapiro's desk?"

"Yeah, Boss. Lots of stuff."

"Well, get the hell out of that bar and bring it to me. *Then* maybe you and Mazou can take the rest of the afternoon off." Cobreaux slammed the phone down.

***

When they reached Mr. C's location, Frank and Mazou were ushered into his office. Frank gave his boss the papers from the lockbox and the envelope from Shapiro's desk.

"The young couple was leaving when we got inside," Frank said, watching for a reaction. "They were ready to walk down the sidewalk."

Mr. C ignored his comment and merely took the envelope, opening it and dumping the contents on his desk.

"Take a break while I look over these papers," he said. "Sit."

As Mr. C examined the material, he gradually sat up straighter in his chair. At one point he picked up the envelope and checked the address.

When he finished, he looked at Frank and Mazou.

"Did you go through his desk? Are you sure you got everything?"

"We got into the house and slipped into his study as he was saying goodbye to the couple. While he was seeing them out, I went through all the drawers except for the file drawer and the one where he kept the lockbox." Frank was already nervous; Mr. C's accusing stare had him on edge. Though he tried, Frank couldn't keep his hands still. And he couldn't stop talking. His mouth seemed to have a mind of its own.

"When Shapiro came back inside, I got his keys and took all the papers from the lockbox while I was talking with him. After he shot himself . . ." Frank smiled at his play on words, "I went through Shapiro's file drawer. The records were just usual stuff. The only items left in the lockbox were a few things he was hoarding: old coins, junk like that. Figured I better leave them so things would look normal. We got everything important; I'm sure of it."

Mr. C narrowed his eyes as Frank spoke. Frank loosened his collar. It felt as though it had started shrinking. Beads of sweat popped out on his forehead, too.

"What about the girl? Did he give her anything?"

"No. Well, I don't think so." Frank thought about the question and hesitated. "We didn't get into the house until the girl and her friend were leaving. We had to contend with Shapiro's dog, too. I didn't see much, but I don't think the woman was carrying anything but her purse." Fidgeting in his chair, Frank noticed that Mazou appeared nervous about the questioning, too.

"But you're really not sure about the girl, are you?" He stared at Frank, waiting for a response. Frank ran a finger along his collar. Now the damn starch was making his neck itch. "You're not sure, are you?" Mr. C shouted at Frank as he slapped the desk.

Startled, Frank jumped up and moved around behind his chair, fearful of what Mr. C might do. Mazou stayed glued to his seat.

"Here's what we need to do," their leader said, glaring at them as he stood and walked around the desk. "Go back out there and look for the girl and her boyfriend. When you find them, do whatever it takes to get rid of them. Just make sure they don't have any information." He pointed at the envelope and its contents.

Frank frowned. "You want them dead?"

As if to give himself time to reconsider, Mr. C turned to the window and ran his fingers through his hair in a quick jerk of frustration. Then he turned back to them, and, in a voice that was eerily calm, said, "No, but get them out of this town. Do whatever you need to, short of killing them. We've got too damn many bodies showing up already. Now get moving." He motioned toward the door.

Mazou almost ran out of the office. Despite his racing heart, Frank was careful to take his time. Still, hearing the door slam behind them, he knew the boss meant business.

***

Cobreaux watched Frank and Mazou leave before he walked back to his chair and sat down. He was concerned that after all these years, things were starting to unravel. If it took every man he had, he could not and would not allow that to happen. Cobreaux felt the hairs stand up on his neck. He shook his head, chasing cobwebs, and reached for the phone.

Staring out the window, he hesitated, then punched in a number. "Shapiro's handled," he said when the call was answered. "I've sent Frank out to find the girl and see if she got away with any of Shapiro's papers. After that, I told him to get her and her friend out of New Orleans. I'll keep you informed."

"How are you going to stop her and her questions?"

Cobreaux hesitated. "If Frank can't get the job done, I'll pick her up, along with the boyfriend, and try to scare them into leaving New Orleans. If that doesn't work, we may have to give them a permanent ticket out."

"The boss doesn't want that."

"We may have no choice. I understand he doesn't want the girl hurt, but there may be no other way."

"Find one."

"I'll work on it."

As Cobreaux hung up, he wondered if he had enough money to get permanently lost. Some days this job wasn't worth the trouble.

***

When Cary and Webster left Shapiro's house, they headed toward the central business district via St. Charles Avenue. They had several things to do. Ed Lawrence at Orleans Laboratories and Ms. Newell at the doctor's office were both on the agenda.

"I can't help feeling sorry for Mr. Shapiro," Cary said. "He's lost everything dear to him; Carolette was his world."

She hadn't figured out exactly what Shapiro intended to do after they had left him, but she had a sneaking suspicion Webster knew. He always seemed to be three steps ahead in his thinking and reasoning. *There has to be an explanation for that.*

"He has a plan," Webster said, confirming her thoughts. "He's going to blow the whistle on everyone and everything."

"How do you know?" she asked, glancing around them. "You sound so sure."

"I saw another envelope on his desk. It was like the one he gave you, and it was addressed to someone at the *Times-Picayune.* I bet when you look in the envelope, you're going to find evidence about your mother and probably a lot more. There's no telling what he knows. And no doubt he's been close to some pretty unpleasant dealings. Mr. Shapiro probably knows where a lot of skeletons are buried. At the least, he knows where to look."

"Pull over," she told Webster. "Let's find out what's in the envelope."

He pulled onto a side street, found a space and parked, all the while watching for anyone who might be following them. Cary already had the envelope open. She immediately reached for the pictures, dropping the envelope in her lap. She began scanning through them.

Webster took a quick peek at them, but after a few seconds, reached for the envelope. "Do you mind?"

"No, go ahead." She was entranced with the photographs of her mother. At long last, Cary could actually *see* her.

She went back to the first snapshot, gazed at it, then stared out the window, her throat tightening at the thought of her mother's young life cut short.

She returned to the pictures. Janice was pretty. They looked alike, she and her mother. Seeing actual pictures made Cary realize how much: the same high cheekbones, the same dark hair and eyes – and both were tall. She noticed Webster peering over her shoulder at the pictures.

When their eyes met, he quickly looked away.

"I'm sorry, I couldn't help it." He hesitated, glancing from Cary to the photographs. "You look so much like her. She's . . . gorgeous." He sounded trapped, like a little boy caught up in something bigger than himself. Cary's eyes lingered on his. That was all the encouragement he needed.

He leaned over, tenderly kissing her. His kiss took her down, drowning her in its emotion. Too soon it ended, and he didn't offer more. As they slowly parted, Cary couldn't help herself; she ran a finger along the line his jaw. She could feel the fine stubble on his chin. She smiled when he took a deep breath, closing his eyes as he did. If they continued on this path, it couldn't bring anything but complications. *Neither of them was prepared for that.*

As though reading her thoughts, Webster gave her one last meaningful look and turned back to Shapiro's papers. He had pulled them out and discarded the empty envelope. The documents were bundled, a rubber band holding them together.

On top was a note to Cary and him. Webster read it to her.

> **Cary Warren and Mike Webster:**
> **Enclosed is an assortment of papers, copies, and other information.**
> **If you should learn that I am no longer alive prior to eight o'clock this evening – Tuesday – please make sure a copy of these papers and information reaches the Times-Picayune. I am aware that two reporters have been investigating certain areas of city government and I believe this information will aid them.**
> **Thank you for your help.**
> **And Cary, I hope you "find" your mother.**
> **Alex Shapiro**

Finally, as Webster finished, Cary put the photographs aside and picked up some of the papers he had already scanned. Among them was a copy of a letter Shapiro had written to Carolette. It was dated nearly twenty-five years ago. They read it together in silence, then exchanged a glance.

The letter laid out in detail what Shapiro had told them. It was all about the red coat and how he had made sure Carolette wore it on the night Janice was killed. The words attempted to explain how he thought his associates just wanted to scare Janice. Shapiro acknowledged his guilt and asked Carolette's forgiveness.

Yet, for all those years, Shapiro had kept his questionable actions a secret – until now.

Along with his confession, numerous other papers and copies of articles detailed various misdeeds. Shapiro had written additional commentary to accompany the basic information. He named several present and former city and state officials. Much of the narrative involved specific crimes; other parts pointed to acts that were not totally aboveboard or were linked to other offenses.

"Look here," Cary said. "In several instances, witnesses dropped out at the last minute under suspicious circumstances."

Reading over her shoulder, Webster whistled. "It says the witnesses were often minor players."

Cary continued aloud. "Other potential, more visible witnesses often changed their testimony, supposedly remembering things differently, or, in many cases, refusing to testify at all. Speculation pointed to most of them having been threatened or bought off." Shapiro had written detailed explanations to go with almost every article and other pieces of information.

A last sheet listed several corporations and holding companies with their states of incorporation. The list didn't make any sense to Cary. She showed the page to Webster, and he shook his head as he read the names. These were obviously entities that the political group had invested in over the years. Trebeck Corporation, Cary and Webster's own employer, was listed under one of the holding companies.

Whether he realized it or not, Shapiro had given Webster one, *or maybe* both, of the reasons for his being at Trebeck. Obviously, the New Orleans group owned Trebeck Corporation. And given Cary's connection to Periot, she was almost certainly the person they were watching at Trebeck. That should be easy enough to verify now that they had Shapiro's list.

On the same page, there was a list of foreign bank accounts keyed to the entities. *Talk about complete and up-to-date information.*

Cary set the bundle down, stunned by its depth and organization. Shapiro had done a masterful job. The *Times-Picayune* would have a field day with his papers.

She found it interesting that Shapiro wanted the information to go to reporters at the *Times-Picayune*. His detailed material would lead a good investigative reporter such as Emile LeBlanc to the evidence and tie together the pieces of several puzzles. A number of people could end up in prison when this material hit the streets.

Cary had finished with the pictures so she read Shapiro's letter to Carolette over again. When she finished, she gazed at Webster and said, "He really did it, didn't he? He killed Janice Talmer."

Webster leaned back against the door before answering. "A lot of people killed your mother, Cary," he said, gently touching her cheek with his fingers. He moved his hand away, saying, "Shapiro was just one of them."

She picked up the note. It pleased her that they were taking the story to LeBlanc.

Now that they had finished scanning Shapiro's papers and discussing them, they were ready to see how the DNA tests had turned out.

***

Webster called Ed Lawrence at Orleans Laboratories. Lawrence told them to come on over; he could meet with them when they arrived.

Before they headed for Metairie, however, Webster called Pam Newell at Dr. Davison's office. When Newell answered, she told them to come on by; she had good news. They decided to see her first since she was closer. A few minutes later, they were seated in her office. "The Troy Weaver file made it to my desk," she said, excitement lacing her words.

"Oh?"

"Yes, and there was a test slide in it with enough scrapings to do several DNA studies," she said. "I've spoken with Dr. Davison and since this slide didn't really belong to Mr. Weaver, Dr. Davison told me we could release it to you. The slide was originally labeled as evidence from an accident. *But*, since no one had requested it in the last twenty-five years, he agreed to let it go."

With the slide in their possession, Webster thanked her and they went out to the SUV. Cary high-fived him as they crossed the parking lot.

From there, they headed for Orleans Laboratories location where Ed Lawrence was waiting for them. He invited them in and placed several charts on the desk. "We analyzed Cary's saliva," he said, "and Jack Robbins' people analyzed the cigar. The DNA extracted from each gives us the information you see here."

The charts appeared complicated to Cary. Lawrence described them and explained the results. He rattled off statistics, including some extremely large numbers, then gave his conclusions – narrowing everything down to two sets of charts. Cary realized those were her own and Periot's.

"These," he said, pointing at them, "are for comparison. In my opinion, the two individuals are direct relatives – this one being the parent and this one," he pointed to Cary's chart, "the offspring." Cary and Webster glanced at each other. She tried to hide it, but she realized Webster could see the news had affected her. *Johnny Periot is my biological father.* It wouldn't hold up in court because of the way they obtained the cigar, but they weren't going to court. *My mother told me the truth.* She glanced at Webster through misty eyes.

Webster asked Lawrence if he could run one more test. He pulled out the slide from Dr. Davison's office and handed it to Lawrence.

"This one's twenty-five years old," Webster told him.

"We've done several older than that. What should we compare it to?" Lawrence asked.

"Compare it to this one," Webster indicated the offspring's chart they had discussed moments earlier – Cary's analysis.

"Who's going to pay for all this?" Lawrence asked. "I forgot to ask Jack about it when I spoke with him earlier."

Webster glanced at Cary and then told Lawrence, "We'll get the Feds to write you a check."

"Works for me," Lawrence said.

Cary looked back and forth between the two of them, her mind obviously spinning. Webster grinned at her.

Damn him. He's so arrogant.

Webster thanked Lawrence for all his help, then Cary let Webster steer her out to their vehicle.

"Why would the Feds be willing to pay for these tests?"

"Because they're nice people?"

"Yeah, right! Really. Why?"

"Jack Robbins works for them. This comes under his job expenses."

She had no idea what he was talking about. Maybe he'd tell her sometime.

Chapter Twenty-Nine

With no immediate plans, they decided to stop, get a sandwich, and discuss their next move. Webster drove them from Orleans Laboratories back to Veterans Highway where they located a little seafood restaurant. After the waiter had taken their orders, Cary leaned in. "We should make copies of everything Shapiro gave me.

Their waiter appeared with a plate of hush puppies for them to munch on while they waited for their sandwiches.

"What do you think we ought to do with the originals?" Cary asked, reaching for one of the hors d'oeuvres. "We can't take a chance on losing them." As she chewed on one of the spicy appetizers, they hashed out the details, deciding to overnight Shapiro's originals to Greg, then set up a meeting with Emile Blanc to go over what they had learned from Shapiro.

Sandwiches arrived, and in no time, they finished their food; each of them leaned back, contented and full. Cary had needed a short break from the uproar of the last few days. Once more she thought of the snapshots. She had gone through them two more times. How could she mourn someone she never knew? Yet she did. In her mind, she compared what she was feeling now with what she felt when her mom and dad were killed. She glanced up to see Webster studying her.

"Janice Talmer really was attractive, wasn't she?"

"Yes," he said smiling. "You have good genes – at least from your mother." Then he said something that tugged at her heart. "I think it would be okay," Webster told her, "if you referred to Janice as your mother." Then he put his hand on hers and gave it a squeeze. Even through her tears, she could see this man's unique inner spirit.

***

Webster started up the SUV and drove out to the street. Once they were moving, he pulled out his phone and called the reporter.

"Can you come down to my office?" LeBlanc asked immediately.

"When?"

"Now. We'll talk when you get here." The phone went dead.

When they arrived, LeBlanc ushered them in. "Sit down," he said, looking past them and then shutting the door. When they were seated, he asked, "Have you heard about Alex Shapiro?"

"What about him?" Webster asked as he glanced at Cary. Her eyes were suddenly wide, her concern evident.

"The police and emergency people are at his house rat now," LeBlanc said. "They say he shot hisself. He gave da staff da day off, but one of da maids had gone back to da house for somethin'. She found him about twelve-thirty. He was sittin' at his desk in da study wit' a gunshot wound to his head. His pistol was on da floor."

"How did you find out?" Webster inquired.

"Came over a scanner here at da paper." LeBlanc said. "It's already on da wire services, too. They're talkin' about him bein' da Mayor's lifelong buddy and all."

"Can you keep something under your hat?" Webster asked. He glanced over at Cary and saw that her face and lips had paled; she was shaking her head as though unable to comprehend what she was hearing.

"Well, can you?" Webster said, glancing back at the reporter.

"If I haf' to."

Seeing how shaken Cary was, Webster placed his hand on hers as he spoke with LeBlanc. "Here's what you need to know," Webster said. "We just left Shapiro's house a couple of hours ago." LeBlanc's eyes grew wide with surprise. "Shapiro called Cary this morning and asked if we could come by. After meeting with us yesterday, he had decided to tell her some things – information he thought Cary needed to know that only *he* could tell her."

"*Today?*" LeBlanc sounded incredulous. "You saw Shapiro today? You talked to him *twice* since we met yesterday afternoon?"

"Yes, but the thing is," Webster said, "we were there until a little after twelve. He must have shot himself immediately after we left. If . . . *if* that's what happened: if he really shot himself, I mean."

"You probably need to tell da police about meetin' wit' him," LeBlanc said, rising and walking around to sit on the edge of the desk.

"I don't think so," Webster told him.

Cary, who had been on the sidelines to this point, appeared restless and tears pooled in her eyes. Webster gave her hand a gentle squeeze.

She shrugged off his hand, wiped her eyes, and squared her shoulders. She was already back in the game.

"Why not go to da police?" LeBlanc asked.

Webster leaned his head back, closing his eyes. It had been a hard several hours. There was a reason he couldn't go to the police, a purely personal one he couldn't divulge: where and how he had met the Mayor. To cover, he said, "Because I'm not sure where the police stand. I don't trust them. Remember Periot's friendship with the Superintendent."

"Yeah, but . . ."

"Not yet," Webster told him. "Take my word for it." Webster remembered what the Mayor had told him. *I never forget a face.* This would not be a good time for Periot to recall where they met.

Cary murmured her agreement.

"Okay, I'm good wit' dat," LeBlanc said. "What else ya got?"

"We have some things to show you," Webster told him.

LeBlanc peered out the frosted glass front of his office and then said, "Let's go someplace more private to talk. Sometimes these walls got ears."

"Let's get out of here then," Webster said. "The fewer people involved, the better."

Catching them both off guard, LeBlanc asked, "Do you think ya'll can trust me now?" This appeared to be directed at Cary.

"Ah . . . Sure," she said, "I guess so. Why?"

"There's something I want to show you."

"Now?" Cary said.

"Yeah, in about an hour."

"Where do you want us to meet you?"

"Canal Street where it goes under I-10. I'll take my ca' and pick you up at da northbound lanes. When can you be there?"

Webster glanced at Cary, then back, and said, "Three-thirty? We need to do something before we meet you."

"Catch ya then."

Five minutes later they were on the sidewalk heading to their vehicle.

"So, we're going to get the copies made, send the originals to Greg, then meet LeBlanc?"

"Yeah," he said, "and I need to tell you something." He paused. "I think I knew Shapiro planned to commit suicide when we left there. I didn't tell you that."

"But what about his note?"

"Yeah. That bothers me, too."

They climbed into the SUV and headed out. Webster was careful to take the backstreets until he was sure no one was following them.

Opening Shapiro's envelope, Cary took out the note and read it aloud before turning to Webster, "He said if something happened to him before eight tonight, we should get a copy of these papers to the *Times-Picayune.*"

Webster dodged a car moving over from the middle lane and dropped back to let the driver in before reminding her, "Notice the note said eight tonight. That sounds like he had some things to do, things that would take some time – maybe several hours. He wanted us to know that."

Cary reached out and grabbed Webster's arm. "My, God. He wanted us to know his timeline in case someone got to him. He had things he needed to do, *and* he wanted to be sure these papers reached the *Times-Picayune.*"

"Yeah, that's how I read it, too."

"What *did* he need to do? That's an eight hour gap."

"First, he needed to mail the envelope." Webster palmed the steering wheel. "But that wouldn't take long. What else?"

"Maybe he needed to contact someone." She raked her dark curls back with her fingers, flipping the hair over her shoulder. "*Or maybe* it was more than just contacting someone," she said. "Maybe he . . ." Cary glanced at Webster, leaving her thoughts unspoken.

"If someone else did this to him, it had to have happened right after we left," Webster said. "I'm going on the theory that someone killed him and made it look like a suicide, and they did it before he had a chance to leave the house."

She looked at him for a moment, her lips drawn and pale, then said in a lowered voice, "Whoever did it could have already been in the house when we left him." They looked at each other and the air suddenly seemed cooler to Cary. From his wide eyes and furrowed brow, she could tell that Webster also recognized they may have avoided peril by leaving Shapiro's house exactly when they did.

As they both breathed a sigh of relief, Cary pointed out a UPS store. Webster swerved across a lane of traffic, causing a couple of horns to blow and one angry driver to wave an obscene gesture in their direction. He pulled up in front of the facility and parked.

"I wouldn't have been surprised if he had committed suicide," she said. "Remember, I told you he was lost without Carolette."

"I remember," Webster said. "We were both concerned for him."

"It's sad," she said.

"We better hurry if we're going to get everything done and still meet LeBlanc on time. He opened his door with Cary on his heels. They went inside the store where Webster handled the copying while Cary prepared an envelope for the overnight run to Greg's house. With the task complete, they drove to meet LeBlanc.

Arriving at the pick-up point, Webster found a parking space only a block away and they hurried to meet Emile. He pulled to the curb as they were about thirty yards away. He touched his horn, and Cary waved as they walked over. Webster opened the front door for her and then slid into the back seat. "Good timing," he said, "we just got here."

"Hear anything new about Shapiro?" Cary asked.

"No one I've talked to seems surprised," LeBlanc said as he merged into the line of cars. "Now, what are these papers you were you going to show me?" he asked, changing the subject.

Cary slid Shapiro's documents across the seat to him.

The reporter flipped through the papers with one eye on the street and the cars around them. Examining them, he let out a low whistle. "He's been keepin' records for a long time."

"Yeah. That's what we thought, too. Pretty detailed, don't you think?" Webster said.

"I'll say."

LeBlanc switched lanes suddenly to avoid a delivery truck. Papers scattered. Webster and Cary held on as LeBlanc fought for control of his vehicle.

"Hey, Dumbo. Watch whatcha doin'."

As LeBlanc changed lanes, Cary began collecting the papers. With most of them in hand, she said, "Why don't we wait until we stop to look at the rest of this."

Webster agreed, and LeBlanc said, "We're almost there anyway. It'll wait."

"By the way, where are we going?" Webster asked.

***

They had reached a large cemetery on Canal Boulevard. LeBlanc slowed, entering the burial grounds beneath a large arch with the word "GREENWOOD" cast in iron. Cary gazed out across acres of tombs and graves spread to the sides and in front of them. Monuments and markers of all shapes covered every open space.

Cary thought immediately of her mother. Had LeBlanc found her grave? *She had a sneaking suspicion.*

Glancing over, Emile confirmed her thoughts. "Cary, have you wondered where Janice Talmer was buried?"

It took a moment to collect herself, then she managed to say, "Oh Emile, I have, but no one seemed to know. Periot even told me he heard she was cremated."

Cary tore her eyes from LeBlanc's and stared out across the thousands of tombs. *The City of the Dead.* She had read that cemeteries were often called that in New Orleans.

Now she turned back toward the reporter, mist clouding her vision. "She's here, isn't she? My mother's here."

Typical for him, Webster reached over the seat without saying anything and touched her shoulder, his fingers firm but gentle.

Oddly enough, the cemetery was beautiful in its own way. The afternoon sun danced off the monuments of white and light-colored marble. The grass had been recently cut; everything was neat and well cared for. Roads and walkways allowed easy access to most of the burial sites. Some appeared new, while others showed rain marks and were obviously very old. A few had crumbled at their corners, leaving dark, foreboding holes as witness to their state of disrepair.

There were gravestones of every size and twist of the imagination. Cary was astounded at their complexity, but mostly she felt as though there was a weight on her chest. She knew the feeling would only go away by seeing where her mother had come to rest . . . twenty-five years ago.

LeBlanc had been watching her. "She's in this place," he said as he stopped the car. "Right down there." He pointed toward one of the long rows of tombs. "Come on. I'll take you to her."

They climbed out of the vehicle. With LeBlanc leading the way and Webster walking beside Cary, the little procession made its way to a simple burial site. Webster remained silent but walked with his arm around Cary. After a few steps, she leaned into him, knowing she would always remember this gesture, its comfort and its warmth. He seemed to gather her to him. *Yes . . . she'd remember.*

The grave rose two feet above the ground, with ornate concrete walls. Cary's thought was that the space was only slightly larger than a coffin. The area on top of the vault was spread neatly with granite chips that came up level with the top of the walls. Her mother's tomb was encased in a small space, but thought had been given to the design. Someone had cared.

And there was something else. Roses – fresh ones – had been spread across the surface of the grave. The fact that they were not in a vase seemed significant to Cary. In her mind they formed a blanket covering someone special. She wondered if that had been the intent of the one who placed them there.

A simple marker declared this to be the final resting place of her mother. Sudden anger touched her because even the marker was ambiguous. The etchings on the stone only gave a name and a date – the day someone had decided Janice Talmer was in the way – *And a threat to their ambitions*. For whatever reason, they didn't even want the world to know the full name of the person buried there. The marker only stated: J. E. Talmer – October 20, 1982.

Cary stood there, elated that she had found her mother, yet angry at Johnny Periot, Eddie Breunoux, Alex Shapiro, and all the others who had put their dreams and ambitions before the life of this young woman. It seemed Janice's only misdeed had been to love the wrong man, in the wrong place, and at the wrong time.

"Why don't we give Cary a few minutes," Webster suggested. "Will you be all right?" he asked her.

"Yes," she said, touching his arm. "Thank you."

***

LeBlanc had already started walking back to the car. Webster fell in step with him. As they neared the reporter's vehicle, Webster stopped, turned back and gazed toward Cary. He couldn't imagine what she must be feeling. Through Emile, she had found her mother, but what an empty victory. Webster could see her in the distance, sitting on the edge of the tomb now, her head down. Watching her, he felt he was intruding, even from here. He turned and joined Emile.

LeBlanc had retrieved Shapiro's papers from the seat, spreading them on the hood. He had begun examining the material, then stopped to take his glasses from a coat pocket. After perching them on his nose, he said, "He has names, addresses, dates, times, everythin'. There's even a list of foreign bank accounts. This could bury a lot of people. It's big stuff, too, not just nickel and dime."

Then, holding Shapiro's confession, LeBlanc said, "It's sad about Cary's mother. Janice's death started everythin'."

"Yeah, I know," Webster agreed.

"What are you gonna do with all this stuff?" LeBlanc asked. "It's gonna hit da' news at some point, you know."

"I need to tell you something else," Webster said. "When we left his house, Shapiro had another envelope on his desk. It was addressed to someone at your paper. I couldn't see who. I just saw a *Times-Picayune* address. It may show up in the next couple of days, but I doubt it. That would be assuming he got it mailed before he was shot. I'm fairly certain he didn't.

"I believe someone entered his house, took the envelope, then shot Shapiro to make to make it look like suicide." Webster glanced at LeBlanc. "I can't imagine what else they may have been looking for."

Stunned, LeBlanc's face paled and his mouth hung open.

"You should also know," Webster said, "that Cary and I are pretty sure Shapiro was going to commit suicide tonight, anyway."

"Why would you think dat?"

At that moment, Cary came walking back from her mother's grave. They turned, acknowledging her. She went over to LeBlanc and hugged him. Smiling, she said, "You'll never know what this means to me. Thank you." She stooped slightly and kissed him on the cheek. "How did you know where to find her?"

Blushing, he told her, "Most of da cemeteries have a list of their residents dat you can access on-line. I found da name Talmer and da initials. I didn't know if it was her 'til this morning. I drove out here and when I saw da date, I knew this was your mother." He smiled.

"Thanks," she said. "This was special."

LeBlanc turned his attention back to Webster.

"About Shapiro's suicide – I think you'll understand when you read this."

Webster showed Cary what he was going to pass to LeBlanc. She nodded and he handed the copy of Shapiro's note to the reporter.

LeBlanc took it, but was still scanning the papers and other information they had given him. "Even with this, you still don't think he shot hisself?" he asked before he glanced down at the note. Then he read the paper Webster had handed him. His eyes grew wide as he neared the end.

"Damn!" He looked at them and grinned.

"I guess you have an exclusive," Cary told him. "Do you know the other reporter very well? Shapiro's note refers to two reporters."

"Yeah, she works wit' me," he said, concentrating on the note. "Ellen Ellison."

"What if the other envelope never shows up?" Webster asked. "What if we're right and someone shot Shapiro and keeps or destroys the material in the other envelope? Then what?"

"I don't know, but as far as Shapiro's information is concerned, I'll only be using it to help with my research. I'll base da articles on what I find. Shapiro's information will just hep me corroborate any evidence I can gather on my own. Deal?"

"Can you keep us in the loop?" Webster asked.

"I think dat's a given, considerin' what you jus' brought me. I'll drop you two at your ca'. I need to get back to my office and see what else has come in."

LeBlanc dropped them off a few minutes later and they headed for their vehicle.

"What time is it?" Webster asked.

Cary looked down at her watch. "Nearly five o'clock."

"Let's go back out to Landie's and get a little rest. Then we'll plan for tomorrow," he suggested.

What else could happen in one day?

Webster pulled over and parked the SUV on the street when they arrived at Landie's. Out of habit, he hadn't killed the engine as he reached into the back seat for Shapiro's envelope.

Cary had gathered their things and started to get out when a panel truck pulled up alongside them. It stopped in the street, effectively blocking the front of their vehicle.

Webster's past experience kicked in; he evaluated the situation without thinking and whispered to Cary, "Make sure your seatbelt's tight and be ready to hold on."

She did it without a second thought.

Chapter Thirty

Webster glanced outside, aware that the truck would keep them from going forward. Cary waited.

The passenger in the other vehicle, dressed in coveralls, got out and stepped over to Webster's window, indicating he wanted to ask a question. A dirty cap was pulled low over his eyes, yet something about him seemed familiar.

Webster's pulse was drumming as he pushed the button lowering the window.

"Can you point me to Hammond Street?"

Webster hedged. "We're just visiting. We don't live in this neighborhood." He gripped the steering wheel with his left hand.

Out of sight, his right hand clutched his pistol under his thigh. His awareness had jumped about thirty degrees when the truck stopped beside them. Being prepared and observant had frequently saved his life. These attributes had been honed in his old profession.

As he talked with the passenger, the driver covertly slipped out of the truck on the other side and started toward the back of the vehicle. Webster kept a wary eye on him. As the man crossed behind their SUV, Webster glanced at Cary, a warning in his expression.

"Hang on!" he told her, jamming their vehicle into reverse and flooring the accelerator. The tires on the SUV screamed, spinning furiously. As they picked up speed, Webster guided their vehicle backward with an expert's touch, brushing the driver, who then tripped and fell – all this as their vehicle began to accelerate.

The SUV's tires caught and it darted backward into the street, roaring toward an oncoming car. The driver, a woman, leaned on her horn in a state of panic, adding to the confusion. She stomped down on her brakes, skidding toward them as Webster hit his own brakes and spun his steering wheel to the right. This caused the front of the SUV to veer sharply to the left with a loud screech of tires and the smell of burning rubber.

With practiced precision, Webster then shifted from reverse into low, gunning the accelerator again and spinning the steering wheel hard to the left. He caught a glimpse of the two men scrambling after them, but at that point, the SUV had completed a rapid 180 degree left turn and was headed back in the direction

Webster and Cary had come from a couple of minutes earlier.

Under Webster's control, their vehicle gained speed, disappearing quickly from the confused activity taking place in front of Landie's house. In the mirror he watched the action in the street for as long as he could. The woman's car had skidded to a halt, sideways, in the middle of the street, blocking any movement by the panel truck. The two men were frantically struggling to get her out of their way. Their efforts didn't seem to be going very well.

Webster gunned it. "You still with me?" he asked as they sped down the street.

"Barely," she said, her face ashen.

"We have a problem."

"I agree."

He could see her nodding. Webster continued to check behind them. He turned a corner and then quickly made several other turns, putting some distance between them and the panel truck. When they had traveled a couple of miles, he wheeled into a strip mall and up to a gas pump at a convenience store.

"Fill the tank as fast as you can and pay for it," he said, handing her a roll of cash. He could tell she wanted to question him, but she just gave him one of her perplexed looks and nodded.

He jumped out of their vehicle and immediately kneeled down, examining the underside of the SUV. Running his hands underneath it, he worked his way around to the rear of the vehicle. As he slowly felt along the undercarriage above the bumper, Webster's fingers struck an object that moved slightly. He leaned over to get a better view, then reached up, removing a small instrument that had been attached to the SUV. He instantly recognized the Global Positioning Satellite transmitter. *A damned GPS device.*

Webster stood up, and looked around, the gadget in his hand. A FedEx truck was parked three vehicles over, giving him idea. Webster walked behind the truck where he stooped down and tugged at his shoe, glancing around to make sure no one was watching. Satisfied, he quickly attached the GPS device to the truck. Getting to his feet, Webster strolled back to the SUV as though he had simply been tying his shoe. They were safe – for now.

***

Cary came rushing across the parking lot. They jumped into the SUV and darted back out to the street.

Cary had made the ride from Landie's house hanging on for dear life. She had listened to Webster, thank goodness, and hadn't removed her seatbelt before all the action started. Finally, now that the excitement had died down, she glanced at him and, with a hint of sarcasm, said, "*That* was interesting."

Without skipping a beat, he asked, "What part did you like best?"

Not to be outdone and with no hint of a smile, she came back with, "The part where my life flashed before my eyes. How 'bout you?"

They both laughed, enjoying the much needed release. It had been a tense several minutes.

"Landie will be okay, won't she?" Cary worried.

"She should be. They're after us," he said. Cary hoped he was right.

"Besides, there's too much going on in front of Landie's house for them to hang around. They'll come looking for us." He sounded as though he was trying to convince himself.

"They had a way of following us?"

"Yeah. Somewhere along the way, they had attached a GPS transmitter to our vehicle."

"And now they're going to be following that FedEx truck?" She had seen him doing something up under the truck.

"Hopefully," he said. "'Til they figure out what I did. We need to change vehicles now that they've seen this one."

"Should we call Greg and ask if he can help us again?" Cary said.

Webster nodded thoughtfully.

Cary picked up his phone and keyed in Greg's number as Webster called it out to her. When Greg answered, she handed the phone back to Webster.

"Greg? Me again . . . yeah, Webster. We have a little problem." He paused. "Oh, you've heard. Yeah. Well, that's what I called about."

While Cary watched for anyone following them, Webster told Greg what had happened and asked about Landie.

Webster listened, then said, "Give me some directions."

He motioned for Cary to write down the information as he called it out. Finished, he thanked Greg and closed the phone.

"Landie's fine," he reassured her, adding, "Greg's going to have Barry trade vehicles with us and store the SUV until we're finished with your search."

"It's a good thing they have a used car lot," she observed.

"Sure is," he said. "Barry's going to meet us with an older model Buick.

It's beat up but inconspicuous, and it has tinted windows."

"Works for me," she said.

"Me, too."

Barry was waiting out front when they reached the meeting place. The Buick was clean but well used, to put it mildly. Greg hadn't been kidding. Barry took the SUV and left them standing beside their new transportation with their envelopes and papers in their hands.

They dumped their things into the back seat and climbed in. Then Webster checked the car out. The engine sounded smooth but much more powerful than the SUV. He hummed, appearing satisfied. Cary liked the fact that it was clean and smelled like oranges.

"Where to?" she asked Webster. "We're homeless again."

"How much money do you have?" he asked. "I'm down to about three hundred bucks. I withdrew some cash in Knoxville but I'm going through it pretty fast. We may have to hit an ATM."

She checked her billfold. "I have a little over six hundred. That gives us almost a thousand, total."

"That's more than enough for a place to stay and some food for a couple of days," Webster said.

Just then his phone rang. Cary could tell by the conversation that it was Greg again. Webster motioned for her to take down more information.

"That's another brother," Webster said to her as he hung up. "Bert Kato," he said as he made a U-turn. "Greg's already talked to him and says he'll put us up for the night over on the West Bank."

"Keeping it in the family, I see," Cary said.

Cary called their new host; Bert said he would be expecting them.

"My wife will have everything ready for you," he told Cary.

"Just come on over. Think you can find the place?" he asked, after giving directions.

"We'll find it."

Cary and Webster arrived at Bert's house just after six-thirty in the evening. It was a medium-sized house located in Terrytown. Two white rockers sat on the front porch, and the house boasted a freshly painted cobalt front door. The house appeared to have been built as far back as the seventies. It had a double garage fronting the street, along with a small yard dotted with flowerbeds. The area appeared to be one of the few that Hurricane Katrina had bypassed. Cary liked the street name – Laurel Avenue.

Susan, Bert's wife, came to the door. She invited them in and showed them to the two bedrooms located along one side of a hallway.

"Landie must have called ahead and told them to separate us," Cary whispered softly to Webster. He smiled and nodded.

They had stopped at a drugstore along the way and purchased tooth-brushes, toothpaste, and sleepwear since their essentials had been left at Landie's. They took turns in the bathroom.

By the time they finished, Cary could hear Susan talking to Bert in their kitchen. She and Webster joined them. Susan had told them earlier that the couple's two children were both off at college, so there was plenty of room. Susan set out some things for sandwiches and they had a quick bite to eat.

Afterwards, the four of them talked for a short time, then Bert and Susan excused themselves. Cary and Webster were free to make whatever plans they needed.

They discussed their situation for a few minutes, but both were tired. Cary suggested they get some sleep and crank up the search again in the morning.

***

Webster was just dropping off when his cell phone rang. His watch showed ten o'clock.

Answering, he heard, "Webster, this is Greg. We have another problem."

"What is it this time?" he said, still groggy.

"Two men have been at my house and over at Landie's looking for you and Cary," Greg said. "They just left us. They threatened Landie, demanding she tell them where you are,"

"What could she tell them?" Webster asked. "She doesn't know anything."

"She told them that, but they searched her house anyway. Same here. They left, but they may check out all of the family. Just to be on the safe side, you better find someplace else to stay – the sooner the better."

"Do you think we should take some precautions concerning Landie? Will she be all right?" He remembered the concern both Greg and Andy had expressed about Landie's involvement on Sunday evening. This was exactly what they had feared.

"Don't worry about Landie," Greg said. "I don't think they'll come back. But just in case, I'll stay over at her house if I can't get her to stay at my place. I know she'll fuss. I'd insist she stay with us, but she'd throw a fit. She's already told me she isn't going anywhere and that she doesn't need a babysitter."

"We need to keep her safe, whatever it takes." Webster rubbed his eyes.

"Whatever we do, I'll at least make sure everything's locked up tight." Greg sounded confident. "You and Cary take care of yourselves."

"I guess you're right. We'll be out of here as fast as we can. We can keep in touch by phone." Webster worried about Landie and her family.

"Let me know if these guys show up again. I have some other help I can call into play." They hung up.

Webster slipped on his shirt and pants and went to tap on Cary's door. She was yawning and having trouble keeping her eyes open when she answered his knock. It took a moment for her to understand what was happening.

"Get your clothes on. We have to get out of here." Webster hurriedly told her about Greg's call and explained why they needed to leave.

"Give me five minutes," she said as she closed the door.

Webster went into the kitchen where Bert sat drinking coffee.

Bert spoke first. "Greg called and explained what happened at Mom's house. Don't worry about her. Greg says he will make sure Mom's okay, so that's handled. Now you two need to disappear for a couple of days."

"Yeah," Webster agreed. "We'll be out of here in a few minutes."

He excused himself and went back to his room where he finished dressing. He dropped the things he had bought earlier into the plastic bag they came in. Cary came out of her bedroom ahead of him. He hurried to the kitchen and joined her.

She was saying goodbye to Bert and Susan. A few parting words, then they slipped out to the Buick.

A panel truck passed them after they had only gone a short distance. Webster watched it pull over in front of Bert's. Two men got out and hurried to the front door. *Too late for a cell call to warn them!*

Cary had also been watching the men and turned to him. "I think one of them is the guy who tried to pull me into the closet at the library. I recognized him this evening."

Webster agreed, angry at himself that he hadn't noticed earlier at Landie's. *I'm slipping, damn it. It's happening all over again.*

The last time he let something like this take place, a young friend was killed. His boss, Jack, had argued that it wasn't Webster's fault, but he knew better. *He knew!*

Webster slowed, watching the men. He turned at the corner and drove down to the middle of the block where he parked and told Cary to stay put.

He hurried back and then, using the darkness, eased toward Bert's house, staying on the opposite side of the street. Webster went to the next house past them, then cautiously crossed back to that side of the street. He eased over to their place, staying in the shadows as much as possible. Slipping between the houses, he moved to a position where he could see in the window of Bert's kitchen. From there he could detect any movement in the family room. Webster hoped none of the neighbors saw him running around in backyards at this time of night. They'd probably call 911.

Webster snuck around a row of bushes and stepped over a short fence into the backyard. The patio windows were shuttered. They allowed him to see in, but he could tell it would be difficult for anyone to see out. He heard Bert telling the men that Webster and Cary had been there but left a few minutes before the men rang the doorbell. "Search the house if you don't believe me," Bert said angrily. He stood with his hands on his hips, defiant. Webster smiled. Landie certainly hadn't raised a family of wusses."

"Take a look," one man told the other. The second man went off toward the bedrooms, coming back shortly. "If they were here, they're gone now. Couple of beds messed up back there."

"I told you that," Bert said heatedly.

"Where were they going?" the second man asked Bert.

"They didn't tell me."

The man glared at the couple but didn't attempt to harm them.

Webster was prepared to burst through the patio door if that happened. The man said something else Webster couldn't make out, then motioned toward the front door. Webster could see through the house and watched them leave. After they were gone, Bert closed and locked the door. Susan, standing nearby, looked as though she was about to cry. Bert walked over and took her in his arms.

Webster eased away and made a run for the Buick. He jumped in as soon as Cary unlocked the door and told her they were going to follow the panel truck.

Her head jerked in his direction. "Why?" she asked. Webster could hear the surprise in her voice.

"Let's see where they go," he said. "Might be interesting." He smiled, thinking, *This isn't my first barbecue.*

The men didn't seem to be in a hurry. When they reached the Westbank Expressway, they turned east, crossed the Mississippi River, and headed toward downtown.

Webster drove along in the old Buick, following the men. The powerful engine allowed him to move around at will in the light traffic, getting close to the panel truck at times, dropping back at others.

They followed the men across the bridge. When the truck exited toward downtown, Webster and Cary tagged along, staying a block behind them.

This was one of the few times Webster had felt in control in the last several days.

The men in the panel truck could lead him to several possibilities. What if they were headed to the main police building or even to the Mayor's office? *That would be interesting.*

Maybe this operation could have a better outcome than the one keeping him awake nights. He'd like that, and Cary deserved it. He couldn't imagine losing one's parents, then finding out your birth mother had been murdered. Cary was strong to be able to handle all that. Webster glanced over at her, betting she was thinking about their destination, too.

Chapter Thirty-One

As they drove into the city, Frank went over what he would say to Mr. C. He dreaded the meeting. Mazou made thinking difficult as he wove through traffic, swearing and honking when another driver cut him off.

Still muttering under his breath about the near miss, Mazou said, "Where ya t'ink they went – da girl and her boyfriend, I mean."

Frowning, Frank said, "They could be sacked out at any sleazebag motel in New Orleans by now." Anxious, he tapped a fist on the door handle. He'd rather take a beating than tell the boss they'd lost the couple again. *Mr. C's gonna be ticked!* To his partner, he said, "They know somebody's looking for them, so they're gonna stay out of sight."

"Yeah," Mazou agreed as he darted in front of a slower driver, ignoring a raised fist and the horn. "What we gotta do is figure out where they gonna pop up next and be there waitin' for them."

"That would help" Frank said. "The boss is gonna be hacked. We spent all kinda time following that damned FedEx truck around." Frank couldn't believe they hadn't picked up on the GPS switch sooner.

"We gonna jus' have to go in there and tell him da truth," Mazou said. "We didn't know they found da damned GPS t'ing. We thought we was still followin' them, Bra."

"You think the boss will care about that?" As much as Frank dreaded telling Mr. C they'd lost them, he hated having to say they had no idea where the couple had gone even more.

Mazou pulled the van over and parked in front of the four-story building where they had received their assignment earlier that day. "So much for taking the afternoon off."

***

Webster parked a half block back between a shiny new Cadillac and an old pickup truck. He told Cary to stay with the car but to move over to the driver's seat and keep the engine running. He had a feeling they would be leaving in a hurry.

As he started to get out, Webster changed his mind. "On second thought, drive up to the intersection, turn the corner, and find a place there. If we have to leave quickly, maybe they won't see which way we go."

Opening the door, he walked around to the sidewalk, keeping an eye on the two men. Careful to stay in the shadows, he moved forward as Cary drove away. Webster eased closer as he watched the two men enter the building and go over to the security desk. They talked to the guard for a moment, then walked to the elevator.

From his vantage point, Webster could see them get on and punch a button for their floor. He waited outside in the darkened entrance until the doors closed. After they had time to start up, he jogged to the entrance and hurried inside. Glancing around as though searching for someone, he approached the security guard and told him he was supposed to meet two guys for an appointment upstairs.

"Oh. You mean Frank and Mazou," the guard volunteered. "They just went up to Mr. Cobreaux's office, number 307."

"That's them. Thanks," Webster said. He headed to the elevator. *Okay, Frank and Mazou.*

"Wait, I should call upstairs and tell 'em you're coming."

Webster's heart sank as he turned. Then the guard said, "Ahhh, you look all right. Go ahead." He waved him to the elevator.

Webster punched the up button and waited. When the doors opened a moment later, he stepped inside. Hitting the button for three, he prayed the men would already be out of the hallway. *Damn, that bell's loud.*

He heard a door close as he stepped out of the elevator. Room 307. Webster peeped around the corner. The company name on the door was Cobreaux Investigations. He walked over to the doorway and flattened himself against the wall, listening. He heard voices, but before he could make out the conversation, he detected footsteps inside the office.

Damn it! One of them was coming back out. Must be going to the restroom. He remembered passing it back near the elevator.

Webster hurried back to the elevator where he frantically punched the down button. Then he punched it again. And a third time. He could hear the doorknob twist open in room 307, then footsteps coming his way.

At that moment, the elevator opened. Someone was still coming. The stairwell! Webster reached into the elevator, punched the first floor button, then the button to close the doors. As quietly as he could, he made a mad dash for the stairs, escaping just as the person turned the corner.

As he reached the second landing, Webster heard the door to the stairwell open upstairs. He stopped in mid-step and held his breath. Everything was quiet for a moment, then a deep voice said, "Hey, is somebody there?" Then silence again. Finally, Webster heard someone say, "Nothin'." At last the door above him closed.

He gave it another thirty seconds before cracking the door open and walking over to the second floor elevator. He would need to be more careful next time – if there *was* a next time.

He got off on the first floor and started toward the front door. As he passed the guard, Webster said, "That didn't take long. Thanks, again."

"You bet."

When he reached the car, he was breathing heavily. He knocked on the passenger window and slid into the seat. Cary was concerned and a little put out. She stared at him as he threw his head back onto the headrest and closed his eyes.

She leaned forward, her arms resting on the steering wheel. "What happened? I was worried."

"They went into a place called Cobreaux Investigations on the third floor."

"Who is this *they* you're talking about?"

"Frank and Mazou. I got their names. They must work for Cobreaux." He glanced over at her.

"Now what?" she asked, sounding calmer.

"We'll see if Emile LeBlanc is familiar with Cobreaux." He told her to start driving as he punched LeBlanc's number into his phone.

***

Twenty minutes later they were in Pat O'Brien's Bar on St. Peter Street in the French Quarter. LeBlanc had been ready to call it a day when Webster phoned and suggested the three of them meet for a drink.

The place was full, even on a Tuesday night. They found a tall table and climbed up on stools. LeBlanc ordered his standard, a Scotch, while Cary asked for a glass of wine, and Webster a beer.

LeBlanc's collar was open and he removed his coat, hanging it on the back of his barstool. Once settled, he wiped his palm across the top of his nearly bald head, a habit Cary had noticed before. As they waited for their drinks, LeBlanc kidded, "Shouldn't you two be asleep?"

"Probably," Cary told him, "but we need your help."

"What can I do?" he asked as their drinks arrived.

"Are you familiar with a company called Cobreaux Investigations?" Cary asked across the table.

The question seemed to startle LeBlanc as he crossed his arms and leaned back. He didn't even pick up his drink. "Cobreaux Investigations," he said in a lowered voice, "also known as Marion Douglas Cobreaux, to be exact. I should tell you somethin', and let this be a warnin'. Stay out of his way. Da man's dangerous, and I know dat from personal experience." Cary noticed that LeBlanc's body language appeared closed, wary. That alarmed her.

"Does he have any connections to Johnny Periot?" she asked, leaning in, her eyes scanning the room as she sipped her wine. She was picking up Webster's traits.

LeBlanc glanced around, too, and tapped his steepled fingers together. "Nothin' proven," he said. "Cobreaux has a bunch of thugs workin' for him. They're careful; there have been a few assault charges, things like that over the years. Never anythin' big."

"What happens when they're caught?" Cary asked.

"Nothin', usually. Witnesses back out and won't testify, decide they didn't really see what they thought they did."

"So," she asked, "do you think Cobreaux and his people work for Johnny Periot?"

LeBlanc rubbed a palm across his head a couple of times, obviously uncomfortable with the question. He bent forward, his elbows on the table, then, although the room was noisy, LeBlanc lowered his voice. "You want my opinion?" Cary and Webster leaned in. "I think dey work for someone who works for da Mayor."

"Any idea who?" Cary pushed him for a name.

"No, but if I had to make a wild guess . . . ?"

"Yeah?" She wanted to reach over and shake him.

"Big Eddie." He sat back and shrugged, his palms toward them. "But it's jus' a guess." Then he reached for his Scotch.

"The Police Superintendent?"

"You got it." He took a sip.

Cary suddenly felt damp under her arms. In a matter of seconds, the temperature seemed to have spiked as though the air conditioning had failed.

They talked for another twenty minutes, then Cary drained the last of her wine and rose to her feet. Webster stood, too.

"Thanks for your help," Cary told the reporter. "We'll be talking with you." As they walked out the door, Cary could see LeBlanc ordering another Scotch.

Once back in the car, they rode for a few blocks without speaking, each of them content with their own thoughts.

"I'm tired," Webster finally said. "We need a place to crash."

"I'll go along with that."

"Can you handle a thirty-minute ride?" he asked. "We can go out to Slidell. They shouldn't be looking for us there."

She leaned her face against the cool glass. The darkness outside was almost a comfort after the stress and danger of recent days.

Thirty-five minutes later they were in Slidell, Louisiana, across Lake Pontchartrain and east of New Orleans. A far enough distance between them and the Mayor . . . she hoped.

***

Frank and Mazou had entered Cobreaux Investigations' office and knocked on Mr. Cobreaux's door.

"C'mon in!" he yelled, motioning for them to take a seat as he talked on the phone.

By his own judgment, Frank was more intelligent than Cobreaux gave him credit for. Frank glanced around, disinterested in the phone call. But without seeming to, he was studying Cobreaux now. The boss was a fascinating subject: short, with a little man's complex. Thinking about him, Frank watched his boss as he talked on the phone. Power and position allowed Cobreaux to be a bully.

While not handsome, and though he was pushing sixty, he did have a full head of dark brown hair. Frank wondered if the color came out of a bottle. What gray Cobreaux had was at his temples, but there was only a smattering of that. His complexion was dark also, and he tended to have a five o'clock shadow long before late afternoon. Frank had once offered to buy the boss a cordless electric razor. That hadn't gone over very well, Frank remembered.

Cobreaux's eyes caused others the most discomfort. His irises were abnormally small and emerald green. Frank had remarked to Mazou one time that you'd need two of Mr. C's eyes to make a normal sized one.

And, as might be expected of a small man, Cobreaux carried a big pistol, an M1911 Colt 45 semi-automatic. The weapon and its shoulder holster caused Cobreaux's left arm to stick out from his short body at an exaggerated angle. Anyone with a knowledge of weapon concealment would know that Cobreaux was carrying – either that or he had a major deformity.

Now Cobreaux was gazing across the desk at Mazou as he continued on the phone. Frank glanced at his cohort. He knew Mazou would do whatever the boss said without question.

"We may have to take them out," Cobreaux said, "and don't tie my hands on this. The Mayor just made his announcement last night. There can't be even a hint of scandal. This is his big chance on the national scene."

Frank heard a sound in the distance. "I thought I heard the elevator bell," he whispered to Mazou. "Go check to make sure no one followed us here."

"You gettin' paranoid, Cher," Mazou said, slipping into his Cajun way of talking, but he did as asked, returning a short time later.

"Nothin'. I even checked da stairwell," he said as he plopped down next to Frank. Cobreaux finally finished his conversation and hung up. He looked across the desk at them, blinking his beady green eyes.

"Tell me you found them and got whatever papers they had."

Frank's stomach sank as he looked at Mazou, then back at Cobreaux.

"No, sir. We didn't get 'em." With all his intuitive intellect, Frank was still scared of the boss. He shook his head and peered down at his shoes. But Mazou bristled. Frank sometimes believed his partner wasn't smart enough to be afraid.

Cobreaux suddenly pounded a fist on the desk, causing the pencil holder to jump about a foot. "I'm going to check with the Audubon Zoo, see if they have a pair of monkeys they can do without. I need to replace you two."

He glared at them for a few moments. Frank averted his eyes, while Mazou stared back at their boss with a dumb grin on his face, probably thinking about those damn monkeys.

"So tell me what happened. How did they get away?" Cobreaux demanded as he settled back into his chair.

Frank squirmed in his seat, then leaned forward. "We nearly got them. We had them blocked in with the van and I was distracting them. The guy must've seen Mazou trying to slip up on them because he peeled out in reverse. Almost hit some broad coming down the street with a baby in her car. When we finally got her and the kid out of the way, the pair was gone. We turned on the GPS and headed after them."

"Okay? So? How did it work?"

"Well . . . it took us a while to catch up with the transmitter. It kept moving around. We thought they were trying to hide."

He glanced over at Mazou. Frank could tell from his partner's relieved expression that he was happy to let someone else do the talking.

"The GPS indicated we'd caught up with them, but we didn't see their vehicle." He hesitated. "They'd obviously found the transmitter and stuck it under the back of a FedEx truck making deliveries in the area. When we figured out what had happened, we looked, and sure enough, there it was up under the rear end of the truck."

Cobreaux stared at Frank for a few moments, then finally said, "Let me get this straight. You two geniuses followed a FedEx truck around for most of the afternoon and evening while the broad and her boyfriend skipped out on you? That *is* what you said, *right?*"

"Yes, sir." They spoke in unison.

After a few moments, Cobreaux burst out laughing. He roared, tears filling his eyes. "I can just see that little scenario playing out."

Frank was afraid to laugh with him so he kept a solemn face, noticing that Mazou did, too.

When Cobreaux finally calmed down, he wiped away tears and said to them, "I've got to admit, it's hard to stay mad at you clowns. You're too damned entertaining." Frank finally allowed himself a small smile, but Mazou kept his expression emotionless.

"I can see how it could happen," Cobreaux mumbled to himself. "Apparently her boyfriend's pretty sharp. He may even be familiar with GPS equipment. We've got to be smarter. I have an idea."

Cobreaux leaned forward, crossing his arms on the desk, and laid out what he wanted them to do. When he finished explaining, Frank looked over at Mazou to gauge his reaction to the boss' plan. Mazou glanced back, eyebrows raised and frowning, doubt in his expression. This was outside their ordinary list of duties, but Frank knew not to ask questions when it came to assignments. Yet this one didn't bode well. Still, Frank knew it was wise to keep his mouth shut and just follow orders.

***

Cary and Webster checked into a Best Western Motel a short distance off I-10 in Slidell. Webster got them each a room. The clerk gave him the two key cards and directions. As they carried their things inside, Cary said, "I'm glad this day is over. I'm going to get a quick shower, slip into my T-shirt, and hit the sack. I'll probably be asleep before I can pull up the covers."

Webster had noticed her eyes were puffy and her clothes rumpled. His were, too. He thought about her plans for a shower, imagined her in that T-shirt, and concluded she had probably told him more than he needed to know. He hoped this new knowledge didn't keep him awake.

They each took a key and headed for their rooms.

Cary had said how drained she was, but Webster was running on pure adrenalin. He knew from experience it would take an hour or more for him to unwind. He'd grab a shower to help him relax, then he could give some thought to a couple of other projects before lying down.

He opened his briefcase, set up the laptop, then jotted his questions down on a legal pad. Number one on the list was Cobreaux and everything he could learn about the people Cobreaux reported to. Webster needed to know if Cobreaux Investigations had any significant contacts outside New Orleans. He also wanted to know about Cobreaux's business interests.

When his list was finished, Webster sent e-mail queries to Jack Robbins and Ray Ward. He expected replies by morning. Now he copied Jim Carson's phone number down and closed the computer. Then he called Jim's number in Virginia and waited.

"I thought you normally worked nights," Webster said when a sleepy sounding Carson answered.

Carson said, "I *was* taking a night off . . . to sleep."

After they had gotten in their licks, Webster settled down to business. "I need you to do a detailed search on a Marion Douglas Cobreaux." He spelled the name.

"His company is Cobreaux Investigations. He seems well connected here in New Orleans. I want to see if he has other associations elsewhere that we should be aware of. I'll take anything you get." Webster didn't tell him about the e-mails to the other two. He wanted independent searches.

"I'll make it the first thing I do in the morning. Shall I e-mail it?" Carson asked.

"E-mail's fine."

Webster took a moment to ask about Jim's family, then hung up.

Tired too, he fell onto the bed. He clicked on the TV, hoping to get the headlines before dropping off to sleep.

Waiting for the news to start, Webster's thoughts drifted. Keeping Cary out of trouble was turning into a full-time job. And keeping a low profile for himself had become a joke – a dangerous one now that the Mayor was involved.

He finally slipped into a restless sleep, his last thought a little prayer that Periot wouldn't remember their meeting.

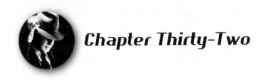

Chapter Thirty-Two

Frank Pinton drove the panel truck to a warehouse out near the airport. Mazou sat quietly in the passenger seat, using a six-inch pocket knife to clean his nails. When they arrived at the building, Frank parked inside.

They were there to pick up a different vehicle and check out a small recreational van parked in the warehouse. Frank opened the door to the camper and climbed in. Mazou followed him, checking for supplies while Frank made sure everything was working. The vehicle was a Class C, complete with a small bed, a micro-bathroom, and basic kitchen. Everything worked as it should. Mazou turned off the lights and they climbed out.

Frank had a special purpose for the camper and an occupant in mind.

Satisfied with their preparations, he drove the second vehicle, a tan Chevy Tahoe, outside. Mazou climbed into the passenger's seat. With a wave of his arm, he said, "Let's do it."

A light rain was falling as Frank eased out and headed to pick up their "guest." Carefully making their way along the damp streets, Mazou ventured, "Good night for this, Cher. There won't be many people out."

"Yeah," Frank agreed as the wipers came on. "Let's get this thing done. Maybe then the boss will forget about the GPS fiasco." He glanced at Mazou. "We ain't never gonna live that down, you know?"

"Yeah, Boo . . . I know."

It was after one in the morning when Frank pulled to the curb several doors down from their target's house. He got out, leaving Mazou to move over into the driver's seat.

He gave his partner a thumbs-up as he walked away.

Then, taking advantage of the shadows, Frank strolled cautiously down the sidewalk toward the darkened house. Once there, he stooped low and eased around to the back of the dwelling. Ever so carefully, he stepped onto the covered porch and over to the back door. Crouching, Frank pulled a folded kerchief from his bag of supplies and stuffed it into his belt.

He turned on a small flashlight to check the lock. Satisfied, he killed the light and pulled a towel from his belt. He wrapped it around his hand, covering it twice. Curling his fingers into a fist, Frank punched the glass pane near the lock, breaking it with very little noise. He reached inside, unlocking the door. Pushing it open, he drew one of his weapons. Then he carefully stepped into the kitchen.

Off to his left he heard someone coming his way. Frank prepared himself. A man burst from a hallway and lunged at him. Frank fired his weapon when the target was no more than six feet away.

Struck in the chest with the Taser charge, the man immediately crumpled to the floor where he thrashed about for several seconds and then lay still.

Frank could hear the old woman stirring in the room off the kitchen. Then she yelled, "Help . . . help! Greg, is that you?" Frank listened to her screams as he holstered the Taser. She was making a helluva lot of noise for someone her age. He scurried into the bedroom.

She was on one elbow when Frank got to her. Knowing she was up in years, he clamped a hand over her mouth and lightly slapped her across the face. *That should shut her up.*

"Keep quiet or you're going to wish you had," Frank whispered. "I'm not here to hurt you, but I will if you don't shut up. Do as I tell you and everything will be okay. Do you understand?" He slowly released her.

In the darkness Frank knew she couldn't see his face. Fear was evident in her voice in spite of his assurances that he wouldn't harm her. He hated doing this to the old lady.

He reached for the kerchief in his belt. "I'm going to cover your eyes," Frank told her, "then I'll help you with your robe. We're going for a ride."

He placed the cloth over her eyes, tying it tight. He was gentle but firm. He didn't want to scare her any more than necessary. Finished, Frank searched for her slippers and robe, finding them at the foot of the bed. She had turned and was swinging her legs down off the bed. Frank placed the slippers on her feet. Then he took her arm to help her stand up. She immediately jerked away from him. *Feisty old broad!*

"What have you done to my son?" she asked in an angry voice.

Ahh, hell! Frank had almost forgotten about the guy on the kitchen floor.

"You sit still," He pushed her back on the bed. "I'll be right back. You move or make a sound and your son's dead. Got it?" She nodded.

Hurrying into the kitchen, Frank found the woman's son starting to stir. The charge from the Taser would wear off slowly. He flipped the semiconscious man over and secured his hands and feet with a wide plastic cable tie. Finally, Frank could return to the bedroom for his supplies.

While he was there, the woman asked about her son again. "He's fine," Frank told her. "We can't take him with us. But someone is going to stay with him . . . in case you decide to be difficult," he added, hoping the bluff would keep her quiet.

Taking his bag, Frank stepped back into the kitchen and pulled out a roll of duct tape. He blindfolded the son and taped his mouth. Finished, Frank dragged the man over to the refrigerator, using two of the plastic ties to secure his legs to the base of the appliance.

Frank didn't want him escaping anytime soon.

Back in the bedroom, Frank helped the woman into her robe, secured her hands behind her with one of the ties, then taped her mouth.

Before leaving the bedroom, he placed an envelope on the empty bed.

Satisfied, he walked the woman through the house to the front door. Frank was following Cobreaux's orders, but he didn't like the idea of kidnapping the old lady and coercing her into silence by threatening her son. They left him struggling against his ties.

Once outside, streetlights would provide all the light he needed. Frank blinked the porch light once and heard Mazou pull their vehicle up to front of the house. He opened the door and started her out to the Tahoe. She tried to pull away from him, but he put an arm around her thin body, forcing her toward the vehicle. She finally quit struggling as he opened the door.

Mazou pulled the Tahoe back into the warehouse at half-past two that morning and parked near the small RV. Frank helped Landie out of their vehicle and supported her as she climbed into the camper.

Once they were inside, Frank said, "Sit here," and helped Landie down on one of the benches at the dining table.

With her situated, Mazou said, "You want I should make some coffee, Cher?"

"You want some coffee?" Frank asked Landie as he removed the tape from her mouth. He left the kerchief covering her eyes while clipping the tie holding her wrists.

She nodded that she would take the coffee. The color had drained from her face and her hands were shaking.

"Yeah, make us some coffee." Frank said.

When the coffee was ready, Mazou poured a cup for Landie and offered her a large powdered donut.

"We're not going to hurt you," Frank told her. "We just want to have a talk with the two young people you've had staying with you."

"Why do you need to talk with Cary and Webster?" Landie demanded. She attempted to take a sip of her coffee. Her hands were still shaking, the coffee spilling onto the table.

"That doesn't concern you," Frank told her.

She wouldn't give up – he had to give her that.

"But why shouldn't Cary be able to find out what happened to her mother?" As she asked the question, Landie made a weak effort to wipe the coffee cup with a paper napkin she found on the table. The donut remained untouched on a paper towel.

"It's just a bad time to be asking questions. That goes for you, too."

Landie mumbled as she dabbed at the coffee she'd sloshed on herself, her face a mixture of anger and indignation. Frank chuckled. She was definitely regaining her composure, but he also noticed her holding a hand to her chest. *Damn Mr. C!*

"If they cooperate, you'll be home in a few hours," Frank said. "We're gonna call them early in the morning to make the arrangements. In the meantime, why don't you settle back with your coffee and donut."

Landie had a few sips of the coffee and even tried the donut. Then she asked if she could lie down. Frank helped her to the small bed and pulled a curtain, giving her some privacy.

Frank and Mazou passed the time drinking coffee, munching donuts, and scanning old magazines they'd found in the camper. They had kept the blindfold on the old lady. What she couldn't see, she couldn't describe.

Thirty minutes after Frank helped her onto the bed, he detected movement and called out, "Are you okay?"

"I'm fine," she said. "I just can't get comfortable, that's all."

"Check on her, Mazou. See if she needs anything." Frank was reading an article in a three-year-old *Car and Driver* magazine about some guy restoring a '55 Ford Thunderbird up in Vermont. He'd like to do that.

Moments later, Mazou called out, "Hey, Cher. Toss me one of those blankets. She's shivering."

***

Greg's normal routine each morning was to walk down to his mother's house around seven o'clock. He'd enter through the back door. Landie always had coffee ready and he would pour them each a cup.

Today was different.

This morning, Greg lay prone in front of the refrigerator and he hadn't heard any sounds from Landie since he'd regained consciousness several hours ago. He was bound up tight as Dick's old hat band and try as he might, Greg couldn't get the damn tape off his mouth. He *had* managed to get the blindfold off.

He wasn't sure about the time. It was getting lighter outside so it must be after six. Hopefully, someone would come to check on them soon.

As he lay there thinking of ways to free himself, he heard the back door open. Then he heard Kathryn call out.

"Greg? Landie? Are you here?" She must have seen the broken glass and was afraid to enter because he heard no further movement. He pounded his heels on the floor to get her attention.

Moments later, she peeked around the refrigerator.

"Oh my God!"

Kathryn quickly kneeled at his side and pulled off the duct tape.

"Grab a knife and cut these bands," he told her.

Finally free and with his wife helping, Greg climbed to his feet. A little shaky, he steadied himself and stumbled in to look for his mother. Kathryn was right in his heels.

By the time they got to Landie's bedroom, Greg had reached a state of near panic. There was no sign of her anywhere, only the empty bed. Then he saw the envelope. It was addressed to the Kato family. He ripped it open and rushed through the enclosed note.

What Greg read sent a shiver of fear through him. They had her. He knew this would happen. He looked around, dropped down on the edge of Landie's bed, and handed the note to Kathryn.

The people who had been here wanted an exchange – Cary and Webster for Landie. The message was clear. They would call at 9:00 A.M. with instructions. If the police were involved, the family would never see his mother alive again.

Kathryn finished reading, then placed a hand on his shoulder.

***

Webster's cell phone rang at a quarter to seven that same morning. He was almost finished dressing; he buttoned the last button on his shirt, then answered.

"Webster, this is Greg." He sounded scared. "Someone kidnapped Landie during the night."

"I thought you stayed with her."

"I did. They tasered me . . . and took her." He sounded choked up.

Greg filled Webster in on what had happened. He also read Webster the note. "What do we do?" Greg asked.

Webster thought for a moment, then said, "Cary and I will head your way. We're in Slidell. We'll be there as fast as we can."

"Webster, we have to get her back. I was afraid something like this would happen if the family got involved."

Webster heard the accusation in his voice. "I know. Don't worry, Greg. We'll get her back." Webster hoped he conveyed more confidence than he felt.

Cary dressed quickly when Webster told her what had happened overnight. While he waited, Webster made a couple of phone calls. They were out of the motel and headed west by seven-fifteen.

Webster called Greg as they reached the edge of the city.

"We're on our way, but the morning traffic is heavy."

"Hurry, Webster. I'm scared to death."

"We will. And, Greg, Cary and I will do whatever it takes to get Landie back. If we need to trade ourselves, that's what we'll do."

"We know that. Just hurry."

"We're on it."

Outside on the expressway, the traffic had slowed, then come to a standstill.

As Webster closed the cell, he told Cary, "We'll have to do whatever these people ask. You know that, don't you?" He glanced over at her.

"I know."

"And we're going to have to give them our copy of the papers Shapiro gave you."

"I know that, too," she said.

"They still may not let us go. They'll know we've read everything, and they'll also know we've probably made copies." Webster tried to think his way through the next several hours.

"We can't let them keep Landie," she said. "We'll have to hope they don't harm us." Cary glanced at him. "Don't they understand I'm just trying to find out what happened to my mother? It's that simple."

"Simple to us," he said, "but we've obviously hit a sore spot with them. Johnny

Periot can't have you showing up on the news with him running for Vice President; his political career would be over. That's especially true if he's connected to Janice Talmer's death."

Cary bit her lip, then turned to stare out the window. Finally, she folded her leg up into the seat and said, "I'm sorry I involved you in all this. It's dangerous and it's personal – personal to me, not you." Cary's anguished expression made it clear how concerned she was.

"I've involved Landie and her family, too," she said softly. Webster could see tears in her eyes. "Now Landie's been kidnapped. Everything Greg and Andy feared has happened."

"We'll get her back."

"I hope so." Cary wiped her eyes. "You know, I think the reason I've pushed this thing with Janice Talmer so hard is because I feel so guilty about pressing Mom and Dad to make that trip to Washington. That wasn't their idea; it was mine. I wanted them to go. Now I'm trying to find Janice's killer to make up for it." She was seeking reassurance. "How screwed up is that?"

"We'll get through it," he assured her. He reached out and touched her on the knee.

The Interstate signs indicated an exit ahead – Read Blvd. Webster swerved over to the outside emergency lane and sped up. A couple of minutes later, they were headed west on Hayne Boulevard at the edge of Lake Pontchartrain. Webster stayed close to the lake, using Lakeshore Drive to save precious minutes getting to Greg and the others.

***

At eight-forty they pulled up in front of Landie's house – time to spare before the nine o'clock call.

Cary hurried toward the door while Webster parked the Buick. Andy opened the door just as Webster was coming up behind her. Kathryn, Barry, and a couple of other grandsons were in the kitchen with Greg. He had just poured himself another cup of coffee, his fourth of the morning, according to Barry. "Want some?" Greg asked them.

Cary took the proffered cup and held it while Greg poured. Then Webster got a cup.

"What are we going to do?" Greg asked, once he set the pot down.

"We're going to do whatever these people want," Cary said. Webster nodded in agreement. "This has to be hard on Landie."

Barry spoke up. "Maw-Maw's tough. She'll be okay."

Greg reluctantly agreed, but Cary could see he was worried. He wanted Landie home – the sooner, the better.

***

While everyone waited for the abductor's call, Webster slipped into the sitting room where he opened his laptop. He pulled up his e-mails and opened the one he was expecting from Jim Carson.

The information Jim had sent was direct and to the point: "Marion Cobreaux and Cobreaux Investigations work almost entirely for the city, but on the quiet side. The company operates on an assignment-only basis. They are sub-contractors of a sort – probably handling the dirty work for whomever they report to. I couldn't find out who that is." The information was pretty much as Webster had expected.

He unplugged the phone line, clearing it for the call they were waiting for, then closed the laptop. He went back into the kitchen with the others.

***

Everyone stood around the table, quietly drinking coffee and watching the clock, waiting for the phone to ring.

And it did ring – at exactly nine o'clock. Cary held her breath as Greg answered.

But the call was from Bert's wife over in Terrytown; she was expecting to speak with Landie as she did every morning. She had no way of knowing Landie had been kidnapped.

Cary could tell Greg was trying to keep frustration from his voice. Soon he hung up. The waiting continued.

Two minutes, three, and then four . . .

Cary tapped out a nervous rhythm with her fingers. Finally, at five minutes after nine the phone rang again. Greg put it on speaker so they could all hear.

"Are you ready to make a trade?" a man's voice asked.

Cary found herself nodding.

"Yes," Greg said.

"Then have the two people standing in front of the Delta entrance to the airport terminal at ten-thirty." Cary read the firmness in the caller's voice. He sounded deadly serious.

"What about my mother?"

"When we get what we want, there'll be a call to this number telling you where to pick her up."

"How do I know you'll do what you say?" Greg asked.

"You don't." There was a pause. Then, "but you don't have your mother now, do you?" Another pause. "You're going to have to trust us. Now you're using up valuable time. Get the couple out to the airport, and don't screw it up by trying to follow us when we pick them up. That could be bad for your mother. And no police, do I make myself clear?"

"Yes! Very clear . . . Delta Terminal. Ten-thirty. "

"Good! Now understand this. We have people watching you. Do as we've told you and everything will be okay." The phone clicked. The caller was gone. Greg looked at the display on the phone – *Blocked Call.*

Cary had been leaning forward, as was Webster, listening to the conversation. Cary noticed that Webster seemed distracted when the phone call ended.

Tension was high, with everyone talking at once. Raising his arm for silence, Greg filled them in on the details.

Webster eased away from the others. Cary watched as he walked down the hall and into his bedroom. He returned a few minutes later. When Cary asked what he was doing, Webster said he was looking for backup. That's all he would tell her.

Final plans were made. Andy would drive them to the airport while Greg waited for a call to pick up Landie. Cary prayed it would come, and soon.

Chapter Thirty-Three

The rain had stopped and sunshine was breaking through the clouds as Andy pulled over to the curb at the airport. The Delta sign was directly above them. Webster and Cary got out and waited as Andy drove away. They were early – five minutes.

"Gives you a strange feeling – like you're being watched." Webster teased as he glanced around.

"Not funny." Her lack of humor told him she would rather be someplace else. So would he for that matter. Cary's search was resembling his old situation a little too much.

At that moment, a Chevy Tahoe stopped in front of them. The driver, a stocky man with sideburns, got out of the vehicle and left the door open. "Get in," he ordered. He pointed to Webster, "You drive." Then to Cary, "In the passenger seat." Finally, addressing both, "Either of you causes a problem, the old lady won't be going home." Cary glanced at Webster. He could see the concern in the lines around her eyes and mouth.

Webster walked around the front of the Tahoe and climbed into the driver's seat. Cary was already in. The man opened the rear door and slid into the seat behind Webster. Before he could put the SUV in gear and pull away, Sideburns reached around the seat and checked him for weapons. The process took only a moment.

As he finished, there was a knock on Cary's window. A security cop sporting a menacing scowl on his face yelled, "Get this thing moving," and motioned Webster away from the curb. After fastening the seatbelt, he followed the officer's command and pulled into traffic.

"Where to?" Webster asked. He was glad he had been able to slip the pistol under his leg as they climbed into the truck.

The inside mirror had been turned so Webster and Cary couldn't easily see into the back seat. "Just drive," the man told Webster. "I'll give you directions." And to Cary, he said, "Keep your eyes to the front."

Webster merged with other vehicles, following traffic toward the airport's exit. He recognized the guy in the back seat as the passenger in the truck that tried to stop them at Landie's house.

"Stay on this road until you get to the light at Veterans Boulevard. Take a right. I'll tell you when to get off."

They rode in silence until they reached the Clearview Shopping Mall. Webster was told to turn into the mall's parking lot. Sideburns had him drive slowly around the mall two times as he watched for anyone who might be tailing them.

On the second circuit, he put a hand on Webster's shoulder and told him to stop, "I think there's a blue Ford Taurus following us." But as the man watched, the Taurus swung into a parking spot. Webster glanced out the rear window as a woman exited the Taurus and opened her rear door. Out came a baby stroller and she started to open it up. As she unfolded the buggy, Sideburns appeared satisfied and told Webster to drive on.

***

The woman glanced at the Tahoe as it pulled away. "They're moving, still headed around the mall clockwise." The small microphone under her collar transmitted her words to each of the three other surveillance vehicles now spread around the shopping center.

Expressing all their concerns, she said, "Don't lose them. We have to know where they're taking Webster and the girl." Then, with the stroller folded away in the backseat, she got into the Taurus and put the key in the ignition – just another shopper.

***

Cary noticed some of their captor's tension seemed to ease as they approached the large Target store located at the side entrance of the mall. Foot traffic appeared light, although lots of vehicles were parked in the area.

From the moment they left the airport, Cary had been working herself up for an escape attempt. She had decided in the confusion, Webster might be able to overpower the man holding them. She knew where Webster had hidden his pistol and suspected he could recover it quickly.

If they reversed the situation and were holding their captor, then they could bargain for Landie's release. But obviously Webster thought differently. As she inched her fingers toward the door lock and handle, she caught his eye, and with an imperceptible movement of his head, he silently told her no. Unconvinced, but giving him the benefit of the doubt, she pulled her fingers back from the handle. She knew he was concerned for Landie, too.

As they passed the Target entrance, Sideburns pointed to the extreme edge of the parking lot, saying, "Drive out there and park it."

When Webster had parked, the man instructed them to get out. "And you," he said, pointing at Cary, "walk around here." All possibilities of escape now gone, she did as she was told, knowing Webster was being held at gunpoint.

"See that van?" Sideburns indicated a light green vehicle. "That's our ride. One yell or a false move and the old lady's history. Now go!" He stayed a couple of steps behind them, the pistol tucked into his jacket pocket.

As they approached the vehicle, Sideburns told Cary to walk around the right side to the sliding door.

"What?" she asked, turning.

Before she could say another word, Sideburns pushed her, causing her to trip and fall to one knee.

Webster immediately grabbed the man's coat, pulling him away from Cary. Sideburns' hand came out of his pocket and he jammed his pistol into Webster's midsection.

Cary sprang to her feet but stayed out of the clash, watching instead.

For what seemed an eternity to her, the two men stared at each other, chests heaving. Webster held fast to the shorter man's collar while Sideburns, in turn, kept his gun pressed to Webster's body. Finally, Webster turned his abductor loose and took a step back with raised hands. By this time, the driver was out of the truck and had them covered, too.

"Put your hands down," Sideburns said to Webster. "You'd love for someone to call the cops, wouldn't you?"

After another staring match, the driver said, "Get in the truck." He pushed open the sliding door, allowing Webster to climb in first, then Cary. They each took a seat. For one brief moment she thought about kicking Sideburns in the face, but Landie's well-being took precedence.

After straightening his coat, the man got in and closed the door; the driver hit a button, locking them in.

Finally situated, Sideburns reached around Webster and again searched his belt and pockets for weapons. Finished with Webster, he frisked Cary. After the body searches, he checked Cary's purse.

Cary wondered what had happened to Webster's pistol this time. Where had he hidden it? Sideburns hadn't found it so it was somewhere in the truck . . . or left behind. Cary glanced at an open toolbox near the door and wondered if the pistol was there. She spied a screwdriver she would try to get as she exited the truck at their destination.

"Let's go downtown," the man sitting behind them said to his accomplice. The driver started the truck and pulled out of the parking lot.

Cary could hear the man behind them as he punched a number into his cell phone. "We're on our way," he said.

***

At eleven-twenty, the telephone rang at Landie's house. Greg grabbed it.

"Is this the Kato residence?"

"Yes. Who is this?"

"I'm the manager at the Exxon - On The Run convenience store, the one on Veteran's Boulevard near I-10."

"Yeah?"

"There's an elderly woman here who says you should come and pick her up. She's wearing a robe," he told Greg. Then he added, "She don't look very happy, either."

"Let me talk to her."

He could hear Landie take the phone. "Greg?"

"Mom! Are you all right?"

"I'm fine," she said. "Just get down here and pick me up."

"I'll be there as fast as I can," he told her. "Are you sure you're okay?"

"Yes. Now hurry." The phone clicked and she was gone.

When Greg arrived at the station, he saw the manager had rolled a chair behind the counter for Landie. She was sitting back there, watching people and tapping her foot.

Greg agreed with the manager – his mother didn't look happy at all.

On the way home, Landie told Greg about the kidnapping, how frightened she had been, and . . . how angry.

"They threatened to kill you if I didn't cooperate," she said, her eyes brimming with tears as she glanced over at him. Greg touched her arm, assuring her he was okay.

"I'm sorry this happened, Mom," he said bitterly, "but I told you we shouldn't get involved with Cary and Webster."

"But don't you see, son, we had to help Cary. I would want someone to help you if you needed it. It was the right thing to do. You know that."

She was right – as usual. Greg sighed. "I know, Mom. I know."

***

The men didn't talk to Cary or Webster on the trip into the city. The silence was difficult because it gave Cary time to worry about what these people would do with her and Webster now that they had them. She wiped her wet palms along the legs of her slacks. This could be their last day; she knew that.

She glanced at Webster and received a wink in return. *Where does he get that confidence?*

One of the things that bothered her most, maybe the most important single item, was that Webster seemed to be in this situation only to help her and he could die for his troubles. Cary didn't know what she would do if that happened, not on top of all the other tragedies in her life.

Every way she examined the situation, she concluded the next half hour could determine her and Webster's fate. She would need to be very careful if they were going to make it out of this alive. She nervously dried her palms again.

The driver exited the Interstate at South Claiborne and drove into an area dotted with warehouses. After a few blocks, the truck pulled into a large fenced yard with a dilapidated-looking building extending along an entire side of the enclosure. They drove to one end just as someone inside raised a garage door. The truck pulled in. Once inside, the driver stopped and the man in back told them to get out.

Cary stepped down and away from the truck. Webster tripped as he was getting out and fell into her, almost causing them both to go down. As they recovered, Webster brushed against her and she felt the hard metal of his pistol against her hip. She realized he had somehow been able to retrieve the weapon without being seen. That was good because she had a sharp screwdriver tucked away in her own sleeve.

Although the outside of the warehouse looked dirty and in disrepair, the inside appeared to be freshly painted. They entered a suite of workspaces and were ushered through a reception area and into a large office. If she hadn't seen the building and was judging from the offices alone, they could have been in any attractive headquarters in the city.

Upon entering the office, Cary immediately noticed several framed photographs on a credenza. The first was an autographed picture of the current New Orleans Saints quarterback; the second, a striking portrait of an attractive woman alongside the man sitting behind the desk. Cary assumed the woman was his wife. The next picture showed the same man posing with the Police Superintendent. Finally, larger and most impressive, was one showing Johnny Periot with his arm draped across the shoulders of their host.

Interesting company.

There were four men in the room – none of them masked. Cary hoped this wasn't a bad sign.

The individual behind the desk was obviously in charge. He looked at Sideburns and asked, "Are they clean, Frank?"

"I checked them when we put them in the van, Mr. Cobreaux," Frank told his boss. Now Cary knew who was behind Cobreaux Investigations: Marion Douglas Cobreaux, in person. And maybe the link to Johnny Periot.

Cobreaux turned his attention to Cary and Webster. Motioning to chairs in front of the desk, he waited for them to be seated before he spoke.

"You have some papers and other information I want," he told them. Then nodding at Cary, he added, "I'm referring to the things Alex Shapiro gave you."

"Where is Mrs. Kato?" Webster asked, showing none of the tension Cary knew he must feel.

Cobreaux glared at him and that's when Cary noticed his eyes. The irises were small and a strange green color. There was a hint of violence in those weird eyes. A shiver ran along her shoulders.

He told Webster, "The old woman should be home by now." He paused, giving Cary time to take stock of him. Then he repeated his query. "Now, where are the papers I want?"

Cary glanced at Webster. She had the envelope in her purse; the originals had been sent to Greg's house. Since those were safe, she saw no reason to put them in further danger by refusing to give him the copies. But . . . Cary also knew that if she turned them over too freely, Cobreaux might think he wasn't getting everything. She had to handle this carefully.

"Mr. Shapiro gave them to me," she told Cobreaux while clutching her purse. "They're about my mother. Why do you want them?"

"*Mom ami*," he said, "We both know they're about a lot more than your mother." He was becoming annoyed. "Listen, we can do this the easy way or the Cobreaux way. Are you going to give them to me or am I going to have somebody search for the envelope?"

Cary glanced at Webster, who nodded almost indiscernibly. She opened her purse and passed the envelope across the desk. Cobreaux took it and removed the documents. He scanned them slowly, looking up at her and Webster from time to time. He apparently wanted to satisfy himself that they had given him everything.

Finished, he said, "Did you read all this?" Then he answered his own question. "Of course you did."

He rubbed at his bottom lip, seeming to consider his words. Finally leaning back, he said, "Shapiro went a little crazy, you know. He decided everyone was crooked, including the Mayor and just about anybody else who passed through City Hall in the last twenty or twenty-five years."

He stared at them as though trying to decide something. "I work for the people downtown," he finally said. "We've known Alex was close to having a mental breakdown for some time. We even tried to help him, but he wouldn't let us." He pointed to Cary's papers. "When his wife died in that robbery last week, it must have driven him over the edge. But you know that because you were there."

"How did you know we had been to see him?" Webster asked.

"We have been watching him since his wife was killed," Cobreaux explained. "You two showed up, and we put two and two together. We knew you were asking questions about your mother," he said, appraising Cary with those odd eyes.

Cary forced herself to return his gaze. She'd give as good as she got.

"I'm sorry about your mother," he told her with what she suspected was false sympathy. "But that was a long time ago. And it was just an unsolved hit and run. No one was trying to kill her. Shapiro's red coat theory was just a part of his breakdown, nothing more. Do you understand?" Cobreaux paused for a moment before adding, "It's important that you do."

Was there a threat in his words? Cary believed there was, and yet he was smiling. He seemed to be waiting for a response.

After brief consideration, Cary said, "Although that sounds like a threat. . .yes, I think I do understand." *I can play the game, too.*

"I'm sorry about the way we had to get you here. You should understand we were concerned someone was going to get hurt. The two of you were very good at giving us the slip." He paused before going on. "Tell Mrs. Kato we're sorry she had to be involved. I trust she's not too upset."

"I hope she's not hurt," Cary said, unable to hide the edge in her voice.

Cobreaux didn't comment.

"Does this mean you're going to let us go?" Webster sounded surprised.

Cary was, too.

"Of course. We only wanted to talk to you, to explain our position and Shapiro's actions and mind-set. You're free to go. We'll hold on to Shapiro's ramblings, though." He motioned at the envelope and papers. "I'll have someone drive you wherever you want. I might add, I think you both would be well served to make arrangements and return to wherever you came from . . . without further contacts here in the city."

There was no misunderstanding the threat in those last words. Cary rubbed her arms in a failed attempt to rid herself of the goosebumps gathering there. But she couldn't let it go.

"What happens if we don't dash right out to the airport and head for Tennessee?" Cary asked, deciding it was time to wave a red cape in front of the bull. Out of the corner of her eye, she could see Webster cringe.

Staring directly at Cobreaux, Cary added, "There are a couple of things I still want to do."

He seemed to consider her words before responding. "I would rather not have another conversation like this," he told her. "In fact, I insist on it. Another encounter of this type would not be in your best interest." Cobreaux took his time, looking at each of them to make his point. "Do we understand each other now?"

Webster's eyes narrowed, but Cary saw him nod.

Cobreaux then turned to Cary, zeroing in on her like an ant under a kid's magnifying glass on a sizzling summer day.

"I understand." She glared at him, unwilling to let him think she was running away like a dog with its tail tucked between its legs.

"Good," he said.

They rose from their chairs and started to leave.

"I have one last question before we go," Webster said, turning as he reached the door.

Cobreaux nodded.

"Were any of your people *with* Shapiro when he shot himself?" The question hung in the air like fog on a fall morning. Cary held her breath and watched as Webster waited for a reaction. She was sure this was the end, especially after all she'd said.

But after a moment, Cobreaux grinned and shook his head as he stared at Webster. Then, without another word to them, he ordered the two men who had brought them to the warehouse to drive Cary and Webster back to Lakeview.

As they rode through the gate and out onto the street, Cary thought she saw Webster taking special note of the traffic. He seemed to have a particular interest in at least two vehicles that were parked on the street. There were several individuals in each of them.

Like the ride into town, no one spoke on the way out to Landie's.

***

When the young couple was gone, Cobreaux chased everyone out of his office. Alone, he reached for the telephone and punched in a number.

"I sent them on their way," he said when his call was answered. As he listened, he shuffled through Shapiro's papers again.

"How did it go?" the man on the other end of the line asked.

"I warned them, but I'd be surprised if they leave town," he said. "Everything I've heard about the girl indicates she's determined. Like her father in that way, I guess."

"Interesting."

"Her boyfriend asked a question as they were leaving." Cobreaux said. "He seems to know Shapiro's death wasn't suicide, but there's no way he could prove it. Still, that makes it a little shaky."

He listened to his long-time client vent his frustrations. He hated the man, but he couldn't abandon his benefactor now.

"Stay on it," he was told.

"Of course," Cobreaux said. Then he added, "You know they've talked to Emile LeBlanc, that reporter at the *Times-Picayune*, don't you?"

Angrily, the other man hissed, "You've got to get rid of the girl and her boyfriend, Marion."

Cobreaux closed his eyes and slowly shook his head. "We can do that if we have to but I'd rather not. The right time would have been when I suggested it earlier. But, no . . . no one wanted to do it then," he said, his voice cloaked with resignation. "Hear me," he said, tapping a finger on the desktop for emphasis.

Chapter Thirty-Four

Greg joined them as Cary and Webster discussed alternatives on the back porch.

"Is Landie really okay?" Cary asked.

"She's fine. Now that it's over, she's talking about her kidnapping like it was a big adventure." He chuckled and seemed to relax, but his forehead wrinkled into a frown as he said, "Mom did say something interesting. She thinks the two men who kidnapped her were the same ones who tried to stop you and Webster yesterday afternoon."

"Is she sure?" Webster asked.

"She said they kept her blindfolded, but she recognized their voices, and she mentioned one of them had a scar on his hand. She noticed it when they searched her house."

"I'm glad you told us," Webster said. "One of them picked us up at the airport today, too. We both recognized him."

"He was the one with the scar," Cary announced. "I saw it."

"You did?" Webster was surprised. "I missed that."

"It was on the side of his right hand. I noticed it when he was searching us in the van," she said. "Women *are* observant, you know."

Greg left them to sort it out and went back inside.

When they were alone, Webster suggested they go some place where they could talk without interruption.

"Let's pick up a couple of sandwiches and go out on the lakefront," she said. Cary remembered driving there with the social worker the night Carolette Shapiro was killed. They could be alone, and that appealed to her.

***

Forty minutes later, they were sitting on the second step of the seawall overlooking Lake Pontchartrain. Cary unwrapped her shrimp po-boy, but Webster had no appetite and laid his beside him, untouched. Waves from the lake lapped at the seawall below them. He watched as she took a bite from her sandwich and chased it with a big swallow of Coke.

Several things were running through his mind. With the danger they faced, he had decided Cary needed to put her full trust in him. To do that, she needed to know more about him. *Therein was the kicker*, he thought. For her to know more, *he* would have to trust *her*.

Webster glanced at her, his mood quiet, almost dark – all his training screaming, "*Don't go there.*" Then her eyes locked on his; she was waiting, clearly sensing something significant was about to occur.

"Okay," he said, "you've wanted to know more about me? I'm going to tell you what I can."

He watched her eyes; they were intense, questioning.

"I'm listening," she said simply. The undulating waves below them made hearing difficult.

"You've almost certainly figured out Mike Webster isn't my name," He began. "I can't tell you my real name. That could endanger others. You'll have to be satisfied with Mike Webster." She nodded, patient for now. She motioned for him to continue.

"I'm in a protection program run by the Feds," he told her. "I've been with the Government for most of my working life, much of that undercover." He felt her glance at him, but kept his eyes on the waves. "My work brought me into contact with some unsavory people," he said, "and some of them want me dead."

He became quiet, still gazing out across the lake. When he continued, his voice was softer. "I've worked all over the world," he said. "I speak five languages and understand enough of several others to get by."

Cary laid her po-boy down and leaned in to hear him better. The wind had picked up, making conversation almost impossible.

"No wonder you didn't want to tell me who you are, "she ventured. "You probably aren't sure yourself,"

He smiled, cutting an eye in her direction. "About Periot . . . he was right. I have met him before – he may not remember. It was a chance meeting that only lasted a couple of minutes. Someone introduced us, but I was using a different name then and I had a beard. The meeting took place in DC. I had been to a symposium on drugs coming into the country from South America. He was there about Hurricane Katrina funding. Anyway, it was just a quick hello. The introduction had nothing to do with the reasons either of us was in Washington. That's why I don't think he'll remember."

Webster opened his own sandwich and took a bite.

"Can you tell me what you do?" Cary asked. "I mean, what kind of work requires you to hide from people?"

Webster picked up his drink and took a sip. "I've already given you an idea but that's all I can say. Sorry." He just shook his head.

She stared at him for a moment. "So, when you came to Trebeck Corporation, you were already in this program?"

"Yes," he said, with a glance in her direction. "I ran into a problem and had to leave my day job, so to speak. That's when I came to Trebeck."

"Do you even know anything about advertising?" There was an edge to her voice that surprised him.

"Actually, I know quite a bit about advertising. I have a Bachelors Degree in marketing and a Masters in advertising with a minor in statistics." He stared out over the water as storm clouds raced across the lake. Pleasure boats in the distance trimmed their sails as they headed for shore.

"Since grad school, I've worked in marketing for about three and a half years, on and off."

With a bitter laugh, Cary shook her head and sighed, "You have more experience than I do, and more degrees, too. Now I have to ask: when was the last time you worked in advertising and what did you do?"

To give himself a moment, Webster turned away, picked up his drink, and took a swallow with a bite of his sandwich. "I was afraid you'd ask that. It's been almost four years . . . and I worked as a copywriter."

"You . . . you what?" Her head jerked around.

His neck tingled with the intensity of her gaze. "Yeah, a copywriter." He turned to face her wrath. "It wasn't my choice to take your job, but the 'powers that be' thought there'd be fewer questions if I came to Trebeck as V.P. of advertising. I could pull it off because of my education and my" – he made quote marks in the air – "leadership experience."

She tossed her sandwich wrapper aside and stood. Stepping over the seawall and onto the grass, Cary walked away, shoulders down and arms swinging back and forth. He heard mumbling but couldn't understand her words. Figuring that was probably a good thing, Webster gathered their trash and dropped it in a nearby waste can. Then he followed her.

As he caught up, she stopped and turned. He raised his arms, palms out in defense.

She remained silent, glaring, fists on her hips – angry. *Damned angry*, if he could read her expression.

"You were in danger," she said, putting the pieces together. "And you're hiding now. Hiding in plain sight." The red in her face was slowly subsiding.

"Yep," he said. "I'm hiding." Then he told her, "Sorry 'bout the job."

"I *am* ticked about that." She closed her eyes and took a deep breath. More composed now, she said, "But you *have* saved me on a couple of occasions. Literally. You've also helped with the search. You didn't have to do that, and it's been dangerous. I have to give you some credit for all that." She raked her hair back. "I'll try not to feel quite as bad about your getting the job."

She turned and started walking, with Webster purposely a step behind. A large sailboat was passing close to shore. They stopped to watch it go by.

He took the lead again, saying, "There's more."

She gave him a suspicious look and started walking again, slowly this time. He kicked at a stone as he followed her. "You need to promise me what I tell you now will be kept secret. Okay?"

Cary glanced back at him with a hint of a smile, "Or what? You'll have to kill me?"

"Something like that." He grinned.

She wasn't pleased, but remained silent as they continued strolling along the seawall. Waves still lapped at the concrete, sometimes sending salty spray up and over them.

"What I'm going to tell you now will be upsetting," he said. "I haven't been totally truthful about helping you."

Cary spun around to stare at him again, the red back in her cheeks. "What the hell are you talking about now?"

"Oh, I've been helping you," he said, ". . . but I've also been working with my old team."

Hands on her hips once again, she glared at him. "How? Or better yet, why?"

Webster kept his voice even. He licked at his dry lips and said, "We think someone was watching you at Trebeck Corporation. Someone related to Periot's political group here in New Orleans. Jack Robbins' people only knew the basics. They initially didn't know who was being watched or why." He watched her put the pieces together.

After a moment he continued. "I was sent in to gather what info I could along with verifying who really owned Trebeck Corporation. Shapiro's information and his list of companies gave me what I needed to come up with some of the answers.

She turned, staring at him with narrowed eyes. He put up his hand, saying,

" Please, let me finish."

She nodded, appearing to calm down a little.

"Robbins' people couldn't imagine why someone from the Mayor's group was interested in an individual at Trebeck."

"So you followed me here. The seminar – just a ruse?"

"Yes," he said and waited for her response.

When she didn't say anything, he added, "When I told Jack Robbins that Johnny Periot is your father, he asked me to keep them informed. I've been reporting to them as we've been in contact with Periot's people. I also told them about Shapiro and his accusations."

He could see her coming apart emotionally. "Damn it, Webster. Here, I thought you were helping me. But you're not. You're *using* me. Is this how it is working undercover; is it all about using people?" She glowered at him, all the while trying to sort things out. "Why are *your* people interested in Periot?"

"It's not just my people, and it's not just Periot. It's the whole New Orleans scene. Government officials have been questioning things here for a long time. This is the first time they've been able to put their hands on something specific. Your mother's death may be the crack in the wall. That and Shapiro."

"What about Shapiro?"

He touched her arm, turning her. They walked over to seawall again and sat down. The waves were higher now. Webster stretched his feet down near the water. "Based on what I'm seeing and from Shapiro's papers, I think drugs and money laundering are a part of how Periot's group is funding itself. Another possibility is protection for drug pipelines. We think that could only happen if the top people in the city, especially the top cop, are running the show. Those are the theories we're working on."

"What brings you to those conclusions?" Cary asked, a little less animosity in her tone.

"Do you remember Shapiro talking about how packages and sometimes people went out on his trucks?"

"Yes."

"That started me thinking about their operations and wondering about the place they took us earlier today. Do you remember much about the warehouse?" He didn't give her a chance to answer. "It was empty except for a few boxes and bundles."

"So?"

"That's a waste of good warehouse space. Whatever they're shipping must have big dollar volume." Webster was still working out the details, but he believed he had the overall picture.

"Let's head back," he said and stood up. Cary had started to shiver, so he casually put an arm around her as they started toward the Buick. She leaned into him, plainly appreciating the warmth.

"Maybe they're between shipments," she said.

"Perhaps, but I'm betting against it," he ventured. "I think there's something else going on. That warehouse didn't look like it was used much. I'm guessing whatever is happening there involves the highest people in their organization, and it probably has nothing to do with shipping and receiving.

"Think about it. If whatever they're doing has approval of the top cop in the city, then nothing can stop them. They just have to keep a low profile." He breathed out a long sigh. *Isn't that ironic. Keeping a low profile is what I should be doing.*

They had reached their vehicle now and leaned against the hood, gazing out at the shoreline. The wind had gathered enough speed that there were whitecaps on the waves. As they stood there, he reached over and took her hand. Without looking at him, she voiced what he was feeling, too.

"When this is finished, maybe then we can consider other things . . . you and me . . . the future."

She took her hand back, smiled up at him, then turned and walked back to open her car door.

Cary slid into the automobile and sat watching the show outside. Webster followed suit. The rain, in the form of an afternoon squall, moved across in front of them, then away, its energy spent. Cary wished her emotions calmed as quickly, but the wheels inside her mind were still churning.

Finally, she turned in the seat, drawing up a leg up under her. "You're saying I lost the position at Trebeck so you could get some questions answered?"

Webster ran a hand through his hair. "There was more to it than that."

"Like what?"

"The people I work for believed Trebeck Corporation is owned by Periot's group in New Orleans. They wanted to verify that, and since I needed to disappear for a while, they sent me. It had to do with the true ownership of your company."

"What? . . . Why would they think his people needed to own a corporation in Tennessee?"

Webster was silent for a moment. Then he explained, "At first they thought it had to do with investing money from the drug and protection business. To find out, they needed someone on the inside: That was me. Then, in the last few days, they picked up a new helper."

"Who would that be?"

"You won't like it."

She grabbed his sleeve. "Tell me before I hurt you!"

". . . You," he said. "You're their new helper."

"Me! What are you talking about?"

Webster placed his arm on the back of the seat, focusing his attention on her.

"A few years ago, Periot's people started thinking about getting him into national politics, like congress or even an ambassadorship. When they did that, they decided they had better check up on you."

"You gotta be kidding." She was genuinely surprised. "Why would they need to know about me?"

"Someone, maybe even the whole group, knew you were Johnny Periot's daughter. So the decision was made to find you and keep an eye on you. They didn't want you showing up in the middle of a national campaign."

She could feel the disbelief written on her face. Her eyes widened and her jaw dropped.

"You weren't hard to locate. They knew the Warrens adopted you, so they followed you to Tennessee."

She slowly shook her head as Webster continued.

"You were finishing college and had been hired to start work at Trebeck Corporation. The company happened to be for sale and they were looking for good investments, so they bought Trebeck under one of their holding companies. They got you in the process. All they had to do from that point on was keep you happy and out of New Orleans."

Stunned, she couldn't speak for a moment – then, "That worked for a while," she said, "until you showed up, right?"

"That's about it. I got your job and you decided to look for your biological family. You got to New Orleans and found Janice Talmer's letter; after that, all hell broke loose."

He watched her as she looked out the window, a myriad of emotions running beneath her calm exterior. "Talk about a bull in the china shop." She glanced hard at Webster, letting him know he wasn't off the hook yet. He might never be.

"What now?" she asked. "Where do I go from here?"

"I don't see how anything's changed for you," she heard him say. "You still don't know who killed your mother."

They were both quiet for several minutes, then Cary broke the silence. "So, do you think Periot was involved in my mother's death?" As she asked the question, she wondered if she was subconsciously trying to distance him from this madness – from her mother's death.

Webster looked at her, a deep sadness in his eyes, as though he had been here before, helping, but not quite making a difference.

Finally, he answered her question, apparently in the best way he knew how. "Do I think he's involved?" He glanced at her before staring across the water. "Not directly. I'm only guessing, and there's nothing verifiable," he told her. "That would be too dangerous. He would need to keep a distance between himself and whatever is going on. Same with the Superintendent." She realized Webster was thinking it through as he talked.

"So, how do they do that?" she asked, although she was beginning to understand.

"That's where Cobreaux comes in. I think he's the operations man. He runs things. Periot or Eddie Breunoux tells him what to do, and Cobreaux finds a way to make it happen." Cary was relatively satisfied now that she understood how the situation worked, yet she couldn't get over Webster's betrayal. He had let her think he was a friend helping her, while in reality he had been following his own agenda.

I'm such a fool. But then again, what should she expect? She was beginning to believe it was a male trait – that all men used women.

But my dad didn't, she reminded herself. *Kenneth Warren didn't!* She brushed a tear away.

No matter. She still planned to learn the truth about Janice Talmer; she would do whatever it took to find her mother's killer. Then she would return to Tennessee and the life she had before New Orleans. She'd even change jobs if she had to. And she would forget Webster and his knack for using people. *Who needed him anyway?*

She paused, reflecting on some of the things he'd told her. "You sound like you've been through this sort of situation before." She watched his expression. It didn't change.

He glanced at her, then away, but made no comment.

Frustrated, Cary thought about the specifics he had given her. "So that's all you can tell me for now?"

"Actually, I've probably told you too much. If I say anything else, I'll only be putting us in even more danger. My own best chance at staying alive is to have as few people as possible know about me. And for you, the answer is, what you don't know can't hurt you. Enough said?"

"I guess." She considered what he'd given her. "I'm still angry that you didn't tell me you work for the government. I thought you were doing this for me."

"I *am* doing it for you," he said, taking her hand, "but they pay the bills."

She nibbled the inside of her lip, willing to leave the discussion there . . . for now. She allowed him to hold her hand.

"But where do we go from here?" she asked. "I still want to know what happened to my mother. Why did they think killing her would solve anything? And who killed her – who ordered it?"

Webster frowned, obviously mulling over Cary's questions. "If you think about when your mother died and what was going on at the time with these people, you have your answer. Johnny Periot, a married man, was just getting ready to begin his career in politics when his girlfriend, Janice Talmer, tells him she's expecting a child. *His child.*"

"Okay."

"You and your mother were a potentially crippling problem to him and the group. The fact that your mother let the Warrens adopt you took care of part of the problem."

"I'm beginning to understand."

"You were now out of the picture, but your mother wasn't. Janice may even have known something they couldn't afford to let out. Whatever the reason, she had no family to concern them, so the choice was made – she had to go.

"Obviously, according to Shapiro, someone made that judgment, but it wouldn't have been Johnny. He would have been above those sorts of decisions. Shapiro himself just followed orders concerning Carolette's red coat, and he probably did think it was going to merely be a warning. Your mother's accident was well organized. Someone high up decided she had to die."

This was still difficult for her to believe, despite everything that had happened over the last few days. She voiced the question. "Just so she could never become a problem for them?"

"That's what I think," Webster told her.

It was warm in the car now, and the nearness of their bodies didn't help. Cary needed to get out of there. "Let's go back and talk to LeBlanc," she said, "and tell him about our visit with Cobreaux."

As she glanced over, Webster reached out, pulling her to him. He held her gently, stroking her cheek softly with his thumb and drowning her emotions with those soft eyes of his. The thrill of their bodies touching sent a roaring sensation through her.

At last he kissed her, tenderly at first, then stronger, his passion evident. After a moment, in spite of earlier admonitions to herself, she kissed him back. When he finally released her, she knew she was in trouble. Still, despite the intensity of her feelings, Cary knew she couldn't let this keep happening.

***

It was mid-afternoon when they called the reporter. Webster tapped the number into his cell phone. Glancing out at a passing yacht, he reflected on his feelings at betraying Cary's trust. It had to be done, and she listened to his explanation. Yet Webster couldn't forget the hurt in her eyes.

His thoughts shifted when LeBlanc answered. Emile asked them to meet him at a small cafe near the *Times-Picayune*. A few minutes later they were sitting across a table from the reporter, a fresh cup of coffee in front of each of them.

"Are you au'rite, dawlin'?" LeBlanc had tuned in on Cary's dark mood.

"I'm fine," she insisted, but Webster had noticed how distant she'd become since their kiss. *Had he gone too far?*

There was no time to dwell on it, though, because they needed to turn the heat up, and the only one who could do that was LeBlanc.

The men discussed the day's developments. Webster told the reporter about Landie's abduction and their forced journey to Cobreaux's warehouse. LeBlanc listened with interest and a question here and there. He frowned when Webster finished. "Why haven't you called da police?"

"Landie was already home when Cobreaux released us," Webster told him, "but the main reason is that I still believe the police are involved. I don't see how everything could work the way it does without top police involvement, and that's Big Eddie Breunoux."

"You're right," the reporter added, tapping a finger on his coffee cup, "if Shapiro was right about half da things he wrote in da material he gave you, then most of what happened could only have gone on with approval from downtown." He paused, evidently thinking it through. When he glanced back at Cary, he said,

"We need to flush out the real boss."

"We agree," she said.

"So, what can we do?" asked LeBlanc, looking back and forth between them. He threw a leg up on the chair next to him, took a sip of his coffee, and waited.

"How safe are you?" Webster asked him. "What I'm asking is this, can you start your series of articles now that you have Shapiro's information?"

"I'm not sure I follow."

"Will they come after you if you start writing the kind of articles we're talking about?"

"I doubt it," LeBlanc said. "Reporters are off-limits."

"Okay. You can use Shapiro's information along with whatever you've found yourself," Cary told him.

LeBlanc put his leg down and turned back to the table. "Webster said we're still off da record."

"We were," Webster told him, "but now it's time to move on. They took our copies of Shapiro's papers, but we sent the originals to ourselves when Shapiro gave Cary the envelope. We'll have those for backup."

"The other envelope hasn't shown up?" Cary asked the reporter.

"Nothing," LeBlanc told her.

"It could still come but I don't think it will." Webster said. "I think someone got to Shapiro, took the envelope, and then killed him – making it look like he shot himself."

LeBlanc nodded, obviously agreeing. He was ready to write the articles. "I've wanted to do a series of exposés like this since I started as a cub."

LeBlanc stood up. "I can probably have da first one in tomorrow's edition," he told them. "Now why don't da two of you let me get back to my office and start writin' it."

Chapter Thirty-Five

"LeBlanc's articles are going to cause an uproar, aren't they," Cary said, as they climbed into the Buick. "They may even flush out other stories."

Fiddling with something inside his coat, Webster added, "At a minimum, Periot's proximity to all these shady dealings will close out his run for Vice President." Cary wondered briefly about Webster's coat problem, then quickly forgot it.

Without a clear-cut next step, Webster's uneasiness was apparent. As though anticipating her thoughts, he said "I'm concerned." He started the car. "It shocked me that Cobreaux let us go so easily." He glanced over at her.

That had surprised her, too. "What about the warning? That sounded real. I mean, they didn't just let us go."

"The warning was meant to jolt us," he said, "but I don't think they understand how dogged you are about this search. They may not have anticipated your stick-to-itiveness."

"So if we stay here and keep on searching for my mother's killer, you think they'll reach out for us again?"

"You can count on it," he told her.

Pulling onto the street, he asked, "Okay, Search Captain, where to?"

At that moment, Cary's stomach growled. "I'm hungry. Let's eat."

He raised a brow. "Again?"

She laughed.

***

Down the block, another vehicle was waiting.

"We need to get them alone," the driver said.

"*Si*, but how?" his passenger wondered aloud.

"Just shut up and watch 'em, Boo." A dark skinned man in the back seat was talking now. In his deep voice, he added, "It'll work itself out. It always does."

The driver pulled out and followed the old Buick..

***

As they left the cafe parking lot, Webster was quiet but appeared thoughtful. Cary watched him, realizing again that he was never off duty. She had been around him enough now to pick up on his caution. He continually glanced in the rear view mirror or over his shoulder when they were walking; he liked to sit with his back to the wall, any wall, and face the door when they were in restaurants and other such places. She couldn't imagine the kind of life that required this degree of vigilance.

He drove them down near the Saint Louis Cathedral where he parked the car. They walked along Decatur Street into the historic district. In the Old Quarter, Webster chose a quaint, open-fronted eatery called Café Pontalba, with tables looking out on Jackson Square.

They sat inside, with a clear avenue of escape if a quick exit was required. After they'd been served a carafe of wine, Cary ordered Crawfish Etouffee while Webster asked for Creole Red Beans and Rice, both New Orleans favorites according to their waiter.

The lighting was dim in the café, and outside, evening was approaching. Guests at other tables talked in hushed tones, soft laughter occasionally punctuating conversation. Square wooden tables and straight-back chairs were pushed close and made walking difficult inside the restaurant. The stucco and brick walls and the floors bore stains of long years in the sun and rain. The weather, especially the storms that so often rolled in from the Gulf of Mexico, had left its mark.

"This structure and the one across the square are the oldest apartment buildings in America," the waiter told them. He pointed past a statue of Andrew Jackson and his horse. "The Pontalba Apartments opened here in 1851."

After the waiter left, Webster smiled and said, "Sort of makes you want to wipe your feet before you come in, doesn't it?" Cary thought he could have come up with a more romantic analogy, but in principle, she agreed.

She wondered if Webster's sense of humor covered feelings he'd rather not reveal. She expected there were also things in his life which were better kept to oneself – *Call it a woman's intuition.*

Sipping at the wine, they sat without talking, watching early evening visitors to the Quarter. Many, it seemed, were just out for a walk – reminding Cary of her mother and Carolette. Others admired paintings and other treasures hanging on the wrought iron fences surrounding the square. A few vendors were starting to pack up their belongings for the evening.

Two young lovers were holding hands as they strolled beneath the giant old oak trees. They appeared to be in their own little world, smiling, sometimes laughing, gently touching, and whispering secrets to each other.

As Cary watched them, she realized Webster was studying her. She flushed when his eyes caught and held hers. After a few seconds, she glanced away, breaking the spell. Then she was sorry she had.

"A penny for your thoughts?" he offered. "A *fortune* if I owned one," tempting her further.

"They're only for sale on Saturdays," she told him with a smile, "and *probably* not that valuable anyway." Then, playfully chastising him, "You should be more careful with your money," adding, "and I'd *probably* be well advised to keep some of my thoughts to myself." Cary blushed again under his piercing look.

She realized this was the first time she'd seriously allowed herself to think of Webster as more than a friend. He was a good person – she didn't doubt that. Still, they had been so busy since his arrival on Friday that romance had not been in the cards. There *had* been some special moments, though. But it was much too soon for real romance. Too difficult to think those thoughts when you're running for your life.

And truthfully, he hadn't been completely honest with her – not telling her his true reasons for helping with her search. That had driven a wedge, leaving them at odds in a way that could be difficult to reconcile.

Their meal came, breaking her thoughts, and they ate in silence. Webster poured the remainder of the wine; they each sipped it slowly, enjoying the brief interlude in an otherwise turbulent several days. The silky strains of a trumpet drifted across the plaza. Off in the distance, a musician was playing a soft, slightly jazzed up version of "Amazing Grace." There was always music in the Quarter.

Knowing he was watching, Cary alluringly ran the tip of her tongue across her lower lip. "I don't think I remember an evening as pleasing as this one," she said.

". . . Nor I," he replied in a low, husky voice.

He kept his eyes on her, enveloping her entire being with an intense stare; his gaze seemed to infer all the wrong things, and yet . . . perhaps a few of the right ones, too. *If only* . . .

After he paid, Webster reached over and took her hand. Cary thought of resisting, but then let him lead her toward the park. As they walked through one of the gates, Webster softly said, "Don't get spooked, but we're being followed." He squeezed her hand; Cary assumed the gesture was meant to keep her from glancing back.

"Act natural," he cautioned. "They're probably just keeping an eye on us

– determining if we took their threat seriously." In the blink of an eye his demeanor had changed.

"If they want a show," he winked at her, "we'll give them one."

Cary wondered what that meant.

They strolled into the park and ambled along, pretending to enjoy the flowers and the evening breeze. Stopping at one especially attractive bed near another gate, Webster whispered for her to bend down and admire a fragrant pink blossom. When she stood, he was quite near her and said something she couldn't hear. As she started to ask him what he said, he turned her ever so slightly; as she glanced up, Webster leaned forward and softly touched his lips to hers.

Surprised, and forgetting their situation for a moment, Cary took a short swing at him. A good slap would let him know she was still upset about his deception. But he was too fast for her. He caught her wrist before she made contact and, deftly turning her hand, kissed the backs of her fingers in a totally European gesture. "They're watching," he said. "We need to look like lovers. Smile!"

Collecting herself, Cary doubted if anyone would be fooled, but after a moment she grinned and relaxed. But, *damn it*, she could still feel the tingle of his lips on hers. The unexpected kiss had left an extraordinary sensation. It was brief, but the memory would linger.

For one brief moment Cary forgot they were being followed. At last she looked away, and with her hand still in his, they walked on. But now she knew they were no longer alone and could almost feel cold eyes following her.

***

From his location across Jackson Square, Coo-Coot watched the couple kiss and let out a low growl of approval. He had picked up his Cajun nickname when he first came to New Orleans.

The moniker didn't really fit him. He was a Latino in his mid thirties, six feet tall, slim, with a dark complexion, and he liked being called Coo-Coot.

The command had come down from Cobreaux's office to end the woman's search. Coo-Coot had been called in and had been following the couple without their knowledge since they left the reporter near the *Times-Picayune* building. He chewed on a toothpick, casually watching the pair as they strolled along the sidewalk.

Knowing they had met with Emile LeBlanc earlier in the week, it was disturbing that the girl and her friend had gone to see him again that afternoon. It had finally been deemed too dangerous to let her continue the search. The man in charge had spoken. Cobreaux had discovered LeBlanc was the same journalist Shapiro had attempted to mail his envelope to. This reporter, even before he met the young couple, had already put himself on a short list of people to be dealt with. Now he had moved up several notches.

Coo-Coot smiled and pulled his fedora lower. Now he stood, trailing after the couple without seeming to do so. His men would follow them, too.

Groups like Coo-Coot's small assemblage had found a place for themselves in New Orleans. Since Hurricane Katrina, there had been an increase in gang activity in the city. It was easy for corrupt individuals in positions of power before the storm to now direct certain types of work to these gangs. Funding special projects with federal and state money was easy. Dollars were coming to the city from all over for storm cleanup and reconstruction. Those in control of the funds were now in a position to have many types of labor performed for them, both legal and not. Arrangements could be agreed upon with a phone call suggesting what needed to be done. The money always showed up timely and in the right bank accounts.

As Webster and Cary walked further into the Quarter, Coo-Coot keyed the radio in his pocket and spoke softly. He gave instructions to the two other Latino men who were part of his team. Fifty yards up the street, a large SUV quietly came to life. The phone calls had been made and now the would-be Cajun was watching, closing in.

Coo-Coot and his team would bring the couple in and then disappear back to the streets. In case anything went wrong, Cobreaux had explained, he didn't want any of his regular people involved in the capture of the young couple. He didn't want any shooting, either. Mr. Cobreaux had said he alone would deal with the girl and her friend once they were in his office.

***

LeBlanc shut down his laptop a few minutes after eight o'clock. It had been a long day; he'd been working for twelve hours straight. An outline of the seven articles he planned to write was organized and filed on his hard drive. He'd even written half of the first article. It was saved to a disc and secured on his computer. He burned a CD containing all the information relating to his investigation and scanned Shapiro's material onto the same disc. Finally, after making a duplicate for himself, the reporter dropped the original CD into an envelope and wrote Cary's and Webster's names and cell numbers on it.

That done, LeBlanc scribbled a note on the envelope's corner telling them how to come up with the password: the first place they had met. He dropped it into his in-box just in case anything happened to him. He always took precautions. He knew they could figure out the password given the information they shared. He always kept his articles secured until they were ready for publication.

LeBlanc's desk had been somewhat cleared, pencils in containers, that sort of thing. He looked forward to writing the remaining commentary on the first article when he returned to his office the next morning.

Contrary to what he told Cary and Webster earlier, LeBlanc was apprehensive. He was definitely concerned the subjects of his investigation might send their thugs after him. It *had* happened before, just never to him. The preponderance of evidence through the years indicated that the people running N'awlins would do whatever it took to retain control. If they decided they needed to take him out, he was reasonably sure they would find a way. LeBlanc also knew he wasn't going to let fear rule his life.

He walked out of the building carrying his laptop and the Shapiro files and got into his car. The reporter headed for his apartment in Metairie as he had done countless times before. When he arrived home and opened the door of his vehicle, LeBlanc noticed a young African-American walking in his direction from across the parking lot. Without conscious thought, LeBlanc felt the hair on his neck stand up as alarm bells went off.

Surprising him, the man spoke LeBlanc's name. Emile squinted, trying to recognize him. With one foot on the pavement but still sitting in the driver's seat, Emile looked up and said, "Yes?"

At the last possible moment, the reporter saw the pistol the man was raising toward LeBlanc's face and quickly threw up his left arm to shield himself. Too little, too late.

The sound of the shot was no louder than an angry cat spitting.

Striking LeBlanc's uplifted hand, the hollow-point round plunged through the palm. The bullet then struck his upper jaw, causing pain as shards of lead pierced the area beneath his left eye. The projectile split, shattering bone and continuing, in pieces, into his face. The force threw his now unconscious body back across the steering wheel.

***

At that moment, two joggers walked out of a nearby apartment. They were laughing as they left for their run. Then, almost in sequence, an automobile carrying three people swung into the complex and parked two spaces over from LeBlanc's vehicle.

The assailant, concerned someone had heard, quickly crouched down. He then decided he couldn't chance the sound of a final head shot. He didn't think it was necessary in this case but disliked having the option taken from him. The reporter was bleeding profusely and was very still.

The attacker stood up near the rear of the reporter's vehicle. Unnoticed, he slid the pistol into his belt and headed back across the pavement to his own car. Once there, he climbed in, started the engine and drove out of the parking lot at a normal pace. In his mirror, he watched as the joggers noticed LeBlanc's car with its door still open. He could almost see their alarm as they discovered the reporter slumped in the seat. After a moment, one of the men ran back into the building.

The shooter smiled as he pulled into the street. He didn't think LeBlanc would be writing those articles for the paper after all.

Chapter Thirty-Six

The unanticipated moment of tenderness in that darkened corner of Jackson Square confused Cary more than she thought possible. How could she feel so let down and yet have such deep feelings for someone who had been less than honest with her? She wasn't sure what to think anymore, but vowed not to let herself be swayed by emotion – danger or no danger. Having decided that, she released her hand from Webster's and tried not to peer over her shoulder at the imagined sound of footsteps behind them.

In spite of the danger and chaos in their lives, *or maybe* because of it, Cary realized how much this early evening time in the Quarter meant to her – even if she didn't want it to. Stealing a glance at Webster, she wondered if he felt the same.

They tried to act casual as they strolled over to Bourbon Street. Peering into some of the clubs as they passed, they were ever mindful of a single individual who seemed to match them step for step.

"Is he still there?"

"Don't look back, but yes, he's still there," Webster whispered.

At around eight-thirty, they started back toward the parking lot and the old Buick. There were less people on the sidewalks away from the entertainment venues. Webster stopped her in front of an antique store along the way, and they pretended to admire the furniture and other treasures in the window. Cary felt as though an icy hand had reached out and tapped her on the arm because in the window's reflection she saw a man watching them from across the street, probably the one Webster noticed earlier. The man stopped and put out his cigarette, grinding it with his shoe.

With Webster's warning still ringing in her ears, Cary pointed out an interesting table inside the store. While keeping up the act, she watched the reflection in the window and saw the man duck into the shadow of a doorway. Then she noticed a second individual several yards back.

Once more she and Webster were the prey.

Touching her arm, Webster pushed her toward the store's entrance. "They're closing in," he whispered urgently. "Let's go inside the store." She saw movement behind them. "Hurry!" he told her.

"No! They'll corner us there." She looked back and saw the two men start their way.

"Run!" She grabbed Webster's coat sleeve and tried to drag him along with her. She had only taken a couple of steps when a shot rang out. Cary felt a burning sensation as pieces of brick and cement stung her face and shoulder. The bullet, fired from across the street, had come close, barely missing her before striking the building. Fragments had struck her arm, too. She touched it – blood!

Another shot rang out, this one closer. Then Cary glimpsed Webster on one knee, holding his pistol in a two-handed grip as he fired a second shot. One of the men across the street dove for cover.

Seconds later, Webster was there, shoving her toward the door of the antique store. Even as he hustled her inside, she saw him fire two more rounds at their pursuers. As they rushed toward the back of the showroom, Webster kept his body between her and the street.

"Where's the backroom?" he shouted at the saleslady.

With stretched eyes and fear in her expression, she pointed past a display of furniture near the middle of the shop.

Webster was now holding onto Cary's hand as they darted between tables, lamps, cabinets, and every other antique imaginable. She was doing her best to keep up. Just then a bullet shattered one of the store's windows. The saleslady screamed. Finally, Cary glimpsed the door to the store's backroom.

She could feel her heart pounding as she ducked low and hurried along. When they were in the backroom, Webster rushed her to another door at the rear of the building. Marked as an exit, it apparently opened out onto an alley. The door had a heavy wooden bar dropped down behind two welded slots. Webster removed the bar, tossed it aside, and kicked the door open. They darted through and he slammed it shut. Cary turned, glimpsing a shadow. She was suddenly face to face with a man rushing toward her.

***

When the crowds started to thin, Coo-Coot and the man with him began closing in. The van was already nearby waiting for the pick-up. Coo-Coot had restrained himself and his team as they followed their quarry. That had worked. They had kept the couple well within reach until they started to run. That's when he fired the first shot.

Cobreaux had said if the couple resisted, Coo-Coot could do anything necessary to end the woman's search. They hadn't realized her companion was armed, though. The guy had almost hit him with his second shot.

When Coo-Coot entered the store brandishing his pistol, the saleslady who was crouching behind a grandfather clock screamed and pointed toward a door in the rear wall. As Coo-Coot cautiously entered the backroom, he saw the back door closing. By the time he reached it, they had moved something heavy against it outside. He beat on the door, pushing and shoving as hard as he could. He soon realized there was no chance of getting out that way.

"Shit!" With one last look at the blocked doorway, Coo-Coot turned and ran back toward the front of the store. Unfortunately, the saleslady had followed him, resulting in a collision at the door to the showroom.

Leaving her on the floor cursing him, Coo-Coot hurried out to the street.

***

Cary gasped even as she realized the old man coming toward her was a transient hoping for a handout. As frightened as she, he turned and hightailed it down the alley.

Seeing a large trash bin adjacent to the doorway, Cary motioned for Webster to help. Soon they had it in front of the exit. Almost immediately there was pounding and pushing by someone from the inside.

Turning, Cary saw another alley a few yards away that ran past other buildings. She pointed and they ran for the nearby opening. Webster held tight to her hand and pulled her along toward the passageway. She kept glancing back, not sure where their pursuers were.

When they were near the end of the second alley, they slowed and walked casually out onto the sidewalk of the next street over. In spite of efforts not to, both of them were breathing hard.

Several bars and restaurants dotted the sidewalks. With Webster still leading, they hurried to a particularly busy tavern a few doors down.

***

Outside the antique store, Coo-Coot radioed his team, starting a new search for the couple. The van appeared almost immediately. He hurried the men, knowing the police would be there soon responding to a "shots fired" call. After grabbing a different jacket and tossing the one he wore and his hat into their vehicle, Coo-Coot sent the Suburban to comb the streets. His other man entered the alley with him in an effort to follow the couple from the time they left the antique store.

Coo-Coot quickly found the rear entrance to the building. As he suspected, the door was blocked. The couple had rolled a dumpster against it.

"What now?" his accomplice asked as they surveyed the scene. Coo-Coot wheeled around, trying to anticipate what direction their targets might have taken. There was an alleyway nearby. Motioning his man to follow, he headed that way. The passage led to another street, this one lined with bars and eateries. Coo-Coot glanced in both directions.

He didn't think the couple would attempt to run for their vehicle. If they did, they wouldn't get far since he had punctured two of their tires. He didn't think they would go in an eating place, either.

Only one thing to do now – start checking out the places where crowds congregate. He suspected the couple was hiding among the partygoers.

"Search the bars to the right. I'll go left." After reloading and checking his weapon, Coo-Coot casually walked into the first busy place he came to.

***

Pushing their way into a packed watering hole, Webster motioned for Cary to follow him toward the back. As they got deeper into the crowd, he told her to keep moving as he stopped to speak with a waitress. He caught up with her a moment later, carrying two half-empty beer mugs.

"What are these for?" she asked, frowning.

"They're for show," he said as he handed one to her. "The waitress let me grab them off a table." Cary followed him to the rear wall and found a spot with a partial view of the entrance.

The small bar was packed with people standing and talking in any space they could find. Cary waited, watching for their pursuers, hoping against hope they wouldn't come.

"Who are they?" she was finally able to ask. "I didn't recognize any of them." She had only glimpsed one man in the store, but that was after the shooting outside and their mad dash to escape.

"Two Latinos," Webster said. "I only saw two. There are probably more."

"Why would Latinos be after us now?"

"They must be working for Cobreaux," Webster said. "He probably doesn't want his regular people involved."

"Wh . . . Why not?" She was afraid she already knew the answer. She expected Webster did, too. They hadn't left the city when Cobreaux told them to – now their search was going to be ended for them . . . permanently.

Webster laid it out, confirming her thoughts.

She watched him. He had shielded her without hesitation when shots were fired, perhaps saving her life again. And he had done it after she had almost gotten them both killed by trying to run. Cary wanted to grab him, put her face in his, and apologize, really tell him how she felt, but instead, she just took his arm in hers and squeezed it really tight.

He looked down, then softly moved his finger across along her cheek. "You're hurt," he said. "A chip must have gotten you." He rubbed a finger across the moisture on the beer mug and touched it to her cheek. "There."

She didn't have the heart to tell him about her arm.

"So what now?" Cary asked, trying hard to hide the tremor in her voice.

Remaining outwardly calm, Webster said, "We wait for the cab I asked the waitress to call. I'm hoping we've lost the Latinos for a few minutes." He took Cary's hand and led her behind a group of people watching a soccer game on a big-screen TV.

Webster knew they hadn't lost their pursuers. At best, they had bought some time. As they waited, he thought of the similarities between this situation and the one involving the kid in Bogotá. In Webster's mind the circumstances were almost the same; he may have waited too long again. *Poor Cary!* He'd give his life to be wrong.

They stood holding their borrowed beers as Webster kept watch on the entrance. He thought he saw the Latino who had been following them come in the front door. Stooping to hide his tall frame, Webster quickly decided he was wrong. The guy chasing them had worn a hat and a different jacket. Still, Webster remained vigilant.

After a few minutes, a barmaid called out that a United Taxi had arrived. Webster scanned the room, then cautiously led Cary through the crowd and approached the front door.

***

As Cary stepped out onto the sidewalk, she felt a hand on her shoulder. She turned, expecting Webster. A chill raced through her when she saw it was a Latino. Unexpectedly, he smiled. "Excuse me," he said, easing by her and continuing down the narrow street.

Immediately, she saw another Latino behind Webster. Before she could warn him, Cary saw the man press something to Webster's back; she assumed it was a weapon. The man steered him away from the taxi waiting at the curb. Then she heard the Latino say, "If you give us a problem, we'll kill her right here."

Neither of them had time to react before a second man moved in from Cary's side. She flinched when he gave her a glimpse of the large pistol concealed under his coat. Not wanting to jeopardize Webster, Cary could only watch and follow.

She glanced around, futilely looking for a way out. The man holding Webster said, "You won't need the taxi. We have a ride for you." He motioned Webster to a large Suburban parked in an alley several car lengths away. Cary was forced to follow as her captor kept his pistol touching her spine. After they were away from the crowd, the man escorting Webster patted him down and removed his weapon.

The men motioned Cary and Webster into the vehicle. There were two sets of captains' chairs. Webster went in back, Cary forward. The two men followed them.

As Webster's captor scrambled in, Cary lashed out at the man beside her. With a vicious right-handed chop, she struck at his pistol. Without hesitation, the thug in the rear shoved his weapon into Webster's side. He glared at Cary. "Do it again and I'll blow your friend away." She glared back, defeated for now.

Webster gave her a slight shake of his head. The gun that had fallen to the floor was once again trained on her, this time touching her side. She felt a prickling at the base of her neck and had to calm her breathing.

Subdued for the moment, she settled back to endure yet one more ride that might be her last.

Even in the near darkness, Cary recognized their location and felt that same sinking feeling she had earlier. They were driven through the same gate and up to the warehouse where they had been taken that morning. The garage door went up and the Suburban pulled inside.

Someone opened the vehicle's door. The man beside Webster stepped out and motioned for him to follow. Cary's guard, more careful this time, climbed down first, and she reluctantly followed him.

The men didn't take them into the office this time. Instead, they were ushered through another door thirty feet away. The Latino in charge and guarding Webster opened the door, motioning them inside.

There were several desk-like tables and half a dozen office chairs in the room. Shelves covered most of one wall and were stacked with plain cardboard boxes and tightly wrapped bundles. Everything appeared ready for shipment.

Cobreaux and another man were waiting for them. Cary reflected that only this morning, he had warned them to return to Tennessee. The second man remained near the door as the three Latinos steered Cary and Webster into the room. The man who had raised the garage door remained outside.

Cobreaux's tie was loose, the first two buttons of his shirt undone, and his sleeves rolled up. His coat lay on one of the tables. Most noticeable now was the shoulder holster he wore and the large pistol in it. The little man appeared primed for a fight. "I thought we had an understanding when you left here today," he growled. "The two of you were going home."

Cary and Webster watched him. Neither of them said anything for several seconds. Finally Webster spoke. "I don't think we realized that was an order."

Glaring at him, Cobreaux argued, "Oh, you knew it was an order, all right. Then, not only did you continue asking questions, you also went back to that newspaper reporter. Did you really think we'd allow you to continue digging up old coffins and stirring things up without taking action?"

Cary's antennae went up. *"Digging up old coffins."* That was what the person said who called and threatened her last Friday. Those exact words . . . *Cobreaux! He was the caller.* She wondered if he had also threatened Janice Talmer twenty-five years ago. It was all she could do to keep quiet. Webster's eyes were boring into her; she could feel them.

Again, neither of them said anything.

"Well, did you?" Cobreaux shouted.

Every man in the room jumped, as did Cary. Only Webster remained calm. She didn't think he'd moved a muscle.

Then, lowering his voice, Cobreaux said in a threatening tone, "I'm talking to you." His anger seemed directed at Webster.

She had to hand it to him. Cobreaux was glaring at him in a way that terrified Cary, and the man wasn't even looking at her. Still, Webster didn't betray any emotions at all, no outward signs indicating he cared one way or another. *Was he really unafraid of this man?*

Judging from his manner, Cobreaux was accustomed to intimidating people and wasn't used to having someone stand up to him – especially someone brought to him by force and under these circumstances. Cary wondered if Cobreaux would tolerate Webster's attitude. Finding out didn't take long.

A couple of the men in the room began to shift their feet as a tingle of dread rose through Cary's body. She was willing to bet her next paycheck the other men had seen Cobreaux react violently with people who had provoked him in the past.

"Son, you don't realize who you're dealing with, do you?"

That one got Webster talking. In a steady voice, he said, "I believe I do. I think I'm dealing . . . with someone's paid thug." Giving his words a moment to register, he continued, "Actually, I'd be surprised if a little man like you could make a decision without checking with someone first."

Cary felt the blood drain from her face. She understood that Webster was pushing Cobreaux into making a mistake. It seemed to be working. The veins in Cobreaux's forehead and neck were pulsating.

"I think you're just an employee," Webster told him, "and a 'yes' man – nothing more." The words hung like smoke in a barroom.

Cary glanced at Webster; she had never seen this side of him or experienced *this* Webster.

Cobreaux exploded out of his chair, sending it spinning against the wall. He rushed around the table and swung at Webster who effortlessly stepped away from the roundhouse blow. Cobreaux's momentum carried him forward and the force of the swing caused him to lose his footing. He crashed heavily onto the wooden arm of a chair, screaming as ribs audibly cracked. Rolling onto his back, Cobreaux moaned as he struggled to catch his breath. Then he tried to turn over and get up.

Two of his men rushed to help. He swatted at their hands and rolled onto his stomach, gingerly rising to his knees and then his feet while grasping the chair. When he was finally standing, Cobreaux reached for his pistol. The men held back, allowing him to play his hand. As he started to point the weapon, Webster took a quick step forward, surprising everyone. Then, with a slapping motion, he snatched the gun from Cobreaux's hand.

The man nearest Cary, her Latino escort, started to reach for his pistol. She, however, shouldered him into the guy next to him, causing them both to lose their balance. By the time they recovered, Webster was in full control.

It had happened too fast for anyone to grasp what Webster was doing and too quickly for them to stop him. In an instant, he had taken Cobreaux's pistol and, snatching his shirt, pulled the man close and jammed his own weapon up under his chin. If the gun discharged now, Cobreaux would be history.

Cary rushed to Webster's side where she had a clear view of the room.

Everyone seemed to be waiting to see what would happen to Cobreaux.

Webster peered down into the shorter man's face. "You want to talk about this?" Webster's tone, though steady and conversational, was somehow frightening – even to Cary.

The little man glared up at his captor with all the hatred he could muster, but beads of sweat were already popping out on his forehead and across his upper lip. Pain from the cracked ribs showed in his expression. "Shoot him, you sum'bitches," Cobreaux screeched, trying to look around at his people. It was difficult because Webster was holding him so only his toes touched the floor.

"If I see another weapon," Webster said as he scanned the room, "he's a dead man." No one appeared interested in causing Cobreaux to get the top of his head blown off. The three Latinos were holding their collective breaths and waiting for the next move. Cobreaux's man near the door had crouched but held his position.

Cary edged closer to Webster and his captive. Just then, she heard the garage door sliding up in the warehouse. Everyone froze, eyes on the door. A vehicle was pulling into the building – they all heard it. Barely able to breathe, Cary listened as the garage door started down again.

Webster held on to Cobreaux and kept the pistol wedged under his jaw. Doors opened and closed on the vehicle outside, then the door to the room opened. Two men walked through the doorway, looked around, then separated with one moving to each side of the room. They checked the situation, their attention then focusing on Webster and his prisoner.

Immediately following the first two was a tall man with broad shoulders who was easily recognizable – the New Orleans Police Superintendent. Eddie Breunoux walked in and stood near the door. From there he appeared to assess the situation, his gaze stopping when it reached Cobreaux.

Cary held her breath. Could Big Eddie be the man running things in New Orleans all these years? Could this be Cobreaux's boss?

***

Coo-Coot had been searching for a way to position himself for a shot. He was surprised when the Superintendent walked in, but Big Eddie had given him what he needed – a distraction. While everyone's attention was on Breunoux, Coo-Coot moved ever so slightly and then he smiled. He would be ready when the opportunity came, and it would come. *It always did if you waited.*

As the Superintendent considered the standoff, Cary glanced around for something that could be used as a weapon, anything, maybe a sharp object. Her eyes were drawn to a letter opener on one of the tables a few inches from her hand. She reached across and grabbed it before anyone could stop her. Big Eddie's attention darted to the movement and his eyes narrowed as he studied her.

Then his attention turned back to Cobreaux and Webster. He glanced at the pistol before focusing on Webster. "Looks like it's your play," he said, after a moment. "Are you going to shoot him or can we talk?"

Webster's manner continued to be calm. "Depends on what you want to talk about," he replied in an even voice.

Superintendent Breunoux, the top cop, was obviously the man in charge, just as Cary had suspected for some time. She knew that was what Webster believed, too.

"I talk much better without a threat," Big Eddie said. "Why don't you let Mr. Cobreaux go? And then let's see if we can reach some sort of reasonable solution here."

Webster stared at the Superintendent. "I don't think so," he said. "There are several of you and only two of us. All of you have weapons. Somehow, giving up our advantage doesn't seem appropriate."

Cary wondered what Webster was up to; she knew she had to trust him and hope he could get them out of this alive.

Big Eddie studied him for a moment before saying, "Well, how 'bout this. You go ahead and shoot Mr. Cobreaux and everyone else can shoot you. Does that work better? And how about Miss Warren? You wouldn't want her to get hurt, would you?"

Big Eddie smiled at Cary, then asked, "How are you this evening, Miss Warren?"

Cary knew they were outmanned but held the letter opener ready for action. It seemed insufficient. Only a miracle could save them now. She looked at Breunoux with contempt but didn't respond to his question about her well-being.

Big Eddie turned back to Webster. "At least loosen up a little, Mr. Webster. Why don't you take the pistol out from under his chin? It could go off unintentionally. We're in a tense situation here; we don't need an accident."

Cary thought about the circumstances, then nodded toward Webster, who was already lowering the pistol. Cobreaux's knees were shaking, his fear probably matching hers – though she was determined not to let hers show. Webster pointed the pistol into Cobreaux's mid-section as he let the man down. Everyone seemed to catch a breath and relax a little. Cary even felt better. Webster still seemed to have the upper hand . . . for now.

He glanced at her and she gave him the slightest smile. He *winked* . . . and for a brief moment her heart melted. Maybe things would work out after all. She realized he was saving her life yet again.

Then, as suddenly and unexpectedly as the wink he had given her, there was a flash and a deafening roar. A shot! And Webster went down.

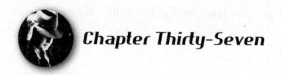

Chapter Thirty-Seven

The shooting happened in a moment – its aftermath took much longer. In terror, Cary crouched down, frozen where she had been standing, traumatized and feeling caught in the midst of some weird urban storm. She watched in disbelief, her mind in slow motion, as Webster spun to his left, turned by the force of a bullet. His grip on Cobreaux torn away, Webster twisted and went to the floor, landing hard. His pistol slipped away – unfired – and skidded across the room.

Immediately, Cary saw a patch of red along the right side of Webster's shirt – blood. There was more under his head. He must have opened a cut when he fell.

Sensing the man nearest her reaching under his coat for a gun, Cary slashed out with the letter opener, striking him below the elbow. He screamed as the sharp point pierced his arm and continued into his body. His fight now gone, the man sagged to his knees, his gun sliding away from him.

Refocusing, Cary dropped down on her knees beside Webster and turned his face toward her. There was a cut on the side of his forehead. His eyes rolled upward, then closed as he struggled for breath. Cradling his head on her knees, she made sure his airway was open. There was a terrifying moment when she was afraid he would die right there in her arms. *So much blood.*

Long moments passed and then a loud crashing noise came from out in the warehouse. Cary glanced up at the sound. Following an initial uproar, she heard people running and yelling.

"Federal Agents! Get down!"

Anticipating that help had come, she hoped it wasn't too late. *Please hurry.*

One of the Superintendent's men drew his weapon and jerked open the door to the warehouse. Instantly, a volley of gunfire cut him down. Following close behind him, two of the others drew their weapons and rushed through the doorway, meeting the same fate. Several of those remaining in the room had reached for their weapons, too, then abruptly changed their minds, raising their hands and backing up to the wall. Cobreaux had also decided the wall was a good option.

The Latino who brought them to Cobreaux glanced about frantically. His awareness focused on Cary as she held Webster's head steady. In his panic, the man glared at her with hatred in his dark eyes. Having already shot Webster, he now had his attention on her. As the agents entered the room, he grabbed Cary, dragging her upright. Turning her toward the door, he brandished his weapon while using her as a shield.

In a flurry of activity, with armed men positioning themselves, another shot rang out. To Cary's surprise, her captor stiffened briefly, then released his grip and fell to the floor. Momentarily stunned, Cary was still glancing about when new arms grabbed her. Eddie Breunoux had taken the Latino's place.

Four men in black uniforms and bulletproof vests were now spread out facing Cary and Big Eddie. Two others covered the men standing against the wall. Each of the agents carried a weapon, and all of them were pointed at Cary and the others in the room.

The agents' leader yelled, "Get on the floor. On your stomachs, hands behind your heads!"

Cary was still being held tight against Breunoux's massive chest. The Superintendent roared, "Back off. Now!" He waved his pistol at the agents. "Who are you?" he shouted.

"*Who are you?*" the agent in charge countered.

"I'm Eddie Breunoux, Superintendent of Police for N'awlins. This is private property and private business. What are you doing here?"

A standoff of sorts had developed but lasted just a few moments – thanks to the only woman in the room.

Her senses were heightened, and Cary still had the letter opener gripped in her right hand. In her traumatized state, she had forgotten it. Taking a deep breath, she struck, plunging her makeshift weapon into Breunoux's upper thigh. He screamed, the pistol flying from his grasp as he released his hold on her.

In that moment, all the anger raged forth, for herself and all the others: her mother, Carolette Shapiro, and now Webster – and what Breunoux and the others had tried to do to her – everything. Now it all centered on Big Eddie Breunoux.

Cary spun around to face him, then brought her knee up into his groin with a furious surge of power. His legs buckled and what fight remained, left him. He dropped to his side on the floor, holding himself and trying to get his breath back.

"On your stomachs with your hands behind your heads," one of the agents yelled again. "Do it now – everyone!"

This time every person in the room, including Cary, did what they were told. Only Superintendent Breunoux failed to obey. He lay there on the floor, groaning and yelling something about his status. His hesitation was rewarded by being slammed into position by a very large and aggressive agent, then having a knee placed in the middle of his back as he was handcuffed.

All the while, Big Eddie yelled, "I'm the Police Superintendent for N'awlins! I was here to stop these people. I even saved the girl," he lied. "I'll have your jobs. You wait and see." There was blood on his leg and hands. Cary smiled, just a little, relieved to see that Big Eddie's plea was going unheeded by the men in the black uniforms.

The federal agents hadn't cuffed her along with the others. One of them touched her shoulder, saying, "You're okay to go." With that, she moved back to Webster's side, hoping no one stopped her this time. He struggled to breathe as she kneeled there smoothing his hair and trying to comfort him. She soon heard sirens outside.

Moments later an agent came over and kneeled beside her.

"Are you Cary Warren?"

She looked up. "Yes." Her voice was weak.

"Come with me, please." She stared down at Webster, not wanting to leave him. The agent insisted, saying their medical personnel would take over now. He helped Cary up, her legs shaky, and moved her out of the way. Two medics rushed in and started working with Webster. He was very pale now, not responding to their efforts. One of them started CPR, trying to keep his heart pumping. Another attached an oxygen mask to his face and also started an intravenous solution. Webster appeared to be fading.

Cary could hear new sirens as she was led from the room. In the warehouse, she could see the garage door had been rammed from outside and torn off its rails. People rushed about, and the place was in chaos.

Her escort walked Cary out to the warehouse yard. She could still see medics working on Webster from where she stood. A bloody bandage now covered the cut on his forehead.

One of the federal agents checked on Webster, then glanced outside – catching Cary's eye. He walked out and directly over to her. This particular agent seemed out of place with all the violence that had happened over the last few minutes. Of medium height and with a boyish face, he might have been a nine-to-five family man who sold computers as his day job. But the large caliber Glock on his hip implied a different profession. He pushed a lock of blond hair away from his eyes before he spoke to her.

"Miss Warren, I'm Deputy Marshal Jack Robbins. Your friend Mike Webster used to work for me."

He hesitated as if considering how much he could say to her. "Mike has been talking with me over the last few days. You probably aren't aware of that. We discussed the search for your mother." Cary felt her stomach tighten. *The unexplained cell phone calls.*

Robbins continued, "My department and others have been interested in the situation here in New Orleans for some time now. For a number of reasons . . . including your search, our activity here has picked up dramatically over the last few days." He glanced inside where the medics were still working. "Mike has helped us gather information to clean up some problems we've been working on here for a very long time." He seemed uncomfortable telling her these things, but he continued: "Mike was able to assist us because of the information and contacts you found in the search for your mother's killer. Whether you realize it or not, you've also helped us a great deal." Cary hadn't fully understood the extent of her own involvement in the criminal investigation.

The agent focused on her eyes and said, "That's about all I can tell you except to say your search has been very useful."

"How is Webster doing?" Cary asked.

"Not good," Robbins said, glancing inside. "The bullet struck him in his right side, went through his abdominal cavity, and pierced a lung. He has significant internal damage and bleeding."

"Oh, no," she said, unconsciously moving a hand to her face.

As the agent finished with her, sirens once again filled the night. With lights flashing an eerie red/blue, an ambulance pulled into the yard. Two attendants jumped out and ran into the building carrying medical cases. Another wheeled a stretcher inside. Cary started to follow, but Robbins put out a hand. "They'll take care of him," the agent said in his southern drawl.

From her location, Cary could see the medics take over for the men who came with Robbins. She watched – helpless – as they worked at keeping Webster alive. A tube had been inserted down his throat. Cary clenched her fists as the second medic attempted to stem the blood loss from the wound in his side. Another medic was trying to get fluids flowing into his arm. Soon after they'd arrived, the medics lifted Webster onto the stretcher and rolled him out to the ambulance.

Cary wanted to be there with him. "Please, Mr. Robbins. I won't get in the way. I need to be with him." There, she said it. Cary *needed* to be with Webster. Now, at this moment!

Robbins opened his mouth as if to say no, but then changed his mind, giving her a slight nod. She rushed over and stood at his side as the medics worked to stabilize him. Cary tucked back the lock of unruly hair he was always fussing with. The bandage on his forehead was loose, allowing her to see that the cut was deep and ragged. His skin felt cool to her touch, sending waves of fear through her.

With her hand on his arm, Cary stayed with them until they lifted him through the back doors and locked the stretcher in place. She started to get in but was told there was not enough room. Two technicians climbed in, the doors were closed, and the ambulance drove away. She watched the flashing lights until they were out of sight. Robbins stood with her.

"Where will they take him?"

"LSU Medical Center's emergency room."

"I'd like to go there now. Is that okay?"

"We need you here for a few more minutes," Robbins said. He didn't really answer her question. When he started to walk away, anger shot through her. She went after him.

Placing a hand on his arm, she pulled him back and said, "Unless you can give me a better answer or you tell me I'm under arrest, I'm going to follow that ambulance. I'll find a way."

Robbins stared at her for so long Cary thought an arrest might be a possibility. Then he lowered his eyes and shook his head. "Miss Warren, I know what you must be feeling," he said. "Webster's my friend, too. I love him like a brother. But we need to ask you some questions and get a statement before we let you go. It won't take long, I promise, then I'll drive you there myself." He smiled, but Cary could see the sadness in his eyes.

"Okay," she said. "I'll wait, but not for long."

Robbins met her eyes, then turned and walked away.

Three other ambulances were now in the warehouse yard. Technicians worked with two of the men who had been shot. They were being treated and prepared for transport. A third already had a sheet pulled over his face.

Sitting at the back of one of the ambulances, the police Superintendent stared at Cary, an angry expression on his face. He had a bandage wrapped around his leg and his hands were still cuffed behind him. She had no sympathy for him.

Cary finally noticed the smears of dark red on her hands and slacks. *Blood, Webster's blood.* She went into the office reception area and found a restroom. As she started to wash the stains from her hands, everything hit her at once. Webster had given all he had to help her . . . and saving her life may have cost him his own.

She put the soap aside, resting her hands on the sink and leaning into them. The tears came slowly at first, mixing with Webster's blood in the sink. She couldn't stop them; God, she hated being like this.

She hadn't felt so alone since she lost her mom and dad. All the old feelings of guilt and emptiness were returning – but she wouldn't go back to that state of mind; she just couldn't. Lowering her head, Cary took a deep breath and pulled herself to the present.

She spent the next few minutes scrubbing up with hot water and lots of soap. Satisfied at last, she reached for the paper towels, drying her hands and then dabbing at her face and eyes. The stains on her clothes would have to be handled later. Cary felt her determination rise as she finished. She resolved to make it through this and find Webster and help him get through it, also. Then she went back outside.

As she stood waiting, another vehicle pulled into the yard and parked. She was surprised to see Greg and Andy climbing out of Greg's SUV. Andy opened the rear door on his side and helped Landie to the ground.

The women hurried toward each other and Landie took Cary in her arms. For several seconds, Cary couldn't say anything. The tears she had managed to stem in the bathroom suddenly returned and ran freely down her face. Thankfully, dear, sweet Landie held the much taller Cary until she could control her emotions.

"How did you know where to find me?" Cary finally asked her friend.

"Mr. Robbins told us. He was at my house all afternoon," Landie said. "He asked lots of questions. He also wanted the papers you sent to Greg's house; he made several calls after reading through them. Later, when he was leaving, Mr. Robbins told Greg, and these are his words, "something big is about to go down." He said he would have someone bring us to you when he could. And here we are. We followed one of his agents over."

Greg and Andy stood nearby looking anxiously at Cary. She released Landie and hugged them both.

"How's Webster?" Greg asked. He peered at her blood-stained clothes with a look of concern. Cary explained about the stains and about Webster.

Jack Robbins had gone inside when Landie and her sons arrived. He was back outside now and came over to Cary.

"Are you going to be okay?"

"I think so," she said. And then she asked, "How did you know where to find Mike and me?"

"We've been following you for the last forty-eight hours," he told her.

"How? Webster would have seen you."

"Webster knew we were there. He wanted us to stay close. He was worried about you, Cary." He chuckled. "He said you don't know when to give up."

Then he leaned close and whispered to her, "This is for your ears only, okay?" He waited for her to agree and then said, "Webster was wearing an audio transmitter this evening. We slipped it into the old Buick for him. He put it on before you had dinner. We heard everything that went on in the warehouse." Cary wanted to speak, but couldn't find the words, her emotions in a turmoil. *How could Webster command that much attention? He must be special to them, too.*

"What happens now?" she asked Robbins.

"Webster told me the two of you sent some papers to Greg's house. He asked me to look them over. I did, and decided to get copies to the state's Attorney General and the Federal Prosecutor. They agree it's not going to be business as usual in New Orleans for a while."

Explaining further, he said, "We came as soon as we could, but we needed to wait for the leader of this operation to show before we hit them. I just hope we didn't wait too long." A knot formed in Cary's throat. Robbins was talking about Webster.

Just then, a large dark limousine pulled into the yard and stopped. The driver and two other men got out and gathered at the rear of the vehicle. One of them opened the back door and out stepped Johnny Periot – *her father* – the Mayor of New Orleans.

He glanced around and, seeing Cary, strolled over to her and Jack Robbins. Periot's bodyguards followed close behind. In his office, Periot had been cocky, self-assured, his shoulders back, letting everyone including Cary know he was untouchable. She sensed something different about him here in the cool night air. His big attitude was gone, replaced by . . . What? Maybe a touch of defeat, something lost? His shoulders had dropped a little, too, and he appeared . . . older.

He stopped close to her and in a subdued voice, asked, "Are you all right?" Concern seemed evident in his voice.

"Yes," she said. His face appeared pale and washed-out now that she could see him in the brighter lights of the warehouse. She was sure he had been keeping up with what happened here. The evening's events had taken their toll on him, too.

"How about your friend, Mr. Webster?"

"He's hurt . . . and it's bad," she told Periot, wanting to wound him the way he had hurt her . . . and Janice Talmer. "Your people shot him," she said. "He's been taken to the emergency room at LSU."

Periot stared at her for a moment before speaking. "They're not *my* people," he said at last, denying her words. "And I'm sorry. Truly." A quiet engulfed them, only the sound of a brisk wind breaking the silence. A thunderstorm appeared to be blowing in as they stood there. Finally, he told her, "By the way, I remembered where I met him. It was in Washington." Periot gave her a knowing glance, then walked off toward the warehouse. Stopping a few steps away, he paused, then turned and said in a voice meant only for her, "Sometimes we all put too much faith in our friends. Even with Webster, things aren't always as they seem, are they?" Letting those words hang in the night air, he left her there.

Robbins, now standing at her shoulder, spoke up when the Mayor was out of earshot. She hadn't realized he was there. "I understand Periot may be your biological father," he said.

"Yes, he is."

"Does he know?"

"I think so."

"That's going to make for an interesting conversation sometime," Robbins ventured.

"Yes, it will, won't it?"

Robbins talked with her for a while longer, asking about her search and answering some of her questions. He seemed satisfied after a few minutes.

"I'll have someone take a short statement, then we'll get you to the hospital," he told her. "As soon as things slow down here, I'll join you."

"If its okay, I'll go to the hospital with my friends," she told him, indicating Landie and her sons.

"Sure, that's fine." Robbins walked back into the warehouse where Cary saw him go over to the Mayor. Neither of them appeared very happy.

Robbins' people took her statement, then let her return to Landie and the boys.

Cary stood apart for a few moments, considering . . . *her father.* It was difficult for her to think of him that way. She reflected on their short conversation. What he had said about "things not always being as they seemed" bothered her. Could he really have been outside all that had happened here in New Orleans? Was it even possible? If he was involved, if they could prove it, why didn't Jack Robbins have him under arrest? She shook her head. So much had taken place, most of it involving her in various ways, but she couldn't learn all the answers in one night. Vowing to follow up on several matters, she turned to her friends.

Cary climbed into the back seat of Greg's SUV along with Landie; the boys were up front. They went directly to the emergency room where she inquired about Webster.

A doctor with big bushy eyebrows – tall, lean, and in his mid-thirties –came out to speak with them. "I handle trauma," he told them. "Mr. Webster's critical. We've already sent him to surgery. I'll keep you updated and let you know as we learn more about his condition." The doctor then asked if any of them were Webster's family. Cary felt her eyes sting with new tears, realizing he had no family of which she was aware. No one to care. *Just like me.*

The doctor gave them directions to the surgical waiting area, said there would be coffee available, and walked away. A coffee pot and cups sat on a table in the corner. Cary poured coffee for each of them and settled down to wait. Anxious and unable to be still for long, she went into the restroom and washed away more of the blood. She wiped at the worst spots on her clothes but soon gave up.

Coffee in hand, Greg and Andy sat in a corner discussing Webster's shooting; Landie, not wanting to hear, browsed through an old magazine. Cary wasn't able to stop worrying. She began pacing the hallway. There were so many things she wanted to say to him. Finally, tired and with her nerves on end, she took a chair and leaned back.

At last, probably an hour later, she dozed off. She was startled when someone gently shook her arm. It was Landie, but Jack Robbins was there, too, both of them looking down at her. He beckoned her to follow him, and they walked out into the hallway.

"How is he?" she asked. The somber look on Robbins' tired face sent uneasy feelings running through Cary. She held her arms crossed at her chest.

Robbins stared at her for several moments before speaking.

"How long have you known Webster?"

Cary cringed, not wanting to answer his question or continue this conversation. She dropped her eyes and looked away. "Only a few weeks," she said, thinking back. It seemed longer. She was starting to realize how much she had begun to care for him. She also sensed the news was not good.

"How is he?" she asked again, fighting back the fear. Then she met Robbins' eyes and let out a long sigh. Then *she* said the words, "He's gone . . . isn't he?"

Robbins turned his face away, gazing down the hallway for a very long time. Cary caught her breath, waiting . . .

"He didn't make it."

"No . . . No!" Cary could feel her emotions crumble as she slowly shook her head, tears flooding her eyes.

"The bullet did too much damage," he said. "They couldn't stop the hemorrhaging. I'm sorry." He appeared downcast, too, as though he had lost a member of his own family or maybe his best friend.

Cary wanted to scream, to hit something or someone, to find a way to shake off the uncontrollable rage she felt at a situation that had gone terribly wrong and a system that allows people to die – all for the sake of money, power, and prestige.

She forced herself to break away from those thoughts.

"Can I see him . . . for a moment," she asked softly, "before . . . before they take him away?"

"It's probably already too late," he said.

Cary stepped in close and placed a hand on his arm. "Please."

A brief hesitation, then, "Let me make a call, but I can't promise anything."

She nodded. "Thanks."

He took out his cell phone and walked off down the hallway. Cary could see him glancing back as he talked. After a few minutes he returned.

"Come with me." He started walking toward the elevator.

As they waited, Robbins tried to prepare her. "There was a lot of swelling," he said, "and they haven't removed the tubes. You might consider being satisfied to just be near him for a few moments, perhaps remembering him the way he was, not like he is now. It will be much easier for you that way." He seemed genuinely concerned.

Cary was anxious, too, but she wanted to see Webster one more time. To not even say goodbye seemed wrong. Cary felt as though she'd taken a blow to her gut.

She tried to think ahead. "Will there be a funeral, and where will he be buried? Will he be returned to his family?" She was rambling. She knew it but couldn't stop.

"He didn't want anyone notified," Robbins told her. "That was his expressed wish. The Marshals Service will hold a small private memorial service back in Washington – no outsiders. Webster always knew this could happen. He didn't want his death 'to be a big deal,' as he put it. His standing instructions were that he wanted to be cremated."

The doors opened and they entered the elevator. She felt it move upward. Robbins stood in the corner, Cary near the door. He said, almost as an afterthought, "He wanted his ashes scattered in the Smokey Mountains. He loved hiking there."

Webster never told me that. I wish he had.

Robbins took her hand. "He cared for you, Cary. He was very concerned about the danger."

"I'll miss him." She wiped at her nose.

"I know," Robbins said. He smiled sadly then, adding, "We all will."

The elevator stopped and the doors opened.

He led her into the cool hallway and stopped at a door marked Trauma Unit.

"Still sure you want to do this?"

She nodded, tears blurring her vision. Robbins held the door open and motioned her inside. Medical personnel were tending to several patients. He went over to a station that had been closed off and held the curtain aside for her.

Hesitantly, she entered. Equipment surrounded the bed. A sheet had been pulled over his face. *Webster!* There was blood in several places. Robbins stood off to the side, giving her freedom to approach the bed. Webster's body was under that sheet. She could sense his presence in this small space. Cary stood there for a moment, then laid a hand on his arm. She was touching him, only the linen separated them.

Cary stood like that for a moment. *He had only wanted to help me.*

Without considering the consequences, Cary reached out to lift the sheet. She hesitated, her fingers scarcely touching the fabric.

"Think about it!" Robbins challenged gently, softly. "Would he want you to see him like this?"

He wouldn't! Cary *knew* that. *Webster would never have allowed this!* After a moment, she pulled her fingers back. Slowly she dropped her hands to her sides. In her mind, she told him goodbye.

There was nothing left to do. *Nothing . . .*

Cary left Robbins there and returned to the waiting room. She told her friends about Webster, giving details as Robbins had given them to her. When she finished, Landie reached out and wiped a tear from Cary's cheek, then took her hand. "You're coming with us, back to my house. You shouldn't be alone at a time like this. You need to be with family."

She smiled at Cary. "We'll be your family now . . . if you'll let us."

Cary fell gratefully into Landie's open embrace and they hugged. Greg and Andy then wrapped their arms around the two women.

Chapter Thirty-Eight

The ride out to Lakeview was a quiet one; Landie and her boys were giving Cary some time to sort out her feelings. Thoughts immediately returned to Webster. For having been with him such a short time, she already knew a lot about him. The guy was certainly courageous and intelligent. So many traits were coming to mind: daring *and* funny: he was handsome, *and* just a little bit bashful. Less than a week of close contact with this man, still Cary realized she knew him better than others she had known for years. Her thoughts also renewed an awareness that she cared deeply for him.

Outside, the mist had turned into a downpour. Biting her lip, she stared out at the driving rain. Somehow the storm with its rolling clouds, thunder, and flashes of lightning fit right in with the emotional tempest going on inside her. Maybe it was only wistful thinking, but she believed Webster had begun to care for her, too.

She recalled the kiss they had shared only hours ago. *That was another nice thing about him.* Webster had put his life on the line for her and, after all the years of danger before she met him, he had lost his life trying to help Cary find hers. Reflected in the window, she watched a tear cascade down her cheek. Wiping it away, she thought how much he had really wanted her to know her mother's story.

What had happened to Webster just wasn't fair. In her mind, Cary still couldn't believe he was gone – it just didn't feel right.

When they arrived at Landie's, Greg and Andy told her again how sorry they were about Webster.

"He was a good man," Greg said. "Yeah," Andy added. They hugged her, then left the women alone.

Cary took a long hot shower and dressed for bed. Then she joined Landie in the kitchen. Coffee was brewing. They each poured a cup and carried them into the living room. Cary knew her friend would understand about losing someone close. As they talked, she realized Landie was waiting for her to take the lead.

"I'll miss Webster," she said. "I'm going to miss him a lot."

"I still think about Roberto," Landie told her, "even now, after all these years."

Then she said, "But you're young. There will be another chance for you, I promise." The women talked into the night, with Landie helping Cary understand these feelings wouldn't go away anytime soon. Still, she would have to go on, despite her loss.

Hours later, they gave in to exhaustion, and Cary hugged her special friend good night. Landie turned off the lights and they each headed off to try and get some sleep. As Cary walked past the room Webster had slept in, she felt a surge of emotion. Pushing the door open, she peered inside. His things lay where he left them. Jack Robbins, she knew, would probably be the one to come and collect them. Cary wondered what would happen to his few personal belongings. Looking at them, a single sob escaped her tired body. A hand covering her mouth, she realized there were so many questions for which she had no answers.

On impulse, Cary stepped over to the vanity and picked up a small bottle of cologne – *Cool Water*. They'd never miss it. She wanted something of his. The cologne would remind her of the Webster she knew – and of better times in New Orleans.

Cary finally climbed into bed and was asleep almost immediately.

A few hours later, Landie knocked on her door and said there was coffee and breakfast in the kitchen. Cary glanced over at the clock and saw it was already nine-thirty in the morning. She couldn't believe it. Yawning and stretching, it seemed she had just gone to bed.

When she walked into the kitchen, Landie was sitting at the table with coffee and a newspaper in front of her.

"Good morning," she said, looking up.

"Would it be too much to hope yesterday was just a bad dream?" Cary ventured.

"I wish that were possible, but I'm afraid you're going to have to settle for a new day," Landie said. "How about starting it off with some breakfast? You have a choice of eggs, toast, bacon, grits, and coffee – or any combination of those. What'll you have?"

Cary wasn't hungry. "Toast and coffee will be fine."

"Are you sure, Child? That doesn't seem like much."

"Maybe later. My body is probably out of whack." This was the first morning in several that someone wasn't after her and Webster. *Webster!*

Her eyes misted.

Landie started the toast and poured Cary some coffee.

"The *Times-Picayune* says the Mayor's going to resign," Landie said. "It also reports that he's told Stuart Daniels he won't be running for Vice President. It looks like his buddy, Big Eddie, has always been the bad guy behind the scenes, with Periot looking the other way. That man Cobreaux is telling everything. It's a mess."

"Will they go to jail?" Cary asked.

"Probably everyone but the Mayor. The article suggests there doesn't seem to be enough evidence against him, but his political career is over." She looked at Cary. "It's sad for all the families involved."

"Yes, it is," Cary answered. She thought it interesting that Landie had never once referred to Johnny Periot as her father.

"One of the *Times-Picayune* reporters was shot last night, too," Landie said. "The paper says he'd been investigating Periot and the others for some time. He was getting ready to release a series of articles."

Cary, still standing, set her coffee down, missing the saucer and splashing it onto the white linen napkin. "What's his name?" In her heart, she already knew.

Landie searched the paper for a moment and then said, "Emile LeBlanc."

Cary's knees went weak. She sat down at the table, putting her face in her hands. Tears seemed to come so easily now.

"What is it? Do you know him?" Landie shuffled to her side and gently patted her shoulder, letting Cary have a moment.

"Emile located my mother's grave for me," she told Landie. "Webster and I were working with him." She glanced up at her friend. "We had given him some of the information he was going to use to write his articles." She dabbed at her eyes. "He was killed?"

"No," Landie exclaimed, "he survived. He's in Intensive Care, I think, but he's alive."

"Do they say how he's doing?"

Landie scanned the article about the reporter and read through the last part again. "He's in critical condition, it says here. He was only shot one time. The bullet went through his hand, then hit him in the face. It shattered a bone under his eye but missed all the important nerves and arteries. He was lucky," Landie said, looking up. "They think the shooter was scared off after the one shot."

"I hope he makes it." Cary hesitated. "Landie, I never imagined a simple search for my birth parents could cause so much death and heartache."

"It's not your fault, Cary, if that's what you're thinking. There are some bad people in this world."

"It still hurts."

"I know it does, Honey. But in reality, you and Webster helped prevent even more killing and sadness. You can be proud of that. And you've found and stopped the men who killed your mother."

Landie was probably right. Yet she knew if she had never come to New Orleans, things would have been different. Better? No, probably not. Just . . . different. *But that's not how life works, is it?* She did come to New Orleans.

"I'll have to think it through. Maybe then I can get on with my life." She remembered something. Pointing at the newspaper, she asked "Is there anything about Webster?"

Landie shook her head. "There's nothing about him specifically, although it does say two men were killed in the shootout. Maybe Mr. Robbins kept Webster out of the news."

"Yes, that's probably it."

"Have you made any plans yet?" Landie asked.

"I'm going to call my office in Knoxville this morning and tell them about Webster. And I want to visit the lady who helped me at the adoption agency. She's been very special. She was adopted, too, so she understood my search. I want to go and say goodbye." Landie nodded as she poured more coffee. "What will you do after that? Are the police through with you?"

"Jack Robbins says I'm free to go home as long as I agree to come back if they need me. If I can get a flight back to Knoxville this evening, I'll go back and try to return to my job. I think the sooner I do that, the easier it will be for me to put everything behind me."

She wanted to go to some sort of service for Webster, a funeral maybe, but Robbins said there wouldn't be one. He had disappeared from her life the way he had come – suddenly and completely. There'd be no goodbyes. That left her feeling empty and alone, the way she had felt when her parents died.

"I hope it hasn't all been bad," Landie said, snapping Cary out of her musing.

She smiled. "Oh no, that isn't what I mean."

"I know," Landie said, smiling, too. The women touched fingers in a caring gesture.

"Will you come back to see us here in N'awlins?" Landie looked at her then and said, "You know, in some ways, Katrina was like all that's happened to you in the last few days. The storm was unexpected and terrible . . . and left a lot of bodies in its wake, and a few broken hearts."

She thought about Landie's unique comparison, then said, "Sure, I'll come back. You're the closest thing I have to family now."

"I hoped you'd say that," Landie told her. "I trust you'll always feel that way about us."

The two women hugged again. They really were becoming more than friends.

Later, as Cary packed her bags, Landie's phone rang. She answered and told Cary the call was for her.

She immediately recognized the voice.

"This is Johnny Periot."

"Yes?"

"Could you come and see me today? *Or* maybe I should ask, *will* you come and see me? I would like to talk to you about Janice Talmer. I think I should answer more of your questions than I did before. Please. Come and see me."

She was surprised to hear from him, but Cary considered his request. *What could it hurt?* Maybe he really would give her some answers. There was nothing he could do to her if she went to his office, not with the press hanging around. His career was already destroyed; now he might feel free to talk about her mother.

"What time?"

"Would one o'clock be all right?"

"One is fine. At your office." It was not a question.

"Yes, please."

"I'll be there."

She hung up and walked into the kitchen. Landie sat at the table, still reading the newspaper and drinking coffee. Cary told her about the call.

"Do you think anyone should go with you?"

"No. I'll be fine. He's in too much of a spotlight to do anything crazy. I think he just wants to talk."

"Well, call me if you have any problems. I'll send Greg and Andy and the boys." They both smiled, but she understood that Landie wouldn't hesitate to send the troops if she called.

She scheduled a flight to Knoxville for five-fifty in the evening. It was decided that Barry would be Cary's driver for the afternoon. He would take her for the appointment with Periot, and then to see Mrs. Hebert. If there was time before her flight, she would ask him to take her by the hospital to see the reporter. Afterwards, he could drive her to the airport.

She packed up and said her goodbyes to Landie just before noon, then got into the vehicle with Barry. They drove away, leaving Landie standing on the porch, waving.

She wished she could have said goodbye to everyone, Kathryn especially. She had put herself on the line for Cary. All the others, too. She could never thank them enough.

Cary rode most of the way to the Mayor's office in silence, wondering what Periot might say about her mother. As they neared the government complex, traffic became congested. When they turned the corner a half block from City Hall, Cary saw the problem.

Chapter Thirty-Nine

There, in front of the main entrance to the government building, milled a crowd of reporters and photographers. Stunned, Cary hoped she could get through them without being turned away.

She could see mobile units from various stations parked all around the city complex. There was even one from a Japanese station and others from Canada, Germany, and South Korea. Obviously the news about Periot's inner circle and his race for the White House had spread across the nation and on to Europe and the Far East. She almost felt sorry for him.

Barry pulled to the curb.

"Should I park and go in with you?" he asked.

She glanced at the crowd again, then shook her head. "I'll be okay. They don't know who I am. Just be here when I come out." She managed a weak smile as Barry gave her a thumbs-up.

Pushing through the reporters and others near the entrance, someone shouted out, asking who she was, but Cary kept moving. Inside at the security point, she had to give her name and show a photo ID. They were expecting her, and she was escorted to the Mayor's office.

When Cary walked into his suite, the place swarmed with staff and security personnel. Periot's secretary recognized her and said he was waiting. Several pairs of eyes appraised her immediately; she could feel people staring. Excusing herself from a reporter, his secretary motioned her toward Periot's office; the door was open. Then, stepping back for Cary to enter, the young woman smiled and quietly closed the door behind her.

Cary stopped after a couple of steps and waited.

He was standing near the windows. "Come in," he said. "Have a seat. Would you like something? Coffee, a Coke?" He glanced out on the plaza as she walked toward his desk. Cary sensed he was uneasy, not showing the degree of confidence he had earlier in the week.

She shook her head at the refreshments as she settled into one of his visitor's chairs.

He turned toward her and started immediately. "I'm sorry for all you've been through here in N'awlins, and I'm sorry about your friend, too. I'm sure he was a good man."

"Yes, he was a special person. I only knew him a short time, but he made a lasting impression." *If only you knew.*

He stared at her for several seconds, his eyes glistening. "Your mother was a special person, too, Cary," Periot said. "We met at City Park. Did she tell you that in your letter?" His hands were stuffed in his pockets, his eyes now cast on the floor.

Cary listened, silent, not wanting to break the spell that seemed to have settled over the room.

"You look very much like her," he said softly, gazing at Cary, obviously comparing the woman in front of him to her mother. "She was very pretty."

"Why was she killed?" Cary asked, her voice low but harsh and accusing. "Did the fact that she was going to have your child present a problem? I guess Janice Talmer and her baby didn't fit into your plans." She was angry and it showed.

With eyebrows raised, he appeared surprised but then understanding as he glanced thoughtfully at her.

"That's part of it, I'm sure," he said. He walked to his desk and sat down before he spoke again. He appeared ready to answer her questions, and maybe he would answer them truthfully.

He continued. "When she told me she was pregnant, I panicked. I told her to get out of my life and stay out." He leaned forward then, elbows on his desk. "I even warned her not to make trouble."

Then he hesitated, appearing to want her full attention. "But, Cary, I had nothing to do with her death. I would never have done that." He closed his eyes as though trying to gather his thoughts, *and* his courage. Then, he opened his eyes and sighed. "I know this will be hard to understand, but I think you should hear it. I've never said this to anyone else." Again, he hesitated, gazing into Cary's eyes this time. "I loved your mother. I really did," he said, "but I was young and in that instant after she told me about you, I could see everything going up in smoke, all I had dreamed about since I was a young boy." He stared down at his hands, then back at her. "I said some terrible things to Janice . . . but I didn't kill her."

"Then who did?" She didn't give him a chance to recover.

He looked up at the ceiling as though he'd find the answer there. "I honestly don't know, but if I had to guess . . ."

Cary hated her father at that moment, and all he stood for, but she held her emotions in check. She wanted to hear him out.

His eyebrows went up and he began speaking again. "Eddie Breunoux probably gave the order," he said softly. "I read about the accident in the newspaper. Being the person I was back then, I didn't ask Eddie or anyone else any questions."

He leaned back. "I guess I didn't have the courage; I just let it pass." He stared out the window and then back at Cary. "I've thought about her almost every day since 1982."

Johnny Periot, Cary's father, then looked at her in a way that caught her by surprise. With love in his eyes, he murmured, "I'm sorry . . . I'm so sorry."

She gazed at him, trying to put it all in perspective. "So am I." She pursed her lips, caught in a moment of sadness for all the misplaced years, for her mother and all the other losses. But, surprising herself, she believed him. *He did love her mother.*

"I have to go." She got up and walked toward the door.

"Are you leaving N'awlins?"

"Yes. I have a Delta flight back to Knoxville at six this evening."

Cary had reached the door; she opened it and walked out without saying goodbye. She didn't even look back.

Cary's visit with Mrs. Hebert was much more pleasant. They talked about the fact that they were both adopted and they had both wanted to find out more about their birth families – and about themselves.

"I tried for years to find my birth family," Mrs. Hebert said, "but I ran into one dead end after another. I thought working for the agency would make it easier but it didn't. Then finally, the laws concerning confidentiality changed. After that, I was able to get the information I needed in order to trace them." She hesitated, becoming thoughtful for a few seconds, then said, "By that time, everyone was gone. All I ended up with were some old headstones in graveyards here and there." She smiled. "I still visit those old graves from time to time." She glanced at Cary and said with sadness, "But it's not like family."

The social worker asked about the shootout at the warehouse and about Webster. Mrs. Hebert had read the morning paper. Cary told her story, then said goodbye to Mrs. Hebert and left the French Quarter. She'd come to love the Quarter with its beauty and charm. Everywhere she looked, there was history. After all, she remembered, over the years, five or six different countries had governed the old city. She would miss walking among the gardens and wrought iron fences separating so many of the old properties.

Fresh memories took her back to Jackson Square and into Webster's arms. Had that only been a few hours ago? It seemed a lifetime. Then she realized – it had been a lifetime for Webster.

After she left Mrs. Hebert, Barry drove her to the hospital where Emile LeBlanc was recovering. Cary had decided she had time to visit him. He was probably still sedated but she wanted to see him anyway.

Surprisingly, LeBlanc was sitting upright in his bed. He didn't look critical. Although groggy, he recognized Cary and gave her a thumbs-up with his right hand. His left hand was heavily bandaged, as were his face and head. He looked terrible. She told him so and smiled. He gave her another thumbs-up. This was certainly the Emile LeBlanc she knew. After a few minutes of one-sided conversation, she told him good luck and goodbye. She patted his arm, smiled again, and left him there.

With Barry at the wheel, they headed to the airport. Afternoon traffic was heavy, but it continued moving and there were few delays. They arrived with time to spare, and Barry left the vehicle in short-term parking. He insisted on carrying her bags and seeing her off.

Cary went to the Delta ticket counter, confirming her flight and checking her bags. Afterwards, the two of them started to the concourse. When they turned a corner near the security area, a large crowd was gathered, holding aloft a big sign. It read: **HURRY BACK, CARY – YOU'RE PART OF THE FAMILY!**

Landie, Greg, Kathryn, Andy, Bert, Susan, and the grandsons – they were all there – everyone. Just standing there grinning. Cary's adopted family! *Her family*. She looked at Barry. He was grinning, too, from ear to ear. *He knew about this*. He had walked her right into it.

Landie stepped forward and hugged Cary. "You didn't think you could leave without saying goodbye to all of us, did you? It's something families do." Everyone crowded around with their own hugs and goodbyes. It was wonderful.

As everyone talked excitedly, Cary became aware of a lone individual standing some distance away, watching them. She looked closely, recognizing him.

The topcoat, hat, and sunglasses didn't fool her. She excused herself and walked over to him.

"What are you doing here?"

It was Johnny Periot. No bodyguards, no assistants – just her father.

"I wanted to come and see you off."

"Were you afraid I wouldn't go?" she asked. She wondered how he had escaped the media.

"I wanted to see you one more time, that's all. I had hoped you wouldn't see me." He paused. "I'm sorry, Cary, for all the pain. Your mother was a good person. You needed to know that."

She nodded. Then she surprised him. "You arranged for her burial, didn't you. I visited her grave, you know."

He stared at Cary for a long moment, then said softly, "It was the least I could do."

"And the roses?"

" . . . Yes."

With those few words and a sad smile, Johnny Periot turned and walked out of her life. Cary watched him go, feeling a slight tug at her heart. Other than herself, he was all that was left of her mother's story.

When he was out of sight, she returned to her new family.

Soon, it was time for Cary to board. Everyone said goodbye again and she walked away, waving as she did.

"I'll be back!" *My family lives in N'awlins.*

Epilogue

Cary received a call two days after she returned to Knoxville.

"Miss Warren? This is Ellen Ellison. I'm a reporter for the *Times-Picayune*."

Cary caught her breath. "Yes?"

"I've been working with Emile LeBlanc on the investigation of Johnny Periot and City Hall here in New Orleans."

"How can I help you?" Cary asked. "And how is Emile?"

"He's doing great," the reporter answered. "They took him off the critical list last night."

Cary breathed a sigh of relief, a silent prayer on her lips. She liked LeBlanc. "Good. Tell him hello for me. Now how can I help you?"

"Unfortunately, Emile won't be able to give me much information for several days and I'm trying not to bother him. That's where you come in. He left a disc for you and Webster containing information on the Shapiro research in case anything happened to him. Maybe he had a premonition. There was a note about a password on the envelope. Let me read the note to you and see if you can figure out the password."

She read the note to Cary.

Just to make sure everything was on the level, she told Miss Ellison she would try to come up with the password and get back to her.

Upon hanging up, she called Kathryn Kato. Kathryn confirmed the reporter had been working with LeBlanc. Cary called Ellison back and gave her the password.

"I've been working on the articles and getting them ready for Emile to approve," Ellison said. Cary was pleased. Emile would still get his exclusive.

She had one more question for the reporter: "Were you able to keep Webster and me out of the stories?"

"Yes. Emile insisted on that."

Word about Webster's death had spread at Trebeck Corporation. Only Webster and Cary's friend Rita had known about Cary's search. Rita kept that information to herself. As for Webster's death, everyone thought he had just been in the wrong place at the wrong time. She didn't tell anyone differently – nor did Rita.

A few days after she returned to work, Cary was called upstairs by Mr. Stocks. "Webster's death has left an opening in advertising management," the CEO said, stating the obvious. With his hands in his pockets, and his eyes everywhere except on her, she could tell he was nervous about asking her to take the job. "Since you were in line for the position before, we hope you will consider taking it now."

She was still unsettled and not yet sure she wanted to be as tied down as the position required. "I need a few days to think about it. I'll let you know." She wasn't sure, either, if she wanted to work for Trebeck, given what she knew about the corporate ownership. She really did want to think about it.

Mr. Stocks was okay with that. "Ms. Ammons has been doing a good job in the interim," he said.

In the days after New Orleans, Cary and Rita spent some time catching up. She told Rita everything. Her friend couldn't believe all that had happened in New Orleans. She even shared her mother's letter with Rita. They were both sad when Rita finished.

Cary reminisced about how helpful Webster was in the search for her family. Then she told Rita about the budding relationship with Webster. She also talked about Landie and her family. But it was a while before she could talk about New Orleans without reliving the tragedies that had occurred there.

New Orleans had changed her. She would never be the same, but she had learned to take things as they come. She no longer felt as driven as before. Going to Louisiana had been the right thing to do.

She often thought about Webster, but tried to let that be a part of her past.

A month after she returned home, Cary heard from Jack Robbins one last time. He phoned her at the apartment one Saturday morning. They chatted for a few minutes, then Robbins asked how she was doing and if she had gone back to Trebeck Corporation.

She told him she had been asked to take Webster's job in the advertising department. "Emotionally, I'm not where I want to be, but I'll get there."

Robbins congratulated her for hanging in there. "Webster would have wanted it that way." He paused as if deciding whether to tell her something else. Finally, he said, "Webster really cared for you. He told me he felt very fortunate to have met you – that he thought you two might even have a future together."

Cary was still uncomfortable discussing her feelings for Webster – she was still not sure of them herself. She just knew that he was an extraordinary man who's death had left a real hole in her life. She tried to change the subject.

"How's the investigation going?" she asked.

"Cobreaux has turned and is giving information to the prosecuting authorities by the handful. He knew more than Alex Shapiro about what went on in the last twenty-five years and he's telling everything."

Without giving Cary the details, he told her Eddie Breunoux had always pulled the strings. The Mayor had been the front man. Periot, as Big Eddie's puppet, had never questioned how things were handled. He just took care of his people from his position at the top. Cobreaux got things done. Superintendent Breunoux gave the orders and ran the show.

Webster had been right. They had run drugs, laundered money, and, in many cases, created legitimate businesses to handle the operations. But the biggest thing Big Eddie had going was the protection business.

"Your search for your mother's killer put pressure in the right spots to make their organization unravel. Who knows how long it might have gone on if you hadn't come to New Orleans?"

Finally, Robbins told Cary the real reason he had called.

"Webster's keen eye for detail led him to follow through on some important items. Remember the blood scrapings the two of you found in Dr. Davison's office? The samples had been taken from a damaged car left at a body shop those many years ago. I had Webster's cell phone, and apparently Ed Lawrence called that number looking for Webster. He wanted to report on the DNA analysis Webster had requested."

Robbins said he told Lawrence about Webster's shooting, then took the information and followed up on it.

"You may want to sit down for the rest of it," he told her.

Cary didn't say that she was already sitting. From the beginning of their conversation, she had the strangest feeling Robbins had something important to pass on. "Go on. Tell me."

"Ed Lawrence said the blood DNA from the automobile had been analyzed and compared to yours." She held her breath. "The results confirmed that the automobile was the one that struck Janice Talmer and killed her." Cary shivered as though a cold hand had reached across time and touched her. It took a moment for her to regain her concentration.

As Robbins talked, Cary could hear children playing in the background. He must be calling from home – it *was* a Saturday morning. He finished the story. "The repair shop had grown over the years and remained in business. The present owner helped us search old records, and we turned up a tag number that could be traced. The owner of the car had been an employee of Cobreaux's, and the reason he didn't return for the vehicle was because he had been shot and killed in a domestic disturbance."

One piece at a time, the puzzle had come together.

"One last question." Cary said.

"Sure."

"What will happen to their holdings?" Clarifying, she said, "Companies like Trebeck Corporation and the others."

"New owners," Robbins explained. "Several holding companies have already made inquiries. The investors held some prime money-makers, valuable and saleable." He assured her Trebeck Corporation would be around for years to come.

Finally, she changed the subject. "Did Webster make it back to the mountains like he wanted?" Cary asked, choking back tears. Robbins said he had. Then they said their goodbyes.

She did some research and satisfied herself about the future of Trebeck. With those concerns out of the way, she said yes to the CEO and settled into running the advertising department. She was immediately effective at helping the company move forward. Top management let her know they were pleased with their choice. She named Rita as her permanent assistant, and the two of them started exploring new possibilities for Trebeck Corporation. The women were having fun.

Mr. Stocks never mentioned what he may have known about Webster. Cary followed the CEO's lead concerning her departed friend.

Cary and Landie talked on the phone two or three times each week. One of them called the other almost every Saturday. By now, Landie had become the elderly grandmother Cary never had in real life. Often, she took a Friday off and caught a plane to New Orleans. Someone would pick her up at the airport and drive her to Landie's house. 'Everyone's grandmother' usually had a meal prepared, and there was always a crowd around the table. Cary had become just another member of Landie's big family.

When everyone went home, she and Landie would sit in the old woman's living room and talk. Landie listened to Cary's problems and helped her solve them. Cary learned to take life one day at a time. Through Landie, she had found what she came to New Orleans looking for – her family.

Everything finally settled down at the office, and Cary developed a routine that worked for her. She went through her mail early each morning. Next, she reviewed her to-do list, crossing out tasks she had completed and adding new ones. The remainder of each day she worked with Rita and their staff to take everyone's ideas and develop them, always taking care to give credit for those ideas. Cary was becoming a proficient executive.

On a certain Friday, as Cary sorted through her mail, she picked up a postcard. The picture showed a panoramic night view of Houston, Texas. Flipping it over, she found a short handwritten note addressed to Cary Anne Warren at Trebeck Corporation. The message read:

> **Dear Miss Warren,**
> **You should know that Texas is a beef loving state. People here like their steaks and burgers in many forms, all the way from rare to well-done. Some even tell us to just dehorn the steer, hose him down, and run him in.**
> **Do you still like your burgers done medium well?**

Cary's heart skipped a beat as she recalled the night Webster arrived in New Orleans. They had gone to Ruby's Grill for Steak Burgers and fries. *That's how he had ordered his burger.*

But this couldn't be from Webster . . . could it? He died there in New Orleans. She had stood beside his body, touched his arm under the sheet. She had even told him goodbye! *But . . . but she hadn't looked at his face.*

This simply wasn't possible. Webster was *killed* in New Orleans!

Her fingers were trembling, the card unsteady in her hand. Cary stared at the signature.

> **A Friend**

There was no return address . . .

September 2011
Dear Reader:

As many of you are aware, *A Letter to Die For* is the first of the "*Letter Series*" novels. Future books in the series will follow some of the original characters as they find themselves involved in other conflicts. Additionally, on my website and in my blogs, you can learn about the day-to-day lives of individuals in the novels. I think you will find the details appealing, but I offer this caveat – be careful, you could find yourself falling for some of them. On the other hand, you could discover particulars you might wish to pass on to someone else in the novels – a warning, perhaps. Sometimes, even a hero needs a little help.

So, without further chatter, I would like to present the first chapter of the second novel in the "**Letter Series.**" This one is titled, "*The Lost Letter.*"

One more thing – be on the lookout for someone wearing a fedora, a leather jacket, and shades. It could be Rage Doyle, aka **The Author**, or it may be me. Either way, stop and say hello.

Cheers and good reading,

Joe Shumock

Scan this QR code for more information
www.Silver-Sage-Media.com

The Lost Letter

Book Two

By Joe Shumock

Publisher: Silver Sage Media LLC

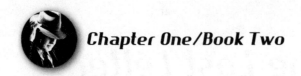

He could hear a conversation in the distance. People were talking about him, but he couldn't make sense of what they were saying. They seemed too far away.

And his head hurt. Damn, his head hurt.

Then everything became quiet again, and in his mind, he walked back into the fog. As he drifted away, he tried to remember what had happened.

The shot that almost killed Webster may actually have saved his life. His recent enemies had been close to locating him when a bullet brought him down in New Orleans. With Webster critically wounded, leaders in U.S. the Marshals Service saw a chance to get him out of immediate danger and into deeper security. Prior to being shot, he had been furnishing information to the Marshals on a case involving several city leaders. Faking his death provided a perfect opportunity to hide him.

While working with the Marshals, Webster also aided Cary Anne Warren in her pursuit of those responsible for her mother's death. In a final show-down with the killers, the couple's situation became desperate. The Marshals were after the same group for other illegal activities. Deputy U.S. Marshal Jack Robbins, a close friend of Webster's, had commanded the team due to sweep in and arrest the group's leadership while rescuing Webster and the girl.

Problem was, the Marshals were almost too late.

The raid's main purpose was to bring down local corrupt politicians who fronted and supervised a clandestine pipeline and protection racket for drugs coming into the southeastern United States from Central and South America. Over the last several years the organization had flourished, operating with impunity due to its strategically placed leadership. For the raid to be effective, the group's leader, the city's police superintendent, had to arrive before Robbins' team could move in.

After the Superintendent arrived but before the U.S. Marshals rolled in, someone got off a shot, taking Webster out. He almost died before the trauma team could get him to surgery.

Robbins now stood in a darkened corner watching as a nurse took Webster's vital signs. He had not regained complete consciousness since being wounded five nights ago. His trauma surgeon, Dr. Best operated almost immediately and had looked in on him several times each day since. The LSU Medical Center in New Orleans was a teaching hospital, so Webster was getting the best care the city could offer. The damage to his body was extensive and would probably have killed most men. Webster's conditioning and will to live probably made the difference between life and death. The surgeon's orders were to keep him sedated and immobile. Toward that end, he had been isolated in a small, dimly lit room within the Surgical Intensive Care unit since leaving the O/R.

However, within the last few hours the situation had changed dramatically. Now hurried preparations were in progress in Webster's room and elsewhere in the SIC unit. Dr. Best and others were making arrangements for his relocation. An armed officer stood at the door to Webster's room and another was stationed at the main entrance to the intensive care unit.

Even with the security, Jack Robbins was still worried. Some violent people were searching for Webster, and it was Robbins assignment to keep them from locating and killing his friend.

Two recent communications had everyone on edge. The latest, a note, had been intercepted in Atlanta only five hours earlier. Robbins carried a copy in his pocket. The short enigmatic message, mailed from outside the country, carried a warning for Webster. There was no signature – only a brusque four words in Spanish: "Ellos vienen, mi amigo." *They are coming, my friend.*

Robbins and his boss assumed the note was from someone inside the drug cartel Webster had infiltrated and where he operated undercover until a few months ago. The note had come on the heels of another possible threat. Sources had recently sent word to Robbins that a suspicious communication had been recorded in a telephone exchange in Central America. Although Webster's name had not been used, there was concern the discussion was about him. With those two pieces of information in hand, Robbins chose to err on the side of caution.

Webster would be out of New Orleans within the hour. His name had already been changed for security purposes. All paperwork listed the patient being transferred as Webb M. Michaels.

Robbins paced the hallway, worrying and keeping tabs on the preparations for the move. For the moment, at least, everything was going as expected.

Elaborate planning had led the public, including Cary Warren, to believe Mike Webster had died as a result of the clash inside the New Orleans warehouse. There was also a concerted effort afoot to make sure old enemies knew of his "untimely demise." Misinformation had been flowing since the morning after Webster's shooting – even before discussions of moving him.

Robbins hated lying to Cary because Webster had started to care for her, but there had been no other way.

A short obituary in the New Orleans newspaper listed Webster as a resident of Knoxville, Tennessee. According to the article, the deceased's body would be cremated, and there would be no service.

***

Across the gulf and some distance outside the city of Vera Cruz, Mexico, a telephone rang in the early morning.

The location, a sprawling estate on a bluff overlooking the Bay of Campeche, belonged to the head of a large drug cartel. A smooth, ten foot stucco wall surrounded the property. The top of the barrier was capped with broken glass and three feet of razor wire. Sentries, in vehicles and on foot, patrolled the grounds 24/7.

The phone conversation was short.

"Hola?"

"I am sorry to wake you, mi amigo. Do you know my voice?"

"Si."

"My sources tell me the man you have been searching for has been shot in New Orleans. It happened last Wednesday evening. I am told he is dead." The caller provided details.

"Is your information reliable?"

"Si." There was a pause. ". . . Usually."

"I will check it out."

"I expected that you would."

"I will be in touch."

The phone clicked and the caller was gone.

***

Careful measures now called for Webster to be known as Webb Michaels until he reached the medical facility where he would be recuperating. On a need-to-know basis, only the U.S. Marshals Service and Webster's doctor knew the true situation.

A stretcher was wheeled into the small room where several pairs of hands lifted

Webster onto it. All the necessary tubes, monitors, and machines were ready to go. Robbins watched from the doorway, aware that an ambulance waited on the outskirts of the Emergency Room entrance area.

The two security officers and Robbins spread out and accompanied the little procession as it left the SICU. Two nurses and Dr. Best quietly walked from the building behind Webster's stretcher. Pre-dawn darkness provided cover as they hurried him out to the ambulance.

With the patient and equipment loaded, an attendant closed the doors, tapped twice, and the vehicle drove away. Though its lights were flashing, the siren remained silent. No official cars, either. Three unmarked vehicles left the parking lot from separate locations, one leading the way and the others moving along in the light traffic.

The little procession drove out to the New Orleans Lakefront Airport where a specially equipped Lear jet sat waiting. All four vehicles pulled up close to the aircraft. Five men quickly spread out, taking up guard positions while two others helped the medical personnel load Webster onto the jet.

As the stretcher was secured, Robbins pulled one of the men aside and gave him instructions. Josh Hamlin, one of Robbins' team members and a Deputy U.S. Marshal himself, would accompany Webster, aka Webb Michaels, to his destination. No one expected problems, but Robbins remained apprehensive.

"Stay with him until he's safely settled into his new facility," Robbins told Hamlin. "You're in charge, but other agents will meet you and act as security."

"Got it." Hamlin boarded the aircraft and took a seat at the rear of the cabin. The doctor and nurses finished tending the patient and took their seats, too. With the right engine spooling up, the pilot and first officer worked through their preflight checklist. At last, the doors were closed and the left engine screamed to life. The aircraft began to move even as the first officer requested permission to taxi.

"Lear Delta Bravo 57 Echo requesting taxi and take-off instructions."

He received an immediate response, and a couple of minutes later, the crew lifted the landing gear as the aircraft clawed its way into the early morning sky over Lake Pontchatrain. A flight plan had initially been filed for Memphis but was revised with Houston Center as soon as they attained altitude – their new destination: Charlotte, North Carolina.

***

Pablo Perez lifted his arm from the shoulders of the caramel-skinned beauty seated beside him. Known as The Merchant throughout Central and South America and the United States, Perez was medium height, five-eight or nine, and slim. He wore a short beard giving him a youthful look, although facial wrinkles and a receding hairline suggested middle age. The woman smiled as she stood and walked toward the extraordinarily large swimming pool that resembled a small lake. The area was striking, with its mature trees and numerous waterfalls surrounding the indigo surface.

At poolside, several young men and women sat talking at tables and in lounge chairs. Others playfully splashed each other, enjoying the water and the weather. A few of the women wore tiny bikinis, while others sported only thong bottoms. Several were totally nude. The woman who had been sitting with The Merchant was in the latter group.

Perez motioned for a man sitting alone on the opposite side of the pool to join him. Several others had been glancing his way from time to time on the chance he might require their attention.

The Merchant watched with satisfaction as the individual he summoned strolled to his side. Casually pulling a chaise lounge close, the young man sat down and leaned in to listen. Perez asked him a question, then followed with some instructions.

"Do you remember much about our friend who closed down our Gulf Coast operation?"

"Si, Pablo. I remember him. The tall one."

"Yes, the tall one." Perez frowned as he continued. "I have been told that he was killed in New Orleans a few days ago. I want you to go and find out if this is true."

The man stood and simply said, "I will leave today."

"Good . . . If he is dead, we will celebrate. But, if my information is not true, find out where he is hiding." Thinking of Webster, Perez's voice rose in anger as he talked to Enrique.

Unaffected, the young man looked back at Perez, his arms crossed at his chest. Though Enrique had proven himself many times over, Perez was continuously surprised by his protégé's total lack of fear. It was uncanny.

"My information says our friend is using the name Mike Webster," Perez said. "He was employed at Trebeck Corporation out of Knoxville, in Tennessee. It appears he was helping a woman look for her relatives in New Orleans. The woman's name is Cary Warren. She works at the same company. My sources tell me Webster was shot and killed during a raid involving this woman's search." Perez stood and lightly jabbed the young man with his finger. "I must know if this is true!"

"Si, senor. I will find out for you."

"Don't fail me, Enrique. I depend on you."

"No, Senor Pablo. I will not fail." The younger man continued to stare at Perez. "If I find he is alive, what do you want me to do? Shall I kill him or bring the information back to you?"

"Let me know what you discover. If you find him alive, I will come to meet you. I want to be there when this one is finished," The Merchant said. His face was red now, attesting to his fury. "I will slit his throat and then spit on him as he takes his last breath. Do you understand?"

"Si, te entiendo perfectamente."

Acknowledgements

Many individuals have had a part in making this book a reality. Several editors have worked with me: Carol Craig of Eugene, Oregon: Kathleen Barnes of Brevard, North Carolina: Charlene Hodgin of Tellico Plains, Tennessee: and most recently, Nancy Thomas, English Professor, Tusculum College, Greenville, Tennessee. Dr. Thomas has worked tirelessly to have me punctuate correctly and arrange my words in some proper order. Thanks, Nancy.

Readers are ultra important in a project like this. They catch so many things the author missed – like when a street should be a boulevard, right Rosie? I know I will inevitably leave someone out but here goes: Kathy Shumock (1940-2010), Judy Regan, Diane French, Debra Fillipo, Caroline Barney, Rosie Mistretta, Susanne Mortimer, Larry Harris, Elmira Tanner, and Barry Hodgin. A special thanks to those I may have missed.

A great amount of appreciation also goes to Barry Hodgin for his graphic and design work on the cover, his photography and website efforts, and his continuing internet marketing expertise. And, too, for his council and business advise.

And to all those who have encouraged me, I thank them, too.

Publisher: Silver Sage Media LLC

Book Web site:
www.Silver-Sage-Media.com
E-mail: info@Silver-Sage-Media.com

Give feedback on the book at:
feedback@Silver-Sage-Media.com

Scan this QR code for more information
www.Silver-Sage-Media.com